THE
REVEREND

THE REVEREND

By D.H. Robbins

First electronic and bound edition published 2015

ISBN-13: 978-7330722-0-5 (print)
ISBN-10: 978-1-7330722-1-2 (Kindle e-book)

All trademarks are the property of their respective owners.

Published by D. H. Robbins

Cover photos, treatment and design by D. H. Robbins
Part opener photo collages and design by D. H. Robbins
Book design by D.H. Robbins—Typeface: Palatino 1i /15

Edited by Roberta J. Buland, Right Words Unlimited,
West Hartford, CT 06117

23456

Published by

To my brothers and sisters in the room.
Their encouragement is everlasting.

A special and enduring acknowledgement to my wife, Kate, for her unceasing understanding that writing requires as much action as thought.

Special thanks and kudos to Roberta Buland of Right Words Unlimited for her editorial skills and expertise–and encouragement. I also wish to thank Catherine, Norm, Julie, Andy and The West Hartford Fiction Writers Group for their advice and support.

Part 1

May 1963 –October 1963

Two Bridges

Chapter 1

Leaving Iowa

Hanson, Iowa, mid-May 1963

Not since he had embraced Mother as she died nearly 30 years before had the Reverend Thomas Barragan felt such a release. Now, as he held John Bass' dying body beneath the water of the baptismal tank, he realized that a life taken through baptism is one also redeemed.

Gazing into John's limpid, light-blue eyes—his skin whitened beneath the chill of the wavering surface of the water—he recognized the countenance of faith. The Reverend then felt the passage of John's departing soul ebb warmly throughout him to nourish and consecrate his own neglected spirit. He basked in the epiphany that he'd discovered the inner light of his own soul. After a lifetime of searching, he'd finally come to feel the presence of his personal god.

Thomas roused a trembling smile as he raised John's body toward him, then looked at the corpse of the boy who had raped and forced Regina, his daughter, to leave home bearing his Lucifer's seed. He brushed a strand of the John's matted blond hair away from his puckered cheek, scarred prematurely from his years in the shadows cast upon him by the underbelly of society. Gazing deep into John's pleading and peaceful eyes, Thomas witnessed the last glimmer of his life extinguish into the vacancy that death leaves in its wake. He pulled the corpse closer to him into an embrace and kissed him fully on his chilled lips. He then anointed his forehead from the tin vial of concentrated lavender he always carried, as though it were holy water. "Blessings, dear heart," he whispered.

Thomas's inner god had provided him with a plan to go away—to leave his past behind here in Hanson, Iowa. The Reverend might have chosen to resume his life in his long-ago Irish home in Ballycannough, County Liaos, that mythical place of his childhood where Mother had raised him as the daughter she wanted, and he yearned to be. But his god had demanded differently. His god had directed him to knit himself into an anonymous new life in the quagmire of a large city to carry on his work, for it was far from finished.

The former Reverend Thomas Barragan planned to build his church and resume his calling with the blessing of his god in the Gomorrah of New York City with a new identity under the name he had chosen for himself: Reverend Thomas Deavers, a liberator of fallen souls.

The newly devised Reverend Thomas Barragan-Deavers finally got underway toward New York a day later than he'd planned. The swelter of a heatwave that had set in during the week hadn't eased since Tuesday, and the early morning humidity ushered in another hot day, according to the morning farm reports crackling from the car radio's speaker. He wondered bitterly why he'd left John's body to moulder in the car's trunk since he'd liberated him a day-and-a-half before. To make matters more unbearable, the trunk of Regina's Corvair was in the front, and the rank smell of decomposing flesh wafted into his face and throughout the car. He opened the windows to release the thick stench that had gathered around him, not concerned that it would flow into the open windows of other passing cars to possibly arouse suspicion.

He remembered a park he had once visited called Backbone in Strawberry Point north of Cedar Rapids, about five hours away. It was a remote enough place to leave John's corpse for the elements to decompose, perhaps to be discovered, unrecognizable, months from now. Since the boy had been a drifter who had fallen through the cracks of society anyway, he would have been little missed.

Twenty minutes out from Council Bluffs, he picked up Interstate 80 where it forked due east toward Des Moines. The glint of the rising sun rudely assaulted his vision as he adjusted the windshield visor to mask the glare that streamed through striated slivers of soft orange clouds in the deep blue sky of late dawn. He remembered Regina had kept a spare pair of sunglasses in her car and he fumbled his hand around in the glove box until he found them as he squinted down the road ahead. The glasses were the large-lens aviator type—maybe practical for driving, but not very feminine. Thomas reasoned that the glasses must have originally belonged to his rancid cargo.

The pale risen sunlight now skimmed the tops of the alternating expanses of the new corn and wheat that blanketed the distance on either side of the Interstate. Roving gusts of wind from the east ruffled the tips of the crops, creating irregular moving waves of light and shadow. The stench had become unbearable. He considered getting off at the next exit to drive far into the oceanic desolation of the corn to leave John's decomposing body like an abandoned scarecrow. No, that wouldn't work; it would be too quickly discovered and traced. Backbone Park would be perfect. Once the Bach concerto through the portable tape player resting on the front seat ended, he pulled into a rest stop to thread his tape of

Grieg's "In the Hall of the Mountain King" into the player, and then continued driving east into the rising morning light.

To take his mind off the smell, he tried to think about his vacation in Jamaica ten years before with his wife, Jillian, and ten-year-old Regina. It was to be the last time he saw Jillian, and the beginning of Regina's estrangement from him.

———

Jillian's rich Catholic guilt had gotten to her.

As he and she lay on the beach, she calmly admitted to an affair she had with a married Jewish lawyer from Chicago. The news of her affair had not bothered Thomas as deeply as the idea that it had been with a Jew. And then came the worst admission of all — Jillian was three-months pregnant. Thomas knew it was not him, because he and Jillian had not shared a bed nearly since Regina had been born.

Thomas did not dare to look at his wife. He stared down at the gold crucifix hanging around his neck. It glimmered in the lowering Caribbean sun. He soon stared over at Jillian who had fallen into a doze under the sun's influence. He had never forgotten the craft of hypnosis that his mother taught him as a child back in Ballycannough. He lifted the crucifix from around his neck. He dangled it lightly before his wife and watched its reflection waver across Jillian's face. The glimmers seemed more radiant against her tan. He knew when God's light had brought her under his control.

As it was approaching sunset, the beach had cleared and there was no one around. He commanded Jillian to walk into the water and not to stop until God's embrace baptized her sins away.

While she was still entranced, Thomas helped her walk to the shore and into the water. He directed her to continue walking. He watched as she strode intently into the water, then farther out until she disappeared beneath. He watched her struggle defenselessly against the waves, as though she had come to realize her plight. Finally, she stopped struggling as she yielded to the pull of the ocean.

Thomas wiped away a tear, which came not as much from grief but from gratitude. He looked down at the crucifix in his hand. "I renounce you!" he said to it and then closed his fingers around it. He then lifted his hand and flung the holy relic into the ocean. "I RENOUNCE you!!!" he shouted as though whatever god of the firmament might hear him.

The Corvair was nearly side swiped by a passing pick-up truck, bringing Thomas' thoughts away from the tropics and back to his driving. He glanced at his watch and reasoned he would reach Iowa City by 11:15; where he could finally open the car widows after he turned off North toward Cedar Rapids to reach Backbone Park a little after noon. By then it would have been a long eighteen hours with very little to eat.

Though the increasing stench from the trunk might have done nothing to arouse his appetite, the Reverend's thoughts turned in that direction, anyway. Once John's body was in its final resting place, Thomas would be ready to grab a bite of lunch. He hadn't had a chilidog in years, as proper men of the cloth were expected to eat little but demure bites of food with a desert of humble pie. He decided on the chilidog, maybe two, topped off with a desert of cherry pie! And a thick vanilla frappe! Thomas smiled for the first time in what seemed to be weeks. He felt relieved to be finally free of false pretension after all these years. Now that he had donned his pastoral collar and was costumed in flannel and denim, he could claim his space among typical human beings.

The sun had risen high with the heat by 12:30, when he found a copse of cedars and pines a few hundred feet south of a narrow dirt access road that appeared unused for years through all the overgrowth in Backbone Park. As he opened the trunk and lifted the altar cloth he'd used to cover John's body, he was assaulted with a fetid waft of piss, shit and rot. He quickly replaced the cloth. Coughing, he rushed to his duffel bag in the back seat and grabbed the first piece of material he could, a pair of Jillian's underpants. Holding the silky garment to his nose, he made his way to the open trunk of the car.

With his free hand he picked up the crimson altar cloth and laid it open on the ground. Then, holding his breath, he lifted the body from the trunk and laid it upon the cloth, which he dragged into the refreshing scent of pines and cedars. He eased the cloth from beneath the body then laid the folded corpse prone. Though rigor mortis had already started its grip, the task of straitening the body was not as difficult as he had assumed. Still holding his breath against the stench, he placed John's rigid and oddly weightless hands over his heart in repose, then straitened and flattened out the still damp baptismal garb he wore. He rolled up the alter cloth, placed it under John's head like a pillow, and then brushed a thickened strand of damp hair from his cheek. With Jillian's panties held to his nose, he bowed his head in a final gesture and said, "Blessings, dear heart. Now rest in peace, and may you find your own god." He blanketed the corpse in a thick covering of earth, leaves and pine needles, hoping their earthy fragrances would swallow the stench, but to also allow for the smell to attract a frenzy of woodland predators. The thought of now three chilidogs two slices of cherry pie, and the double-thick vanilla frappe overcame the leftover odor of decay and his dark feelings of the past days and months.

He put in a tape of Orff's *Carmina Burana*, and then drove southeast toward Davenport on the border of Iowa and Illinois. He felt as free as the fragrance of freshening air now flowing liberally through the fully opened car windows, as the tinny blare of the cantata's dramatic choral reprise, *O Fortuna* filled the atmosphere around him.

Soon happily stated with his sinful meal and the sweet residue of vanilla frappe on his tongue, Thomas stopped at a farm outfitters' general store north of Davenport. There he brought a change of clothes: a Chambray shirt, khaki windbreaker, a few pairs of chinos and brown tie-shoes to replace his fouled denim, flannel and work boot ensemble. He stopped at a nearby Sinclair gas station washroom to clean up a little and change into his new outfit. He balled up what he had been wearing, and then soaked them in the bathroom sink to subdue their smell. He stared at his wavering reflection in the polished steel mirror above the dirt-smudged little sink. His face appeared gaunt around his wide-set steely green eyes. He ran his hand through the close crop of his soft, nappy, mousey-brown hair. It was damp with perspiration. He hadn't seen his reflection since the night before, and relaized he needed a coating of lanolin after a hot, lingering soak in a tub.

He lifted the soggy wad from the from the sink and stuffed it into the paper shopping bag from the general store to drop into the gas station's garbage bin, whose stench far overpowered that of his discards. Finally, he made his way to the fuel pumps to gas up the Corvair for the planned two-hour trip south to Peoria, Illinois, where he would find some much needed rest. He reached into his valise and took out the bottle of lavender cologne, and sprayed a little of its scent around the car.

He arrived in Peoria around three hours later. The audio of one of Bach's Brandenburg Concertos strained and wavered to the death to the recorder's batteries, but this didn't bother him as he marveled like a visiting hick at the mechanics and culture of the small metropolis. He had hardly ever gone cross-river to Omaha during the time he lived in Hanson, so it had been far too long since he had been in a real city. The most spectacular structure in Hanson had been the industrially bland, eighty-foot tall cement parapets of the twenty connected grain silos and elevators along the train yard at the north end of Center Street where it ended at the Missouri River. In Hanson, the grain silos represented something more like the end of the world despite the hazy view of Omaha on the western bank.

Like Hanson, Iowa, Peoria was also on a river, the Illinois River, which separated the cosmopolitan downtown area in the west from the industrial area on the eastern bank. Thomas realized that this small Illinois city would prove to be a sufficient slice of urbanity in preparation for the soaring massive expanse of his final destination of Manhattan.

A long-ago parishioner at The Church of The Holy Waters who had once been to Peoria had raved about The Pere Marquette, a grand old downtown hotel. A fourteen-story turn-of-the century red brick and concrete corniced structure, it seethed a classical elegance that would have been as foreign as Machu Picchu in back in Hanson. Thomas rationalized that, like he deserved the chilidogs, he deserved this kind of luxury for at least the next few weeks while he honed his and his god's plans for his future.

The lobby was thick in the lavishness of alternating red-carpeted and ornate marble-inlaid floors, high and columned walls rich with marble adornments, vaulted ceilings, and chandeliers dripping in crystallized cut glass pinpointed with light. The lobby desk was of dark oak wood inlaid with light marble panels with a thick matching marble slab top. Thomas sighed in gratitude that in this ambiance he felt far away from the gritty ordeal of the past few days. He celebrated his liberation as god's reward for him and signed for a one-week stay in a $90 a night room on the twelfth floor.

The bellhop who helped him with his bags groaned over the weight of the duffle bag as he placed it on the luggage rack at the foot of the king-sized bed. After he neatly turned down the thick green silk comforter, Thomas handed him a five-dollar tip, probably double what it should be, but gratitude doesn't come cheap. Once the bellhop had bowed gratefully as he backed out of the room and shut the door, Thomas went to the window above the desk and stared out at the stout, rugged skyline of Peoria. Most of the city lights had come on against the gray ambiguity of sky that rose the dusk into nightfall. A thin, muffled concerto of car horns echoed up from the street through the large windowpanes. He placed a hand to his cheek and smelled the lavender he had spayed in the car and on himself. He prepared for his hot bath and a transformation of his appearance into that of a woman; more precisely, Jillian. It was his pleasure and his curse that she had remained with him so.

After a long hot soak in the tub, he stood before the bathroom mirror in his with a towel draped over his thin, bare, shoulders. Even at 47 years old, Thomas had been blessed with soft, youthful, delicate feminine features, with a light bone structure and high, sallow cheeks. He had already closely shaved his tender face, chest and shapely legs and thinned his brows. He had put on a knee-length gray skirt he brought along from Jillian's wardrobe, then delicately applied some rouge from the tin in the top tray of the worn leather valise of female things that his mother had bequeathed him. He had taped a photo of Jillian to the mirror then stared more intently at it than at his reflection. He had already sprayed the bathroom with sprits of lavender, and the scent started to naturally arouse him in an unwomanly way as he felt a thickening in his groin.

He closed his left eye and the lid trembled as he applied a subtle layer of light blue eye shadow, and then repeated the process for the right eye. He dabbed a thin layer of makeup to cover up the pores on his nose, then added a deep red gloss to his lips to match that he had already painted on his long, slim nails. He spread a little more foundation on his forehead to reduce the glare. Finally, he reached behind and then took up Jillian's wig and placed it carefully upon his head. He glanced down at his feet, upon which he wore some pumps that did not quite go with the skirt. He gazed at his hairless chest bound with Jillian's white bra with its cups stuffed with hotel washcloths, and realized he didn't have a blouse to go with the skirt. He liked the idea of a pink silk blouse, and imagined how slithery soft it would feel against his skin. He made a mental note to buy one in the morning.

He glanced again at the photo of Jillian, then at his own reflection. He flexed the muscles in his cheeks a little to hollow them out. The likeness was close. He realized his next challenge would be to work on modulating his voice and inflection to raise it half an octave. He smiled wryly over the accomplishment of his disguise as his deceased wife. "Blessings, dear heart," he said to Jillian's photo. Then he repeated the statement in a little bit higher, and realized that the timbre of his voice needed a little practice before he could make his public debut as a woman.

During his first week at the Pere Marquette, Thomas trained himself into becoming more adept at acting somewhat cultured. He took many of his meals in the Chemenee Ballroom restaurant, where he dined on thick, well-done slabs of Kansas City steak and butter-and bacon drenched baked potatoes. He shopped for clothes in the better stores on Main Street to update his wardrobe from the country to the city. Several times he drove the newly polished Corvair north to Bergner's Department store to buy some women's fashions "for his wife."

Toward the end of the week, Thomas was suddenly seized with the thought that he had been overspending. He began taking his meals at various restaurants along the riverfront. The surface of the Illinois River glittered with the lights of passing dinner cruises and their soft sounds of dance music. He originally thought he was going to the popular riverfront for the charming ambiance of the frontage.

He ate his meals in the seedier bars. It turned out he was drawn more to what was going on from within the dinginess around him than the view outside, which he hardly saw through the film of grime covering the windows of the bars in which he ate. One of these dives, The One-Eyed Pelican, smelled moist and musty through the dense clouds of cigarette smoke that stung his eyes. He squinted over his greasy dry hamburger and wet French fries, then glanced down the bar at the patrons. Many of them seemed to be lonely people huddling sullenly over their drinks, as though protecting them.

Maybe it was the residual of his religious training, but he strongly sensed that a few of the down-and out patrons seemed to be unstrung from their lives as they desperately clung to their drinks and beer bottles. They may have ended up with the brittle realization that this was one of the last stops in their lives before disappearing into the coarse shadows of the streets and alleys across the river. They were the vulnerable ones who might welcome his help. He was seized with a passion to liberate them, but knew that, at least for now, it would turn sloppy if he tried.

But he would try, he decided, even if it were not tonight. Thomas felt that the hole in his spirit, once temporarily filled by the soul of John Bass, was now wearing off. Sweating off the sudden heat of desire, he slapped a twenty-dollar bill on the bar—twice the price of the meal—then rushed anxiously out the door for some fresh air.

Chapter 2

Pedro's frustration

Outskirts of Oklahoma City, Oklahoma, early June, 1963

Hellie Laine's character had been forged by the spirit of Oklahoma. Her birthright flowed through six generations, beginning with the 1830 Indian Removal Act evacuating the Cherokee from Georgia along the Trail of Tears. Those who did not die along the way settled in the expanse of the featureless, scrubby plains forming the Oklahoma Territory. Then came the westward migration under the banner of Manifest Destiny, followed by the Land Rush of 1889. Next came the settlement of ranchers, who legally entitled themselves to much of the land settled by the earlier arrived Sooners.

Then there was an oil strike in 1901 near Tulsa, which ushered in the new American Century and scores of speculators hoping to strike it rich. Vast basins, two-to-six miles deep below the plateaus of Oklahoma, were richer in crude than any other place in the nation. Some of the more devious speculators outwitted a greater number of unsuspecting rubes and wildcatters, as the many started working for the few. Hellie's father, Timothy "Timbo" Laine, and now Hellie, had been among the many.

A vault of deep-blue sky, garnished with thin, fleecy strands of high stratus clouds hung motionlessly and into forever above the acreage she'd been charged to oversee. Eighteen pumpers were rooted haphazardly among some phone poles and the 50-odd head of grazing cattle around the dried-out plot. Gusts of hot wind stirred up small twisters of dust that rose as fuzzes of dry mists coating the sparsely grassed plateau of range. Hellie lounged farther back in the wicker rocking chair on her porch and propped her booted feet upon the railing as she trained a pair of binoculars at a pumper unit in the northeast sector.

A chain-link fence surrounded each pump unit to keep the cattle away, but that never seemed to stop Pedro, one of the four longhorns, from bumping his one-and-a-half-ton body against the fences as he futilely tried to challenge the pumps through his attempts to knock them down. Today Pedro had succeeded in mutilating the western side of the fence surrounding pumper twelve.

Hellie put aside her binoculars and then lifted the work-shack handset from the rusty little wire-topped table at her side. She held down its contact button to ring up Heck Tanner, the field foreman.

His voice sounded dry and craggy, hungover. "Hellie? Everythin' okay at your end?"

"Gather up some of your roughnecks, Heck," she said in her characteristically flinty tone that some men found seductive. "Looks like Pedro's been at them fences again. This time it's unit twelve."

"Sure, it was him?"

"'less some of your wildcatters got drunk and Rickie-raced around the range in them little tractor things of yours to play chicken with the pump jacks."

"Now, Hellie, it was just that one time a few weeks back."

"Twice. You forgot about back in April."

"The boys was just blowin' off a little steam is all," Heck said.

"Well, now it's Pedro. None of them other bull beeves got the spit to charge the jacks like Pedro does. 'Sides, he's standin' right there next to the carnage like he's proud of it. Fence's kinda leaning on its side. I'd get some of your fellahs out there mending it before nightfall."

"Yez, boss," Heck said.

"And Heck. Don't let 'em roust ol' Pedro. He has been known to charge at man-meat, time and again."

"Yez, boss," Heck repeated.

She snickered and said, "An' don't you forget that, darlin'. This is your boss sayin': 'over and out'." She raised half of her wide mouth in a little simper as she released the button on the handset. "Boys!" she muttered peevishly under her breath.

Hellie identified with Pedro's frustration. Timbo had been a small-range cattle rancher who once owned this section of land until 30-year- young Nate "Flapjack" Robertson bought it out from him below prime under some sort of rangeland technicality back in the early 1930s, just before she was born. Her older sister, Jillian, remembered and would often relate to Hellie how Flapjack Robertson had cheated their daddy out of a fortune in mineral rights. Timbo politely hardly ever spoke of it. Hellie remembered back to when she was nine or ten, just be- fore eighteen-year-old Jillian set out for Bible college over in the mystical east coast, when the derricks started to sprout up from the seeds of Flapjack's oil leases. Eighteen of the 22 of them struck, and the 4 non-producers remained as dormant testaments awaiting the possibility of reactivation to strike more crude.

To Hellie, they were more like four tombstones memorializing what might have been for the companies that still paid off their leases to seventy-six-year-old Flapjack Robertson. Now Hellie was paid by the same nameless people from a large oil conglomerate to oversee a field she might rightfully have owned.

Jillian had possessed more worldly desires—the type of which had led her east to Vermont, the rocky, topographical opposite of the oil- rich plains. In her junior year, she went further astray to Ireland to continue her studies in religious philosophy. In Athy, Ireland, she met and married that preacher man who had turned away from Catholicism to develop his own church. Hellie had determined that something was off-kilter the one time she met him shortly after Jillian and he moved to Hanson, Iowa with their 6-year-old daughter, Regina. Jillian's frustration turned to woe over her life with her holy husband and grew deeper with each of her weekly phone calls to Hellie, until one mid- April week nearly ten years before, the calls ceased altogether.

Hellie held on to her suspicion over Jillian's drowning. Her older sister had hated the water, as she, like Hellie, was more of the land. More of a wader who couldn't even hardly tread water, Jillian would have never made a conscious decision to swim a half-mile out into the shark-infested Caribbean waters, even if she could swim. The drowning amplified Hellie's uncertainties over the Reverend Thomas Barragan, and in time she had come to worry about the fate of his daughter, and her niece, Regina.

She ran a calloused, work-hardened hand through the unruly, maze of blonde curls that tufted out from the folds and tucks of the green bandana that held her hair somewhat in place. She heard the nickering from Clarence, her seven-year-old roan quarter horse, from the open stall where he had been grazing at his oats next to his stall mate, Philadelphia, a brown and white pinto mare, who was nearly half again Clarence's age and twice as gentle. Next to the little open barn—next to his friends—her fat yellow Labrador retriever lolled fecklessly in the shade of a small pin oak.

The dog had wandered into her home through the open glass porch doors two years back, while Hellie was fixing up a rice and bean salad for herself. She decided he was emaciated and scruffy looking enough to have been abandoned, and she took him in. He needed a name, and she glanced down at the can from which the beans had come. Since then, Garbanzo had hardly left her side and she knew he would be eternally loyal. She counted him and Clarence among her only true male friends.

Off from the right came some feather-light cries from her six-month old adopted son who had arrived here under more dire circumstances than had Garbanzo. Back in February, Hellie received a breathlessly urgent call from Regina, who had just been released from a Tulsa Hospital. Regina told her aunt that she had left her home in Hanson, Iowa "for good, and under painful circumstances." She had just given birth to a baby boy and had nowhere else to turn. Hellie took her and the infant into her home, only to realize that in all her inexperience and youth, aside from the routine feedings, Regina had little patience to tend to her baby. Regina gratefully allowed Hellie to take care of her unnamed infant. Hellie named him Timbo, after her father.

Hellie knew there was much work to be done on her damaged niece as she stayed on. Regina's ambivalence toward her baby didn't surprise her. Hellie gathered she had inherited the trait of her insensitivity from her preacher father; a man who had systematically drained her of any ability to care. She had seen the same detachment swallow Jillian's spirit after she had married that preacher bastard.

The grinding of gears and the heavy bass beat of "South Street" sung by The Orlons came from the radio of Hellie's truck as it invaded her sphere of reflection. The truck's engine stuttered to a stop, and Hellie watched Regina approach the porch. "How was work?"

"I got a raise, and a promotion to associate convention planner, which sounds a lot more than what it means," Regina answered as

---

she ascended the rasping steps, leaned against a supporting corner post and lit a cigarette.

Hellie knew that Regina had been carrying on with her boss, so the news of her promotion didn't come as any surprise. "Well, ain't that somethin'! Congratulations, and I could use a little more help with the finances for the feed around here."

Regina ran a hand through her sun-lightened hair. Hellie sometimes wished she could recapture the plush, silky suppleness of Regina's youthful appearance. In contrast, her complexion has been hardened by work and weather.

When Regina had arrived six months before, anorexia had enlarged her facial features through pools of shadow, like those of a refugee who had lost the sense of caring. To Hellie, as Regina's features fleshed out, she had come to resemble Jillian at nineteen.

Regina stared passively down at Timbo in his bassinet and watched him ball his little fists. "Yeah, I owe you a lot, Hellie."

"Well, hon, you've done lots to spike up my boring days of sitting around here watching them ol' pumping jacks all the time."

Regina's look turned bashful. "I, uh, think I broke the truck," she admitted. "I hit a wicked pothole on route two-seventy this side of Mc- Loud and something started to rattle around somewhere in the engine." Hellie glanced over at her eight-year-old red Ford pickup, which was beginning to show its age through scabs of rust forming below the driver's door. "That muscular old fellah? Hell, he's like an ol' free horse that cain't be broken. That ol' boy's been known to run on fumes and raw crude alone without complaint. If you broke anything, it's that radio speaker; loud's you keep that stuff you listen to. Guess the shocks could use a little attention, though."

"Okay, Hellie, I just hope I didn't throw something outta whack when I hit that fuckin' pothole."

When she had first showed up, Regina would curse like a sailor on liberty. Hellie didn't like it when Regina used words such as "fuck" and "shit" or even "Goddamn." But the grit of her niece's nature seemed to have eased over time as some maturity soaked in. "I'll keep an eye on it, hon. Anyway, I was thinking about tacking up Clarence and taking him out to survey the pumps. You wanna join me and tell me about your new city slicker job promotion?"

"Sure, why not?" Regina answered. "If you don't mind saddling up Philadelphia for me while I change."

"I wouldn't have it any other way. You never seem to cinch her tight enough. Phillie's not that real tender in the tummy. You gotta remember that. You go tog up, now. I'll have her ready for you in about fifteen minutes." Regina fluttered a smile. "Thanks, Hellie."

As Regina opened the sliding glass door separating the porch from the living room, Hellie felt a frigid blast of air-conditioning on the back of her neck. She heard the phone's annoying ring as Regina shut the door and went to the kitchen to answer it. Through the half-opened kitchen window Hellie heard her say, "Hello?"

She donned her old wide-brimmed fedora with an eagle feather sticking from its cowhide hatband. Then she unfolded herself to a stand and made her way over to the barn to ready Clarence. She heard Regina's voice became more of a gasp. "Deacon Barnstable? How'd you get this number?"

Hellie could hear mounting numbers of "Holee shits!" escalating through the window from 20 feet away as she saddled Clarence. She sensed their horseback conversation would be about more than Regina's job promotion.

Chapter 3

The whirly-bird

Regina and Hellie rode the field. Philadelphia nickered away the annoyance of a fly and Regina felt the little mare's little shiver rumble through her thighs. She talked guardedly about her promotion at The Oklahoma Tourist Bureau but isolated the phone call from Deacon Barnstable away from the conversation.

"Not much but a bunch of pumping jacks, derricks and a few head of underfed beeves to draw many tourists here," Hellie remarked. She drew down the brim of her fedora. "And the twisters," she added toward the changing weather disguised in a magnificent sunset. The balmy swells of wind from earlier in the day had shifted to the northeast and hardened into the soft and chilly gusts of a late summer twilight. A confusion of wispy orange and blue-gray cirrus clouds bloomed up from the puffy high cumulous. The background sky blended from light cyan on the horizon up into a rich blue.

"And those fucking twisters," Regina echoed absently. She was no stranger to them herself. The lush cornfield-covered Iowan flatlands seemed to draw tornadoes equally as forcefully as the sparse plains of central Oklahoma. The prime difference might have been that the tornadoes didn't stay on the ground as long in Iowa, as low hillocks and bluffs broke them up.

Leather creaked against leather as they rode silently into an orchestration of cicadas, a few whippoorwills, mockingbirds, peeper frogs and at least one bullfrog from the small bog on the northern end of the range. Hellie reached forward to pat Clarence's neck. "God, I do love it here this time of day," she said as she fingered his mane. "So peaceful. And that smell of earth and oil and leather and horse."

Regina adjusted her aviator sunglasses as she looked ahead at Garbanzo investigating one of the many piles of cow leavings. "And cow shit," she added. She didn't share her aunt's sentiment about this unique place. She came of age in corn-fed Hanson and the relative thrill promised by Omaha just across the Missouri River. By comparison, McLoud, Oklahoma had little to offer except for Hellie's comforting presence and its being the "Blackberry Capital" purely by coincidence. She was relieved to have found her job in Oklahoma City, wherever it may lead beyond the routine-turned-boring Wildcatter Motel trysts with Trevor.

Timbo rustled in the denim papoose Hellie had secured around her front where the baby could snuggle against the softness of her ample breasts. "This boy's gonna be a rancher yet."

"You think so?" Regina answered distractedly as Philadelphia shook her head to ward off another fly.

"Oh, yeah. Timbo Senior had me riding a fourteen-hand-high quarter horse at six years old. I'm gonna see Timbo Junior doing the same by five." She dipped her hand into the breast pocket of her chambray shirt and took out a home-rolled cheroot and a couple of wooden matches. She struck one against a rough part of Clarence's saddle. She lit the cheroot, pinched out the dying match flames and then put the extinguished match in the fore pocket of her jeans and then drew in a languorous puff. "Yeah, a rancher," she reminisced. "My daddy was a rancher, as will be his namesake, here," she mused into the distance. "Never a one of them oilmen. When all the oil's gone, as it will be someday, what's gonna be left is beeves to graze on the new grass here on the plains."

Regina didn't want to say anything about young Timbo's true father, John Bass, even though his name had just recently come up in her phone conversation with Deacon Barnstable. As though to shield herself from the thought, she lowered the brim of her black Stetson and changed the subject. "You ever think of going out, Hellie? I mean, I rarely see you going much farther away than McLoud." She suffused a private laugh. "Do you ever think about going out to Oklahoma City and finding a good fuck for yourself? Even for just one night? I mean we all do need it from time to time."

If Hellie ever broke out in a blush, it would be hard to tell beneath her weary, natural bronze complexion. She pinched a bit of loose tobacco from her lower lip. "Any time, hon, I wanna go find a tumble buddy for the night, I take a hot soak in the tub, lather up with a cake of Lava soap and some DEET, and then drive Ol' Red into Okie City. I get a little drunk, find me a cowboy, and then let him poke at me a few times, get a little more drunk from the experience, and then drive back here where I'm good for another month or so." She squinted at Regina who, captivated by her reply, brushed a stray wisp of hair from her cheek.

"You can go for a whole month without it?"

Hellie smiled as she glanced at Regina. "I don't cotton much to alcohol, though I know it's a necessary evil time and again. I need that month to douse out my hangover with lotsa black coffee."

"I meant the fucking. You can go a whole month without it."

"At least that. My hormones don't rage much as yours, no more, Reg. Stopped kickin' 'round like that sometime in my late twenties. You'll find that out after you've had your fill of men mucking up your life." She stole another look over toward her adopted sister. "Besides, lately I've had my share of responsibilities to keep me bound here. Not that I mind."

Regina wet her lips, then leaned forward on the saddle to stroke Philadelphia's mane. "Look, Hellie. What I meant was, if you ever feel the urge come upon you, I can take watch over things around here."

"You mean Timbo."

Regina kept a thoughtful silence as she glanced down at her son. "Well, yeah. Him, too, I guess. And the pumps. I just don't want to stop you from carrying out what a woman finds, you know, natural. We all get that way, sometimes. Well, you know." She decided to let the conversation die away, as Timbo reached out his fragile little hand toward her. She had felt his touch before, often inadvertently. She remembered how soft and tenuous it felt. Innocent and clean. She pursed her lips and looked away.

Hellie stuck to her point. "You think you're ready to look after Timbo on your own?"

"Well, yeah, why not? I mean I used to babysit back in Hanson."

"Reg, sweetie. This ain't the same and you know it."

Regina glowered at her. "I wanna make this clear, Hellie. Timbo's yours. Honestly. I could never mother him the way you have. It wouldn't be fair to any of us. All I was saying is that if you want some time off to go out and get fucked, I'm okay with looking over things here while you're gone."

Hellie admired her niece's spunk and conviction. She could see that she was coming into her own. "Okay, sweetie," she said after some thought. "I'll think on it. Now you wanna tell me about that phone call?"

"No."

"But you'll tell me, anyway."

Regina collected her thoughts as she looped and swung Philadelphia's reins against her withers to nudge the mare forward.

She soon sensed Hellie riding beside her. "You remember about four months ago when you told me to contact someone I knew back in Hanson?"

"Yeah, so you could keep in touch and to let that person know you were doin' fine."

"I did. A friend of mine, Connie Mueller, who goes to that church I used to have to go to. I told her to not tell anyone about me."

"Your father's church."

"Yeah, his church." She stroked Philadelphia's mane. "Anyway, the deacon there, Gary Barnstable, must have gotten our number from her because he just called to give me some news. You got a cigarette, Hellie?"

"Just my hand rolled's. You want one?"

Regina tightened her expression in disgust. "Shit, no! I don't know how you can smoke those foul things."

"It's an acquired taste, like over thirty years. What sort of news did this deacon tell you?"

Regina shook her head and sighed. She stared out at some distant erratic tines of dry lightning striking off in the east. "It took them a little time to find me here, in that I swore my friend Connie to secrecy. She's the only one I could trust, and she hid me well. Anyway, it looks as though my father, ex-father, whatever, went and killed him- self about two weeks ago."

"Really!" said Hellie. "The Holy Father? How'd he do it? Nail him- self to a cross?"

"They think he drowned himself in the Missouri River."

"Another drowning," Hellie said as she recalled Jillian's death. Like it runs in the family. She told herself.

"They found his car in the river, anyway. But no trace of him. Guess they figured he washed up all un-recognizable down river, maybe around St. Louis or someplace."

"Well. How about that? How to you feel about it?"

"Honestly, Hellie? I don't know what to feel right now. I'm really not fazed by it, one way or another. I'll probably feel differently in the morning. Anyway, he left a note, leaving me the house."

"Jesus wept, Reg. You're not going back to that place!"

"'Course not. I've had my fill of Hanson and its too many bad memories. He's just one less one. I don't know what I'm gonna do about all this. The deacon told me there's to be some sort of memorial next Saturday, I guess I'll have to go, now that they know he's gone for sure. I have to go there anyway, to sign some papers."

Hellie chuckled softly. "The whole world is one big stack of paperwork that needs signin'," she said as she snuffed out the remains of her cheroot with a pinch of her thumb and forefinger and then flicked it off into the field.

"I wish you wouldn't do that; put out those shit-sticks you smoke with your fingers."

"Can't feel a thing."

"What are you, Hellie? Made of steel?"

"And a little grit. So what're gonna do about all this? Rent out the house? Can you at least get your car back, so you can stop abusing Ol' Red, there?" she said, motioning back in the general direction of her truck.

"My little blue and white Corvair," she reminisced. "Connie once told me that it was gone. He must've sold it or something."

"Freakin' bastard. Did he say anything else in his note? Other than: 'Hi, and goodbye. My house and its taxes belong to my long-lost daughter?'"

"Actually, Gary read it to me. Said he respected me and couldn't live with the fact I was gone. Something like that."

"So now he's blamin' you, the bastard. Dammit! 'Respected

you,' — his own daughter, an' that's the best he could come up with? I just know he had something to do with Jillian's drowning —"

"Oh, shit, Hellie!" Regina flared, wondering if she should start believing her, as off in the stratosphere as her theory was. "Don't start going down that rutted road again. That's the dumbest thing I ever heard. He loved my mother, in his own way. He'd never try to —"

"Drown her?"

"No. Never! Now you stop that! Anyway, Gary did have some more good news."

"Better than the death of the His Holiness?"

Regina shook away Hellie's quip. "Actually, two pieces of good news. Seems as though a church member wants to buy the house. In cash. Week after next. Right after the memorial, I guess."

"Well! Hell, damn, spit!" Hellie beamed. "Praise to Lord and pass the ammunition! That is great news!"

"Yeah, it is. Plus, there's seventy-five thousand from my dowry and college fund."

"Hell, yeah!" Hellie sputtered. "Now you can buy yourself a car. A pink Coupe De Ville V-8 like a *real* Okie-girl!"

"Anyway, so I'll be signing the house papers and collecting my money when I go back there next week."

"Just don't stay too long. Collect your cash and run. Anyway, you've got that slicker job to come back to."

Regina smiled off into the distance toward where Garbanzo had found another cow-pie to investigate. "And there was another really weird thing to come out of this. I never told you about this particular guy, John Bass. For a reason."

There was a hint of suspicion in Hellie's tone. "What reason?"

"I didn't want you to know —"

"Now you got me curious, hon," said Hellie. Regina looked over at her and down at Timbo, then sighed her answer without saying it. "Oh, shit," Hellie said with one of her rare expletives.

Regina smiled sadly at her little son. Such innocence! She reached out to touch him, then withdrew her hand as if she had performed a forbidden act. "Yeah. He was Timbo's father."

"Was?"

"Gary told me John also turned up dead, right after my father died. Some hikers found his body somewhere in a forest north of Cedar Rapids. Drowned, it seems."

Hellie's features soured into a perplexed look. "Seems to be a lot of that drowning going around up in those parts. How did your church deacon know about that?" she asked. Clarence nickered apprehensively. She felt him tense up beneath her and patted him lightly on the neck. "Easy, boy," she said close to his perked-up ears.

"John's body was wrapped in a baptism robe with a label they traced back to my father's church. They also found some sort of alter cloth that had turned up missing around the time my father died."

"So, Reg. Let me get this straight. There's this fellah—" she choked in suspicion, "Timbo's father—who decided to steal some baptism togs and some sorta tablecloth from your preacher-daddy's church, then drive or hitchhike to this Cedar Rapids place from Hanson—how far away is that?"

"I don't know two hundred fifty, three hundred miles, maybe?"

"Drives or hitchhikes three hundred miles to go wrap himself in a baptism robe from your father's church to go drown himself somewhere in East Nowhere, Iowa, where there probably hardly ain't no water. And then—now drowned and most likely dead, he drags him- self from the water to complete the job off in some woods somewhere."

"Something like that. It's all too weird."

"Reg, hon, there's a lot more to all this than just 'weird.'"

The cattle had begun to act erratically as they might before a twister. Garbanzo started barking hoarsely at the western sky and then am- bled in a bulky gait toward Hellie and Regina. Juan, one of the steers, started bellowing loudly toward the whopping of helicopter blades and an advancing searchlight just above the horizon. Pedro started to anxiously bump his powerful body against another fence. "Oh, crap! Hell, damn, spit!" said Hellie as Clarence nervously tried to circle back toward his stall a half-mile away. "Easy, boy," she tried to calm him.

Philadelphia had started to mimic Clarence's anxiety. Regina, far from being the horsewoman her adopted sister was, felt a nervousness welling within her. "What's the matter?" she asked breathlessly.

"It's probably Jamie Robertson, Rickie-racing his damn whirly-bird toy helicopter, again. Damn drunk bastard."

"Who's Jamie Robertson?"

Hellie tightened the reins as Clarence, his ears now back, began snorting and wheeling around. "Some asshole I went to high school with. He was on the football team, but he never grew out of the locker room." The bubble-nosed cockpit and steel-girded fuselage of the yellow Bell helicopter was now in full view at treetop level. "The horses are gonna *spook*! Hold fast onto Philadelphia. Grip your legs tight around her! Hold tight in the saddle but give her some rein or she'll pull against you!" Hellie shouted over the approaching chop of the rotors.

Jamie lowered the nose of his helicopter to increase its speed as it passed at 70 miles-an-hour. 50 feet above their heads. Philadelphia snorted anxiously and wheeled confusedly as Clarence whinnied and reared. Close above them, Jamie had his boot planted firmly on the helicopter's skid as he leaned his lanky body out of the open door of the cockpit and let out a loud Confederate Rebel yell. He reached behind and slapped the rear of the cockpit bubble with his straw cowboy hat as though he were goading a bronco.

"YEEEEE-*HAAAA*!!!" he shouted as the rotor wash lifted the hat from his grip and it fluttered to the ground about 300 feet from where Hellie and Regina were trying to control their horses.

"JAMIE ROBERTSON! YOU COME BACK HERE!! You lost your *HAT*! SERVES YOU *RIGHT*, YOU DRUNK SON OF A BITCH!!"

Hellie shouted through a gusty laugh at the departing chopper as the livestock began to nervously settle down. Regina detected a certain longing in Hellie's tone.

Even through the rising darkness, Hellie noticed that Pedro had knocked down another fence.

Chapter 4

It hurt…a lot

The Crystals singing "Da-Doo-Ron-Ron" over the radio simmered beneath gushes of girlish conversation from the front seat of Penny Maxwell's DeSoto. Maxie pointed to the corner of her mouth as she squinted at Connie sitting next to her. "You've got some mustard right here, on your lower lip. It's gross, yucky and droolley and everything." She then bit into her Trippple-Burger which smeared a sheen of grease on her chin.

Connie smiled meekly as she daubed away the mustard, then looked up at Regina's reflection in the immense rearview mirror. Over the weekend, the two seemed to have become more closely bound in their secret sorrows in a way that only two emotionally wounded survivors in the battlefield of parental dysfunctions might understand. Connie had kept her friend's secret close, and Maxie suspected none of the tension that had weighed Regina down enough for her to leave home. "Well, Reg, how're you feeling about all this? Your dad dying and all?"

"Just another day, I suppose," Regina said and then sipped her soda. She felt like a grown-up in the company of her adolescent friends. She blinked at the sun-glinted chrome accessories of the dashboard as she felt like a stranger here in the Iowan town she'd once called home. "I guess he was kinda weird for a preacher," said Maxie. "Not to put the guy down or anything."

"His weirdness was a hazard of his job, I guess," said Regina.

"I don't think I ever met a preacher who wasn't, you know, creepy in one way or another," Connie agreed, then bit delicately into a French fry.

Maxie turned and lowered her horn-rimmed glasses on her nose to look at Regina. "So really, Reg. What've you been doin' with yourself since you—you know—like, fell off the face of the earth?"

Regina leveled a vacant stare at her, as though Maxie had stepped into uncharted territory. Then her lips bloomed into a subtle smile. "Well, you heard about John Bass."

"Oh yeah. Sorry," Maxie said, then glanced knowingly at Connie.

"We knew you two were, uh—close, or something."

"Or something," said Regina.

Connie tried on a smile, but it didn't fit. "He was no good for you, Reg. You know that," she said.

Regina sensed a deeper fog of depression lurking in Connie. And the more Connie tried to cover it up with teenage banter, the more woeful it appeared. But she knew enough about her situation to let her be.

"No shit," Regina said, and then lighted a reassuring touch on Connie's frail shoulder.

"No shit," Maxie agreed with an accentual nod. "Still, I guess even shitheads like him don't deserve to up and die like that."

"John got what he wanted," said Regina. "He was headed in that direction, anyway. You know he got me pregnant."

Connie pretended not to know as she lightly grasped Regina's hand. "No kidding, Regina!" she said for appearances sake. "You got pregnant?"

This was big news to Maxie. "No—freaking—way!" Maxie gasped through an impish smile as she choked back a sip of her soda.

"Way," Regina confirmed, realizing the stunning shock of childbirth that set her fundamentally apart from the two girls in the front seat. She watched passively as they munched on French fries and hot dogs and sipped their Solid-Shakes here at the Pit Stop, a drive-in hangout for kids. Back in Oklahoma City, grown men like Trevor took her out to posh candlelit restaurants where she drank mixed drinks and played adult games.

Regina's thoughts became lost to the hoarse, low whistle of a passing eastbound freight hauling creaking boxcars filled with the yields of the Heartland: Iowa corn loaded here, and cattle loaded from the Omaha stock yards across the river. She stared out into the fuzz of humidity and the lowering red sun past the carnival lights of the sign for the Pit Stop and a billboard advertising laxatives. Down at the end of Center Boulevard, rising like monoliths between the Missouri River and the Hanson railroad siding, a cement rampart of grain silos rose ten stories, blocking the view of any landscape beyond. It wasn't too long ago that she'd regarded those grain elevators as the far border of her life.

"—or girl?" she heard Maxie asking over The Shirelles singing "Foolish Little Girl."

"What, Max? Sorry. I was—"

"Did you have a boy or a girl?"

"Oh. A boy."

"Jeeze! What was it like? Being pregnant and giving birth, and all?"

Regina stared solemnly back at the grain elevators. "It hurt," she said, "a lot."

"You shoulda brought him with you," said Connie.

She smiled sadly through the music's refrain. Foolish little girl, she thought, and then said, "He's back home. My aunt's taking care of him." She longed for a brief, endless moment to be beyond the grain silos—back in Oklahoma with Hellie and Timbo where she now be- longed and felt newly safe. She wished Tuesday would hurry up and come so she could leave behind all that Hanson, Iowa had represented for once and for all.

Regina awoke from a doze after another round of Trevor's humping, prodding and squeezing. It wasn't even sex anymore. She stared into the flame of the candle she had placed on her bedside table in their usual room at the Wildcatter Motel. The candle's flame stuttered in a chill that surged a tingling little shiver through her shoulders. The flickering light soothed her and took her into fleeting memories, many involving her mother. She then wondered if there was some semblance of truth in Hellie's suspicion over Jillian's death. Finally, the lure of the little flame eased the thought away.

Trevor rustled himself awake and eased back into his side of the bed. He began picking at his fingernails with a folded matchbook cover. Regina hated this habit of his as he concentrated on gouging his cuticles with the matchbook. He measured out his words. "So, sweetcakes, now that you've inherited all this money, what are you gonna spend it on?"

"Hellie just went and helped me pick out an El Dorado. Baby blue," she answered blithely. The bedsheet slipped from her shoulders by degrees as she propped herself up next to him. The headboard creaked against the wall as she drew her knees protectively to her chest and she lit a cigarette.

"Ah, y'all'll be the belle of Okie-city. You and your car."

"One Cadillac's as good as another around here, I suppose. No matter who's driving it."

"Well, we should celebrate," he said. He made an event of putting aside the matchbook and reaching under the bed to produce a bottle of whiskey and a couple of plastic cups. He poured a drink for himself, then motioned the bottle toward her. "Want some?"

She took the empty cup he offered her and held it toward him. "Is the Pope Jewish?"

"Well, then, darlin'. Here's to the Rabbi Pope and your new-found wealth." He poured a few shots into her cup.

"New-fangled wealth is more like it." She took a healthy sip. "Are we gonna meet again on Friday night, Trev? I should have my new car by then. I'll drive us." Then she let her voice fall off as she remembered one of their conditions. "Oh, yeah, right. Separate cars."

"No more of that beat up old pick-up truck?"

She smiled wryly. "Yeah, if I kept driving that pick-up, people might think you were having an affair with my aunt Hellie." She chuckled at the absurdity.

The passing shadow of a concerned look showed her he didn't find it so amusing. He thought about his schedule for Friday night. "I'll call my wife and tell her I'm going bowling with the boys."

"That's good." She blinked sleepily. "Why don't you tell her the truth? Like the rodeo's back in town? Which it is." She hardly minded that he didn't take her to public functions, unless they were business-related. It was another one of their conditions.

He broke into a smile. "Yee-hahh!" he whispered furtively, then toasted her again.

"Ride 'em cowboy," she indolently whispered back.

He lit a cigarette, and then vigorously shook out his match. "Listen, sweetcakes, beyond all that, I wanted to talk to you about something else. We're talking work, now."

She slipped her cigarette into the bedside ashtray, and then drew up the sheet with her free hand to cover her breasts. "I thought you didn't like to mix work with, well—" She sipped her drink.

"Normally, no, I don't. But this is important. In October we break ground in New York for the Pavilion." He waited for her response.

"Uh, o-kay. Yeah. I know that," she said stiffly. She hadn't realized she'd seemed so tense. It was a reaction she had developed around him lately, but usually just around the office. She took another sip of her drink and savored the softening warmth of the whiskey.

"Well," he smiled lightly, "I want you out there with us."

"In New York? You want me to go to New York?"

"Uh-hunh, yeah. I've cleared it with Marty and his department." Marty Bull was the Director of the Oklahoma Tourist Board. Working with the New York World's Fair Committee office in Manhattan, he had driven the development of the Oklahoma Pavilion.

Regina had reasoned she'd never see New York City in her lifetime. She choked back her excitement. "Honestly? I mean, I thought just all you big shots were going."

"We need support staff, so there'll be others going from Marty's department. I thought it was only natural for you to come, too." Probably more convenient for Trevor, than natural, she thought.

"O-kay, wow. You just need us support staff to set you all up out there? I mean, how long will you need me? A week or so? I'll need to let Hellie know."

"Until October. From mid-April through mid-October."

"The whole fucking summer? Jeezuzz, Trev! What do you need me the whole summer for?" She squinted at him simpering back at her through a stream of his cigarette smoke. "Oh, well—yeah," she realized.

"Why sweetcakes! What do y'all take me for? I am your boss after all. You'll be working there at the Pavilion. Nine to five, just like any other day."

"Doing what, exactly?" She picked up her smoldering cigarette, took one last drag, and then tamped it out.

He thought for a moment. "You like water-skiing?"

"Trev. I'm from Iowa, where they farm and play football and basketball. Or cheerlead. There's not enough water there to support a water-skier. Sort of like here. So, no, Trevor, I don't water-ski."

"You'll learn."

"What are you talking about? I'm a klutz when it comes to shit like sports. Really. I always got an F in gym."

"We're going out to Crandall Lake tomorrow morning, and I'm taking you water-skiing," he insisted.

She reckoned It would be bad for her career to do anything but follow along with his hare-brained scheme, whatever it was. "O-kay, then," she said sourly. "But I'm sure you'll end up being sorry about this. Besides I just think this is all because you want to see me in a bathing suit, which I find kinda creepy 'cause you've already seen me in the altogether."

"That I have, Reg." He pursed a wicked little smile. "Which is why I know you're going to do just fine."

"This really is getting a little weird, Trevor. What's fucking water-skiing got to do with the World's Fair, anyway?"

He crushed out his half-smoked cigarette. "I can't tell you right now, but you'll find out soon enough."

Jesus! Water-skiing, now? Regina slunk back down under the covers, sure that Trevor had another one of his silly ideas cloistered away. His ideas were fine, as long as they didn't involve her. She thought about what three months in New York City might be like. She thought about shopping for clothes as she sipped her drink to relax into a light sleep.

An hour later, Trevor slipped out of bed to leave for his home. His wife. His children. That normal life adorned with secrets that suburban families lived. The last thing Regina needed now was any sort of "sweetcakes" conversation from him. Knowing he would soon slip alone back into the drizzly primordial darkness grown through the twilight from which they arrived, she feigned sleep. She heard the light crinkle of the usual fifteen dollars as he withdrew it from his wallet and placed it on the dresser. He called it "cab fare," but she knew better. And worse, she didn't care—anymore.

She soon saw the muted glow from his headlights filter through the flimsy window curtains, casting a soft swell of eerie shadows as he backed out. She heard the light sizzle of his tires through the open window as he drove from the wet parking lot.

Now alone, she felt a hardening around her eyes and a tight dryness in her throat. She caught her breath as she remembered Timbo's fragile touch upon her cheek as he offered her one of his smiles. Now she felt the trickle of a tear down that place on her cheek where he had touched, and she felt helpless—imprisoned away from a love she felt she might never have.

She choked as more tears began to flow, dampening and softening the coarseness of the pillowcase. She began to sob, once again releasing more of the tears she had steeled away since Jillian had died

Chapter 5

Who...*Me?*

New York City, Lower East Side, early July, 1963

The former Reverend Thomas Barragan from Hanson, Iowa had now become Reverend Thomas Deavers, of New York's Lower East Side. He was repulsed by the acrid smells of piss and old vomit that smudged the atmosphere in the lobby of his hotel. The room wasn't so much of a lobby as it was a squalid, airless chamber with some padded folding chairs and an overstuffed, seemingly abandoned couch, with its gray innards tufting out through its many rips. A large console television in a scarred pine case near the couch provided a soft glow through the moist, festering darkness as it flickered out an episode of "The Patty Duke Show." Cathy, the sophisticated look-alike of her unrulier cousin, Patty, both played by Patty Duke, was trying to reason with her doppelgänger about something, but Thomas couldn't hear the canned laughter because the sound was turned off.

Fred, the broad-faced, pocked-complexioned desk clerk, huddled behind a thick, scarred Plexiglas enclosure with a retractable tray to pass cash back and forth. Thomas held his breath against the human stink as he dared to squint at the old couch. He spied Ishmael, the resident derelict, in his usual place, heaped in tatters and watching the silenced TV show as he snickered noiselessly at the unheard jokes. It was just another evening at home. Thomas shook his head and trudged up the stairs, blistered and aching from his one-man battle with the gutting of his future church a few blocks away.

Thomas's hotel room was squalid. The stench of alley garbage wafted through the open window that looked out onto featureless brick wall six feet away. The open widow also ushered in a crush of heat and humidity along with the incessant tempest of traffic and police sirens. Still, it was a little cleaner and slightly larger than most of those rooms he had stayed in over the past 6 weeks, since leaving his former self behind in Iowa.

The table fan on the pinewood dresser creaked erratically as it pivoted on its iron pedestal, a stirring up the stillness of the settling evening heat. The terry-cloth bedspread looked as though it had come from a thrift shop, yet the bed was surprisingly soft. He lay down upon it, took his bronze and amethyst medallion from his pants pocket and then turned it before his eyes.

As he flicked and rotated the amulet he wondered once again why he chose New York City instead of returning to his childhood home back in Ballycannough, Ireland. Through the swirling color of the amethyst, he imagined the blessed scent of the lavender surrounding the thatch-roofed homestead of his youth. And he thought of Mother, his maker who died in his arms over 30 years before. But it was nothing but a vision. He blithely reasoned that though he would have preferred his ancestral home, he was already known there as a Barragan, from a founding family of Barragans. For his purposes, he needed the protection of the plain sight anonymity as the Reverend Deavers that could only be found in a city such as New York. He gazed into the amulet and meditated away from the stress of his day and the gloomy world he had chosen.

He soon reached that moment of enchantment where he could no longer help himself. His meditation drew up his inner desire with a flaming migraine along with the urge to vomit. Held by the lure, he slipped from his bed, snatched up a photo of his departed wife, Jillian, from the bureau and rushed into the squalid bathroom to make him- self over as her.

After throwing up, and still coughing, he leaned the photo against the mirror, nearly flaked away to its bare slate backing. He reached into the shadows beneath the sink and pulled out Jillian's wig and the ancient valise containing his makeup. The valise and the ingredients he had continued to replace over the years had been a gift from Mother, who had used its contents to make her son over.

Even if he had wanted to suppress his want to be a woman in favor of playing his genetic role as a man, he could not. He was overcome with the need to be the girl who dwelled within for as long as he could remember, when Mother began to mold the daughter she would have preferred from the innocence of her 6-year-old son.

During the day he was the Reverend Thomas Barragan Deavers, a man cast in the image of his god. Yet, even in the light of the day, little surges to become the woman he yearned to be gnawed tenderly into his desire. But the darkness of night was reserved for her—for Camille—the name that Mother had given to him. Making himself over felt like the loving embrace she had saved for him.

He started with the lip-color. The ritual of its application soothed him in the transition from what he hated into what he truly relished. As he delicately applied it, his thoughts drifted into the remembrance of his liberation of John Bass nearly three months back. Thomas knew his god had delivered the boy to him after John had found a fool's solace through the imposter, Jesus. John had come crawling to him, pleading for redemption from the sins of his life and the dumb burden of guilt he bore from the defiling of his daughter, Regina, by planting of his demon seed within her. Thomas had been angered by the prospect of his daughter bringing another tortured life into the world. John de- served liberation, and Thomas made sure the boy got what he deserved by drowning him through baptism. On his journey to New York after feigning his own suicide, Thomas deposited John's sodden corpse, still wrapped in the baptismal robe, in a woodland near Cedar Rapids.

Thomas's remembrance of John's liberation only led him to crave a release of sublime energy into his soul to nurture the god within him. He brushed a flake of mascara from his cheek, then went to the bed- room to begin to dress as his deceased wife.

Street business was scant at 11:45 p.m. and Willard, the night clerk, took his deep sleep seriously. His incessant snoring was softened through the Plexiglas window, now half-covered by a grimy shade. If there had been any traffic at all, it would have been the girls and their Johns sauntering quietly by, as Willard was irritated into surliness when awakened. The girls were on the honor system anyway, as their Johns would slip the five-dollar-an-hour room fee through the window slot.

Tonight, the lobby was quiet and lit only by a few dirty bulbs in the ceiling and the dim blue glow from the broadcast of the "The Steve Allen Show." Ishmael was huddled fetal-like in his putrid, fishy stink within a loose cocoon of rags. The TV audio flowed thinly above the silence. Allen was conducting his "Man on the Street" interview routine, alternating among fellow comics: Tom Poston, Don Knotts, Tim Conway, Louis Nye and Bill Dana. Ishmael's occasional laughter had been expressed more as abrupt, stunted yawns, as he had anxiously bobbed his head up and down.

But now Ishmael concentrated on something closer—the swaying of an amethyst that seemed to bleach out all else around him but its purple radiance. His own stench was softened by the scent of lavender. Thomas, now made up as Jillian—a willowy woman with short auburn hair—stood behind him. He was barefoot and wore his dead wife's pink silk blouse. If he had not been standing in the low gloom, one might, through a squint, have judged his womanly looks as curiously on the debit side of ordinary.

Thomas gently swung the medallion before Ishmael's puffy eyes. "God is with you, Ishmael," he murmured soothingly in a husky whisper. "Stare into God's light. He has come to claim you, because He loves you. Stare into His light. See only this, and nothing else."

From the television, Don Knotts stared in pop-eyed wonder at the audience and pointed at himself. "Who, *me?*" he blurted nervously. The audience laughed through the softened audio.

"Who, *meee?*" Ishmael parroted in a crusty whisper.

"God wants you to come to him," Thomas whispered close to Ishmael's withered ear.

"God, I be here," Ishmael murmured. His flabby, ulcerated lips bloomed into a faint smile. "Waiting fer you."

"Then close your eyes, Ishmael. Sleep now so God's love may embrace you."

"God—love," said Ishmael in release as he trembled into a deepening trance.

"Hold in your breath and feel the kiss of God," Thomas said as he gently covered Ishmael's mouth and nose with a bandana. It felt to Ishmael like a soft cloud, maybe an angel's kiss.

Jillian's wig shifted out of place as Thomas leaned closer and lightly pinched Ishmael's thick nostrils shut and held them closed. Soon he sensed the satisfying grate of the derelict's spirit as it cut into his psyche. It seeped throughout him, then eased into a warm oceanic sensation as it found a home in his soul. Staring down, mesmerized by the lifeless bundle of clothing on the couch, Thomas was overcome by how natural it had felt for him to harvest a soul to liberate his own. He reached into the skirt pocket and pulled out a vial of lavender. He smeared some drops on Ishmael's forehead with his index finger. "Blessings, dear heart," he whispered, as he brushed a tickling strand of Jillian's wig hair from his cheek. "And may you find your own god." Thomas stuffed the bandana and the vial back into the skirt pocket and then tiptoed up the stairs toward his first full night's sleep in weeks.

Chapter 6

In the shadows of the bridge

Bits of the five blocks between the Manhattan and Brooklyn bridges—the Two Bridges District of the Lower East Side—were a grim reminder of post-war Prague. The neighborhood's neglected and boarded-over buildings served as so many four-story tombstones memorializing a bygone age when the streets churned with immigrants. Now the stale odors of old dead fish from the Fulton Fish Market rolled in like a fog from under the shadowy conduits of overpasses which paralleled South Street. The rancid stink of fish was barbed by shards of mid-July heat through the swelter. The thermometer read somewhere above 80 degrees even in whatever might have passed as shade. And it was not yet 10 a.m.

Thomas had come to realize that he might have decided too hastily to buy and refurbish the woebegone building on Front Street that might someday become his church. He had resigned himself to the belief that he was severely conned by the Orthodox Jew who sold him the cruddy, dilapidated structure. Its interior was cast in the gloomy shadows from the FDR Drive overpasses and served only to darken the place's musty aura. But it was in the right neighborhood and the only nearly-intact structure in a row of jagged, crumbling cement and stone walk-ups.

Concentrating so much on the first floor that would house the chapel and his office, Thomas had scarcely seen the second, where he planned to live. Covered in white dust streamed gray in sweat, he had taken on the appearance of a powdery spirit barely coalescing from the gritty cloud that swallowed him up. He had spent over two weeks using a crowbar to remove the first-floor plaster that clung stubbornly to the lath. His once-tender healing hands were now blistered and dry in advance of developing calluses. His knuckles had been scraped raw and he had carelessly chiseled a deep cut into his right ring finger.

Below where he worked in vain to carve out his future sacristy was a huge basement, if one could imagine past the rusted iron monster of a coal-fired boiler, which sprouted root-like ganglia of pipes into the dingy ceiling. Near the 100-year-old furnace was a 4-foot deep, 5 by 10-foot coal storage pit. He had envisioned the coal pit as a baptismal pool, and it was a deciding factor in his paying too much for the building.

The basement had presented a special problem. Though he had swept it clean, its putrid odors clung to him for days after. Even after he had discarded his work clothes, the festering smell that had settled into the basement seemed to have been absorbed into his skin, causing the lavender fragrance he often applied more as a defense to intermingle to produce a fetid aroma of a perfumed dead rodent.

Late morning eventually blended into early afternoon. Even the weather's cooling and the gentility of the Allegro from Bach's "Third Brandenburg Concerto" flowing from a classical music station on his transistor radio did little to relieve the suffocating stifle held fast by the density of grit swarming around him. But at least the environment was brighter now that he had finally removed the boards covering the high windows on the first floor, and he welcomed the pale light like much-needed nourishment.

Coughing and short of breath, he put down the scraper and crowbar and went out into the open air to sit on the front stoop. He wondered if his stiff, labored breathing was anything like the black lung disease he had once described to his now tolerably qualified friend, Fred, the proprietor of the Cherry Street Hotel.

He glanced up at a monolithic brownstone buttress of the Brooklyn Bridge, and marveled over its construction. He came to realize that he could not be any more than the person his god willed him to be and that he could not do this reconstruction task on his own. He resolved to hire a contractor to finish the work that had sapped the strength he had overestimated in himself.

Pleased with his decision to bring in a contractor and a team of builders, he reckoned that this might have been a good day, after all. His mind had been so distracted by his sluggish attempts at renovation that he had neglected some of his newly developing primal spiritual needs. Even though he had liberated Ishmael last night, he still felt a void in his soul. He continued looking into the Two Bridges District that consumed the 5-block distance from the blue-painted Manhattan Bridge to the stone edifices of the Brooklyn Bridge rising above him. He then stared down into the shadows the FDR Drive overpasses cast between the two bridges. He spied darker lumps within the gloom. They were the lost ones—so gone in their crumpled lives that they may not have realized they needed liberation.

Thomas went home to shower and then went out for a late afternoon tea and bagel at a deli on East Broadway. After, he stopped at one of the many open storefronts in the close, bazaar-like environment of Canal Street in Chinatown to buy a red silk caftan he had noticed a few days before. When he came back to the hotel, he found Fred directing two movers as to where to place a newly delivered couch.

"Why howdy, there, stranger!" Fred called to Thomas. "Ishmael kicked the bucket last night. Bad ticker, I guess. I was lookin' for an excuse to replace that old couch he stinked up with all his piss, an' other stuff too ugly to think about. I figgured he'd leave us sooner or later, anyway, one way or another." He nodded toward the new couch being roughly carried through the door. "I been keepin' this new baby in storage for this moment."

"Too bad about Ishmael," Thomas said sullenly. "I was just kind of starting to like him."

"To each his own, I guess. Anyway, preacher, seems I haven't seen you in a coon's age."

"I've been working on constructing my church, but I realized I needed some time away from that devilish chore."

"A lotta work, eh?" Fred scratched at something beneath his ear. "Good idea to take a day off from time to time. Hell, even God did that. Right? On Sunday? You been working too hard at that church of yours, anyways, Preacher Tom."

"I'm no carpenter, for sure, so I realized I couldn't do it on my own. I was going to ask you, Fred. I think I may need a team in on this. You know any building contractors?" He shook his head at the thought of spending even more money on what was becoming a lost cause, then heard himself say: "I'll pay well, in cash, as I aim to be up and running by the holidays."

"Can't do much for you there, Preach. Never even considered remodeling this place, fine as it is."

Thomas conjured up a sly smile as he looked around. "I sort of realized that already, Fred."

"Hey, I might know someone," one of the movers said, "if you're interested."

"Why, I certainly am!"

"Some homo-guy over in the West Village, jest rebuilt an ol' dive into one o' them fruity-queer nightclubs. But I don't think they serve booze there 'cause them homos don't drink, though they might.

Maybe part o' their religion, or sompthin'. Who knows? Sometimes they do that pinko folk music and weird poetry shit. Stuff like: 'My dog shit on the rug; down with America!' Anyways, the builder did a pretty good job, and to code, long's they keep the lights low."

"You mean that builder, what's the name? Santiago? Santana? Somet'ing like that?" the other asked.

"Yeah! That was it, Dantano, no, *Dantana* Contractors over some- where up on Eleventh Ave. They're in the book so's you can look 'em up. Kinda artsy-fartsy, but she does good stuff."

"She?" Fred asked. "I didn't think women was the type of people to get dirt under their pretty nails." He held up both hands and twiddled his stubby fingers.

One of the movers snickered. "Yeah, some broad runs the business. She's just plain friggin' gonzo, if you ax me."

"Nobody axed you," the other one said. "Anyway, I think her name was Debbie. Debbie Dantana. Good lookin' chick. Most likely a girl-homo, too, bein' she runs a construction business."

"We seen her once. She looks I-talian, Latino, or sumpthin'." "Well, she *is* a good-lookin' broad," the second mover said. "Coulda been a fuckin' goddess, maybe, or even at least normal-like if she wasn't so raw. Like I say, she's most likely a homo-broad."

"Dependin' on your state o' mind," the first mover commented. "She's jus' an artsy-fartsy friggin' pinko beatnik-weird chick, if you ax me."

As they jostled the couch into position, Thomas decided to call this Debbie-person at Dantana Contractors.

Chapter 7

The artsy-fartsy pinko beatnik-weird chick

Deborah Dantana's voice projected a coarse, sandy timbre, which she routinely softened as though suddenly remembering she was fundamentally a woman. "A church? Really? Sounds like an interesting project. I've never done a church before," she told Thomas when he called an hour later. "Okay, Reverend Deavers. How about getting together tomorrow at the site to discuss details?"

Thomas found it nearly too easy to say, "Okay, Mrs. Dantana, that would be fine."

She laughed smugly. "Please, Reverend Deavers. Miss Dantana? I'm not a spinster, yet. I notice you have some sort of accent over this garbled-up phone connection. Is it English? Scottish?"

Thomas felt a rise of warm nausea along with an outbreak of sweat on his upper lip. When he became unguardedly nervous, such as when he spoke to a woman stranger, his brogue would filter through. "Irish, Miss Dantana. It's an Irish accent."

"Has a nice tone to it. Okay, Reverend. I'll see you tomorrow."

When he met her the following day, Thomas found that Deborah's exotic allure more than compensated for the roughness of her hands and the hard characteristics of her trade as a contractor. She was in her mid- 30s, about the same age as Jillian when Thomas—when she died. Deborah's dark eyes set behind weighty lids suggested an Asian influence in her lineage, but her smooth, light-coppery complexion with its fine, high, angular facial features softened by gentle waves of light-brown hair, revealed more of a Southern Mediterranean origin.

Except for some initial discussions over the plans for Thomas's church, they barely exchanged words. She sent him away from the building about a week after the construction began, telling him that she and her crew preferred to work alone.

"Your building belongs to me for the next three months or so, Reverend Deavers," she had said in her characteristically crystalline timbre of authority. "Obviously, you can check in from time to time, but for now, vacate yourself. Go shopping for carpet, or go have a drink, or something. We can talk about details of the design once we've gotten rid of this cruddy plaster and lath and've put up some decent walls." She ran a hand down one of the walls. "Man, oh, man! This place is ancient! Urban prehistoric, I'd guess."

She pushed her red painter's cap back on her head as she aimed a small, right angle square like a conductor's baton at a small battalion of workers, whom she directed with precision and an ultra-keen eye. "Too much torque on that drilling, Edwardo!" she called out over the whining grind of a circular saw from upstairs and Jimmy Soul singing "If You Wanna Be Happy (for the Rest of Your Life)" from the overly-loud radio in the kitchen. "Sand *with* the grain, Dave! Not *against* it!" "You're about an eighth-inch off on that framing, Jose!" "Nice, work Jason, keep it up!"

Except for some spot inspections, Thomas stayed out of her way as she had requested. Because of her assertive attitude, he had taken an embarrassed liking to her, which was distanced by an uneasy sense that she might consume him if he got too close.

Perhaps because of her, he exchanged his traditional hill country look of jeans and chambray shirts for pressed khaki pants, oxford shirts and occasional open-collar sport jerseys. He continued wearing his well-healed John Deere ball cap as a personal statement.

He relished the idea of having more time to himself to search for the lost souls in the bowels of the vicinity across South Street— under the overpass of the FDR Drive.

―――――――――

Dressed covertly in a pair of dark-blue jeans and a gray shirt, Thomas drew down the bill of his threadbare green ball cap to shadow his eyes to become one with the surrounding darkness. It was nearing 2:15 a.m. and he was frustrated from having worked for nearly ten minutes on hypnotizing a dazed man who remained propped up against an abutment and stared beyond the amulet Thomas swayed before his eyes. Along with intermittent glowing swells from the headlights passing overhead, the twittering reflection from the medallion seemed to be the only light setting the roughened man apart from the shadows.

A nearby voice finally slurred, "No use trine t'waken that one. He been sittin' up there dead fer near three days, now. "

Thomas realized there was little point in reacting to the voice from the unseen vagrant. He quietly wound the chain around his medallion, slipped it back into his jeans pocket and sauntered away toward another abutment.

He next found a muddied clump of humanity wrapped in a tattered overcoat of undetermined color. A stained New York Yankees cap, circa Joe DiMaggio, was flattened to his head as though it had grown there. He was mumbling quietly in a monotone over the sound of his little transistor radio—a rebroadcast of the second game of the Yankees-Indians double header. "Fuggin' Pepitone!" he slurred from a doze. "*Stupri strike ou' rex es. Alla te parcere whack at the stupri in pila!* Jus' whack at the fuggin' ballga, ya fuggin' rookie!"

Thomas took the amulet from his pocket as he crept upon the mutterer and then stooped down. He swung it casually before the man's heavily lidded eyes.

The vagrant continued mumbling. "Friggin' Yankees *potest non etiam ludere gamiata*, namore! Forgot how to play the fuggin' *gamiata*!" His muttering fell off as Thomas's fatigued voice rose softly over the whiffling of the traffic overhead.

"See into God's light. God has come for you—" The amethyst in its bronze setting caught the dim undulations of radiance from the highway lights which sent irregular waves of illumination across the man's broad, thick-featured, blackened face. His deeply browed eyes remained nearly closed within the hard shadows of his pockmarked face.

"Whatahelluia?" he muttered.

Misinterpreting his comment, Thomas said softly, "Yes, brother. Alleluia. God has come to take you to paradise."

The man jolted upright and opened wide his rheumy eyes. He swept the medallion away with a knurled hand. "What th' *fug*! Ge' that fuggin' *aliquid ex faciem meam*! Outta my face wi' dat yalunda you're waving! Wha' th' fug's *matter* wit' chu?"

Thomas shielded the amulet. "I'm trying to help you to find God."

"*Deus non est necessaria.* Don't need yer godwindo," he sputtered bitterly. "*Vocavit Baggada Intradato.* Got my own, called th' Baggada Intradato. Don' need th' one *yer* sellin'!"

Thomas rose and stood back as he glared intently at his prey, wondering if that was Italian chopping into his English, but then recognized it as a crude blend of Latin.

"Dei tui non inducitis in Yankees de hanc stupri 'ludum! No—yer godwindo canno' bring th' Yanklados outta this fuggin' gamiata! May stan' a chance wit' meo Baggada Intradato. Meo Baggada Intradato bring in Yogi Berra. Yer godwindo make 'im to go down strikin'. *Yer Deus eum ut descenderet, percutientes..."*

Phil Rizzuto, the Yankee announcer, called out from the tiny radio's speaker: *"Holy cow!* Yogi's hit a double!"

"...sometimes," the vagrant finished.

At a loss for words, Thomas could only mumble. "Sorry. I didn't know you were awake, I thought you were, uh, talking in your sleep."

"Ego semper vigilantis! I em always waked up! Gotta be, roun' here in the low-tow dstric'. Elsewise you in *morte, habens lunch cum Baggada Intradato*: be in death an' havin' a lunch wi' the Baggada Intradato— maybe not a bad t'ing—but not for me, *ne tamen."*

"Okay?" Thomas answered tenuously, not comprehending this arena of dead or vaguely awake souls such as this one speaking in broken Latin.

"Maybe okay fer me, mister. Ain't so much fer you."

"My god is fine for me," Thomas defended.

"Bene, sis pinna tuum godwindo: may you fin' yer godwindo right now, then. There be some sinners right behin' yer ass."

Thomas swung around to face three Latino boys. Even through the murk of darkness, he saw that they were vividly dressed and coiffed with highly preened ebony hairdos. The short, lithe and sallow one in the center held a menacing knife at his thigh. Its blade gleamed in the passing headlights from above.

"Buenos noches, señor," he said through a smirk. "Nice night, no?"

"Yes? It is." Thomas answered tensely as he stepped back.

"Si. But we are a little short on *dinero* to enjoy it. Very sad. You

can help us, no?" The lights from the FDR Drive reflected off the blade as he turned his knife and then slowly lifted its tip to the right corner of Thomas's mouth. "Maybe I do not cut you a nice big smile *por su dinero*, no? For your money?"

"I-I don't have any. No! Wait! Maybe I have some Traveler's Cheques." As he reached back for his wallet, he felt the tip of the knife pressing harder against his cheek. Thomas stilled his hand at his side. "*Muchachos!*" the gang leader called back to his subordinates. "*Tiene Traveler Cheques!*" They laughed unctuously as the knifepoint drew some drops of Thomas's blood.

Thomas watched helplessly as the two others stepped behind him and grabbed his arms. The leader slowly shook his head. "Ungh-ungh. *No, no, hombre viejo...*"

"That's all I have," Thomas said.

"No. No. You have more. You have a jewel. We have seen it. It is in your pocket. Here, let me find it for you."

Thomas clenched his fists. "*No!* You can't take that!"

"Oh, no?" The gang leader challenged calmly as he reached into Thomas's jean's pocket and withdrew the amulet by its chain. "*Si,*" he said admiring it in the light as his lieutenants tightened their grips on his arms. "*Si, viejo hombre.* I can take it. *Comprendre?*"

In the corner of his vision, Thomas saw the form of a large, dark-skinned man in a porkpie hat rise and coalesce from the gloom behind the gang leader. The broken bottles he held by their necks in each hand glinted harshly in the lights from above. The hefty black man stealthily and quickly approached the little Latino leader until he was close enough to raise one of the broken bottles to the side of his neck.

The gang leader stiffened as he felt the prickling sting of broken glass below his jaw. "Neh, Bernardo," came a whisper from behind him on a whiff of fetid breath. "Neh, ya can no take." He pushed the jagged edge of the broken bottle deeper into his neck until a trickle of Bernardo's blood rolled down to his collarbone.

Bernardo inched his knife slightly away from Thomas's cheek and froze in position. "I keel you for this, *sucio* Negro scum!" he seethed.

"Neh, li'l broder. I'm da one in control here in da Two Bridges, not you," the big man said as he brought the second bottle to the other side of his throat and pushed them deeper into both sides of Bernardo's neck. "You know who I might be, then, eh?" Slow drools of glistening, dark blood dribbled from where the broken bottles cut below the skin. "The *hedorpodrido* of your breath tells me everything," Bernardo seethed. The slow motion of his knife blade caught the light flowing from above.

"*Yoseréla muerte* to you if you move your blade to me. You turn your head; you bleed to det 'fore you can cut me."

Thomas felt the anxious grips on his arms grow limp. "*¿Qué es esto*, Bernardo? *¿Qué quieres que hagamos?*" one of them whispered nervously.

"Shh!" Bernardo spat. "*Que se vaya!*"

Suddenly, Thomas felt the grips on his arms loosen completely and fall away, as the castoff he had been talking to a few minutes earlier swung a four-foot long lead pipe hard against the backs of their knees. "*Et stupri* Pepitone whacks the fuggin' *pila* outta de *parco!*" he shouted.

"*¡Mierda!*" one of them cried as the two gang members collapsed backward to the ground.

The derelict then arced the pipe down hard on one of their shoulders, as the other gang member quickly crawled in a lopsided gait into the darkness. "*Ac turpis* hit *a* Tony Kubeck! A base hit from Kubeck! Holy cow!"

As the one gang member ran away, the derelict behind Bernardo twisted both broken bottles deeply into his neck, severing his carotid arteries. Bernardo's knife clattered to the ground as he crumbled to his knees. His blood pumped out forcefully as he groped for air. *"El Diablo Negro!"* he grunted.

"Yea," said the vagrant who was taking Bernardo's life. "I be dat: *El Diablo Negro!"*

Thomas was so mesmerized by the sight of Bernardo dying, he hardly noticed Bernardo's grip loosening on the medallion as it dribbled into a glittering heap upon the dirty asphalt. Thomas stooped to pick it up to place it back in his pocket as *El Diablo Negro* and the other vagrant stood high above him. *El Diablo Negro* then crouched to pick up Bernardo's fallen switchblade. He held it out to Thomas.

"He be yours to take, now, Broder," *El Diablo Negro* told him.

"Eta the rivralinto: float him *in ipso fluminis!"* the other added as he pointed his pipe in the direction of the East River. He then brought it down hard on his victim's spine. The gang member groaned away into semi consciousness as he slowly began to give up his life.

Thomas took Bernardo's switchblade knife and slipped it into his pocket. "Thank you, Brothers!" he said. "But I don't need to use the knife now. I have my own way." He withdrew the bandana from another pocket and placed it over Bernardo's nose and mouth, and then squeezed his nostrils shut. His dying resistance diminished, then stopped as Thomas felt the lurching shudder of the Latino's soul pass into his body. He took the little vial of lavender perfume, he now always carried, from his pocket and swiped some across Bernardo's forehead. "Blessings, dear heart," he whispered coarsely, then closed his eyes in prayer and let out a sigh. He held the bandana up to the light. It and his hand glistened in blood.

"Mortuus nunc: He gone, now." The other derelict pointed his

lead pipe to the one lying at his feet. "*Hoc bastardus, etiam*: This ono-chita, too, almost. Good riddance to bad shitata-cacca. I wish de ever'one dem be gonitono forever!"

Thomas looked up at him. "What's your name, brother?"

"*Meum nomen est* Milio!" he announced proudly. The iron pipe clattered to the ground as he stood at attention and saluted. "I seen da warrino and fight enta Europea in worl' warrino two, twenty year ago. I seen blood. Ete I seen da Germano det camps fer da Hebrewtos. I am Americanino, *ete meum nomen* stays to be Milio."

Thomas mulled this over. "Milio? Is that your name?"

The vagrant slacked his stance. "Milio, ya!"

"Thank you for your service, bother," Thomas groaned as he stood, shaken from his ordeal. "I am Rever-, uh, I am a preacher,'" he told them. "And I'll help you, if you ask. '*El Diablo Negro*', do you go by another name?"

"Before dey call me '*El Diablo Negro*,' me name went like dis: Juan Trout."

Milio chuckled. "Troutalino! *Sicut pisces!*" He blew out his cheeks in imitation.

Thomas swallowed back a pang of anxiety as he stooped over the second fallen gang member. He yelped out in pain when Thomas rolled him over. "!*Ayeee! No siento las piernas!*" he groaned. Thomas looked over at Milio and Juan, who now stood next to one another. Milio seemed ambivalent, but indignation bristled in Juan's eyes.

"He no feel his legs," Juan interpreted.

Thomas returned his gaze to the fallen boy and saw that his pink-satin shirt was open to the third button. A large silver crucifix suspended from a gold chain around his neck glimmered against the gloss of perspiration on his hairless chest. His glistening eyes were wide in fright. "Son, you probably don't understand when I tell you that your spine is broken. God has returned your sins to you so that you may never walk again. I am a man of God and can relieve you of your pain by bringing you to Him." He tapped himself in the chest. "*Padre*." He held his bloody hand over his heart. "Last rites," he pointed at his victim, then back at himself. "I am a *Padre*."

"*Él es un padre y le puede dar la extremaunción*," Juan translated for the dying gang member.

The young Latino's breathing quickened then stopped. He spat back at Thomas. The scant discharge landed on his hand to blend with Bernardo's blood. "*Tú no eres un sacerdote!*" he seethed. "*Usted es el* diablo!"

"He tells you: You are the devil," Juan said.

Thomas sighed in resignation as he routinely covered the young man's nose and mouth with the bloodied bandana until he felt the surge of another soul crumble into his. "Blessings, dear heart," he mumbled passively over the body. He anointed his forehead with a smear of lavender and then looked up at Milio and Juan. "Will you help me set these two into the river?"

Chapter 8

The simple joy of the game

Thomas visited the site of his future church once the plaster and lath were off the walls. The large room that would serve as the chapel had been framed and set up to be covered by wallboard, then painted. New electrical wires were already in place and meandering among the perpendicular arrangements of studs and joists. Deborah's concentrated expression softened as she spied Thomas and smiled self-assuredly. "G'morning, Mr. Reverend Deavers! We're making some progress."

"I can see that," he said.

"Electricians should be finishing up here in a couple of weeks. The existing wiring's for shit. Amazing this place hasn't burnt down. Come to think of it, it's pretty amazing it hasn't been condemned. Or maybe it already has. This city never keeps tabs on places like these. I guess Robert Moses and his city planners just hope they'll crumble away into obscurity to save demolition costs."

Thomas sniffed in deeply the scent of fresh wood — and a new beginning. "Probably so, Miss Dantana. But you'll make it right."

She relaxed against a door frame and folded her arms. "'*Miss Dan- tana?*' Who the hell is that? I already told you, Miss Dantana sounds like the name of my fourth-grade teacher — some bad memories, there. Please call me Deborah, for now." Her plush lips grew into a puckish smirk while she looked him over as if for the first time. "Let's just see how it goes."

Thomas was flushed through by a wave of anxiety. Through his naïveté about the workings of a coy woman, he didn't know how to interpret her comment. "Right, then, Deborah. You can call me Thomas—for now."

"How *cute*! You're blushing. I've broken through the reverend's reserve. Okay, Thomas Deavers. I've got some work to do here. You can walk around a little if you want to, so long as you don't trip over any wires—or any of my guys. If all goes well, we should have the insulated walls up and the electric running before early October. Have you picked the carpeting out, yet? I'd go with a dark beige. And don't forget about the plumbing fixtures," she called back to him as she made her way into the large room that was to become the sanctuary. "I'll help you out with the kitchen appliances..." Her voice trailed off behind her as it was drowned out by the rasping buzz of a circular saw.

He saw a clear space to stand in the old parlor, which would serve as his office, to the right of the stairway and went there to pore over an electrical schematic rolled out on the drafting table. He realized a further aspect of Deborah's skill as he gazed at the color-penciled mappings of a ganglion of wires broken up by circuitry symbols and icons representing the language of an electrician. It was all a confusing hieroglyphic to him, representing something that only she could decipher. While staring at the plans, he overheard a gush of whispers between two Latinos working on a nearby window casing.

"*Me he enterado encontró cadáver de Bernardo e Hernando ayer por la mañana. Ellos hicieron flotar en el* East River," the one with hammer said.

"*Si. Cerca* Hell Gate *cerca el muelle en* Astoria," nodded the other as he fitted a level to the side of the casing.

"*Dicen que 'El Diablo Negro' asesinato Bernardo e Hernando.*"

"*Después ellos auxiliar encontrar y matanza 'El Diablo Negro'.*" He drew a finger across his throat to emphasize his point.

Thomas hardly needed a translation to understand what the two workers were discussing. The mention of Bernardo and *El Diablo Negro*, along with the hand signal for death prompted him to go out and buy some newspapers to pore through them for anything on the death of the two Latino gang members.

He left quietly and then walked up to a newsstand on Delancey Street and bought the four major New York City newspapers. He found a bench and then began to scour the papers. There was nothing in the New York Times, The Daily News or yesterday's evening edition of The New York Post. But he did find a blurb in the police blotter of *The New York Knickerbocker*, a daily gossip and crime tabloid.

More Scum Washes up at Hell Gate —

By Frank Malone,

Senior Editor, The New York Knickerbocker

New York City — August 29, 1963

Police found two bodies washed up near Hell Gate in the East River, near the boat piers in Astoria, Queens, yesterday. The two Latinos, reputed gang members from the Lower East Side, were the victims of a gangland-style killing, presumably the work of one of their own, or a rival gang. The bodies were tightly tied together with the pants of one of the victims, whose pockets and legs were weighted down with stones and debris for ballast. Their shoes were missing" (Milio had claimed Bernardo's red sneakers) *"as was all the glittery junk that gang members wear as their brand. Nevertheless, the bodies were identified as those of Ra- mon 'Bernardo' Hernandez and Hernardo Trevez-Villa. They are reputed to be key members of the Lower East Side Latino gang, Los Lobos*

Solitarios ("The Lone Wolves").

Who knows? Maybe this is the sign of better things to come. Maybe these lowlifes will end up killing themselves off!"

Thomas found Milio basking in a thin slant of sunlight near his abutment. His little radio was silent, as Milio became aware of some- one standing before him and opened his puffy, bloodshot eyes. *"Abite, vos!* Go 'way, you!" he groaned huskily, and then shut his eyes again. Now in daylight, Thomas saw that he was not a Negro, as he had suspected, but a white man covered in filth, with sad, deep-set eyes that had seen too many of life's darkened recesses. He had the appearance of one who had given up, yet who needed to be spared.

"Milio, it's me, the preacher. Don't you remember me?"

Milio shrugged deeper into his pile of clothing and turned on his side.

"We, uh, sent Bernardo and his gang member into the river a few weeks ago. You, El Diablo Negro and me. Remember?"

"Bernardo, he is bad shitata-cacca," Milio mumbled from his fetal position within the heap of his clothing.

"He's dead now, Milio. He can't bother you anymore. Bernardo is gone."

Milio rolled back over to face him. "Bernardo? *Abiit?"* He deepened into thought as he fingered the rough brim of his Yankee cap. "No. *Ante biduum, vidi.* I seen he two days before dis."

"No, brother. He's gone. *Abiit.* We sent him away last week," Thomas assured him, realizing that people like Milio most likely had no sense of time. He nodded toward the silent transistor radio. "No baseball game today?"

"*Ballaga gamiata,* yes. Yanklados an' Chicagito White Socklitos." He reached behind him and held up a nine-volt battery. *"Mi* radio, *frangitur*—broken. *Non sonus*—no sound."

"Can I have that?" Thomas asked as he reached out for the battery.

"Ya." He dropped it into Thomas's open palm. "Non worklino for me no more."

"I'll be right back," Thomas told him as he pocketed the battery and walked with purpose back toward the site of his church.

He returned in a little over an hour with a ten-pack of nine-volt batteries, opened it, and handed one to Milio, who had hardly moved. "Wasa dis—*Quid est hoc*?"

"For your radio. So you can listen to your Yanklados game."

Milio offered up a scant-toothed smile. "*Tu es* Baggada Intradato!" he said as he eagerly reached behind him for his radio and then plugged in the battery.

Thomas remembered that Milio had referred to his higher power as the 'Baggadda Intradato.' "No, Milio, I am only the preacher."

Milio hadn't heard him as he held the radio to his ear. Thomas heard that the Yankees were ahead, three to zero. Catcher Elston Howard, after having batted two men in at his last at-bat, was up, and Milio was lost and grinning through the simple joy of the game.

Chapter 9

The sanctity of a marriage

A one-night stand with Alice after not having seen or heard from her since their divorce did nothing to lift Ray Nealy's frustration over her. Before last night, he had felt the benign warmth of her presence in his memory, but now, after finally seeing her, he tried to shake this morning's image of her walking away—this time for good. He was plagued by sight of her retreating stiffly toward the Waldorf Astoria lobby with her head held high like the place was built for her departure. It crushed Nealy's 15-year-old reminiscence of her laughing in the sunshine of being 25. She was all he saw among the swirl of people milling around the hollow marble environment of the gilded concourse as she wove her way toward and finally down the stairs to the hotel exit. She soon softened into the bustle of reality, coalescing back into life like a translucent spirit and leaving only the crumbs of Nealy's reflection upon last night behind.

For now, this was a perfect place to forget. And to be forgotten. Nealy had been nursing his first and second drinks for the last hour-and-a-half, since settling into the leather comfort of a bar stool in the Waldorf's Bull and Bear Bar. To an outsider, it looked as if he might be praying over the altar of his drink as he stared down at his hands. They were and the smooth, sinuous hands of a 20-year-old, rather than those of a man in his mid-forties. One of them clenched a damp cocktail napkin, the other his tumbler of Scotch on the rocks. His hands were still shaking in the aftershock of Alice's leaving, which registered as a delicate tinkle of the ice against ice in his drink.

Nealy felt smothered by the deep oak and mahogany environment decorated with trinkets suggesting the stock market; ornate bronze pedestal clocks and glass-domed stock tickers. The din of conversations meandered throughout the otherwise soft and respectful mid-afternoon silence. The place was decidedly masculine, with thorough- bred horse portraits on the walls and suffused in the rich, manly scents of cigars, bourbon and Vitalis. He glanced up the high nest of liquor bottles arranged behind the bar in typical Waldorf Astoria style—clear to the left; increasingly darker to the right—in an organized, logical purpose. Above the bottles of booze stood a bronze statuette of a bull and a bear standing beside one another and looking off into a distance. He smelled the mellow sweetness of some cigar smoke from three stools over, where a porcine man with a deep voice was chatting with a willowy, overly done-up woman with her hair highly piled. This enticed Nealy to light up a cigar for himself.

Though his divorce from Alice had been as amicable as it was mis- understood, it had been tearful for them both. They clearly loved one another but were just were not growing well together. They had become uncomfortable in each other's presence. It happens in marriage. They had run out of words, but not out of love.

And then she called him last week to say she'd be in town. She had told him her purpose in coming to New York was to be with him for the final night they had denied themselves years ago. And why not in a room at the Waldorf, where they had their honeymoon? Alice needed closure. Nealy needed closure. It was a nice touch that quickly turned to a stab at his heart.

Their pillow chat after an uninspired second round of sex—their last—led her to talk about her life as it was now. She had married the man who had led her away from him. She and her husband moved to Fort Worth, of all places. He brought a four-year-old son into the marriage, and she had given birth two years ago to their daughter.

Kids. Somehow Nealy never imagined Alice with kids.

During their marriage they had decided against children; she more than he. She reasoned that his being a New York City cop would be bad for a child. As it was, he had spent away his time on 16-hour days and was rarely home. Besides—God forbid—he could get killed in duty. That, more than anything, was what made her so uncomfortable and increasingly led her to keep her distance. In the fifth year of their marriage she found her next husband, an oil broker down on Wall Street. That was safe. Last night Alice got the closure she had wanted, only to leave Nealy swaying in the wind. She could now be whole again to raise her children. Through the confection of his memories of her, Nealy had forgotten how subtly cruel she could be. It left him loving her more.

He sipped his Scotch and decided he would try to take his mind off Alice by calling Jenny, the receptionist from his days at the 20th precinct, where they had had a platonic fling. Jenny became concerned that she might be getting too close to Nealy, a married man. Being a good Catholic, her guilt led her to transfer to the 2nd down on the Lower East Side—as far away as she could get from the 20th on 82nd Street.

Nealy realized he was absurdly free now, and he knew Jenny, now a cop herself, had not yet married. Jenny Pretroni from the 2nd precinct. He used to joke with her that hers was more the name of a Mafia Moll. He decided to call her on the pretense of congratulating her on the promotion to street cop, on her way to the detective she had always wanted to be. That would be a cause for a belated celebration, and more closure for him.

He flattened out his napkin on the bar and then downed the rest of his Scotch. He ordered another. "Do you have a phone booth in here?" he asked the bartender as he put Nealy's fresh drink on the bar.

"They're in the lobby, sir."

"Okay, thanks," Nealy said as he rose from his bar stool and snubbed out his cigar. He took up his drink. "Save my seat. I'll be back in about ten minutes."

"Very well, sir," the bartender solemnly answered, in a peevish, Waldorf Astoria style.

***

Jenny seemed overjoyed to hear from her old compadre from the 20th precinct. Of *course* she would love to see him again. She needed the break. She told him it would take her mind off her having to study for the detective's exam in three weeks. They agreed he would pick her up at 7 p.m. at her apartment on East 79th street.

Thoughts about his guilt over cheating on Alice, or her memory, turned to those about his work and Francesca, his secretary and associate. He called his office over on 1st Avenue to hear Francesca's voice to reclaim some sort of normalcy, and to check in to find out what was not happening in his caseload. It seemed that, lately, nothing ever happened. "Raymond," Francesca asked after a few minutes of listening to him, "are you hungover again? You sound hungover."

Private investigator that he was, Nealy knew when Francesca was privately investigating him. He swallowed a sip of his drink and felt the warmth of it soothe his throat. "I am not hungover, Frannie," he said, his voice registering as a low echo in the warm confines of the booth.

"You're sounding a little bit slurry to me," she said. "I've come to know you too well over the last twelve years. I can tell when you're coming down from a bender. The booze is killing you, Raymond. Stop it. Now!"

"Yeah, okay Frannie, I will," he lied. He sensed Francesca was about to engulf him in another one of her lectures. He felt a rising sweat begin to seep through his fingers and palm clasping the handset. "You can't go on like this, Raymond. If you become a lost cause, you'll lose all of us who love you. Well, maybe all except Marty, because you're his favorite barfly. And that's pretty pathetic."

Francesca had taken up the annoying, yet increasingly necessary habit of mothering him, even though she was 12 years younger than he. One of the concerns that filtered through the fog of booze and hangovers was his growing dependence upon her for matters beyond their work. He secretly wished for both of their sakes that she would find herself a steady boyfriend upon whom to bestow her draconian coddling.

She had just asked him something. "What, Frannie? I didn't hear you," he said.

"Have you been taking your vitamin C and B-twelve?"

He winced through a dull surge of a headache. "Yes, Frannie. Have you been taking your Valium?"

"Shut up," she said over a suffused giggle. "Anyway, I know what all of what you're doing to yourself is about. It's about that ex-wife of yours. Raymond, forget her. Alice is probably happily living in a place like Kansas…"

Fort Worth, Fort Worth, Texas. Jesus! he thought.

"…with her current husband and golden retriever while she does something like sell cosmetics to win a pink Cadillac. She's probably forgotten all about you. Over and out."

Nealy reasoned: Yes. She has now forgotten all about me. To turn his thoughts away from that, he turned them back to Francesca.

"Well, hon," he said, "you're being awfully intense this morning."

"It's 'cause I'm really worried about you, Raymond. Where the hell are you, anyway? You haven't been here for two days, and I can't run this business of ours, for what it is, all on my own—" Her voice fell short.

"What is it, hon? You sound choked up."

"You're doing too much drinking. I fucking *hate* it. What it does to some people." She sniffed. "My father was a drunk and did some horrible things to me and my mother. She divorced him for it."

His concern for her seemed to remedy his headache and bring him out of his funk. "I never knew your parents were divorced. You always told me your father died."

"Well, he did—for me. And he did for everyone else a few years later when I was fourteen and they found him dead and drunk in a gutter in front of a Naples whorehouse during the war."

"Frannie, hon, I'm so sorry."

"Well, I've had a really terrific step-father for the last sixteen years, so don't be sorry for me. Take that sorrow to yourself and do some- thing about your problem. Anyway, Raymond. There's a lot you don't know about me that I want to tell you. But I can't. Why? Because I don't know if I can trust a—a drunk."

He was stung by this. He never realized that she might not trust him after all the years of knowing him.

She tried to diffuse the land mines lurking in her admission. "I'm sorry, Raymond. I guess I've been having too many childhood night- mares, lately. I don't mean to be so tough on you. You know I trust you. I just want you to know I care. Anyway, you as well as anyone knows I can tie one on myself from time to time. I just hope I can know when I've had enough."

"Apology accepted, Frannie," he said pensively. "Any calls?"

"Just the usual. It's been a quiet day in the naked city. Marty called. He said it was business that could keep until you got back to honor the lunch you promised him for Friday."

Police Sergeant Marty Cohansen and Ray Nealy shared the dubious distinction of having been friends since criminal justice school. "I did? I promised him a lunch?"

"He thought that might confuse you, so he said for me to remind you that the Red Sox beat the Yankees on Wednesday."

"What a leech," Nealy mumbled as he remembered their bet.

"That's it?"

"That's all, Raymond." She sniffed.

He realized she needed to relax her tension as much as he needed to nurse his wounds from last night. "Listen, Frannie. You need a day off. Why don't you turn our calls over to the service and go home to rest? I'll be in tomorrow, okay?"

"Thanks, Raymond. I might do that. Are we still friends?"

"Sure, hon, of course. Kiss, kiss." he said, then hung up the phone. He hadn't realized that he had tensed up so. He relaxed his shoulders and took another sip of his Scotch.

Chapter 10

The sorrows of denial

Con Edison Electric was digging up the street again. The drilling and pounding had slogged on for nearly a week outside Nealy's second floor apartment in the Upper West Side. An incessant and angry cacophony of honking horns from the traffic rose above all the construction noise of jackhammers and the clanking and groaning of the gear they used. The noise had continued into the night as it interrupted Nealy's sleep and inflamed his morning hangovers.

Tonight, drink in hand, Nealy languished in the quiet oasis of his East Side mid-town office. In this womb of a place, he found it comfortable to sink into the deep end of his depression. And since that desperate night he spent with Jenny after the bitter-sweet one with Alice last week, there had been an increasing number of depressions.

He relaxed back into the plush office couch. He savored the close, cozy softness along with the scent of worn leather and the warm relief offered through his drink. He extended his legs out onto the cock- tail table, then leaned back luxuriantly as he stared across the room at his hulking mahogany desk in front of two, tall-arched windows. They displayed the warm and impassive lights of Queens coalescing through the misty pre-midnight sky across the East River.

Hamlet, his parti-colored, blue-eyed basset hound, lay

seemingly just as at ease in his dog-smelly bundle of blankets off to the side of the room. His loud snoring was punctuated by low wheezes, and even an occasional whimper as Nealy reasoned he was dreaming of chasing squirrels in his sister's back yard in Rhode Island a few weeks back.

But it wasn't Hamlet's snoring or the view from across the river that kept Nealy's mind occupied. It was still Alice. He was continually plagued by the uneasy belief that he could not fall out of love with her. But tonight, especially tonight for some reason, he found himself wishing that she might have returned to her life in Texas to realize she loved him still. His "Alice-remembrances" had begun to scare the hell out of him, more so than any case he had worked on with Marty Cohansen up in the 20th.

Hamlet began whimpering again as he flailed his stubby legs in the air from where he lay on his back. Thankful for the interruption, Nealy reached over and turned on the lamp on the end table, dousing the room with muted light that flooded the panoramic view of Queens with a dull glare. He groaned as he sluggishly swung his long legs from the table. His right knee had commonly complained from a tiny scrap of shrapnel that had wedged itself near there as a 19-year-old remembrance from some forgotten and insignificant battle in eastern France.

He swigged the remaining contents of his glass of Scotch. The aura became further wrecked from the hi-fi through the jazz meant to soothe the mood of the evening. Dexter Gordon's mellow version of "In a Sentimental Mood" began to play. It had been one of Alice's favorite pieces. Nealy was besieged by a swell of frustration. He threw his glass against the brick wall above the hi-fi as a release. It didn't help. The glass shattered into six pieces when it hit. One its pieces careened off the wall and disrespectfully streaked the needle through the song.

In further frustration he kicked the cocktail table away. The bottle of Johnny Walker fell to the floor and its treasure seeped into the carpet. "Shit!" he grumbled in protest, hoping there was another bottle to replace it. Even if there was more stash, the only tumbler he had left was lying broken into shards on the floor near where he had flung it. Even in times like these he preferred to soften up the hard edges of his gnawing addiction to alcohol through the dignity of drinking it from a glass.

Nealy limped over to Hamlet's water bowl, picked it up, and then went to the bathroom sink to fill it. The harsh light from the little bath- room woke Hamlet up, and Nealy heard his collar jangle as he shook himself fully awake. He realized that maybe a walk down First Avenue would do them both some good despite the weight of the heat and humidity that had thickened the night.

Francesca arrived at the office at around 10 AM to find her boss disheveled and trying to work at his desk while nursing a cup of coffee. She sighed. It didn't take much imagination for her to conjure up the feeling that it had been another rough night for him.

From even a short distance, petite, sultry, yet wholesome-looking Francesca Cancelli might be mistaken for a teenager. In truth, she was 33 years old, but, like a teen, she carried a nearly perpetual expression of adolescent innocence bordering at times on wonderment. Though she was only five-one and a bit stocky, she took weekly karate lessons and worked out or jogged four times a week, and her stoutness was mostly muscle tone. Her cherubic features were framed by a volume of lush, dark-russet-brown hair, which hung smoothly by its weight to a few inches below her shoulders. She had sleepy, deep brown eyes. Marty Cohansen once had called them "bedroom eyes." Those eyes, and a seductively husky voice that belied her small size had come close to ensnaring

Nealy more than a few times. But he and Francesca both knew better than to mix church and state. Besides, she knew that Nealy had been suffering from the plague of Alice. So, Francesca remained a colleague, sometimes a confidante, and his friend of 11 years.

She glanced over at the couch piled high with a muss of pillows. A tumbled bedsheet was draped from the couch to the cocktail table to the floor. Under the table was the overturned empty Johnny Walker bottle and a plastic picnic glass, a quarter-filled with murky, stale Scotch. She spied the shards of the broken glass below the splatter on the wall. There was a stain on the rug that hadn't been there yesterday. The ashtray on the couch's end table was piled to overflowing with half-smoked cigars. Among them were a few cigarettes, which she knew Nealy smoked only when he was troubled or really drunk. A long horizontal photo of the Brooklyn skyline from the Manhattan Bridge hung cockeyed above the low bookshelf serving as the coffee making counter in the makeshift kitchen. The coffee percolator's basket splayed out a small pile of muddy grounds from where it lay next to the pot.

The still-damp stain in the carpet felt mushy beneath her right foot. She hoped Nealy hadn't neglected Hamlet enough for the dog to pro- duce it. She looked around from the crooked picture on the wall and then to him sitting silently and unshaven at his desk, staring fixedly into his coffee mug as if trying to read the grounds. "Love what you've done to the place, here, Raymond," she said wryly as she removed her shoes. She picked up the empty bottle and put it on the coffee table.

"Trying to land us a slot in next month's *Town and Country*'s interior design feature?"

He answered her with a mellow grunt while he stared more intently into his mug, seemingly afraid to move lest his head roll off onto his desk.

Hamlet rose from his bed with a groan, then waddled over to greet Francesca with his characteristic welcome: a hoarse hound dog noise caught between a short low howl and a bark. "Hey there, Hamlet!" she whispered excitedly at him as he approached with his tail up and wagging in a languid circle. She knelt to his level and rustled the velveteen fur on his low-hanging ears. He licked her face and smeared her mascara. She felt the dampness of the stain in the rug seep through her stocking to her right knee. She reluctantly dipped a finger toward it and then lifted it to her nose, grateful that it wasn't Hamlet's pee, but booze. She glanced back at her boss. "So, you slept here in your clothes again last night? Or didn't sleep, as the case may be. I'm sensing another obvious problem here, Raymond." she said through her attention to Hamlet. Then she stood up and leveled a gaze at her boss. "You know that damn couch is no good for your back."

"I find it cuddles me like my mamma used to," he grumbled as he painfully looked up at her and attempted a forlorn grin.

"There's no future in going back to the womb, Raymond. And I gotta tell you. From a woman's standpoint? It would hurt like hell."

"Ouch!" he cringed.

"How old's that coffee you're drinking, Raymond?"

He stared reflectively at the stained white mug with the 20th precinct's emblem on it. The mug was a souvenir; cracked and soiled from years of his badly-brewed coffee, but it had remained amazingly intact despite his tending toward clumsiness brought on through hangovers. "I think I'm down to the sludge."

"Amazing there's any sludge in that weak brown disaster you pass off as coffee, sweetie," said Francesca as she made her way toward the percolator. She picked up the fallen grounds basket, wiped up the mess on the counter, then approached him and reached out a hand. "Here, gimme. I'll make something we both can drink that will actually help you to wake up to the day." He handed her his precious mug. She walked to the bathroom sink to wash it out and to fill the percolator.

"Oh, yeah. Late yesterday, while you were gone, Marty called again," she called over the running water. "He said it was nothing import- ant—nothing that copious amounts of bourbon couldn't cure and that he'd catch you at The Back Page. Did you see him there? I assumed that's where you went last night. You know, Raymond?" she caught herself from delivering another lecture. "Never mind." She carried the cup and percolator to the counter.

"I didn't go there last night. So, I didn't see Marty."

She couldn't help herself. "So, you came right here to drown yourself in that—" she glanced down at the empty bottle under the coffee table, "that shit?"

"Who are you? My *mother*?" Nealy groused. He winced over the dry, feverish pain shadowboxing in his head.

"Sore subject, eh? Well. Marty called. That's it," she repeated as she walked over to him. "No million-dollar case this week. Or last. Or the one before that. Or since time began."

"It's okay, Frannie. Don't worry. I'm sure our caseload will pick up soon enough."

"Really, sweetie? Are you predicting a murder spree coming up? Or maybe even just some unfaithful husband that we need to spy on? You know? Why is it only the husbands that are scum? What about wives? You ever notice that, Raymond? It's never the wives?" She walked back to the bookcase next to the humming refrigerator where the coffee was kept.

"Don't know, Frannie. You tell me."

"It's because we broads are perfect," she said smugly.

"It's because you're broads," he chuckled back at her over another wince. It hurt to laugh.

"Spoken like the true idiot you are, sweetie. You're such a pig sometimes." She dished what looked to be ten scoops of coffee into the percolator basket.

"You baited me. Oink, oink."

She turned on the coffeepot and then trained her gaze intently on him, as he scratched at an unshaven cheek. "Seriously, Raymond. You look like shit. When was the last time you got any real sleep?"

"I don't know. Are the Dodgers still playing at Ebbets Field?"

"I thought so." She took a little time for thought. "You know, I'd invite you back to my place for the night, if I didn't think your psyche would object."

Nealy had stayed at Francesca's apartment on York Street once or twice before, after the two of them went out drinking and he needed a place to pass out. But she hadn't been this candid with him before, and the look on her face broadcast a serious intention. Nealy felt a dim jolt flow though his body, as the thought of them together even for just one night crossed his mind. "I, uh, don't know, Frannie. I don't think—you know since Alice and I broke it off. I'm still kinda, well, you know."

"Shit, Raymond. That was over six years ago. Get over it, already," she said, then coquettishly put her hands on her hips as she caught the mistake in her invitation. She felt the need to dig her way out from the embarrassment of her pointed suggestion. "Wait. What were you thinking, Raymond? You think I was offering you the 'fun-bad-leave- me-in-the-morning experience,' because you need some sorta sexual reassurance, or something? You just need a good night's sleep is all. And a stiff drink isn't working. I wasn't talking about sexing you to sleep. I was thinking I have a mallet in my kitchen and I would knock you out with it, so you could sleep. Any hanky-panky would just keep you awake. Shit. I may use the mallet on you anyway, now that you've thought those evil thoughts. You should be ashamed." It was more wishful thinking on her part. Her lower lip quivered. Thinking she had overplayed her scold, she turned back to face the coffeepot, as if her staring at it would speed up the brewing process. "You know, I've seen you stand up to some of the toughest guys and crimes in the city. But one woman? You're a squashed bug on a windshield."

When Francesca became flustered in conversation, her natural defense was to deflect the subject. But this time she walked over to him and planted a warm friendly kiss on his forehead. "I'm sorry you thought I—" he began.

She investigated his bleary eyes and smiled brightly. "Have some coffee when it's ready and come back to life a little, Raymond," she said. "I'm gonna take my little buddy, here, for a walk." She slipped on her shoes and then patted her thigh. "C'mon, Hamlet!"

Beyond his feelings for Alice, Nealy truly loved two things in his life because they hardly ever complained, except for an occasional biscuit, or a carburetor change. One of these, Hamlet, was shaking his sleep as he stood up from the pile of dog blankets where he had been resting. The other was the two-tone maroon and cream-colored Night Bird, his 1939 Fairchild Warner amphibious float plane. He gazed at the picture of plane on his desk. He imagined the chattering of its pontoons on the choppy, fresh-smelling water that shivered and rattled the fuselage around him as he came up to speed for takeoff from Rangeley Lake in central Maine where he had a cabin. The thought eased his pain.

Chapter 11

Deborah's time clock

The high whine and grating ring of circular-sawing and power-drilling had finally stopped as Deborah's crew broke for the day. A radio playing overly loud had been plugged into the new circuitry in the kitchen and streamed out the closing chords of Leslie Gore's "You Don't Own Me," through the disk jockey's interruptive quips.

Then a semi-hourly newscast recapped Dr. Martin Luther King Jr.'s speech delivered the day before in the Washington, D.C. Mall crammed with peaceful demonstrators. "I had a dream…," it began, and continued about the days when race would no longer be a barrier for anyone who wanted to truly live in peace. "Dr. King's speech was viewed by some on Capitol Hill as grandstanding for the masses," the newscaster reported. "But overall, the demonstration was peaceful, featuring performances by Mahalia Jackson and Peter, Paul and Mary. Joan Biaz and Bob Dylan performed their own brand of protest folk songs."

The Moscow-to-Washington, D.C. hotline would soon go into service for the President and the Soviet Premier to talk directly to one another, and to avoid the kind of tension that took place nearly a year ago during the Cuban Missile Crisis.

Many Americans were confused by the new "Zip Code" postal service that had begun in early July. "Soo—Oh-*kay*! So be the news.

Now it's time to 'zip' you back to the Dan Ingram Show here on: (cue jingle) *Seventy-seven. W-A-B-Ceeee!*"

Thomas turned to see Deborah leaning against the baluster. "Well, Reverend, what do you think of your new church?"

He nodded timidly. "I see the walls are up."

She relaxed her stance, smiled coquettishly and loosely folded her well-toned arms. "Yeah, down here and on the second floor they are. We're still putting up some studs on the third floor, and there's some more wiring to be done. The fridge and six-burner stove'll probably be coming in tomorrow or Saturday. Did you see the island we put up in the center of the kitchen? I designed it. It's got lots of cabinet space." She directed a dark-eyed gaze at him as though mining for something she knew lay deeper.

Unnerved that they were alone, Thomas looked bashfully away. He scratched his chin and then ran a hand through his hair, which had filled out stylishly from the brush cut he had over 4 months before, when he arrived in Manhattan. "You've done beautiful work here, Deborah, much more than I could've expected. Really—good—work. I've, uh, picked out some oak wood pews. I, uh—just need to know how many I'll need."

"Okay," she acknowledged casually with a little nod. "Uh, Thom- as. There's something I've been meaning to ask you, and I hope you don't mind. "

Caught between fear and hope, he said, "Uh, o-kay?" "We've done a pretty good job on this place."

"A very good job, Deborah. Excellent."

"Yeah, well I almost hate to ask this, but it's time for our second payment."

He relaxed his shoulders as he sighed in relief. "How much do you need?"

"I've estimated about—uh, nineteen thousand?" Then she

added quickly, "I mean if you want to pay it over time, we can work something out."

Thomas had just received another $100,000 check from the trust fund in Dublin that his barrister, Shamus, was handling. A few hours before, he cashed it though a shadow account that Shamus had set up in The Upper East Side and was on his way to deposit the money in his legitimate Chase Manhattan Account. "Okay. I'll pay you in cash. You sure you won't need a little more?"

She offered up another coy smile. "Jesus, Thomas! Why can't *all* my clients be like you?"

He smiled back at her, nodded approvingly and then turned to leave. "I believe in paying a person his due, Deborah. I hope your other clients would do the same. Actually. I have the money in my parked right outside. I was—just on the way to the bank to deposit it."

"Are you *crazy*, Reverend?" she scolded. "You should *never* drive around this neighborhood with a carload of cash! Christ Almighty, a guy gets mugged for a dime here in the Two Bridges District. Or cops could arrest you for getting the cash from a drug deal!"

"I was just bringing it to the bank."

"Who cares! You know what you need, my friend? You need an urban mentor. I can help you there."

"Sorry, Deborah, I didn't—" His voice fell off in embarrassment.

Deborah realized she might have come down too hard on this ten- der man—a rube in the big town. She glanced down at the floor, and then leaned over to pick up a stray wood shaving. "Actually, Thomas," she muttered wistfully as she concentrated on the little curl of wood she held up to the light between her thumb and forefinger. "Now that you mentioned your car, I was wondering if you could give me a ride back to my place up on Mercer Street in the Village. The guys took my truck back to the shop and —"

Thomas answered her with numb enthusiasm. "Okay, of course."

"Then maybe we could talk about the rest of the project over dinner? I know a nice little place on West Fourth. My treat."

Thomas felt caught in a loop. "Okay — of course, Deborah. Why not?"

Deborah's brick-faced townhouse was nestled into a row of similar structures near New York University on a close-knit, shaded street in the heart of Greenwich Village. She brought her talent for design into her home — a generous mix of light, space and orderly clutter. Thomas might have expected this style of her through the precise, ordered approach to her work. The far wall was of glass divided into a perpendicular arrangement of asymmetric panes along the lines of a Mondrian *De Stijl* grid. Through it, he saw a backdrop of lush foliage fringing a narrow brick patio.

The open style of her home was in contrast to in the opulent window hangings and drapes — a confusion of primary colors and prints. These little and large clashes of color were accentuated by the near-sterility of the walls and scarcity of furniture consisting largely of over-sized cushions placed on the thickly carpeted floors, around polished short-legged teak tables. Even the dining room was an arrangement of purple and beige pillows scattered haphazardly around a large table sunk into a well for diners to extend their legs. He might have written this unusual quasi-Asian style off as a woman's touch, had it not seemed so unique to Deborah.

She gestured toward the living room, "Go ahead and make yourself comfy while I run upstairs to wash up and change. Make a drink or grab a beer from the mini-fridge under the bar, whatev — I don't know, do you preacher-types drink? I don't want you to burn in hell for—oh yeah, that's right. Jesus drank—all that water into wine last supper mumbo jumbo." Her breathy, restive voice trailed behind her into the open hollow of the second-floor landing as she walked up to her bedroom.

"*Jesus—last supper mumbo jumbo.*" Thomas repeated quietly and liked her even more.

Deborah did not need Thomas's money, as she normally paid her loyal crew in advance. The Dantana Construction Company had been passed down through the family for nearly a century. Having had a hand in the construction of Penn Station, The Metropolitan Museum of Art and Madison Square Garden, among other city icons, the company first made its mark in the late 19th century as her grandfather's construction company aided in the shaping of the city. Many turn- of-the-century architects requested Dantana Construction for its understanding of the neoclassical style. The company had worked with such landscape and architectural luminaries as Stanford White, Frederic Law Olmsted, Cass Gilbert and Henry J. Hardenbergh. Despite the setbacks and backroom political interests of the Tammany Hall machine, the Dantana Construction Company grew its business into a medium-large enterprise over its 30-year heyday.

Domenico Dantana, Deborah's father, was a second-generation Italian and the son of Salvatore Dantana, who had started the construction business in New York in 1862 with his Japanese wife, Shimita. Salvatore died in 1918, leaving Domenico, his only son, as the heir of his company. In 1926, shortly after his father's death, Domenico married nineteen-year-old Celita Epricanasio, a Spanish Castilian beauty, whose father had been a highly placed Moor married to a Sicilian. Soon after his marriage, Domenico partnered with a fellow builder and investor, Massimo Corelli.

Deborah was born in 1928, followed a year later by her brother, Benny, who was destined to be the primary inheritor of much of the company. Deborah would be the secondary heir with a trust fund, and the primary beneficiary of an exotic attractiveness gained from her mixed heritage.

Domenico died suddenly of a heart attack in 1946 while attempting to lift a heavy beam on his own. Massimo Corelli assumed the task of running the Dantana & Corelli Company in 1948. While most of the company had been willed to Benny, he had gone off to fight in Korea and left the running of the business to Massimo. In 1953, Benny died from shrapnel which had lodged into his stomach from an explosion of a land mine.

On paper at least, Deborah had inherited her brother's share in the construction company, though she wasn't anxious to run it. She naively left its operations in Massimo's hands, which had made sense, given his working experience with Domenico.

But she soon found out that Massimo had been bilking company funds since before Domenico died. While Benny was in Korea, Massimo had been the sole watchdog of expenses and profits and kept two sets of books. When Deborah finally came into her father's business after graduating from The Pratt School of Design, it was open season for Massimo's cooking of the books until a careless accounting error brought his transgressions to the surface, along with a lengthy court procedure. The Dantana & Corelli Construction Company, once valued in the hundreds of millions, even before Massimo rearranged the funds, was now truly worth only $620,000. It was not until around 1959, when Massimo was finally convicted, that Deborah's company became worth $120 million on the residuals from all its buildings' leases and the firm's core worth. The money was now faithfully handled through the law offices that had convicted Massimo.

Still, Deborah had no interest in running a large construction company. Set for life, and knowing her limits, she downsized the once giant Dantana & Corelli Construction Company to simply: Dantana Contracting, Ltd. To keep busy, Deborah chose only a few, more eclectic, jobs. What she loved to do most was apply her own assorted tastes to the detail work and the interior designs.

Now 35, Deborah's biological timeclock was ticking, and she wanted only to be loved wholesomely for herself. The men she had been with before showed feint affection as they tried using her position as a means toward claiming her as a trophy. She sought someone different—a man who knew nothing of her well-publicized worth—someone from outside the world in which she had come to feel so lonely. She wanted to learn more about The Reverend Thomas Deavers.

She gazed at her reflection in the shower-steamed mirror. Some short, light-brown curls clung damply to her cheeks. She gently swept them aside and applied lanolin to soften her skin. She then searched the cabinet above the sink and found a neglected bottle of lavender fragrance and daubed it beneath her jaw to feel less like a dusty construction worker and more like the tender woman she aimed to be.

Dave Farragut's, a plush, rich mahogany wood bistro on West 4th Street, was designed in a maritime theme. Thomas and Deborah sat in a small corner booth and chatted idly over their single-malt Scotches, tilapia and baked stuffed lobster. After toasting to the success of the project, they casually discussed its future as a church, the layout of the upstairs, and, Deborah's favorite topic, the interior design. Though Thomas had some reservations about her excessive design plans, he remained respectfully quiet as the pleasantly foreign effects of the Scotch set in to dissolve his uneasiness.

Their conversation about the plans of the building worked its way down from the rooms of the third floor and then the nearly completed second, and then the first, where the sacristy, office and kitchen would be. Finally, there was the basement. Here she had planned a parish hall featuring a large dumbwaiter to lower meals down from the kitchen. She brought up the subject of the large bin in the floor near the old coal boiler, which she already had replaced with a propane gas-fired furnace and water heater. "We should probably cement over that dirty old coal bin to add more floor space."

"Actually, Deborah, I was thinking the bin could be converted into a baptismal tank."

She smiled tightly over the rim of her glass. "You mean a swimming pool, don't you? That's one hell of a big hole in the floor."

"No, really. I'll be performing baptisms, and I think it's a nice size for it."

She furrowed her brows. "Really, Thomas? How many baptisms are you gonna do at one time? You could fit about ten people in there." He simpered uncertainly. "Well, I suppose it could double as a swimming pool when it's not Sunday," he said. "No, really, Deborah. I have this idea that I could cover the bottom with smooth stones and some live aquatic plants."

"What? Like the Jordan River?"

"Exactly," he answered. "The Jordan River. Is there a way you can do that?"

She sipped her drink. "I can do anything you want," she said, then stared down at her dinnerplate in thought. "I'm beginning to like your way of weird thinking, Thomas. A swimming pool built to mimic a lake."

"The Jordan River. Or a piece of it," he corrected her. "With under- water lights."

"Yeah. You'd need small heating and filtration systems, just like a large swimming pool. Hah! I'm really beginning to like this idea! It could be a really neat soaking tub, when you're not using it to wash away sins. A soaking tub of holy water. What a great advertising ploy! 'Wash away your guilt in our Holy Water Soaking Tub!'" She placed her hand over his, and he stiffened with apprehension. "You're crazy, Thomas, you know that." She raised her glass. "To the Holy Water Soaking Tub!"

Thomas slid his hand from beneath hers and raised his glass. "The Holy Water Soaking Tub, hear, hear!" he said, and then added, "You know I really like your perfume. I love the smell of lavender."

"Yet another thing we have in common." she said.

Chapter 12

Los Lobos Solitarios

The Tide Washes up Some Trash on Welfare Island—

By Frank Malone,
Senior Editor, The New York Knickerbocker

New York City —September 14, 1963

It seems like good things happen in twos in the Upper East River. About two weeks ago, this reporter wrote about two Latino gang lieutenants, members of Los Lobos Solitarios, *washing up dead in Hells Gate in Astoria. They were tied together by their pants and weighted down with rocks. Now it appears two more members of the same gang, identified as Geraldo Lopez-Anchito and Chico Maldinaro have washed ashore, also wrapped in weighted-down burlap bags, on Welfare Island. Like the two earlier gang members, Bernardo Hernandez and Hernardo Trevez-Villa, who floated ashore in Astoria last month, Lopez-Anchito and Maldinero had also been deliberately stabbed.*

I suggested then that these low-life gang members might be killing one another off. But I've changed my opinion on this and am now going out on a limb to suggest that, due to the similar M.O.s, this could be the work of a vigilante; a Good Samatitan in my book. If so, keep up the good work, fellah! And may you never be caught!

Thomas folded up *The New York Knickerbocker,* smiled smugly and then flipped it into a trash can.

He often visited Milio during the day to bring batteries, coffee and crullers, then sit with him while he contentedly cradled the large new radio Thomas had bought for him. After a time, the big, burly Juan Trout, *El Diablo Negro*, sheepishly sneaked in to join them to bask in the waning warmth of summer. There they would sit in the cool, musty shadows of Milio's space to discuss baseball and the dwindling of gang activity in the area as big band music played over Milio's radio.

Today, Thomas dropped in to tell them about the piece he had read in *The Knickerbocker*. "We've become vigilante heroes, now!" he told them. His comment was lost on Milio, who, though he remembered the preacher for his generosity, had already forgotten about these latest incidents that had prompted the preacher's uncharacteristic glee.

Juan listened intently. "We might be doing it again tonight," he said as he inclined his head toward the glimmer of a bumper of a partially concealed, apple-green ship of a car parked half a block away on South Street. "Me, I have feeling dey be plannin' at sumpthin' now."

Nestled deeply into the white Naugahyde interior of their metallic-flaked green Buick 88, three of the *Los Lobos Solitarios* members listened to the full blast of Ray Barretto's Latino hit, "*El Watusi*," as they discussed their plans for the coming night with the driver, Julio "*Jalinqo*" Fontana, the gang leader.

After losing four of his key members and having read their eulogies in *The Knickerbocker*, he was determined to take down those responsible for killing off his gang lieutenants. He squinted out toward the three men who sat under the highway. "*El grande bajo el puente. The big one. He ees El Diablo Negro. Él está hablando con uno llamado.* And the ahtter one, Milio, ees wearing Bernardo's red shoes. I do not know *el gringo*—the white one."

One of the gang members lit a cigarette. "*Han matado a cuatro de nosotros, Julio.* There are now only six of us."

"Tonight we take care of that—we take care of them!" Julio seethed. He stole a drag from his comprador's cigarette. "*Van a estar muerto!* By tomorrow! *Muerto!* El Diabo Negro and Milio. All of them!"

At around 1:30 a.m., five *Los Lobos Solitarios*, including Julio, stood over Milio and taunted him by demanding he tell them where they could find El Diablo Negro.

"Non *El Diablo Negro.* Do no knowen him," Milio said tiredly as he reached behind to place his hand on one of his metal pipes.

"You do, *eres tonto borracho*! We saw you today with him!"

"*Quod scire non viti!* Dozie no mean I knowen which placindo he lives!"

One of the gang members reached toward Milio's new radio. "No, no—li'l boy!" Milio warned as he raised the short iron pipe in his left hand.

The gang member threatened him with his knife. "That fuckin' little pipe do no good for you, tonight, *borracho.*"

"Aye," Milio told him as he reached behind again as he stood. "Bu' *dis* do!" He rapidly produced a baseball bat as he adroitly lumbered to a stand and then expertly swung it as though swinging for a home run into the *Los Lobos Solitarios* member's midsection, and then quickly jammed its end into the stomach of the one standing next to him.

Julio and the two others would have rushed toward Milio if they hadn't been restrained by sudden, thick hammerlocks from behind by Juan and Thomas. Thomas tightened his hold while he held a knife to Julio's stomach, as Juan held his broken bottle to the other's jugular. "I am *El Diablo Negro*," he told him as he jammed the bottle's broken edge into the side of his throat. Julio screamed sharply at the gush of blood from his fellow member's neck, as Thomas thrust his knife deep into Julio's belly, and hooked him in that position as he jabbed the knife repeatedly into Julio's gastro-intestinal works, as though trying to mash them up.

"No, no, preacher!" Juan scolded him. "Dat way you jus' geeve heem bad stomach ache! He still be alive. Here, let me show." He grabbed Thomas's bloodied knife, thrust a downward stroke deep into the side of Julio's neck, held it there until he collapsed limply into near-death. Juan lifted the knife and demonstrated the thrust twice in the air. "In da neck artery like dis." He told Thomas, then handed him the knife. "Here. Now you show me how."

Thomas raised the knife and arced it down timidly into Julio's pulsating esophagus, as Julio finally died.

"A little better, preacher," Juan said. "We work on it, okay?"

"Okay. Thank you, Juan," Thomas breathed as he felt the dull sting of Julio's soul passing into him.

"Maybe next time, we use gun, no? From distance?"

Thomas considered this as he thought of Seamus and his connections back in Dublin. "Maybe we should. I may be able to get some."

Juan stopped the looting of Julio's body and glanced thoughtfully at Thomas. "For true, preacher? Of course I cannot get—but you can?"

Thomas smiled brightly through his blood-spattered face and as he interrupted his last rites over Julio. "Aye, Juan. I think I can. I might have—connections." Juan smiled back at him and nodded as he went back to his pillage. Thomas glanced back down at Julio. "Blessings, dear heart," he muttered impassively, then rolled the body away.

A fifth gang member who had backed off to the side in horror finally scrambled frantically toward Julio's Buick parked a block away. Juan turned from his prey moaning on the ground as he bled out and drove a fatal thrust of Thomas's knife into his neck. He then quickly rose to follow the stray member running for the car.

Thomas motioned him to stay. "Leave him be, Juan, let him go. No, wait..." He reached into the right pocket of Julio's silver pants and drew out his car keys. "Here, give him these to drive back to warn the few that are left."

And the Hits Just Keep on Coming!

By Frank Malone,
Senior Editor, The New York Knickerbocker

New York City —September 30, 1963

I learned yesterday that last week some Brooklyn cops found two more Los Lobos Solitarios *bodies washed up, this time in Red Hook. They were also tied up in weighted burlap bags. To add icing to this cake, a few days later, two additional members floated to the river's surface near Greenpoint. The cherry on the icing is that one of these dead scum was Julio "Jalinqo" Fontana, the gang's primary kingpin, who has eight homicides credited to him (arraigned but never convicted due to loop- holes in the investigations), along with a slew of robberies. Also, gang ac- tivity in the Lower East Side has significantly decreased as these deaths have mounted. Is it possible that* Los Lobos Solitarios *have been eliminated? The only one I now know who can tell us is the vigilante that I'm now certain is responsible. Thanks again, buddy! Stay hidden; stay safe!*

Chapter 13

The Back-Page

The 20th precinct cops drank while some reporters pretended to play cards as they listened in for stories at the Back-Page Bar on Broadway and 31st Street. The penumbral watering hole was redolent in an aura of seasoned masculinity, saturated with the sweet and peppery fragrances of bourbon, beer, cigarettes and cigars. The bar's colorless, wooden-beamed, tin ceiling and creaking wide-planked floor seemed to groan under the weight of decades of the printed rumors and exaggerated crime stories that had been discussed around the marred tables.

The late-afternoon crusty irregulars were there: Double-talking Nick Pesipio, who repeated some of what he said like an echo; Willie Faraday of the Hat, who never took off his time-worn brown fedora; Mighty Joe Kanowski, who resembled the famous gorilla of nearly the same name; and Stogie Frank Malone, who claimed he was born with a Havana Supreme in his fat lips. They had the look of a ragtag collection of B-movie bit-part character-actors, but were in truth four of the hottest crime beat reporters at *The New York Knickerbocker*. At 4:30 p.m., the drop-dead hour for the city edition, they and some other city scoops retreated uptown to The Back-Page to discuss their breaking stories over bourbon, brews and smokes.

Nick, Willie, Joe and Frank made their afternoon home there to eavesdrop on tidbits for tomorrow's morning edition, now that the day shift in crime was ending. Although the 20th precinct—the "Two-Oh," as it was known—was located inconveniently about 50 blocks north of West 31st, this was where the Two-Oh detectives, cops and other assorted gumshoes met to soften the edge of the day away from their beat. Though reporters and cops respected their different spheres, at The Back-Page, it was what was heard, not what was seen, that counted.

Other than the smoke-fluffed green clouds of illumination under the lamps overhanging the bar, the dim carnival glow from the round, old Wurlitzer jukebox provided what seemed to be the only illumination in the place. No Rock n' Roll was permitted in this shrine. The Wurlitzer was stocked with Benny Goodman, Frank Sinatra and Vic Damone tunes. Sinatra singing "I Wish I Were in Love Again" meandered softly through the atmosphere and provided a mellow audio background.

"Anyway, Jack's sister had this cat," Nick was saying, "this cat, I swear to God."

"I believe this, what you are saying, Nick," Mighty Joe intoned interestedly in his spent, dry voice. "Jack's sister had a cat..."

"A *cat*," Nick repeated. "She taught the thing to shit in the toilet... shit in the toilet."

"Christ, so damn, friggin' what?" Frank Malone crabbed wetly through his smoldering stogie as he looked down at the poker hand he had dealt himself. It was a nervous habit he performed with the worn-out deck of cards he carried around in his pocket. He picked a five-card stud hand from the deck while pretending not to listen to the cops at the adjacent tables. He sure as hell didn't want to listen to Nick talk about Jack's sister's cat taking a dump in the toilet. "We all gotta shit somewheres. Frankly I prefer a terlet myself."

Mighty Joe took the most unimportant topics acutely, as though there might be a story in it. "Yeah, Frank," he said, "but you're not a cat."

"Jeeezuss, Joe," Malone sighed down at his two of a kind.

"Then he'd flush it...flush it," Nick continued, "all by hisself. A friggin' *cat!*"

"Now that sure as hell is a scoop," muttered Malone as he started to deal himself another hand. "Let's stop the fuckin' run of the City-Ed and put that one on the front page."

"Maybe the second page," suggested Mighty Joe.

"Joe?" said Malone as he stopped dealing long enough to squint at him. "As long as you continue to take this shit that Nick is saying seriously, I'm gonna continue to worry what sort of sickness is payin' rent in your head."

"Anyway, I thought it was important," Nick said with a little flinch as he tightened his tie. "You know, human interest...human interest."

"Screw human interest," Malone said darkly from the depths of some perpetually mysterious chip on his shoulder.

Willie fingered his hat brim and then sipped his beer as he tried to break through the developing ice. "Hell, I'm more interested in Jack's wife."

"Jack's been livin' off the fat of her income...the fat of her income," said Nick. "All he does is send her to work, unless he's waitin' for her to cook his dinner. You know, work and dinner—dinner and work. That's her whole relationship to him. I'd never treat a woman like that. Never treat her that way."

"That's why you ain't never had a woman, Nick," Malone told his cards. "They *like* bein' treated like shit. It's like a motherhood kinda thing. They always seem to gotta take care of something—or someone, then they gotta complain about it. Jeee-zuz! How they *love* to friggin' complain."

"Were you and Myrna like that, Frank?" Nick asked. "Always com- plainin' at each other?"

"Nah—we were above all that shit."

"So, that's why she left you, hunh?" Willie asked through a tone of light condescension and the haze of his cigarette smoke. "You weren't paying enough attention to her?"

"Anyways," said Malone, as though briefly absorbed in thought. "Ya know, since history began women are only savvy to what they can care for, even if their husband is a deadbeat like Jack."

"That's very profound of you, Frank. Very profound," Nick said as he winked at Willie. For a moment, Malone faltered in drawing a card from the overworked deck.

Willie tamped out his cigarette and lit another. "Anyways, so Frank—I see you're still holding on to your, like, premonitions about them gang killings on the Lower East Side." He blew out a stream of smoke as Malone deepened his concentration on his cards. "Like some sort of vigilante's at work keeping the place safe for democracy, or at least for the tourists who never go there?"

"…Or our Cosa Nostra buddies who run the fish business down there," Nick added and then sipped his beer.

"Shit. A one, a four, a three, nine, and a five! Fuckin' lousy hand!" Malone grumbled as he slapped his cards face down and then looked over at Willie, then at Joe sitting next to him. "Vigilante. That's what it smells like to me. Why? You guys got a problem about that?"

"Not me—not me, Frank," said Nick.

Willie looked passively over at the detective, Marty Cohansen, and his buddy, Ray Nealy, the private investigator, sitting a few tables away nursing their respective bourbon and Scotch. "I heard one of 'em was stabbed right through the prunes. Twice."

"Ouch!" Nick said.

"I know you heard it, Willie, 'cause I told you," Malone reminded him. "And the guy, their leader, 'Jalinquo' Fontana, was ripped open at the stomach. His guts was falling out."

"Shit, Frank," said Mighty Joe. "I find that to be, like, really disgusting."

"Hard world, down there, Joe," Willie said.

"Hard world," Nick agreed.

Willie continued, "At least they was wrapped in burlap bags. Right? Like I don't know, scarecrows, or some shit, right? Maybe that's what you should call your vigilante guy, 'The Burlap Bag Avenger.'"

Nick raised his glass to the passing waiter to indicated he wanted another beer. "Kinda goofy-soundin' to me—'The Burlap Bag Avenger.' Goofy-soundin'."

"Pro'lly ain't a bad idea, though, Frank," said Willie. "Sorta like a hook for your scoops. To give your guy a name like that."

"This ain't some sorta Superman character," said Malone. "The M.O.s are the same and concentrated on them *Los Lobos Solitarios*. I think I've fuckin' hit on something."

"Why don't you call him 'The Scarecrow' because of the burlap bag thing?" suggested Mighty Joe. "It's got, like, a ring to it."

"Oh, yeah, right," Malone said as he sipped his whiskey. "Maybe we could run it in the Sunday comics."

"Why not?" Nick said thoughtfully. "Why not? That sorta shit worked for J. Edgar Hoover back in the Twenties an' Thirties."

"G-men comics," Willie reminisced. "I usta *love* them freakin' things. Then I got old."

"That's ridiculous about the comics," said Malone. "I was just kiddin', ya galoots."

Willie shouted over his shoulder at Cohansen and Nealy. "Yo! Marty! What do you think? Think we should turn them killings down on the Lower East Side into a comic strip?"

"Oh, crap, Willie," Malone mumbled around his cigar. "Don't get *them* guys involved."

"Not my precinct, Willie," Cohansen called back huskily from where he stared down at his drink. He then leaned back in his chair and held his glass of bourbon loose in his hands. His neck bloomed around his frayed blue-shirt collar. His cheeks were lush and fit into the fullness of his fattening chin.

Nealy sipped his Johnny Walker Black. "What do you make of those gang killings, Marty?"

Cohansen pursed his lips in contemplation. He widened his eyes and gazed across at Nealy. "Not much, Ray. Every once in a while, the gangs do their own housecleaning. Maybe more efficiently than the Department does. 'Specially down there in Frontier-Land."

"You think there's any juice in that vigilante theory?"

"Like I said, those gang creeps take care of their own, for better or for worse. Long's they stay out of the Two-Oh, I'm fine with it. Speaking of for better or for worse. You gotten over Alice, yet?"

Nealy let out a little sigh. "Yes. No. Shit, I don't know."

"Well, buddy you been pining long enough, now. You should get on with the rest of your personal life."

"I'm trying, Marty." He thought about what to say next, as he measured out his words. "Ya know? Alice showed up in town last month— "

"No shit!"

"I didn't want to tell you back then, for some reason. Anyway, we spent the night together. At the Waldorf. Just like our honeymoon."

"For Christ's sake, Ray! Why you go an' do a stupid thing like *that*? Ain't she married again, or sompthin', by now?"

Nealy huffed out a sorrowful laugh. "Yeah. Anyway, the result equaled me wanting her more. And now she's back in Fort Worth with her husband and kids."

"She got *kids*?"

"Two. One from his old marriage and one from—the two of them. Now I wake up every morning thinking about her." Nealy smiled reflectively. "That's not all. She messed up my mind so much that I spent the next night with Jenny Patrone. You remember her."

"From the Second down on the East Side? Shit, Ray...I'd say it's about time if it weren't so fuckin' pathetic."

"Yeah, that just made matters worse in my head."

"Ray, you gotta get yourself a life outta this funk o' yours. It's gonna affect your judgement like..." Cohansen stopped in mid-sentence.

"Like what, Marty?" Nealy challenged mildly. "Like why I left the force?" He recalled the time a little over five years back when he and Cohansen had chased a 15-year-old kid up to 90th Street after a robbery. The kid, backed against a wall, wielded his pocket jack-knife, which in the dark, Nealy took as a stiletto. He pulled his gun and then the trigger. The kid only got winged in the arm, thanks to Cohansen pushing Nealy's gun arm away. The only thing the kid was guilty of was being scared. Nealy could have been guilty of a lot worse, but the NYPD's Internal Affairs Department swept it under the rug. The kid was black, after all, and that kind of stuff always happened up in Harlem where the kid was from and where incidents like that were best forgotten.

"Well," Cohansen pondered delicately. "You had just split with Alice. Your judgment was fuzzy."

Nealy stared down at his drink and smiled sadly. He concentrated on Tony Bennett singing "Old Devil Moon" circulating from the jukebox into the haze of the environment. "I was drunk," he said.

"You was cleared, Ray. You know I wish you'd come back to the Two-Oh. It's time."

Nealy dismissed Cohansen's invitation—again. "Yeah. Look, Marty, you won't say anything to Franny about what I just told about me spending that night with Jenny, okay?"

Cohansen smiled with half his mouth. "What about Alice?"

Nealy shot him a threatening squint. "That goes without saying. Don't tell Frannie about any of it. Okay?"

Cohansen wondered why Nealy cared so much about Francesca not knowing about his friend's little dalliance with Jenny and goes-without-saying Alice. Nealy was only human, and Jenny was a step in the right direction. He put down his drink and tapped his temples. "Womb to tomb, Ray—It's locked here in the vault. Though I don't know why you'd care if Frannie knew."

"I just want to keep things businesslike between us. "

"Hell, she's your right arm. She reads your mind. She prob'ly already knows. You done with that Scotch? I'll get you anudder." He lifted his empty class and wiggled it. "As for me, I could use anudder Jim Beam."

"Why not, buddy? If you're buying," said Nealy. "Anyway, how many guys did that so-called vigilante take down?"

Cohansen rolled his shoulders. "We'll if you're to believe Frank Malone over there, six, maybe seven." He glanced over at the table of reporters. "Yo, Frank! How many them gang members you say was found floatin' up the river?"

With his broad back still to them as he stared at his poker hand, Frank held up five fingers of his free hand, then clenched it and held up three more. The whole thing had become a fish story.

Nick called back. "Eight. Frank said eight, Marty. Hey Marty! What's your cop opinion say? You think we should call Frank's guy 'The Scarecrow?'"

"It's a stupid idea, Nick." Then he said to Nealy, "There's no vigilante, Ray. Them gangs are just cleaning out the closet down there, like I said. And them snoops over there just wanna make a comic strip out of it to back up the one they've already made up in their so-called true crime stories." He looked over at the door. "Ah, here she comes, Miss America."

Nealy looked across the room and spied Francesca making her way toward them. "Don't tell her about that thing, no matter how drunk you get, Marty," he reminded him.

Cohansen tapped his temple. "In the vault, buddy." He flagged a passing waiter. "Sam! Pour us another round, and a vodka grapefruit for Miss America, there."

"Sure thing, Marty," the waiter mumbled as he made his way to- ward the bar.

Francesca looked over Frank's shoulder as she passed. "Lousy hand, Frank. Not even worth bluffing over. Better deal yourself another."

"Why, I oughtta..." he grumbled.

She lightly patted the pate of his balding head. "Now, now Frank, be a gentleman. Here," she said as she quickly rubbed where she had patted. "That's for luck."

"Thanks, Frannie," he muttered though a slight smile. "You don't know how much that fuckin' means to me."

"Frank don't have the stuff to be a gent like you asked, Frannie," Willie said. "Now, *me* on the other hand..."

"In your dreams, Willie boy, in your dreams," she scoffed through a loose little smirk, and then made her way over to where her boss and his best friend were sitting. "Hey," she said as she pulled an empty chair from the table next to them and sat. "Miss me?"

"I ordered you a vodka grapefruit," Cohansen said.

"Well, then, skip the formalities and marry me now, Marty." Her deep red nail-polish glittered in the scant light as she scissored her right index and middle finger together. "You gotta ciggie for me?"

Cohansen fished out a Pall Mall and his lighter from his breast pocket. "You really wanna get married to me, Frannie?" He then peered deliberately over at Nealy.

"Marty's already married, again, and living in Flushing with the rest of suburban America," said Nealy.

She placed her hand over Nealy's. "Well, I guess that just leaves you." The waiter put her drink in front of her. "Thanks, Sam."

"'Welcome, sweetie."

"Don't tempt me, Frannie," Nealy chided.

"Yeah, by all means, Frannie. Don't tempt the man," Cohansen said and then sipped his drink. "He's not the marrying kind—yet."

"That's why I asked him, Marty," she said. "He's safe."

"Knock it off, you two," Nealy said. "Any calls?"

"Just some woman—again. She's been callin' for a week now. Says it's personal." She looked slyly at him. "You been holdin' out on me, or something, Raymond? Well, anyway, good for you, buddy. How come you never call her back? Maybe you should."

Cohansen cast Nealy a smug look, tapped his temple and mouthed the words: in the vault.

"Been too busy, I guess." He thought that maybe he should call Jenny back—maybe it would be something they both needed.

She sipped her drink. "Well the truth be told, I'm uncomfortable as your go-between. So, call her back, already, will ya?" It sounded like a challenge.

"No" he said.

Francesca smiled dejectedly down at her drink. "Still love your ex that much, eh, Raymond?"

"No, I'm not going to call her back, that's all."

"Why not?"

"Don't want to," he pouted.

She shot an accusing glance at him. "For shit's sake, old man! You trying to prove some sorta point not calling her? For the life of me, I'll never know what makes men tick."

Nealy took a healthy sip of his Scotch.

"And you're doing a lot more of that shit, lately. Drinking. Marty, will you talk some sense into this galoot of a friend of yours?"

"I stopped following up on domestic calls years ago, Frannie."

"Marty?" she whined.

"Okay, o-kay. Jeeze-Louise." He leaned across to Nealy to confide in him. "Stop drinking, Ray. But not too much."

Francesca's look turned smug. "Fat lotta help, Marty!" She looked around for Sam the waiter. "Whadda they have for eats here, tonight?"

"Humble pie," Nealy grumbled.

"Just shut up, you, and call your girlfriend, ex—whatever. See if I care."

Cohansen held up his hand. "Wait. Listen to me. Ray, they got the same ol' crappy bar food for dinner here they always have. Look, why don't you take Frannie, here, for dinner at The Gaucho's Bull Pit over on fifty-seventh? Just tell Arturo at the front desk that I sent you. He knows me, and he'll find you a nice, quiet table where the two o' you's can hash all this out." He looked over at Francesca, who was biting her lower lip. He winked back at her. "Oh, yeah, and Ray, don't drink too much around her, okay? The lady don't like it. Then finish this discussion of yours, which is kinda startin' to give me *agita*." He gazed over at her. "You like steak, right, Frannie?"

"Red meat," she motioned as she lightly pounded her chest. "Me,

Tarzan, Kimosabe."

"That was Tonto, not Tarzan," Nealy said.

"Well, I'm sure if the two of them ever met, they'd thoroughly enjoy each other's company, as I do yours, Raymond. I'd say you owe me a dinner about now, anyway. So, how 'bout it? I could use a steak."

Nealy simpered as he leveled his gaze as if he was searching for her intent. He could only hope. "Steak it is, then."

Chapter 14

The Holy Water soaking tub

Pop music seemed to follow Deborah's crew around, and now Kyu Sakamoto sang "Sukiyaki" from the radio on the serving ledge of the newly constructed parish hall in the basement. She had spent the past five weeks directing the construction of the parish hall, along with supervising the swimming pool builders contracted out of New Rochelle to convert the grimy coal bin into a baptismal pool. Now that it was finished, she stood back to admire the work they had done.

A cluster of circular tables surrounded by red-cushioned folding chairs had been set up in the large, green-carpeted parish common area, which was flanked on the far wall with the steam table and serving counter set upon a section of highly varnished parquet flooring. Behind the steam counter, the housing for the large dumbwaiter ascended to the stainless-steel industrial kitchen above.

A severe-looking accordion panel cordoned off the baptismal pool and a sacristy where The Reverend would hang his vestments and store some of the ceremonial trappings of his service. The room's white-washed walls glimmered in wavering reflections from the water. The floor around the baptismal pool was a random configuration of large brown and white terra-cotta tiles laid at 45-degree angles. Track lighting surrounded its circumference. At Thomas's request, a brighter spotlight was controlled by a dimmer switch connected to the pool's access steps' railing. He claimed that this light would serve to add drama to his baptisms, but in truth it was meant to catch the twirling facets of his amulet as he baptized his supplicants.

Smooth large and medium-sized flat stones covered the pool's bottom. They were placed upon an under-lay of clay soil and gravel into which the aquatic plants had taken root as they wavered lazily beneath soft eddies of the water. Sea grass rose three feet above the water's sur- face in the far-right corner of the pool.

Deborah had never designed such a thing before. She was proud of her success in having created a hybrid of man-made and natural elements as inviting as the little pool. She fixed her gaze upon the subtle swirls of foam that gushed lazily from the eight outlet nozzles beneath the heated water. Her guys had left for the day, and despite the mid-October coolness in the air outside, she felt the heat of fatigue. She daubed at the perspiration on her brow with her painter's cap. Her chronic, dull backache was also flaring up. The water was inviting. Why not? She wondered. Who would know? She slipped her bare feet from her dirty work boots and stripped off her white coveralls and shirt. Down to her flimsy white bra and cotton panties, she eased into the pool and treaded water toward the sea grass where she slid luxuriantly down to soak into the soft churn of water from the jets.

She closed her eyes to shut herself away from the noises that flowed distantly from the radio and dehumidifiers, as she called up tender memories of those Augusts in her childhood when Domenico and Celita brought her and Benny to their cabin on Canandaigua Lake in upstate New York's hilly wine country. She remembered sliding into the warm fresh water of the lake and letting the undulations of underwater growth tickle her body, just like this. And just like then, she felt truly at peace.

The nearly completed church smelled of new wood, fresh paint and carpeting. Thomas was struck by the realization it was now finally ready for service. The plush, reddish-brown broadloom relaxed under his footsteps, and the red-cushioned, light-oaken pews were in place in the airy chapel. Deborah had argued for floor pillows instead of the pews, but Thomas stood up to her and was adamant about keeping the pews—at least enough to compromise.

Five full-length rows of pews were set in the rear part of the plank- floored room, while another four rows of puffy red and orange pillows were arranged in front of them. The seating faced a freestanding light-oak podium behind a dark cherrywood post and brass altar rail. An icon; a cherrywood cross inlaid with chrome with short slats connecting the transepts at 45-degree angles, hung discreetly on the wall behind the podium.

The corridor carpet ended at the black and white tiled kitchen housing the oversized gleaming stainless-steel appliances and the center island with its many drawers. The carpet also ended at the office opposite the chapel. He thought the parish office, with its parquet floor and large gray oval rug was a little overstated with its heavy mahogany desk, plush beige leather chairs and the rich mahogany credenza. Against the far wall was a floor to ceiling mahogany bookshelf. He felt the room had more the look of an office for a high-priced lawyer than a humble pastor, but, again, he had ignored his own preferences over those of Deborah. He remembered the endless days just over four months before when he thought his church was a hopeless project. He was as amazed over the transformation as he was perplexed about his developing feelings for her.

Making his way toward the kitchen, he noticed the basement door was ajar, so he went down the carpeted stairs to inspect the handiwork and discuss it with Deborah. He knew she would still be working there, for he heard the radio blaring, and her truck was still parked outside.

He found her relaxed in the water among the rushes at the far end of the baptismal pool. On seeing him, she slouched lower until the water came up to her chin. "Come on in and join me, Thomas. The water's just right."

The unexpected sight of her near nakedness beneath the shimmering water shocked him as much as he felt confounded by desire. He felt the slightest stirrings in his groin, which were swiftly repressed by his weakening sense of indifference. He looked bashfully down at the tiled floor. "The pool is meant for baptisms, not swimming, Deborah. We discussed this."

"Oh, Thomas." She splashed some water toward him. "Don't act like such a prude. It's not as if I'm swimming laps or having a game of water polo. Why don't you take off your clothes and join me? It's really restful."

He was sure his god had cunningly wormed this temptation into his psyche, and he was shaken numb by her suggestion. He cleared his throat. "Deborah, please," he croaked softly as he suppressed an urge to seize her body among the rushes like a Bathsheba in the Edenesque setting of the Holy Water Soaking Tub. He wondered why he should feel so limp and helpless in the presence of a disarmingly beautiful woman yet feel nothing of slicing into a gang member's stomach to kill him with the prospect of ridding him of his soul. "I—can't. Really. You know I can't."

"Thomas!" she scolded. "Don't be ridiculous. Come in here. Now." He glanced toward the stairs, then toward the steam table in the common room. Anywhere but at her. "I—really shouldn't, Deborah.

I'll just go back upstairs while you get dressed. Maybe we can go out to dinner or something."

"Jesus, Thomas! All *right*. At least bring me my shirt. It's right over there." He walked over to where she had piled her clothing. As he lifted her shirt from the floor, he heard the slosh of her standing up. He bashfully extended the shirt to her. "Look at me, for chrissake. You're acting like a little kid! I'm your friend. I'm not going to bite you." Thomas slowly raised his eyes to her as she unclasped her wet bra and held it out to him. "Thanks," she said tersely as she took her shirt. "Here, take my bra. I can't wear it. It's wet."

Though the time it took for her to take the shirt and slip it over her shoulders may have been only a second, to him it seemed much longer as the image of her dampened, glistening nudity indwelled itself in his mind. Her light-copper complexion was flawless and smooth. Her small breasts were firm and highly toned, like the rest of her conditioned body. Their pudgy, subtly fringed magenta aureoles were nearly the circumference of a half-dollar around the rigid little dark stems of her nipples. A deep navel with a protruding little lip rimming its top accented her flattened stomach. Her pubis, visible beneath the wet translucent panties, was covered by a light mist of dark hair. Her thighs and calves were taut and muscular. He was seized with envying her body more than coveting it. He wished he could possess it, to somehow dive into it and make it his own.

She swiftly draped the chambray shirt over her shoulders and covered up the depth of his desire. "Okay, Thomas. You're on for dinner," she said as she boosted herself onto the coping and over to her coveralls. "You honestly should try out your Holy Water Soaking Tub sometime," she said as she stepped out of her wet panties. "It's really relaxing, especially near the water jets. I heard someone out in California is trying to package this kind of thing." She drew up her coveralls. "California—where else would they come up with something like this?"

Thomas could not contain himself. "You're beautiful."

"What?" she said indifferently as she concentrated on buttoning her shirt.

"I think you're beautiful, Deborah. Please don't take my reluctance personally. It's just that—"

"I know. You've got to check in with God to get His permission before you act on any of your primal earthly desires," she said.

"No. It's not that. I just need a little more time."

She stopped buttoning her shirt and reached out to tenderly touch his cheek. "I know, Thomas. I'm sorry. Believe it or not, I'm a little rusty at all this, myself. Here," she said as she leaned closer and pecked his cheek with a dry, kiss. It felt like the soft tickle of a feather. Deborah then leaned away to finish buttoning her shirt. "That will have to do for now, I suppose. I'm in no hurry; well, maybe, but not now, at least not yet. Look. I'm all flustered. I didn't mean to—"

"Really, dear heart, it's fine. All we need is a little time—and patience."

She drew back in a sudden recollection of something to change the subject. "Um! I just remembered. A friend of mine who runs a little club I designed for him on MacDougall Street has invited us to a Halloween party a week from Friday."

"Halloween?" Thomas scoffed. "You mean we have to dress up like hoboes and princesses? Bob for apples?"

"Something like that. But these types of Village folk take Halloween really seriously. It's like a part of their culture."

Thomas frowned in apprehension.

"Hey! Don't act so glum! It'll be fun! We all need some fun in our lives, and we need to celebrate all this—," she waved her hand around in the air "—this crowning achievement of ours. You can take me to The Twenty-One Club or something later. But first let me introduce you to my crowd at this party. You don't even have to dress up. You can go as a reverend, with the backwards collar and all. It's Halloween, and that'll scare the hell out of a lot of the godless atheists and agnostics who'll be there." She simpered at the thought. "There's nothing more horrifying for them than a guilt trip."

He stiffened in the reluctance to make up his mind, as he kept his eyes on her.

She planted another kiss on his cheek. "You old party-poop! Come on! I've decided for both of us. We're going." She walked across the room to the radio and turned it off. "Come on, now, Thomas. We'll stop off at my place and I can change. Then you can buy me dinner at Farragut's." She then went up the stairs, leaving Thomas to get over the shocks of going to a Halloween party and of having seen her nude.

Part 2

November 1963 – March 1964

The
Glitz & Glitter Club

Chapter 15

Camille's coming out party

The ferule of the tiny brush felt ticklish as Thomas applied a thin layer of eyeliner above the extended lashes he had glued onto his right eyelid. The lining served to accent the subtle application of the teal eye shadow that brought out the green of his eyes. He swirled the brush upward toward the end of its stroke. Once he had applied this finishing touch, he replaced the brush on its periwinkle-print porcelain holder and relaxed to admire his magnified handiwork in the round makeup mirror on the desk in his hotel room.

As he referred to Jillian's the worn-edged photo propped up against the stem of the mirror, he saw that he had become much better at capturing her looks. He mussed up the auburn wig around his thin, softened face to add a little excitement to the look. He pinched and puffed out his cheeks, and then ran his tongue lightly around the coloring on his lips, tasting a hint of cherry. Finally, he applied some lavender *eau de toilette* around the underside of his jaw.

He carefully replaced his makeup tools, the picture of Jillian and the bottle of lavender perfume into the valise Mother had given him, and then hid it under the sink. After adjusting the padding in his bra and tugging up a nylon stocking, he ran a cherry-red varnished-nailed finger under the binding brim of the girdle around his waist.

Over the past few days, he had practiced wrapping a crimson

and white print sarong he had bought at week ago at Gimbel's Department Store. Now he accomplished the task with ease as he adjusted its droop over his left shoulder. The curve of his bared right shoulder reflected a soft sheen from the thin light in from the dresser. Finally, he slipped his slender feet into a pair of lavender-blue, medium-heeled satin pumps, and then went downstairs to hail a cab to take him to Deborah's apartment.

Fred looked up from calculating his weekly receipts. His voice was muffled from behind the Plexiglas enclosure. "Holy shit, padre! You clean up pretty good as a broad! If I didn't know you was such a shit-kicker guy from East Homerville, Kentucky, I'd date 'cha myself! "

Thomas smiled politely. "Why thank you, Fred—I think. It's a good thing Halloween comes along only once a year, though."

"Never was much on Halloween, and all. Too many weirdos around here as it is! Anyway, ol' boy, girl, whatever. Have a good date. I'll leave the light on. You remember your key, this time?"

Thomas simpered and raised his sequined handbag. "In my purse."

"Put it in your pocket, then, padre, if you got any pockets on that dress of yours. Purses have a tendency to get picked off around here."

Thomas looked out through the door toward the street and saw a cab approaching. "Gotta go!" he said as he rushed through the front door. The cab driver noticed Thomas behind him as he pulled over to the curb. "Twenty-three Mercer Street," Thomas commanded in what might have been taken as a woman's voice as he got into the cab.

Dressed as Thomas's male "date," Deborah was waiting for him on her front stoop. Her short hair was blackened and slicked high and back with a little too much Vitalis. She had pasted a scrawny, Chaplin-esque black mustache above her thinned-out upper lip and had applied a hint of color to her cheeks to give herself a cherubic look. A pair of small, round, thick-framed eyeglasses neutralized the look of innocence with one of intellect. She wore a tight fitting, gray pinstriped suit, a pink dress shirt with a high winged collar and a garish-colored necktie done up in a thick Windsor knot. She held a black felt bowler hat down at her side.

She slid in next to Thomas and directed the cabdriver to take them to The Glitz & Glitter Club on MacDougall Street in Greenwich Village. "Well, Thomas. You certainly look pretty good as a woman. Why if I were a lesbian, I'd—"

He chortled privately and spied the cabdriver's bewildered expression reflected in the rearview mirror. "Watch that kind of talk, Deborah. You could spend your life in the fires of damnation for thinking like that."

"Oh, you preacher men! So provincial," she said peevishly as she patted her hand upon his.

Thomas took one look at the burlesque being played out around him at the The Glitz & Glitter Club and knew he had found a home. The place seemed to glisten with constellations of shiny things set into the darkness of the ceiling, as it was draped with huge feathers in a pastel palette of pinks and cyans that were attached to the to the left and right walls. The room was populated by people in exotic costumes that made Deborah's and Thomas's seem tame. Colors swirled all around them. The dancefloor was bathed in a dull confusion of col- or from the swells of lighting muted by a haze that was redolent in the harsh and sweet fragrances of cigarettes and marijuana. The music from the 16-piece orchestra on the dais of the dancefloor thumped like a heartbeat through an echoing sibilance loaded with the sounds of the exuberance from the assortment of patrons.

Couples of gaily-costumed men and couples of women embraced and sometimes kissed as they danced in and out of the swells of the dim, leisurely roving beams from the spotlights above the dance floor. Thomas tried to divert his stare from a glittering male couple dressed identically in gold togas. They were locked in a passionate kiss as they danced.

The members of the band were seated behind their black music stands, each emblazoned with a "Bonne-Aires" logo in cursive gold type. A recent addition to the Bonne-Aires, Big Eunice, a zaftig negro singer, who bulged out of her silver-sequined evening dress, commanded the place with the finish of her brassy rendition of Ruth Brown's "Help a Good Girl Go Bad."

The music soon switched to a blaring instrumental of Dizzy Gilles- pie's "Manteca." Loud, dueling trumpets intensely sibilated the atmosphere over a tribal Latin percussion beat that rumbled the floor as two couples cleared the others on the floor and swirled into competitive mambos. Thomas rightly assumed they were professionals by their tight, concentrated grace and practiced Madison Avenue smiles. They swizzled around through the swirling pink and blue rays of the spot- lights that kept pace with them.

"So, Thomas. Welcome to The Glitz & Glitter Club!" Deborah called over the din as she donned her bowler hat.

He smiled with half his mouth. "I feel like I've died and gone to Purgatory."

"That's your second reference to the underworld since you picked me up tonight. Feeling guilty, are we?" Thomas's smile turned wry and he patted her hand as she adjusted her hat. "Well, if that's the case, you should, then. Feel guilty. Maybe we'll both end up in hell despite your presumed saintliness. Such is life."

Someone costumed as Louis the 14th approached them and planted a light kiss on Deborah's cheek. His sibilant voice came out in a series of gushes. "Hera, dah-link! It's been ages!"

"Teddie?" she said.

"Why, none other, my dear! Well, it's Theo-*dora*, actually, in my *essence de plume* state" he looked over at Thomas. "And who is this gorgeous slice of cheesecake you brought with you?"

Thomas gazed bashfully around as Deborah took on a vague expression. "How did you know it was me, Teddie?"

"Why, Hera! I recognized your tie. It looks like it was chopped from those hideous drapes in your townhou—sorry, dear girl, but it's *absolutely* true. Those curtains are simply awful! Bobbie and I had to throw them out. But I see you must have retrieved them from the trash to make that hideous necktie." He lifted his flamboyantly-feathered sequined mask to blink his exaggeratedly long-lashed eyes. "How did you recognize me?"

"Who but you would dress as Louis the Fourteenth, king of your own establishment?" He winked at Thomas. "Let her eat cake!" he proclaimed in a whisper. Deborah squinted into the gloom toward the bar. "Wrong, Louis. Teddie. You're such a Francophile, you should know that. Anyway, it was Marie Antoinette who said that. Ah! I see her over there, tending bar. Is that Bobbie?"

"The very one. And who are you supposed to be, dah-link? Franz Kafka or James Joyce, or perhaps Charlie Chaplin? Or Trotsky, maybe?"

"Neither and none—Georges Sand, or Collette, take your pick."

"*Touché*, my adorable little Hera! "He looked again at Thomas. "And you, there, beeeu-ti-ful–looking woman! Don't tell me you're Alice Toklas' object de desire, Gertrude Stein. She was such a frumpy old boor, who resembled a flabby cross between Ma Kettle and Grandma Joad. And all that phony pretentious intellect! You're far too pretty to be her. So, who are you to be tonight, sweetie?"

Thomas cleared his throat and tried out his woman voice. He remembered the name Mother had given him. "Uh, I'm, uh, Camille, Debb—Georges Sand's date."

Teddie thoughtfully tapped the dark beauty mole on his cheek with the edge of his mask. "Well, Camille, my sweet." He winked again. "Your drinks are on me tonight. Yours, too, Hera—Georges, Al- ice, whatever. Hah, yes, you're Alice! Welcome to my Wonderland!" He planted another peck on Deborah's cheek and then a more tenuous one on Thomas's, and then headed off toward the tables to make his rounds. Thomas drew his chin to his neck as he scrutinized Deborah.

"Hera? Where did that name come from?"

"Greek Goddess—Zeus's wife, I think, or at least one of them, for those who believe Zeus may have been a polygamist. She's believed to be the perfection of wife and mother." She cast Thomas a sideways glance that served only to confound him. She lightly cleared her throat. "Anyway. The name just sort of came up and stuck. These are all old friends of mine, so I let them call me that. And you, Camille?

"Long story," he said.

"Ex-girlfriend? Ex-wife?" she pressed, then cringed. "Current wife? Maybe living where you came from back in Illinois?"

"Iowa," he corrected. "And no, Deborah, nothing like that. I'll tell you sometime. Maybe." He ventured a quick, reassuring kiss on her cheek. "Let me go get us some of those free drinks. Scotch?"

"Chivas if they have it, Dewar's if they don't. Neat, please." She pointed toward where Teddie had disappeared into the smoky darkness. "I'll go find us a table over there."

As Thomas approached the bar, he meandered through a cotillion of he-shes, some draped in enormous white feathers and sparkling in glitter and fragranced in a floral bouquet of perfumes. He was certain he spied Grace Kelly chatting with Marilyn Monroe. Passing closer by, he heard them talking in hushed male voices. He

---

looked around and saw other starlets and divas in private discussions as some of them kissed others' cheeks in passing. Among them: Bette Davis (two of them), Joan Crawford, Kim Novak (sort of), Natalie Wood, Ginger Rogers, Josephine Baker, Eartha Kitt, maybe three kitschy Cleopatras (though no Elizabeth Taylors) and one lonely Kate Smith. And of course, there was Marie Antoinette tending the bar.

Bobbie sauntered over to him. "What'll it be, beautiful?" He patted his highly piled white wig as he puffed on his cherrywood briar pipe.

"Two Scotches. Neat. Chivas, if you have it." Thomas said. Bobbie's voice was deeply masculine, garnished with a characteristic lisp.

"Did I see you over there, with Hera?"

"You did. I'm her date. How did you know it was Deb—Hera— from this distance?" He glanced once again toward the dance floor. He shot a glance toward on the mambo dancers who were cheered as they twirled into a multicolored blur to the closing crescendo of the music. Thomas smelled a bloom of cherry as Bobbie took a draw on his pipe. "Wasn't too hard. She's wearing a piece of her horrible drapery around her neck. I'd know that hideousness from twelve blocks away! But we love her here. Anyway, nothing's too grand for our dear Hera! Glenlivit for both of you! Doubles, even."

As Bobbie poured the drinks, Thomas looked down the length of the bar and observed the wide array of Halloween costumes glittering in the scant lighting. One person in the top-heavy headdress of a giraffe was conversing with another in that of a unicorn. Las Vegas chorus girls dripping in sequins in ornately feathered head-wear abounded. And there were a few men. Standing next to him, a shirt-less John Wayne cowboy look-alike sporting an orange bandana was talking to a Robert Taylor in a toga. Bobbie placed the drinks before him. "Interesting place here, isn't it?"

"I've never seen anything quite like it. But I'm new to the area. I'm from, uh, Iowa."

Bobbie winked at Thomas, then held his pipe off to the side. "You'll learn to love it, sweetheart. This place kinda grows on you. The Glitz & Glitter's a little like Rick's American Cafe in 'Casablanca.' It'll shock you, but you'll collect your chips at the end of the night. It probably isn't like anything in Peoria, for sure!"

"Iowa," Thomas corrected as he took up the drinks. "Peoria's somewhere in Illinois."

"Same place, darling. At least when you're viewing it from here in the Big Apple," Bobbie said, and then put his pipe back in the corner of his mouth.

Thomas smiled uncertainly and then walked back toward where he squinted and spied Deborah sitting in a semicircular booth near the stage. Dancing Eddie, the Bonne-Aires' lead singer, was jauntily belting out the recent Jack Jones hit, "Wives and Lovers," as he swirled around on the stage. Deborah was talking to a leather and denim clad James Dean and a T-shirted Marlon Brando, who appeared as Stanley Kowal- ski from the set of "A Streetcar Named Desire." Contrary to the image of Stanley Kowalski, this Brando sipped from a frosted martini glass. Thomas slid in next to Deborah. She faced him with a concerned look. "I didn't know this, but Jean Cocteau and Edith Piaf died within hours of one another a few weeks ago."

Thomas pursed his lips and raised up a little shrug of his bared right shoulder. "I don't know who—"

"Goodness!" Brando gasped, doing his best to imitate the star's lisp. "Jean Cocteau? Director of 'Beauty and the Beast' and 'Orpheus?' And you've never heard of Edith Piaf? 'The Little Sparrow' and *chanteuse extraordinaire*? Heavens, darling! Where have you been? Under a rock?"

Thomas remained silently perplexed on how to approach such a catty criticism from a Marlon Brando look-alike so badly trying to stay in character. Deborah came to his rescue. "Aw, come on, Silva. Camille's a little new to all this. Camille, say 'hi' to Silva, here and his partner, James Dean. They may act tough, but they're pussycats through and through."

"Thanks for the compliment, Hera," said Silva.

"Mee-ow!" said James Dean, as he put a clenched, open-fingered hand up like a claw.

"I'm from Iowa," Thomas said, as though to qualify himself.

"Oh, peaches!" said James Dean. "I'm so sorry about that!" He turned to Silva. "Silva, you must mind your manners! Iowa doesn't know that Edith Piaf, Cocteau and France weren't somewhere in Canada."

Thomas licked his lips and winced a grin. "Well, they do speak French in parts of Canada, so the confusion is valid."

Silva looked at James Dean and then he fixed his gaze on Thomas. "Well, her prettiness makes up for her lack of au couture. Your name is Camille?"

"Uh, yes."

Silva reached across to fondle the fabric of Thomas's dress. "I love that sarong you're wearing, sweets!"

Thomas was bemused that he didn't recoil from Silva's flimsy touch. "Thirty-four ninety-five at Gimbel's."

Silva quickly withdrew his hand as though from a dirty toilet bowl. "*Gim*-bel's?" he scowled.

James Dean brought his hand worriedly to his mouth. "Oh, dear Camille! You poor little pirate! Hera! Haven't you introduced our sweet Camille to Bergdorf's, Saks or at least Best and Company? *Gim*-bel's! God forbid!"

"Actually, it never crossed my mind," Deborah said sourly from behind the rim of her glass of Scotch.

Silva leaned back and crossed his muscular arms. "Well, prepare yourself, Camille, honey. I may ask you out to show you around this Gotham. Build a little haute-couture into your beautiful brain."

Thomas looked helplessly at Deborah. "I don't—"

Deborah shot Silva a threatening gaze. "She belongs to me, Silva." "Share and share alike, Hera," Silva tisked.

Deborah took a quick sip of her Scotch and then grasped Thomas's hand, as she stood up. "Come on, Camille. Let's dance."

"Party crasher!" James Dean scolded as Deborah led Thomas into the misty lights of the dance floor.

They began to dance apart from one another. "Silva's a big jerk, but he's totally harmless." She glanced down at Thomas's clumsy foot- work and smiled. "You're not very good at this. Dancing."

He smiled bashfully. "I know. It was never one of my strong points.

Not much call for it behind the pulpit."

She shook her head and placed her hand on his bared shoulder. "You'll learn to dance, and other things, Thomas. This is a hard city to live in. Brutal at times."

"I know," he answered knowingly, now that he had become a part of the brutality.

The music then shifted to "It Never Entered My Mind," in the subdued, soft style of Miles Davis. Deborah drew him to her and felt a twinge of his defiance. "Please, Thomas, don't resist," she whispered reassuringly. "Don't be afraid. Everything'll turn out fine." She hugged him gently and lightly placed her head on his naked shoulder. "We will be fine," she whispered succinctly and then sighed contentedly.

Thomas realized he could not keep himself in check any longer.

He tenuously drew his hand up to the back of Deborah's glimmering hair and lightly stroked its oil-slicked stiffness. He raised his head up, as she did hers, and they stared richly into one another's eyes—his light green into her deep brown. She twitched her usually plush, but tonight thinned-out, lips into a nervous twitter of a smile, as he tried to relax his lips. She draped her arms over his shoulders. They ceased dancing and stood still in an embrace. She gently pulled him toward her. Her lips bloomed into the depth of a kiss, while his remained rig- id. She tasted the cherry on his; he, the hint of plum on hers as their separate scents of lavender commingled into a swarm of a fragrance that finally drew them that much closer together. She relaxed her body into a tender attachment, as he relaxed from the years of his dungeon of sexual confusion.

They soon became weightless as one; fitting into one another like the long-missing ingredients of an emotional riddle as their bodies warmed and seemed to float together. The fact that he was costumed as Camille, and she as Georges Sand or Alice B. Toklas— anyone but Kafka!—made the tender moment seem all the more real. Thomas realized through their kiss that if they had not been disguised as they were, in such a surreal environment like The Glitz & Glitter Club on Halloween, this all-encompassing, lovely, heartfelt cuddle may have never felt as right as it did now.

Deborah finally reluctantly pulled away and stroked his cheek. "I'm gonna finish my drink and we'll go back to my place," she whispered closely. "It's time for us, now, Thomas. But, really, I need to finish my drink, first."

"I do, too," he said in a hoarse whisper. "You'll be patient with me?

It's been a very long time."

She placed two fingers on his lips. "I'll be as patient for as long as it takes."

She drew him into another little kiss, and they remained in their embrace until the song ended.

Making love was a uniquely peculiar experience for them both. Until Thomas reluctantly stumbled into her life, Deborah had not felt a need to risk another intimate relationship. Her frequent thirsts for socializing with a neat Scotch in hand were quenched at nightclubs such as The Glitz & Glitter with its mainly homosexual regulars. She had come to learn to not trust the quickly passing heterosexual male instinct, and to feel comfortable and safe in the company of queers. The fact that she had constructed, designed and owned the place made it that much easier to hide away from men who craved what they thought she could offer them. It had been a hard lesson for her.

Thomas had paralyzed himself away from passions beyond those immediate ones that salvaged his needy soul. Playing the part of a Reverend for nearly 25 years, he was not conditioned to act on the passions of the heart. But tonight he had found a new sort of comfort there.

The act of penetrating her body perplexed him. He felt a surging, godlike involvement through her intimate moistures and the slick sheen of her perspiration as she wrapped herself spider-like around him, flexing her arms and legs as she gasped. Her surging embraces weakened him like a Samson to her Delilah as their sexes damply joined and throbbed in urgent satisfaction. He became enraptured by her gasps for breath and the loud cries from her pent-up frustrations. Then he felt the surge of their mutual orgasms, and he sensed an out- right exchange of their souls. When they finished, she gratefully fes- tooned his face with a torrent of moist, desperate kisses of release.

"OH God! Oh, God!" she panted. "Thank you, Thomas! Thank

you! I *feel* like Hera, now!" she gasped through tearful laughter.

Making love to Deborah left him in a breathless, surreal silence. He looked over at her face, thinly glossed with a luster of perspiration and smudged with clots of mascara. Her pasted-on mustache had become displaced to her cheek. He realized how smudged his makeup must have appeared to her, as he felt the tickle of one of his formerly attached eyelashes off to the side of his right eye. He tried to neaten himself up by straightening Jillian's wig upon his head.

Chapter 16

Cowgirl boot-prints in the snow

The one-and-a-half-acre plot allocated for the Oklahoma Pavilion was outlined in green on the plan of the New York World's Fair spread out on the long mahogany table in the conference room. Members of the Oklahoma State Tourist Bureau, along with architects from the team who designed the pavilion, stood around the table.

The Oklahoma State exhibit and its pavilion would be situated off the Avenue of the States, north of the Hollywood Pavilion and west of the sprawling New Jersey Pavilion on the Avenue of the Nations. The Oklahoma plot was close to the fair's iconic metal Unisphere, an immense sculpted world globe surrounded by a ring of fountains.

The plan was mostly covered over with intricately-detailed schematics and point-of-view drawings. The pavilion sketches depicted a band shell, two small lagoons and a waterfall to highlight Oklahoma's water development program. A 100-foot-long topographic relief map of the state recessed into the ground was the feature attraction. Plots of grass and a picnic area fringed and dotted with indigenous mistletoe and redbud trees comprised the rest of the pavilion grounds.

Marty Bull, the director of the Bureau, stared at an artist's rendering of the project. He swept a beefy hand over the drawings as if consecrating them. "This is one hell of a lot of the state to fit in an acre and a half, eh?"

"Well, we've got a lot to show," Trevor answered.

This all had become a bore to Regina, who stood sullenly off to the side yet near her boss, while taking in what she could. Four months of overtime, concentration and pillow talk with Trevor over this silly fair had sapped her of the time and energy she felt she might have better-used toward carousing around in the nightlife of Okie-City.

Dave Kiefer, a representative from the New York World's Fair Committee, stared sourly at a watercolor rendering that depicted some willowy mistletoe trees nearly obscuring the little waterways, the band shell and the small Will Rogers Exhibit building in the distance. "Kind of out of keeping with the pavilions around it," he critiqued in a whisper tinged with a case of laryngitis he had picked up from the week- end's Oklahoma State-Alabama football game.

"That's the point, Dave," Trevor said. "We want a park-like oasis among some of those more carnival-like exhibits around us. Open spaces for fair-goers to go and sit a spell. Anyway, there'll be enough activity in our park to make it just as exciting as any other exhibit — things a little more, uh, kinetic — live scenario performances."

"Like what?"

Marty rolled his eyes furtively and clenched a little at what he knew was coming.

"Well, we plan on having three mock cattle auctions a day." "Really, Trevor? Cattle auctions?" Dave muttered dubiously. "Yeah." Trevor said and then pointed to the larger of the two lagoons, "and see our lake, here? We're gonna have a water-skier pulled around in it."

"In *that* little thing? It's no bigger than a swimming pool!"

"It's big enough. Over a half-acre," Bobbie Selis, one of the architects, said.

"And maybe a liability lawsuit in waiting," Dave mused. "How deep is this lagoon of yours?"

"Around five feet," Bobbie answered.

Dave shook his head. "Where are you going to keep the cows when they're not being 'auctioned?' Not too many pastures around Flushing Meadows, even though that's what they call it."

"We're gonna rotate three lots of five cattle from a grazing plot we rented in Westchester County. We'll trailer in five each day," Trevor said.

"A cattle-drive down the Avenue of the States?"

"God almighty, Dave! That's a great idea!" Marty blurted.

Trevor shook his head and sighed. "No, Marty, forget it. We don't want this turning into the running of the bulls in Pamplona, for Pete's sake. The cattle will be sedated."

"I was just being sarcastic, Marty," said Dave. "I'm from New York, and sarcasm's one of our strong points. You know, most of the state's pavilions are featuring their industrial strengths. Maybe instead of the swimming pool with the water-skier, you could put up an oil derrick." Marty pointed at the rendering in his hand. "I was thinking the exact same thing, Dave. Except maybe a working oil jack, you know, one of those pumps you see in our fields all over the place."

Trevor glanced over his shoulder at Regina and cast her a smirk as he rolled his eyes. She smiled half-heartedly back at him.

Dave sighed. "Pumping oil in Flushing Meadows? Shouldn't be too difficult—all that sludge that floats around in the bay. I don't think you'd get a very useful product, though."

"I was thinking more of a mock functioning pump; not doing much but moving up and down like a real one."

Dave brought a hand to his cheek. "Actually, Marty. That's not a bad idea. Sure beats having a water-skier being pulled around in a bathtub." "A half-acre, five-foot deep lagoon," Trevor corrected dryly. "Besides, everyone knows Oklahoma pumps oil. We're trying to sell our recreational benefits."

"Trevor, I'm still a little worried. I mean, the cows are going to be enough of a problem," said Dave. He cast a casual look at Regina. She smiled timidly back at him.

"*Cattle,*" Trevor said. "Here west of the Mississippi we call them cattle."

"Whatever. They both moo, and we make no real distinction in Manhattan. Anyway, I'm still stuck on the liability issue about the water-skier. I can't imagine a boat and the skier are even going to fit in your lagoon." Dave glanced at the architects. "You guys figure that in?"

"Of course," Bobbie answered. "The boat's a nine-foot mini-speed boat with a twenty-five-horsepower engine, going slow at about 20 miles per hour. Tow-line's about another five, seven feet. And plenty of room in there for one skier."

Trevor lifted his coffee mug from the table and sipped. "It's not going to be like one of those Cyprus Garden things they do in Florida, Dave, where fifty water-skiers stand on each other's shoulders. We've done a lot of testing in one of our small ponds out in El Reno."

"Okay, then who's going to do the all the water-skiing?" Dave glanced over at Regina. "How about you? Do you water-ski?"

She looked expectantly at Trevor who shrugged his shoulders. She demurely cleared her throat. "Uh, yeah, I do," she said lightly.

"What do you think about this? Would you try this sort of thing?" "Yeah, I might. It's a pretty big pond, I think. I'll probably be one of them. The skiers, I mean. I've skied a few times in the test pond. It's fine."

Dave smiled at her. "Okay, then. Who are you again?"

"Regina Barragan. I'm Mr. Nevins' secretary."

"Well, then you're a very brave young woman for trying this, Regina." He looked around at the rest of them. "Okay, cows and water-skier, you all have the Committee's blessing. Just don't let your cowherd loose to go messing with the flamingoes at the Florida Pavilion." He smiled slightly as he shook his head. "I'm beginning to wonder if this is a World's Fair or a freaking zoo."

"Thanks, Dave," Trevor said. "Is it even going to be a World's Fair? Did Robert Moses work out his spat with the International Committee?"

"You heard about that."

"Oh, yeah. We heard that the international committee thinks it's a 'crass commercial adventure' and not a real World's Fair at all."

"Well, I suppose my boss's publicly expressing his feelings about the draconian rules of the International Board didn't help too much. If there's one thing to like or not about Bob Moses, it's that he is bullishly determined to pull off The New York World's Fair. And he always gets his way. They're trying to work things out, but for now it's all beyond the talking phase. I'm sure it'll work out when we open at the end of April." "Excuse me?" came a timidly respectful voice from Marty's secretary standing in the conference room doorway. "Regina? You have a call from a Gary Barnstable? Says it's real important." Regina felt suddenly numb. "Okay, Marcy. I'll take it."

"Take it in my office, hon," Trevor told her.

Regina placed the handset back in the cradle. She stood stiffened in place as shr stared out the window down at North West Fourth Street. She wasn't seeing anything in particular, for her vision was blurred with tears. She felt the trickle of one trailing down her cheek.

Deacon Barnstable had just told her about Connie Mueller's suicide, and how the Iowa State Troopers had found her body in her friend Penny Maxwell's two-tone DeSoto with a hose running from the exhaust through the car window and the engine still running. The car had been covered in newly fallen snow far out in the field fronting her father's former church.

Regina didn't know exactly why she felt the loss so closely, but for the fact she might have come to love Connie for their shared secrets. Connie's virtue was the opposite Regina's and her presumed infamy over being John Bass's girlfriend and sex-slave.

She realized through her tears she might have loved Connie as a friend, but never allowed herself the chance. She might have learned the value of the kind of love shared among friends, rather than the raw emotion she had wasted upon John—and now Trevor; a development they both secretly felt would naturally form the moment he hired her.

She heard Trevor and the other five meeting attendees filing out of the conference room. Over Marty's insistence that they have lunch, Dave reminded him that he had to catch a flight back to LaGuardia in a few hours. Trevor noticed Regina staring out his office window and went into his office and closed the door. She inclined her head to rest upon the hand he had lightly placed on her shoulder. "You okay?" he whispered. She bit her lower lip as she focused her view on one of the oil der- ricks rising about the city. "I just found out one of my good friends back in Iowa went and killed herself last week," she said.

"Oh, honey, I'm so sorry."

"I just don't know how to deal with it."

"Look, sweetcakes. Why don't you take the rest of the day off? We're okay here, for now."

"I think I need to do that. I'll be okay by tomorrow." Trevor kissed the crown of her head. "Good. Go ahead home, then. Take as much time as you need."

Through Regina's detachment over Connie's death, her baby blue El Dorado seemed to glide by itself through the barely-trafficked route home. She had been looking for an apartment, but still lived at Hellie's place despite Jamie Robertson's increasing number of visits there. By now often extended to overnight stays.

She saw Jamie's helicopter on the field in front of the house when she parked near Hellie's truck. Beyond it, the cattle had been let out to graze among the clots of snow. She glanced over to where Philadelphia and Clarence, wrapped in their dirt smudged green blankets, munched contentedly from the feed trough in the open stable. Philadelphia let out a huff and a nicker, and then shook her head as if shaking away the chill.

Once Regina was in the living room, she saw Jamie seated at the Formica dining table, holding a bottle of Lone Star beer in one hand and a Lucky Strike cigarette in the other. He lifted the cigarette cupped in his hand, jabbed a puff and then took a languorous sip of beer. His scrawny body was dressed only in his oversized Jockey shorts, cowboy boots and a pair of crusty riding chaps. His beat-up straw cowboy hat rested back on his head within the shaggy nest of his dirty- blond hair.

She sighed. "You look ridiculous, sitting there all dressed like that, Jamie."

He lifted his beer bottle. "Cheers, Reggie. They let you out of school early today?" His voice crackled, as though he had just woken up, or had been made hoarse from grunting out expletives of ecstasy, such as the late-night ones Regina sometimes heard him bleat from Hellie's bedroom. By contrast, Hellie took on her sexual involvements very quietly, occasionally ordering Jamie to shut up.

Regina glared at him and pursed her lips. "I don't even want to know why you're all got up like some sort of porno star, Jamie."

Hellie padded from her bedroom wrapped in a large bath towel and wearing her worn-out moccasins. She cocked her head as she dried her ears with a hand towel. "You're home early, Reg. Everything okay?"

"Could be better, I guess," she said. "I see you two've been playing cowboys and Indians again."

"Well? So?" Jamie challenged.

"Quiet! I don't want my niece thinkin' you and I've been acting like perverts." She scissored her index and forefinger to indicate she wanted a puff from Jamie's cigarette.

"Oh, I think that little cat's been long out of the bag, Hellie," Regina said through a knowing half-smile as Jamie handed Hellie his cigarette.

"Ain't nothing she probably ain't imagined before," he said.

Hellie scowled in warning as she glared at him. "Jamie. Whyn't you get your clothes on and fly away in that little toy hello-copter of yours?" "Kin I at least finish my beer, fir—?"

She deposited the smoldering cigarette into the mouth of his beer bottle. "No." She snapped her wet towel at him. "Go on, now. Git!"

"Damn and hell!" he muttered as he rose from his chair.

"Don't worry, little baby, you can come back in a few days. An' don't go scaring my beeves this time when you fly outta here."

After Jamie went to the bedroom to dress, Regina went to the kitchen to get herself a beer as Hellie shuffled to the second bedroom to see about Timbo.

Regina stared out at the horses huddling in their stalls against the chilly blasts of wind. The torrents were complicated by the gusts caused by Jamie's helicopter rotors. He then flew west at 50 feet above the ground, shuddering walls of the house as he passed overhead. But Regina heard or felt nothing of this as she grappled with how she should understand Connie's death. She was also sadly confounded by why she had so much trouble feeling anything deeper.

Garbanzo was curled up on his blanket in his usual place beneath the Formica table now that his favorite spot in the bedroom had been usurped by the intrusion of Jamie. He sniffed for any stray table scraps, then lifted his head and perked up his ears when he heard the living room couch cushion sigh as Hellie sat.

She was dressed her usual way, now—in a flannel calico shirt and loose jeans. She had turbaned her wet hair in a towel. Regina turned to face her as Hellie lit up a cigarette from the pack of Luckies Jamie had left behind.

"Timbo's been put up in your room for now."

"You've been doing more of that, Hellie," Regina said distantly.

"More of—what? Putting Timbo up to nap?"

"Smoking. You're smoking more."

"Yeah. Jamie converted me to these factory-made ones. They're better than the ones I tried to roll myself. Never was very good at it."

"Uh-hunh. But you're doing it more."

"Must have something to do with too much Jamie. Anyway, what's eating at you? How come you're home so early?"

Regina sighed, and then sipped her beer as she made her way around the dining area furniture toward the living room. She slumped down into an overstuffed relic of an easy chair next to the couch. "Trevor let me leave early."

Hellie smirked knowingly. "Guess that's the advantage of sleeping with your boss. Lets you leave work when you want."

"That's not it. I got some bad news."

"She-*it*! The creep didn't go an' fire you, did he? I told you, you should never go messin' with a married man you work for. Guilt usually ends up gettin' the best of them in the end. And so, they solve the problem by firin' the innocent part of the equation."

"No. Nothing like that. I found out my friend Connie from Hanson killed herself. Wrapped herself up in a running car with a hose attached to the tailpipe."

"Oh, hon!" Hellie said as she leaned forward and placed a hand on Regina's knee. "I'm so sorry to hear that! Connie's the one you were communicatin' with back there?"

"Yeah."

"I kinda knew somethin' was up when that church deacon called here to ask for your work number. I was hoping he mighta found a little more money for you, but not somethin' like this. I'm real sorry. I know you two were close."

"Not really. I mean, I guess I'll miss her a little. What really worries me is that I don't know how I should feel. Or what to feel. I just feel kinda, I don't know, frozen in time."

"What can I do to help, Reg?"

"Nothing, sis. I just gotta deal with this myself. Maybe I'll take Philadelphia out for a ride."

"Sure, why not? I'll join you."

"Is it okay I just go alone this time? I just wanna be by myself." Hellie leaned back and took a puff on her cigarette. "Sure, sweetie, you go right ahead. Just don't forget to cinch her right, and try to keep your distance from the cattle. Now Pedro's been actin' a little horny, I think it might be he's havin' his time."

Regina simpered a private smile. "Seems a lot of that's going around here."

Hellie's smile matched Regina's. "I know. I'm trying' to keep Jamie quiet in there so you and Timbo can get some sleep, but the man treats tumbling around in sex like some sorta one-man rodeo."

Connie's grave was set away from the others in a new section of the Hanson Inter-Denominational Cemetery. A fresh red rose stood resolutely upright where it had been just placed against her headstone. Earlier roses, worn and desaturated by time, lay on her grave and were dusted over by a new-fallen snow. But the new rose stood out. Clusters of footprints surrounded the grave. They were from the people who had laid down the earlier roses. They had become softened by the passing climate.

Among them was another more recent set of footprints; sharp-toed, deep-heeled cowgirl boot prints. The fresh prints wandered off into the wind-blown mists of snow, back toward the road from which they came. From there, Regina's Cadillac inched wearily away, a smudge of baby-blue through the early morning fog, as if fatigued by the eight- hour drive that brought it here. It moved further into the obscurity of the atmosphere, then headed back south, toward home.

Chapter 17

Nineteen sixty-four

The Bonne-Aires were playing through their full 16-piece complement tonight as they backed up Dancing Eddie. His nasal tone was hollowed-out through a small megaphone as he sang Ruth Etting's 1926 "You've Got Those Wanna Go Back Again Blues." His blackened hair was slicked back tight in a 1920s cabaret style to match his black tux with its glimmering sequined tail. The two professional male dance couples featured the same smiles they wore on Halloween as they danced an exaggerated three-step waltz to the muted, brassy music. Dressed in tight evening clothes that glimmered in the roving slants of green, orange and blue rays of light, the dancers circled, whirled and dipped their partners to the downbeats. The men dressed as the women in the couples wore clinging sequined evening dresses, matching masques, glistening feathers in their highly-piled wigs.

Deborah, Thomas, James Dean, who was now dressed opulently as a red-headed woman in a magenta evening gown, and Silva, seemingly still dressed as Brando, had nestled in over their drinks in one of the circular booths to the right of the dance floor. Thomas stared fixedly at the rotating mirrored ball above as he recalled the miniature version of it above the pulpit of his Church of the Holy Waters back in Hanson. The memory brought on another of Regina, and he wondered how she was. The annoying thought passed as quickly as it came on. That picture seemed out of place here at The Glitz & Glitter Club.

James Dean had been timing the minutes since 11:20. "Ten minutes!" he announced as he looked at his watch.

Deborah glowered at him through her glinting white masque. "J.D.!

Will you stop doing that, please! It's been bugging the hell out of us."

"Right, sweetie," said Silva. "You've been counting down the minutes for the last half hour. Like a fickin' timekeeper."

"But Darling Silva!" he said to his partner. "Nineteen sixty-four is going to be our year. I can feel it."

"I remember sitting here last year when you said the same thing about nineteen sixty-three," Deborah said sourly, still emotionally stung by the president's assassination in Dallas almost six weeks before. "And look how that turned out."

"Probably best we put nineteen sixty-three behind us," Silva said.

"It was a shitty year, anyway."

Deborah had told them about Thomas's calling, partly so the entourage would regard him as a hetero male. "Well, what has God to say about all that, Reverend Camille?" James Dean asked. "Was it the shitty year my darling Silva said it was?"

Thomas was mildly perturbed by the reference. "My name's Thomas, not Camille."

"Why, sweetie pie!" James Dean said. "In this place in our hearts and minds you'll always be Camille."

Deborah patted Thomas's knee. "Just ignore them and they'll go away."

"It's the name you gave when we first met you. So, it sticks," Silva said.

"Nine more minutes!" James Dean called out.

"Like a flecking town crier," Silva grumbled, "but we love you, anyway." Finally, it turned midnight and the Bonne-Aires played a Dixieland rendition of "Auld Lang Syne" as a sexy, zaftig nurse rolled Father Time in a wheelchair out onto the dance floor. The patrons applauded and booed the passing of the year as they showered one an- other with kisses.

Silva kissed James Dean on the cheek.

Then James Dean kissed Silva full on the lips.

Deborah kissed Thomas on the lips, as he tried demurely to pull back. James Dean kissed Thomas on the cheek.

A large cardboard cake was rolled out from the darkness into the shocking pink spotlights. The applause loudened, and some boos turned to cheers and catcalls. Bobbie, dressed in diapers and a gold sash emblazoned with "1964" hatched from the top of the cake. "HELLO EVERYBODY!!" he shouted sibilantly. HAPPY NINETEEN SIXTY-FOUR!!!" He hopped out of the cake and pranced around the floor a few times, then stopped to slide into the booth next to Deborah. He planted a dry kiss on her cheek. "Happy New Year, dear Hera!"

"Another grand entrance this year, Bobbie," Silva said.

"Yes," Bobbie pouted. "And I'm seeing it in all alone. My dear Pauline is up with her sister in the frigid wilds of Vermont for the holidays!"

"How *rude!*" James Dean quipped.

"*Isn't* it?" Bobbie said. He pulled his pipe from the brim of his diaper and then turned his attention to Thomas. "I think I've seen you before."

"Halloween," he answered. "You were tending bar."

"Ah, yes! As Marie Antoinette, and you were the one from Peoria, Iowa. Hera's friend." He stuck the unlit pipe into the corner of his mouth.

"Illinois," Thomas corrected.

"I'm Bobbie, a passing member of this motley group." He waved his hand around the table. Then he held away his pipe to take a sip from James Dean's pink squirrel drink.

"Hey!" James Dean complained.

Bobbie tousled his hair, upsetting his wig. "Oh, darling. It's only a little sip."

Teddie bounded into the stage wearing a white top hat and tails. He tapped the mike for attention. "Listen up, all you queers! I have a special guest tonight." He motioned toward the wings as a frail young blonde in a green satin evening gown shyly emerged and took her place next to him. "I'd like to introduce Mademoiselle Marie Trudeau, an absolutely fabulous chanteuse I found in Montreal." He touched her tenderly on her bare shoulder. She reacted with a bit of tension as though wondering if she belonged in this place. "So—" Teddie went on, as he appeared to be eating the mike. "Here now I introduce to you, formerly from Montreal and now our own Little Sparrow, Mademoiselle Marie Trudeau!"

The patrons applauded as she took the mike he handed to her. She coddled it affectionately in her little hands as if it were her only friend in this alien environment. "Merci, T'eedadoree," she said in a tiny voice cradled in a French accent.

Teddie leaned into the mike. "Now come out here and dance the New Year in, all you homos!" he bellowed before he left the stage.

"So much for our anonymity," Silva said darkly.

"Teddie is such our little ringmaster," Bobbie said in Thomas's ear. His breath smelled of rose-scented tobacco.

The lights dimmed, leaving only a blue beam to bathe Marie as she began singing the Johnny Mercer-Ziggy Elman 1944 standard, "And the Angles Sing." Her words flowed like light syrup through the dimmed, smoked-up atmosphere. She alternated the verses in French and English with a low, sultry, breathy tone that belied her size. From her first words she seemed to spellbind the patrons into a respectful quiet. No one danced because they were too busy listening. She then morphed the song into its sound-alike, the Frank Loesser 1950 hit, "I've Never Been in Love Before."

Teddie had been jouncing around among the tables to chat. When he got to Deborah's and Thomas's booth, he pulled up a stray chair and sat down. "Isn't Marie absolutely *fabulous?*" he gushed.

"She is," Bobbie agreed with a stout nod, and then a draw on his pipe. "I love the way she sings in French-to-English and back again."

"I found her singing in a dump up in Montreal last October and convinced her to sing for us. Our Bonne-Aires adore her, and she them." He glanced lovingly up toward the stage. Marie, now with her eyes closed was caught in the ecstasy of music. She was adapting well to the environment. "They work so well together," he added thoughtfully, and then turned back toward the table. "I've signed her to a six-month, five-night-a-week contract." He beamed at Deborah and Thomas. "Isn't that *won*-derful?"

"Good for you, Teddie," Deborah said as she nuzzled into Thomas's shoulder. "She is really good." Like many others in the room, Thomas's attention was drawn to Marie as the mirrored ball above the dance floor loped into a slow revolution.

When Marie finished her song to a round of applause, she handed the microphone over to Dancing Eddie and he began to sing Tommy Edward's 1958 hit, "It's All in The Game." Couples filtered out into the dance floor, as moving pinpoint beams of colored light filled the room. Deborah leaned closer to Thomas. "Come on, let's dance. Then we can leave and see nineteen sixty-four in the right way."

Thomas wanted to dance with her, as long as he could fake it, as bad a dancer as he was. But he was brushed by the sensation that he did not want to leave this comfortable atmosphere. Then, oddly enough, his thoughts turned briefly back to Regina, who was only ten when her mother drowned. He reminded himself that Deborah was about the same age as Jillian when he had watched her slip beneath the water ten years ago, today.

Chapter 18

Les Misérables

Juan appeared misshapen in the great coat he wore in defense of the cold. He then grasped the collar of his dirt-colored coat close around his neck and shivered away a gust through the hard, frigid air. The rugged brown skin of his face with its high cheeks, large puffy, dull-pink chapped lips and dense wooly black beard suggested the look of a Saint Petersburg war refugee. The brim of his signature porkpie hat shaded his forehead and eyes.

Above, the sounds of traffic sizzled on the wet overpasses of the FDR Drive. The city was grayed in snow and slush. A thickening mass of tight, gray clouds conspired to flail out a tempest that was forecast to begin the following afternoon.

"But me, I dunno want to exit me home, preacher," he said to Thomas's offer. "This place be where I live."

Thomas leaned against the highway abutment and drew his woolen muffler up through the collar of his Loden coat to cover his chin. He glanced down at Milio huddling against the cold as he sat on a clump of dirty snow. The frivolous sound from his radio might have been polka music—something um-pah, at any rate—just to fill a void that only Milio could sense. "What about you, Milio? Don't you want a nice warm home?"

"I no knowen, preacher. *Me fecit Deus me hic de ratione.* Here is my godwindo's plan for me. He tellen me why he do this dis to me when I see him someday."

Thomas remembered a Hindu salutation: *The God in me greets the God in you.* "No, Milio, your godwindo put me here to help you."

Milio shrugged mightily against a frosty tuft of snow that had swept through the cavern of the overpass and seemed to channel into

him. He pulled the brim of his Yankees cap over his rheumy eyes. "Alla I knowen be that I be frozen mia aswanda off! *Hic est in malis meis ab tergo!*"

"Because ye be sitting on dat pile o' snow," Juan said as he bent the thin brim of his hat over his eyes to shield them from another small blowing mist of snow.

Thomas's voice was muffled thickly though his muffler and coat. "You both need to get out of this weather and move to a new home. It's not going to get any better out here. I built the apartment for you, anyway."

"You din't no ask us if you could do dat, preacher. Coulda saved you some time, dere."

"Will I hafta taken a bat to keepen me cleana alla time?" Milio asked. "*Ad balneum arbitrio?*"

"Probably, yes, Milio. A hot bath will make you feel new." "Then I lika where here I make me home."

Juan lightly shook his head. "Me, I do not need a new home. Here unner da bridge is where I can live."

The music on the radio cut through the static to a weather forecast as the announcer warned of tomorrow's impending blizzard. Up to 15 inches of snow. "*Malis meis ab tergo!* I be frozen mia fokinda aswinda off!!" Milio repeated.

"We be staying here, preacher, where we know how to live a life. We be fine, right, Milio?"

Milio tightened his collar and turned up the radio volume to lose himself away from the conversation.

"Suit yourselves, then. You know where you can find the church if you change your minds," Thomas said as he shivered away a wind- blast, then turned to go.

"I be thankin' you for carin' bout us though, preacher man!" Juan called after him as he walked back to the warmth of the church he had named "Heaven's Doorway."

Thomas was weathering out the storm when he heard an incessant knocking on the church's front door. He rolled himself from his bed, wrapped a terry cloth robe tightly around his body and then slipped his feet into a pair of house shoes. He hastily shuffled down to the foyer, intersecting the path of his curate, Francis, whom he had recruited from The Glitz & Glitter Club's kitchen. The curate opened the door and a dense swirl of snow blew in through the hard-wet aura of the late afternoon chill. The swells of wind seemed to pluck at the shrouds of the Brooklyn Bridge like a harp in the snow-hazed distance. Through the frosty fog of the snow, Thomas recognized the vague, hunched forms of Milio and Juan.

Juan's voice was clipped by the weather. "Okay, preacher. We stay here, now." He swept his hand behind him. "We bring some friends wid us to stay, too. Just for tonight."

Francis opened the door wider and let in another large waft of blowing snow. "Blessings, all of you!" he proclaimed loudly. "Come in! Please come in and be welcomed into Heaven's Doorway!"

Juan cocked his head quizzically at Thomas who canted a tight, knowing smile over Francis's enthusiastic welcome, as he, Milio and eight others filed by.

Thomas herded the ten of them into the sanctuary and told them to sit down. Juan folded his arms and leaned against the chapel door- way. Five of the others sat reluctantly in the pews, while Milio and the three others took to the puffy cushions in front to fall asleep. Thomas motioned to Francis and introduced him to the disinterested, shuddering assemblage, then instructed the curate to find some blankets and then fire up the stove to put up some stew and hot coffee.

"Ya got any beahs?" one of them called out in a fizzling voice.

Thomas remembered Deborah had left two full six-packs of Rheingold in the refrigerator after her last visit three days before. "Uh, we do," Thomas answered tenuously.

"Fuck the stew, then, man! I'll have me a coupla beahs!"

"An' some hard stuff," another said. "Got any, like, Wile Turkey or anythin'?"

"Nothing like that, no."

"Any wine? Ripple?" grumbled another. "Muscatel? Any o' dat?"
"Sorry, brothers, this isn't a bar. All I can offer is coffee and stew."

"He'll, preach. Ain't this a chuch? Ain't cha *spozta* have wine an' shit?"

"Shud-dup, mon!" Juan growled threateningly. "Da preacher be off'rin us up shelter from da beeg storm out dere! You assho's wanna go back inta it, leave you now, oddarise, shuddup an' do like da preacher say!"

There were grumbles of acquiescence throughout the room.

"Now, preacher, wha' da ya wanna us ta do? Maybe Spider over dere, who wanna da beer, can help wi' da cookin'. "

"Oh, okay," Spider agreed solemnly. He sat up from where he lay on his cushion. "Jes' tell me where ta go to help, boss," he said to Thomas.

"Please, all of you. Just call me Reverend Tom, or just simply 'preacher,' and think of Heaven's Doorway, here, as your home. Tonight you need only food and rest."

"I t'ink Milio c'n help all us by takin' a bat'! He be stinkin' da room!" another said.

"Neh—No! Neh bat'! *Nec balneum pro me*! Me, I dunno do no damn *bat's*!"

"Yeah, we nodiced!" There were sputters of laughter.

"There are two showers downstairs, if any of you want to wash off," Thomas said. "And Francis will show you where there are some robes for you to wear while your, uh, clothes dry out," He motioned to Juan. " I need to show you and Milio where you'll be staying."

The three-room apartment suite with its kitchenette and separate bath still smelled of the fresh paint that had been applied in December. The beds had crisp new sheets and coverings. New and donated clothing Deborah and Francis had found through local charities had been placed in the drawers and hung in the closets. There was a radio on the bedside table in the room that would be Milio's, along with an almost-new portable television in the suite's common area. "Welcome to your new home," Thomas said to his dumb-founded potential tenants. Their silence was accentuated by tufts of snow scattering against the windowpanes that, on clearer days, looked out on the Brooklyn Bridge.

"You do all dis for us?" Juan finally managed to say.

"Why not? You've done a lot for me, and we've done a lot together."

"I dunna knowen how to answer you, about alla dis."

Thomas grinned at Milio, then inclined his head toward the portable TV. "Now you'll be able to watch your Yanklados on television. You can see what they look like."

Tears welled in Milio's rheumy eyes. "*Ita sum felix*! I be so happiness now! You do be my Baggada Intradato, preacher man!" He leaned towards Thomas to hug him.

Thomas stepped back from his advancing hug. "Okay, Milio, you can show me how happy you are by taking a shower. You both can clean up, change into some fresh clothes and come down for a hot dinner, if you want, or just stay up here and rest. Tomorrow or the next day when the snow clears up, we'll go to my barber in Brooklyn. Then we can talk about how we can all help each other out. There's a lot to do."

"A bat'?" Milio complained nervously. "Now?" "Yes!" Thomas and Juan agreed unanimously. "And one for me, too," Juan added.

"Oh, shitata-cacca!"

"I just lost my power and heat," Deborah pouted over the phone. "Well, dear heart, you could come here to the church, but you probably won't find a cab at midnight in this blizzard."

"Actually," she pouted, "I was hoping you would come here. I'm getting all cold and I need you to warm me up."

"Oh, dear heart, there's nothing I'd love more. But my hands are full at the church. I've got a troupe of homeless souls sleeping in the chapel."

"Christ, Thomas! *That* must stink a little!"

"Hazards of the trade. Maybe I can start to finally build my congregation from them."

"Tonight's probably the last time you'll see any of those people. Until the next blizzard. Lock your valuables away. Half of them will eat you out of house and home while the other half robs you blind."

"Oh, ye of little faith."

"Okay, Thomas. So, you've fallen for a heathen. Someone has to be the voice of reason in this relationship."

Her remark sent a pang of anxiety through him. He realized soon after they had first made love that he did not care how their affair would end, he only knew, and maybe hoped, that it soon would. But for now, it was a comfort to him. He had become aware that he was playing the part of a loving suitor to her, just as he had played the same role of a dutiful husband to Jillian.

He heard something crash to the floor below him. "Oh, damn!"

"Ooh. I love it when the preacher talks dirty to me. What was that?"

"Something fell."

"Yeah, one of your Jean Valjeans just dropped the candlestick he was trying to steal. You'd better go check on it, Thomas. I'll try to stop by tomorrow if they ever get around to clearing the streets."

He cracked a wry smile. "Bye, dear heart. I love you, as usual," he said without emotion.

"Kiss, kiss, Reverend Thomas Deavers. Bye, 'til tomorrow." She hung up the phone.

Chapter 19

Heaven's Doorway

By mid-morning, the blizzard had swept out and up toward Nova Scotia leaving dull white mounds of nearly 15 inches of snow behind. Outside Thomas's office window, everything appeared pristine. The brownstone buttresses of the Brooklyn Bridge were festooned with clumps of snow and glistening ice, now melting away in the sunlight shining through the streaks of blue sky amid departing thick striations of light gray clouds. It seemed quiet, too, with no traffic except for the occasional grinding of snow- plows fitted to the green-gray New York City garbage trucks. Even that sound was muffled through the insulation of the thick blanket of snow.

The resonance of snoring and wheezing coming from the chapel distracted him from writing the sermon that he may or may not deliver to the homeless foundlings who made their way into Heaven's Door- way. Six of the eight now resting in the chapel had showered and were cloaked in the white baptismal robes he stored in the sacristy next to the bathrooms. Their gritty street clothes were drying out downstairs in the parish hall, which Thomas had sprayed liberally with the scent of lavender and Lysol from aerosol cans. The remaining two people who chose not to shower stayed in their sodden clothing. Thomas had looked in on them a few hours earlier, where they huddled together like lovers in a back corner. They were shivering, perhaps with low- grade hyperthermia.

Thomas gently drew a few extra blankets over them as he held his breath against their smell and then sprayed the chapel again with lavender-scented deodorizer.

Checking in again on the soundly sleeping assemblage 15 minutes before, he noticed the two of them had stopped shivering and were now loudly snoring. He reasoned that night in the streets had normally kept them awake and quietly diligent against its dangers. He felt it best to let them all sleep in safety a little longer.

But the threat was only replaced with another. Juan had recently told Thomas that with the relative annoyance of *Los Lobos Solitarios* out of the way, an unopposed rival gang, The White Cobras, had be- gun to re-infiltrate the district. They now posed a slight but gnawing threat. Representing their own version of the White Supremacy, The White Cobras were godless, therefore less prone to liberation. They numbered about the same as *Los Lobos Solitarios* — between 8 and 15—but they were more threatening because they wielded a more menacing arsenal of pistols and machetes. And they were more organized. The White Cobras were in the business of dealing drugs, and recruited their runners from among those who lived under the bridges and FDR Drive. Their leader was a shaven headed, sunken-eye ghoul they called "Führer."

Thomas sensed a presence in the doorway and looked up to see someone who might have once been Juan. This version was washed to a couple of shades lighter and dressed in pressed chinos, thick woolen gray sweater and a green-flannel shirt with sleeves rolled to the el- bows. Had it not been for the porkpie hat upon his graying disarrayed mass of hair, he might have passed as a rugged North Sea fisherman.

His forearms were tufted in hair and thick with muscle. Thomas reckoned that with his build, coupled with his quick adroitness and precision with broken bottles he dealt to the necks of his victims, he might have been a boxer in his former life. He noticed clusters of sores among the scars on his arms.

"'Morning, Juan. How're you feeling today? Better?"

"I dunno know, preacher. Me, I feel like I be standin' here lookin' funny."

"You look good, brother. Don't worry." "Ain't not me, though."

"It is now."

"We see 'bout dat."

Thomas motioned to him. "Come on in. Have a seat."

Juan cautiously did as Thomas told him. The leather chair across from the desk creaked under his weight as it swiveled a little to the right and then settled to the left. He quickly stood. "Oh, shit! I break dis chair!"

"It's okay, Juan. Sit back down. It's supposed to swing around like that."

He cautiously lowered himself back down. "Den what is its job as a chair, if ye canno sit down in it?"

"Hell if I know," Thomas told him after a little thought, and a quirky half-smile. "The chair was Deborah's idea."

"Deborah?"

"My friend. She helped to build this church."

Juan's broad lips shimmied to the right in what might have been a knowing smile. "Friend? Your woman?" He reached up to scratch his ear, but when the chair moved, he quickly put his hand back down to grip its arm to anchor himself.

Thomas shook his head. "Not 'my woman.' It's not like I own her."

"You married to her? Like a wife?"

"No. Nothing like that."

"Have you done da fuck wid her?"

"Okay, Juan. Enough about Deborah."

Now Juan truly became enlightened, grinning broadly as he playfully wagged a gnarled index finger at Thomas. "A-hah, preacher! You did do the fuck wid her. Den she is your wife! Me, I would like ta meet her someday."

"Someday you might."

Milio appeared in the hall with his chino pant legs drooping and dragging down below his bare feet. His short-sleeved shirt, with buttons misaligned by two holes, was worn inside out. Beneath his treasured Paleolithic Yankee ball cap, his light-brown hair was raked out in all directions as if he had been electrocuted. He was several shades cleaner because he had stood motionlessly for a half hour in the shower stall the night before, not knowing what to do but watch the water fall upon him. Juan finally had to show him how to use the soap and when and how to get out of the once warm, but then chilling, stream of water.

"I dunno known who I be nomore," he complained. "*Ergo sum, et non erit ultra* Milio no more!"

"You're still Milio," Thomas assured him. "Just a new and better version of him. I'll get you both to a barber tomorrow for a shave and a haircut. This is the beginning of your new lives. Come on in, Milio."

"But dunno sit down!" Juan warned. "Deese chairs have da devil in dem, dey will kill you and make you sick."

Thomas was dressed casually to not let the symbolism of his vestments stand between him and reluctant motley crew of visitors who sat uneasily in the pews and on the cushions. They seemed uncomfortably stunned, as though wondering what the preacher man was going to do to them. He wore the medallion around his neck but had tucked the amulet into his shirt pocket. He placed his hand lightly on the pocket to feel the amulet's reassuring presence, and then smiled warmly out at the assembly, most of whom were anxious to get back out into the streets where they felt more at ease. Though two of them, one being the one called "Spider," remained in the white robes they had put on after their last night's shower, the remainder of them had changed back into their musty-smelling street clothes.

Thomas had pulled a chair out to the front of the room, and now stood behind it, bracing himself forward on the backrest. He looked off to the side where Juan and Milio sat. Juan remained at attention, as though gratified not to be sitting in a chair that moved around beneath him, as Milio tried to doze off into a relaxed concentration.

"Okay," Thomas began. He turned the chair around and sat, resting his bare forearms on the backrest in front of him. "How are y'all feeling today?" Sometimes his lingering Midwestern accent through the touch of his Irish brogue was hard to shake. There remained a si- lence, brushed by a few nods of some heads.

"*Hey!*" Juan shouted as though at his troops. "Da preacher man wanna know how you do *feel* today!"

This was followed by a scatter of more enthusiastic affirmations of: "Fine—Good—Okay," and one "Praise the Lord!"

Thomas simpered back approvingly. "Don't worry. This isn't going to be a sermon, or even a lecture. I just wanted to welcome you all to this place—your place, really—known as Heaven's Doorway. Think of it as your home when you want to get in out of the weather, or even just out of the night for a while. A place where you can come in for a meal, or to wash up," he glanced out at the two who had not cleaned themselves up. They remained close together where they sat in the rear pew. "—and be safe."

"Bros, ah culn't sleep cause of all dat stink you was puttin' out all night!" someone complained loudly, as some others laughed.

"But all of you—think of this as your home away from the

streets. There will always be hot a meal, a place out of the weather, and to watch a ballgame, maybe. A place to sleep, to be among your friends; as many others as you want to bring here to Heaven's Doorway. And think of me as your friend—as one of you. Juan and Milio, they'll be here to help you out."

"*El Diablo Negro*?" someone asked. "You be a churchman now?"

"No!" Juan said emphatically. He looked over at Thomas. "We see 'bout dat, preacher."

"Well, for the time being at least," Thomas said.

"Okay, jus' fer now, den. Whaddabout you, Milio? You stay here wid da preacher man?"

Milio jolted awake. "Huhn?"

Thomas continued, "Never be afraid to come here, and never be afraid to bring your friends. As you know. It can be rough out there with all the gangs—and whatever else."

"Damn right! Oops! Sorry, preacher," one of them said back.

"Damn right!" Thomas's voice echoed through a little smile over a muffle of nervous laughter filtering through the room. "We need to watch out for each other. I'll depend on you as much as you agree to depend on me. We'll all help each other, and Heaven's Doorway will be our recluse and our fortress."

"A fort?" someone wanted to know.

"Yes, a fort, just as much as a church."

"You know, Preacher. Las' time a church was aroun' here, dat Reverend, he be killed by da White Cobras gang. We no wan' that happen to you again."

Thomas faltered in his address. He didn't know about that. "Well," he cleared his throat, "it won't happen because this time we'll be pre- pared. You know we can take them on, right?"

"Yes."

"Pow!" said Milio as he swung an invisible pipe from where he was waking up. "A homer runingo, oudda da park. Pepitone has done it again! Holy Cow!"

"Juan, Milio and I, we will train you to fight back if you want us to. We'll be like soldiers in the fortress."

"I too lazy to fight. Me just wanna be left alone wid my stuff," someone said through a sleepy voice.

"You won't be, as long as there are gangs out there."

One of them in the back began clapping with his heavy hands. His clap echoed loudly through the chapel. No one else joined in.

"Okay, then, we'll work on it," Thomas said. "Because of the gangs, I have to keep Heaven's Doorway locked up at night. So, here's a code knock to be let in." Thomas stood up and walked to the pulpit. "Knock loudly on the door like this." He demonstrated on the side of the wooden lectern. "Three slow knocks, followed by two quick ones. Once again, like this: "Knock—knock—knock, knock-knock," he demonstrated again. Now I want each of you to try it one by one, then you can go if you want. But you might want to stay, because Francis is making a hot lunch for you all."

Thomas inclined his head to the right of the room. "Starting with you on the pillow, and then going to you next to him, show me how to knock on Heaven's Doorway if it's locked." The first of the eight knocked tenuously on the floor. "Okay good, but a little louder." He knocked again. "Great. Now you." The one next to him demonstrated the knock with an exaggerated gusto as it continued around the room.

Chapter 20

Sugar treats

"A ceiling fan. The coldest day of the year and you want a ceiling fan." Deborah sipped on her drink where she sat across from Thomas at The Glitz & Glitter.

"Yes. Right above my pulpit. There's a real stench hanging in the chapel from all the unfortunates who are starting to come to the Friday and Sunday gatherings. Most times the smell gets really oppressive." Smoking had become a developing divergence for him. He twiddled two fingers together. "You got a cigarette?"

"Since when did you take up smoking?" Deborah asked him as she rifled through her handbag for her pack of Marlboros. "I wish I never had. But I've got this addictive nature, so I guess it's okay, for me." She handed him a cigarette and her battered Zippo. "I thought Men of God are supposed to be the paragon of virtue and an example for all us heathens and other druids. Sip on your drink, Thomas. The ice is watering it down."

Thomas lit his cigarette from the lighter's huge flame and blew a stream of smoke upward to join the rest of the glittering smaze that had been magnetically drawn toward the dark ceiling. "Stress of the trade, I guess. And smoking plays its part in blending me in with the hipsters of New York."

"Not to worry, Thomas. You're not that hip. Anyway, sure. I can have my guys put a fan in for you. Maybe two. You'll most likely need one in the back. You probably really should have some sort of air-conditioning, but it can't be central air, because we'd have to go rip the walls apart. I guess we could put in some window units."

"Window units?" he asked distractedly as he inexpertly puffed his cigarette.

"Air conditioning. Something a little more potent than ceiling fans."

"I'll be okay with just ceiling fans, Deborah," he said through a plume of smoke. "Just one above the pulpit."

"Well! Hello, you two!" James Dean intruded as he sat down in the single empty chair at their table. He was adorned as a blonde in a loose green satin blouse and black sateen lounge pants, "Have you seen Silva? He's being an elusive little demon tonight. One minute I spy him, then the next he disappears like some sort of silly spook."

Deborah demurely sipped her drink. "Have you tried downstairs in The Cavern?" She then lit a cigarette from the overgrown flare of her Zippo. "He likes to hang out down there when there's a jazz combo."

"Oh, that. Well, leave it to my dear Silva. I never could stomach all that screeching impressionism some people call music. But I do like those cute little cockney Beatles touring around here from across the pond." He mooched one of Deborah's cigarettes, lit it, and then attempted to blow a smoke ring. "I love their moppy hair. Especially Peter, that doe-eyed guitar player."

"Paul," Deborah corrected him.

"Which?" James Dean said as he rolled the filter of his cigarette between his thumb and forefinger.

"The doe-eyed Beatle. Paul. Paul McCartney."

Thomas leaned back in his chair and draped his arm around Deborah's shoulders. "I think it's all nonsense. Those silly Beatles. A faddish flash in the pan. They'll be forgotten by August."

James Dean smirked at him. "You'd look stunning in one of those Beatle wigs, Camille, especially along with that sarong you wore on Halloween."

Deborah took another puff and coughed. "For Pete's sake. Are you all still talking about that?"

"Why, Dah-ling, haven't you heard? That's all we've been talking about."

"Then you need to get on with your lives, dear hearts. It was Halloween, for pity's sake."

"We don't care about that. Wear that dress again with a Beatle wig and you'll make more friends than you can count around here. And we still want to take you shopping and then for a proper makeover at Pauline's place over on Christopher Street."

"Who? Pauline?" Deborah said as she flagged a passing waiter for another round. "Not on your life! Don't listen to them, Thomas."

"Don't know about the Beatle wig, James Dean," Thomas said. "I'd probably look more like that Stooge, Moe, in drag, anyway,"

"I'll have a pink squirrel," said James Dean to the waiter.

"Where have you been?" Silva said to James Dean as he coalesced from the surrounding obscurity and sat on the edge of his James Dean's seat.

"Here, obviously, darling. Don't you think Camille would look *ador*-able in one of those Beatle wigs?"

Silva squinted intently at Thomas. "Frankly, he'd look more like Moe of the Three Stooges," he said dourly.

Thomas sipped his Scotch and soda. "That's what I thought."

"I thought you were down in The Cavern with all that jazz music of yours."

"Haven't you heard, dear James? They've taken a break." The waiter returned with the drinks. "Take your pink drink and come back down there with me. Batwoman brought some of those sugar treats you like, and she's saving some for us."

"Really? Oh goodie!" James Dean said as his rose abruptly from his seat. "I'm totally ready for those sweets of hers!"

"Deborah? Camille?" Silva offered.

"His name's Thomas, and maybe some other time. You kids go have your fun and be home by two."

James Dean referred to his watch. "It's already two."

"Whatever, then," she said after them as they retreated toward the stairs leading to The Cavern.

"Sugar treats?" Thomas asked her. "Sugar cubes laced with LSD." "LSD?"

"Their magic potion. I'm sure Silva and James will tell you about it soon enough, sweetie. For now, let's finish our drinks and go back to my place. I'm starting to feel a little frisky."

Chapter 21

Angel

Dull shards of soft, purplish light roamed through the muted darkness as the ceiling fan above the pulpit rotated a small mirrored ball attached to its center post. Thomas cleared his throat to address his congregation of street dwellers, most of whom had showed up only for the promise of a meal following his talk. Some of them seemed easily mesmerized by the repetitive flows of lavender light, the two ceiling fans served to mellow the musty, fish-tainted aroma rising from sleepy congregation.

He talked softly in a tempo geared to the subtle surges of the light, just as he had perfected back at his Church of the Holy Waters in Iowa. "The street has burdened you with a cold, bitter life, but whatever has dragged you there no longer matters. You are here because you want to find out who you are—who you can be. You are who you are. Say after me: 'I am who I am.'"

Refrains of "I am who I am," filtered into the silence left in the wake of Thomas's directive. "Say it again."

Sluggish mumbles of "I am who I am," filtered throughout the room.

"'I am who I am.' That is how God, in the form of a burning bush, answered the prophet Moses, who wanted to make sure he was talking to God." Actually, God had said 'I am that I am' to Moses, at least according to the Hebrew Torah and the King

James version of the Bible. While the "Who" addressed a personal God—perhaps an inner one—the "That" referred to a God of the cosmos. But one pronoun of difference meant little to Thomas. "I am who I am." He waited for a response from the assemblage. A few more scattered rejoinders floated around the room: "I am who I am."

Squinting into the penumbral darkness, Thomas could tell who might have fallen more under his influence through the depth of their responses. One of the parishioners who was not at all enthralled captured his interest. Sitting off in a corner and in another world and shivering away a drug reaction, was a dirt-smudged, wild-haired, emaciated waif in her mid-20s. A loose, oversized army field jacket weighted down her fragile shoulders. She wore a woolen cap drawn down below her eyes, as if to shield them, and her, from the light.

"Then you are who God is. You are His children, and you are Him. You have His kind of power over your lives. This is true whether you shiver out your days under the overpasses or languish in a Fifth Avenue penthouse. You are who you are. You are all God within and you are your own god. Say it again: I am who I am."

"I am who I am."

"You are God. Accept your fate. Your inner god, every bit as powerful as the one in your imagination, will see you through. The god who lives within you is the way to the all-powerful one in heaven. So, children, accept your fate." He signaled Francis to turn up the room lights, and the congregation slowly blinked awake.

Thomas singled out the drugged girl carrying her field jacket as she plodded down the hall with the others toward the parish hall. "I haven't seen you around here before. What's your name?"

She slid the wool cap off her head and stared blankly back at him but seemed to see nothing through her daze. "I am who I am," she said. "Okay," said Thomas, trying to douse her sarcasm with his own. "I get that, dear heart. But what is your name?"

"Angelina," she said hoarsely from too little sleep and too much of a hardened life. "Angel."

She shrugged as she looked down at the floor. "What-ever. If you say so. Can I go, now?"

"Go and get yourself something to eat, Angel, and stop by my office on your way out. I have a valuable gift for you."

She brightened, in that she could, and cocked her head. "Money?"

He smiled. "Perhaps. But you'll have to see me to find out."

All the others had filed to down to the parish hall by now, and he and she were alone. She looked around and then lowered her head. She appeared as though she'd lived a life that had reduced her to a mere existence. Varying ratty lengths of loose hair, which had been contained beneath her cap, now shielded her face.

"Sex? You want to fuck me," she sighed dejectedly as she dropped her field jacket to the floor and began to routinely unbutton her shirt to display a sunken collarbone covered by raw, roughened skin.

"Heavens not, dear heart!" he whispered coarsely. "Now stop that!" "You find me not pretty? Even a little?" she croaked weakly as she gazed up at him and re-buttoned her shirt.

"Of course, you're pretty; too pretty for me to consider you as some sort of object. Let's just say I find you—special." He placed his hand lightly upon her shoulder and felt the trembling knobs and blades of her bones beneath the feeble layer of her shirt. "Now, Angel," he felt her cringe at the mention of her name. "Just go and get something warm to eat. As much as you want. Then stop by my office on your way back out." He kissed her lightly high on her forehead, tasting the salt of her skin beneath a stale coat of dirt and the dryness of her hair. She gazed sheepishly back at him.

He realized that she reminded him of a cadaverous version of his long-gone daughter. She might have been Regina's ghost. At any rate, he thought it his duty to finish the job that Angel's wretched circum- stances had begun. She smiled mirthlessly and went down to the hall as he picked up her field jacket.

Thomas ran the hardened fabric of Angel's jacket through his fingers as he relaxed in his office listening to the Allegretto from Beethoven's Seventh. He put her coat gently to the side near a Bible he hardly used any more. He had dismissed the Good Book as so much fiction that was for him no deeper than a pulp mystery story. There was a time before he found his god when he referred to it for inspiration. Now, like the fables it told, the book was unused, worn and wrinkled soft with age. He picked it up and a snapshot he'd used as a bookmark fell out on his desk.

The picture had been taken around 10 years before on a beach in Negril, Jamaica. Eleven-year-old Regina and her mother, Jillian, all smiles and teeth, stood tanned and refreshed in the vivid saturation of a late tropical morning. He stared closely at the large yet subtle birth- mark on Regina's stomach. It dribbled in a path from her navel to her hip to beneath the brim of her frilly, modest, two-piece pink bathing suit. Standing next to their daughter, Jillian appeared as nonexistent as she would become eight hours later when he would watch her go for a swim—and then watch her drown.

He opened the Bible to where another photo poked out. It was Regina's graduation photo, taken a month before she left Hanson. It revealed a deep-eyed, dour-faced girl who had lost the happy innocence of the younger one in the snapshot, as she stared narrowly at some vagary far beyond the lens. Loose hefts of her long, dull auburn hair hung disarrayed over her shoulders. Her jaw was set tightly in a show of mistrust. Here was a 19-year-old who had seen far too much of the darker side of life too soon, as had Angel. Thomas glanced back at the child in the snapshot. "What has become of you, dear heart?" he asked it in a hoarse whisper.

He slipped the photos back into the Bible and allowed the music's softness to carry him away into its ebb and flow until he sensed An- gel's presence in the doorway. She was still trembling from the residue of whatever drugs she had taken, but food had brought some color to her dirty cheeks and a dim glisten to her eyes.

Thomas laid her jacket upon the Bible and motioned her to one of the chairs. "Please, dear heart. Sit."

He walked around and leaned against the front of his desk as she sunk into one of the leather chairs. She suddenly stiffened in a wave of fright. "Am I in trouble? You din't call the cops on my ass!"

"No, dear heart, no," Thomas said. "This is the safest place you can be right now."

"What do you want, then?"

"I want you to stay here. In Heaven's Doorway."

"What? No! I have my own home!"

Thomas did not want to imagine what her place must look like. "Just for today, where it's safe and quiet. There's a room upstairs where you can clean up and rest. You need rest."

"Damn it, mister! I knew it!" she blurted tiredly. "'F'you want to fuck me, just say so. We'll do it, and I'll go back to my place. And then everyone's happy. Okay?"

He doubted whether she had any capacity left to feel happiness. "No. I do not want to have sex with you!" he flared. "I'm a Reverend, for God's sake! I'm sworn to celibacy."

"Okay, then. So, I ain't worth you going to hell for. Can I please go now?" She seemed to muster up all her strength to rise from her chair.

"You are worth everything. You are one of God's children." "Well, he's been one hell of a fuckin' papa to me," she seethed quietly as she stood away from the chair—and him. She clutched up her jacket from where he had placed it on his desk. "My own daddy would beat me and then fuck me, but he even treated me better than this frickin' god you're tryin' to lay on me. 'God is within me,'" she seethed scornfully. "Bull-shit! At least my real daddy din't sentence me to the street four years ago!"

"Well then, who did, Angel? Who sentenced you to the streets?"

She folded her arms and stared at the floor. "Well it certainly wasn't me, a sixteen-year-old kid. It was my frickin' mother; like it was my fault when she caught me and daddy fuckin' in her bed one night. No time to pack. 'Just leave right now, Angel. And never fuckin' come back!' That was what she said. And so I'd appreciate it if space cadets like you din't call me 'Angel.' Too many bad remembrances. So, preacher man, either fuck me now, or let me leave. And I wouldn't mind a little money on the way out."

"You're just worn out, Angelina," Thomas said as he went around to the back of his desk. She watched in shadowy curiosity as he unlocked a drawer and then brightened when he pulled out two $50 bills. "These hundred dollars is yours if you stay and rest; just rest and wash up a little to bring out all that prettiness of yours. I promise I'll make no advances on you. Can you do that for one hundred dollars? Can you get through the rest of the day without whatever it is you rely on to ruin your life? For just one day? If you really need some sort of, I don't know, something to help you sleep, I've got some bourbon in the kitchen."

"Is it Jack Daniels?"

He smiled slyly in the realization that she seemed to be coming around. "How should I know? I'm not supposed to drink either, or I'll end up in hell as soon as if I had sex with you."

She looked down again and smiled broadly. "I might be startin' to like you, preacher."

"Can you trust me then, Angelina? Trust me not to hurt you?"

"I don't know," she said. Her mouth began to twitch as though she might cry, but there were no tears left for her to shed. "Okay. I'll stay here. Just for tonight."

The filter and dehumidifiers droned soothingly as the jets beneath the water created delicate ripples on the surface of the baptismal pool. A shimmering turquoise glow from beneath the lit waters softened the fine darkness of the room divided by accordion panels. Two voices filtered through the drawn panels from the far end of the parish hall. Thomas's was sonorous and loose, Angel's was timid and spare.

They sat at one of the smaller tables, scantly lit by the wavering light from two thick candles that shimmered off the planes of their faces and the bottles of Scotch and bourbon between them.

"May God forgive me," Thomas toasted with a grin as he lifted his freshly made drink to Angel, who sipped her bourbon as she guarded her glass like it was the last valuable thing left in her world.

Angel had showered away the dirt that had nearly disguised her earlier in the day. Her dark-blonde hair, now washed and softened, hung in a mass of ringlets to her shoulders. The pocked skin of her gaunt face was covered in a light film of freckles. Her dim green eyes were sunken in the shadow of wear and delusion. She was naked beneath the plush terry-cloth robe Francis had placed in her bedroom. The sight of her obliquely reminded Thomas all the more of Regina.

From the laundry closet above, the soft cycling of her street clothes tumbling in the drier along with the whirr of machinery servicing the pool from the closed off baptismal area on the other side of the room added a soothing element to their lapses of conversation. After Francis had put her clothes in the drier, he had left for the night to work in The Glitz & Glitter Club's kitchen. Milio and Juan were out somewhere beneath the overpasses communing with Spider and the rest of their street friends.

Angel had begun to relax. She smiled wearily over the rim of her glass. "So, this god of yours really don't care if you take a drink, like you said he would," she said in a ragged tone caught between a whisper and a choke.

"Oh, He does, really. But the god within me—my god—says it's okay. He accepts that we men of the pulpit are nothing more than mortals, trying to do our best. So, deep inside we're all only human. You, me—everyone else."

She thought about this for a moment. "That's what you were talkin' about earlier, then."

She remembered more from his sermon than he had. He searched his memory back a few hours, as he sipped his drink. "Yeah, something like that. What or who controls us from within is more forgiving than that lightning-bolt-hurling God we imagine up there above us all."

"Seems you don't think much about Him. The One above, I mean." "Oh, but I do, Angelina. I wouldn't be a Reverend if I didn't."

She slurped her bourbon and then stared at the flickering candle flame. "I get the feelin' this's more like a job to you, not like a—a what-cha-ma-call-it."

"Calling?"

"I 'spose."

"What do you feel about God, Angelina?"

Still staring into the candle flame she said, "I already told you. I think he's a fuckin' prick, because of what he does to people. People like me, for instance. I don't, like, belong—like I don't exist." She sighed in resignation.

Thomas glanced at her, then down into his drink. "Then you probably don't exist to Him, Angelina," he said.

Her lips trembled as her eyes teared up.

"God doesn't listen to those who don't exist for him. You've been forgotten in this life, Angelina. God forgot about you the day you left your home for the streets. And the day your father first took you into his bed."

Her eyes began to glisten, but she shed no tears.

"Look," he continued calmly through a thin, benign smile. "You can't even cry anymore. God has taken all your emotions back and left you as an empty shell of a person." His smile broadened wryly as he sipped his drink. He reached subtly into his pocket and felt the roughened bronze edge of the medallion. He then drew it from his pocket to the table and shielded it with his hand. "Maybe there's really nothing left for you."

Finally, a tear rolled down her cheek. "I'm scared," she whispered. Another image of Regina flashed through his mind. He felt as though he might as well be talking to her. "You ought to be scared, daughter," he said. "What are you thinking, now? Do you believe your life is worth living the way it is?"

She stared more intently into the candle flame as she brushed away the trickle of a tiny tear. Her answer came through her question. "Can you help me?"

He turned the medallion in his hand. "Yes, I can."

"How?"

"I can renew your life for you." He stood up and then extended a hand. "Here, Angelina, come with me."

Another few tears rolled down a cheek as she stood, sniffled and took his hand. He led her to the far side of the room and slid open the panel separating the pool. He guided her to the its edge. "Now, Angel," he said closely, "I want you to stand here, and follow what I tell you. Within a few minutes, you'll be completely renewed. You'll meet the god within who cares about you." He reached over to the railing of the pool steps and flicked on the switch for the small spotlight to catch the reflections from the amulet he slowly twiddled before her eyes. He inflected his soft voice to the surges of glow across her face. "Concentrate on the lavender light from the gem. The god in you lives in this gem. Look deep into God's eyes. He is waiting for you, Angel. His arms are open to embrace you. Look and see—look and see—look and seeee."

Soon, her lids began to close. "Daddee?" she said weakly as she became entranced.

"I will ask you to do what your god channels through me," he whispered. "I am the voice of your god who sees you, feels your pain. Let him take all your pain and change it into joy."

Her lips blossomed into the genuine emotion of a suppliant smile. "God… joy."

"Now, dear heart, remove your robe." She let her robe slip to the floor. Her emaciated body was covered in scars, sores, track marks and cigarette burns. "What a loveless life you must have lived, Angel," he said as he looked at her shivering body. "You deserve your god's love. Now step into the water and be embraced by the love of your god." She did as she was told as Thomas stooped to lay the amulet on the tile

floor. He then stood and undressed. "Do you feel your god's loving embrace?"

"Yesss…" she said through another shiver. "So warm…so warm." He stripped down to his shorts and stepped into the water to stand next to her. "Lower yourself into his embrace." He helped her to lower herself into the water, as he picked up his shirt from the floor and positioned himself behind her. "Angel, dear heart, you are ready for a new life, a loving life, a life free from pain and anyone who would hurt you."

"Free from everyone," she whispered in a voice bristling into the fear of acceptance of the unknown.

He soaked his shirt in the water, wadded it up and brought it closer to her face. "God will kiss you now, to fill you with a new life and take you into his arms. Now feel the kiss and the embrace of your loving god."

"Kiss of my god…"

Thomas brought his wet shirt to her face and held it tightly over her nose and mouth as he dunked and held her beneath the water. Too weakened to fight, she succumbed quickly. Thomas held her under the water long after he felt the warm, feathery tremble of her liberated soul enter his.

But this was not at all like the liberation of a man's soul. Angel's soul instantly bloomed within him, engulfing him from the inside out. Her soul released a primeval sense of himself as a woman. It embraced him in a kind of heat he had not felt since Mother huddled him to her near the warmth of the sod-burning hearth in Ballycannough. Angel's soul had overtaken him with such a primal power that he unleashed the bestial orgasm of his entire manhood as a murky flowering cloud into the water. He released a hard sigh of relief. Finally, he lifted her limp body from the water and kissed her damp, thin lips. "Blessings, dear heart," he whispered breathlessly. "Thank you for helping me to become the one I truly need to be."

He lovingly lifted Angel's corpse from the water, laid it on the tile and then pat it dry with the robe she had worn. He then anointed her forehead with lavender to consecrate the act. He covered her body with the robe, put on his shoes and pants and went to find a fresh vestment shirt in the changing room. He took a large burlap bag from a folded heap of them he kept on the floor of the utility closet next to some un- opened boxes of Bibles. He rolled the hand truck from the far corner of the closet out to where Angel's half-covered naked body lay amid splattered pools of baptismal water. As though he had rehearsed the process before, he went up to the laundry room to retrieve her dried clothes, then dressed her and pulled the burlap bag over her body.

He propped and secured her body onto the hand truck and wheeled it up the ramp through the basement service entrance. The Chevy Corvair that had once been Regina's was parked near the egress from the basement, in the shadows of the side of the building. He folded Angel's body into the trunk, as he had done with John Bass' so long ago.

He backed out into the empty street, flickering under low lamp-light, and drove a block and a half into the thickness of the 1 a.m. dark- ness toward the bowels of the Two Bridges district. He parked close to the edge of the East River. Cloaked by darkness, he emptied her body from the burlap bag into the river.

Still overcome with the smooth exhilaration brought on by the passion of a woman's soul within him, he drove the Corvair back to the church. He realized he needed to bum a cigarette from Juan and walked back out toward the FDR overpass in search of him.

The low voice from behind carried an unsettling musk with it. "Well, pilgrim, what brings you to the depths of hell?" The voice was followed immediately by two sets of hands grabbing him harshly from behind. They flung him face down into the course gravel and the stench of the slush-covered ground.

Through one opened eye, Thomas saw wads of paper, shards of broken glass, and the steel-toed shoes of his assailants. He felt the hard, quick drive of one of the metal boots into his midsection. "You're that preacher man," was all he heard of the watery voice before he felt another two sharp kicks to his arm, along with a hard third one that dislocated his shoulder. A fourth kick grazed his cheek and then three more landed deep into his midsection. Finally, he felt the kicks suddenly subside, as another voice said, "What the *fuck*!?"

Thomas mustered what energy he could to roll away from his wounded shoulder to stare into the terrified face of a tall, wiry white man dressed in black. Blood spurted from either side of his neck as he crumpled stiffly to the ground inches from where Thomas lay. He felt the warm welter of the victim's blood soak his vestment and stared up blankly to see Spider standing behind where the attacker fell, legs apart and holding a barber's razor, sheeted in blood, in each hand.

Thomas could barely see out of his other eye, but thought he saw the blur of Milio pummeling another attacker with his baseball bat, as the third ran off into the darkness, yelling: "You will fuckin' *pay* for this, fuckin' bastards!!"

Juan stepped out from behind Spider. His voice echoed as though through a tunnel. "Me, I teach Spider how to shave a mon."

Spider smiled smugly as he folded the razors closed. Thomas thought he heard him say. "Ya got any more beahs in dat church?"

"Do no worry 'bout the beers, dere, Spider. You go help da preacher man to da church, while Milio an' me, we know wadda do wid dese White Cobras."

"All I wanna was a cigarah," Thomas mumbled drunkenly. "Juan you gol-lah cigarah?"

"White Cobra. Shitata *cacca*!" Milio said from a distance. It was the last voice Thomas heard before the searing pain in his abdomen lowered him into a blackout.

Chapter 22

The absolute truth

As Deborah nursed Thomas back to health in her apartment, Juan, Milio, Spider and some others put themselves up in Heaven's Doorway. Francis had given up on resisting their occupation as he spent more of his time working in The Glitz & Glitter's kitchen.

The chapel had become a lounge for those from the underpasses, including the wiry Spider; the bulky, lumbering Lumpyman; Squinty, the myopic one, who saw better in the dark than most of the others, and Saxman, who insisted he had once backed up Charlie Parker. His voice was brassy as if to replicate the sound that may have once come from the now rusted and useless instrument on to which he clung.

They loafed around drinking beers and smoking cigars and cigarettes. Saxman smoked a battered pipe, and the air was redolent with rotten tobacco and the prevailing mix of sweat, urine and the fishy stink that had attached to their clothing. Juan, the self-appointed leader in Thomas's absence, interrupted the course and erratic flow of conversation. "Dem White Cobras," he announced as he sprung up to a stand from where he had sprawled half-asleep behind the pulpit.

"So?" Spider said back from the rear of the chapel.

Juan lit a cigar and flicked the smoldering match to the carpet. "What we plan to do about dem?"

"Nutin'," said someone in a raspy voice. "Dey pay me sometime fer runnin' dere chores."

"Runnin' *drugs* you mean," the Saxman piped in. "Soma which you pro'lly keep for yerself."

"Like I says, dey pay me."

"Me, too," said another.

"We gotta take dem down, anyways," Juan said. "Dey startin' to make life worse for most of us. An' dey almost kilt da preacher man."

Squinty's voice sounded small from the rear of the room. "We need not to mess with thim White Cobras,"

"Yeah we shoulda," Milio said. "Lika Juan say, the preacher man *nuntii quando miserunt occiderunt*. Them hit a doublata, an' scoreoa two runs, when dem took down dea Preacher las' mont'."

"What? Wha'd he jus' say?" blurted someone in a hooded sweatshirt from where he was huddled in the back of the room.

"Nuttin'," Juan said. "What matters be us. We gotta run dem White Cobras away."

"Maybe dey run demselves 'way. Like dem Solotos Lassos last year did to demselves, too," Saxman said.

Juan squinted at Saxman. "It be *Los Lobos Solitarios*, Saxman," he corrected. "Us, we can take down da White Cobras. I know we can."

"An' how mightchya know this, Mr. *Diablo Negro*?" asked the hooded one from the back of the room.

"'Cause us—me, Milio an' da preacher—we got ridda *Los Lobos Solitarios*. We did it. Kilt seven or eight of dem and floated dere bodies off inta da river," Juan admitted.

"*Et interfecerunt eos, et octo*. Eight...ita be eight a dat shitita cacca bunch we floated," Milio said.

"They did," Spider emphasized, and then slurped his beer. "I know dis. Jus' like we did to two of dem Cobras after dey jumped the preacher man las' mont'."

"That preacher helped you take down the two Cobras?" said the hooded street person.

Juan nodded. "Well, dem Los Lobos Solitarios, anyhow. He give dem las' rites after we started dem to die, den he finish dem off and floated dem down da river. Oh, yeah, an' he be good wid the knife. Well, *almost* good."

"Though I be better," Spider said.

"De White Cobras. Dey got guns," said Lumpyman. "Dem P.R.s juz had switchblade knifes."

Juan picked a half-smoked butt from his pocket. "Us, we have guns now. Preacher helped us get dem. To sen' dem Cobras away." He lit his smoke.

"You have guns," said the voice from the hooded sweatshirt.

"Yeah, ours and like da one like dis I take from dat Cobra who hurt da preacher," Juan said as he reached deep into one of his coat pockets and pulled out a chrome-plated .38 caliber handgun.

"Hooooly shit!" said the one in the sweatshirt.

"An' razors, in case their necks need a close shave, like dey did a last mont'." Spider added. "I agree with *El Diablo Negro*. If we team up—"

"Us, we can sen' dem down da river like *Los Lobos Solitarios*." Juan continued. "Us all, we can live our lifes—no more fear. Us, we really can do dis. And wid da preacher's help. He got money fer more guns, too—an' knifes. So, who is wid' us tonight, huhn? Me, Spider an' Milio an' de preacher, when he get better?"

Milio's and Spider's hands shot up, joined cautiously by those of Saxman, Lumpyman and then Squinty, followed by four of the ten remaining people in the room. A few others, inspired by the show of hands, reluctantly raised theirs half-way. Juan offered up a smug smile. "Okay, den. We meet here again at sundown—aroun' six— in two nights to start to figger out how to do dis. Spider and me be da only ones using guns. Milio, he be good wid da pipe and de bat. An' da rest o' you, me and Spider train wid the knife."

"I wanna gun!" Squinty shouted.

"Ya godda learn ta *see* first, Squinty," Juan said.

Spider eased himself up by degrees from his cushion with a groan. "I need me anudder beah. Anyone else want anudder one?" Most of the remaining hands shot decisively up, as Spider surveyed the room. "What? I look like some sorta *barkeep* to you?" he said. "'Getchure own, ya lazy bastids!" He walked out toward the kitchen refrigerator that Thomas had Deborah stock with bottles of Pabst Blue Ribbon. He had rightly reasoned that ample quantities of beer would be one thing that would keep his congregation coming to Heaven's Doorway.

The hooded street person in the back of the room folded his arms tightly across his stomach. He glanced down at his left hand from which the sleeve of his oversized sweatshirt had ridden up on his wrist. On his hand was a small tattoo of a Swastika within a circle; the tag of a White Cobra. He subtly pulled his sleeve down to cover it as he sorted out his thoughts on his report to the *Führer*.

After Deborah had rushed Thomas to the NYU Medical Center three weeks before, half of his damaged and spleen had to be removed. A hot pain seared through what was left of it and his five broken ribs as he tried to wake up. The broadcast from Deborah's bed-side clock radio sometimes bristled into static, even picking up pilot transmissions as planes lowered into their approach over the East River into LaGuardia Airport. Another of The Beatles' current hits, "She Loves You," played beneath the in and out crackle of transmissions like: "Eastern Airlines DC 6 flight 251, on final, LaGuardia, Runway 4." Beatles songs occupied eight of the top 25 slots on the charts, as the music and antics of the four cheeky, moppy-haired Liverpudlian lads roiled through the American culture in what was now commonly referred to as "The British Invasion."

Thomas turned sluggishly away from the radio and the dull stubs of pain in his shoulder to face Deborah who was propped up on her side as she stared at him.

She kissed him lightly on his forehead. "All that's gotta really feel like shit to you," she said. "How does the cast feel today?"

"Like my arm's caught in a mold of stinging mosquitoes. Godless creatures!"

She patted his arm. "Poor Thomas. Always the flair for the dramatic. You've got only two more days to bear with it. Dr. Andreessen said he'd take the cast off and put a lighter one on this Friday."

Thomas rolled over on his back and sunk his head into the pillow.

He sighed deeply. "I'll believe it when I feel it."

Deborah swung her legs out of bed. Her smooth naked figure gleamed like dull copper in the flow of the early-April morning light through the windows. "Come on, sweetie, let's get you up and rolling," she said as she stood and slipped into her blue satin robe.

"I'm an invalid," he pouted as she rolled a wheelchair to his side of the bed.

"And I'm here to take care of you." She drew back the covers, took a light hold of his calves, and helped him to pivot into a sitting position on the edge of the bed. He braced himself with his left hand.

Deborah's robe had slipped open as she leaned forward, exposing her firm breasts as they hung as though weighed by their bulbous, pink areoles and thickened nipples. The sight of them gave him the energy to hoist himself up and into the wheelchair.

"I'm gonna get these bastards for this," he muttered bitterly. "What happened to turning the other cheek, Reverend?" she said as she positioned him in the chair.

"That old saw doesn't count for preachers who are attacked by Lucifer's disciples."

She laughed. "Well, then. Praise the Lord and pass the ammunition!" That sounded familiar to him, as an electric surge rose through the pain when he remembered it was one of those family phrases Jillian had frequently used. "Damn right and amen!" he ventured through the swell of his pain as he grasped her hand. She had worked at softening her work-coarsened hands, and her skin had come to feel pleasently soft.

Deborah had designed The Glitz & Glitter Club from the shell of an 80-year-old restaurant. It had originally been one of the southernmost places that slumming up-towners would go to boast they had entered the northern fringes and dangers of the Five Points and the legendary Lower East Side gangs that had worked its streets. Nevertheless, the restaurant had been a classy place, with a vaulted wine cellar that had been converted to The Glitz & Glitter's Cavern. It was now a place where folk singers, poets and jazz musicians on their way up or down or in between gigs showed up to jam with the Bonne-Aires' four-piece house combo.

The Cavern was doused in a primeval climate punctuated by smoky rays from two blue spotlights illuminating the performer on the stage. Tonight, Big Eunice, looking extremely overweight and *zaftig* in a tight red satin dress trundled breathing heavily onto the stage. Her chubby ebony features shimmered from the sheen of her perspiration under the graze of a spotlight as she breathlessly labored onto the stool on center-stage. She leaned forward into the microphone. She heaved louder, irregular breaths. The small crowd throughout the smoky din quieted as though not sure whether the entertainment for tonight was going to be Big Eunice performing a heart attack on stage. "Phew!" she finally gasped as she wiped the expanse of her forehead dry with a gold handkerchief.

"That was one long walk out to the stage, my chillen!" She tucked the hankie into her bodice, between where her enormous breasts bub- bled over its top. She took another breath and then brought the mike to her lips. "You!...Ain't!...NUH-thin...!," she began singing in a raspy bellow that only someone of her size could produce, "...but a hound dog!" The crowd broke into cheers and catcalls, as some flicked their lighters into the darkness. This was not the hit commercialized by Elvis Presley. This was the brassy original Big Momma Thornton blues version from 1952.

Big Eunice had fallen into the song; becoming one with it as she closed her eyes and let her singing carry her away. She breathed just as heavily as before, but now her breaths were exhaled to the downbeats, as the Bonne-Aires combo provided a gentle, yet unnecessary, backup. Big Eunice's thundering, soul-filled voice seriated the atmosphere and cut through the smoke.

Silva, Bobbie, James Dean, Deborah and Thomas, who had now graduated from the wheelchair to a crutch for his left side, celebrated his improved condition over drinks. He now wore a smaller and lighter sling and cast around his dislocated shoulder, but the new bandage around his waist bit uncomfortably around his midsection. It shortened his breathing and his short bouts of speech were garnished with wheezes.

James Dean's senses had been dulled by pot being passed around their table. "Each time I hear Big Eunice I about pee in my panties," he said. "I forgot. Where'd Teddy find her?"

"I think he found her at one of those blues dives down on Beale

Street in Memphis," Bobbie said, as he tapped the bowl of his pipe on the edge of the table to dislodge some tobacco.

"There's too…much light…on her," Thomas wheezed. "No won- der…the poor dear is sweating…so much."

"Any less light and we'd be in a coal mine, wearing one of those pit helmets with flashlights on the front," Silva said.

"Whoo, now that would be totally groovy!"

"Christ! He's even starting to talk like a teenybopper," Silva said. "Too much of that British music, J-D. Maybe I should start dressing you up Carnaby Street-style."

"You can dress me any way you want, sweetie."

"Don't get him started, Silva," Deborah said as she took a puff on the communal joint. "You'll never turn him off." She passed the glowing-tipped reefer to Thomas, who handed it off to Bobbie.

"Ah," Silva sparked in remembrance. "I still haven't forgotten to take you shopping, Camille."

"S'okay," Thomas said. "Don't…need to."

"He doesn't need women's clothes, Silva," Deborah said. "Dressing my man like a woman creeps me out."

"Speak for yourself, George Sand," said James Dean.

"Jesus. It was just a Halloween costume. This year we'll dress as hoboes and dissolve that image you all have of me and Thomas as cross-dressers."

"Nothing wrong with trannies," Silva said.

Bobbie drew in some shortened wet puffs as he lit his newly-packed pipe and then trained a concerned look at Thomas. "Poor Camille. You seem in so much pain. Are you still hurting, sweetie?"

"I'll live."

"Yeah, but there's no reason you have to live in pain like that." He pinched his thumb and forefinger in James Dean's direction. "James, be a dear and pass me back that reefer. We need to absolve

Camille of his hurt." James Dean passed the marijuana back to Silva, who held it up to Thomas's lips. "Here, take a deep puff on this. It'll help."

"I…don't smoke…that stuff."

"Actually, Thomas, it may really help you," Deborah said.

Silva lightly waved the joint in front of Thomas's face. "She's right. Tell you what, missy. You take a small puff of this, and Bobbie'll tell you a little secret about our dear Hera."

"Thomas knows just about everything he needs to about me."

"Then he probably knows this." Bobbie gestured the stem of his briarwood toward Thomas. "Listen to your girlfreind, sweetie, take your medicine. You'll be glad you did. Think of it like smoking one of your cigarettes." Thomas took a weak puff.

"That's it, sweetie." James Dean said. "Now another one. A deeper one. And hold it in. Savor it."

Deborah glowered at Bobbie. "God damnit, Bobbie, if you tell him one of those things you think you know about me—" she warned. "For Christ's sake, Thomas, exhale! You're turning red. I can tell, even in this light."

Thomas gratefully puffed out a small bit of smoke. Bobbie had been right about the remedy. He felt the burn in his lungs, but a little less physical pain. "Good…now…tell me…about Hera."

Bobbie caught Deborah's glare, then smirked at her. "Oh, come on, sweetie! It's time he knew, if you haven't told him."

"Shit, Bobbie. You'd better keep this neat. Thomas and I are starting to develop something here."

"Nuptials, perhaps?" James Dean asked.

Even through his pain, Thomas felt a numbing sensation rumble through him.

Deborah looked at Thomas. "Hunh? Well I hadn't thought about that, but—"

"Holy double groovy!" James Dean blurted through an epiphany. "We could have the wedding right here at Glitz and Glitter! The event of the season! Camille could be dressed as the bride and Hera as the groom!"

"No!" Thomas gasped in a winded panted, then coughed. "No marriage…Not yet…at least."

Bobbie smirked. "Maybe this will change your mind." "Bobbie, I'm warning you," Deborah said.

"Now I'm…really curious…What about…Deborah?" Thomas wheezed. He would listen to anything to take the conversation away from marriage.

"Well, sweetie. Hera more than just designed this place— "

"She owns it," Silva said. "This building, and the one next to it." He sipped his martini.

"Shit!" Deborah grumbled.

Thomas took on a befuddled look, as James Dean joined the banter. "And some of half the buildings in the city, at least anything built before the nineteen-thirties. Midtown to the lower West Eighties."

"Jesus! That is so not true!" Deborah cried. "Thomas, don't believe them!"

"Interesting," Thomas said as he looked at her.

"Okay, God dammit! It's only *partially* true," she admitted. "I have tiny little stakes in some of buildings my grandfather's company helped construct in the in the forty years between the late eighteen-hundreds and into the nineteen-thirties. But only a little bit of it, and that's the absolute truth, Thomas."

"Like the New York City Library, Penn Station, The Metropolitan Museum," James Dean said.

"And all those upper West Side apartment buildings, including The Dakota," said Silva.

"Oh, shit. Please, Thomas, don't misread any of this."

"The sweet thing is, Camille," Bobbie said, his voice muffled as he puffed on his pipe, "your girlfriend, and hopefully intended, is filthy rich—and miserably frugal."

"So, Thomas," said Deborah as she glowered around the table. "Do you want to propose to me now in front of all these fucking idiots, or wait until after we screw tonight?"

"Dahling! Don't be so hard on yourself!" Silva said. "You should be proud of your part in the heritage of this deranged Gotham we call home. There's absolutely nothing wrong with being rich. Especially in this town."

"I hate you all!" Deborah seethed lovingly.

"A harmless invective," said Silva. "To be forgiven and forgotten by morning."

This new information did not seem to faze Thomas at all. "I feel for you...no more...or no less...Hera-Deborah...than I always have," he coughed. "For what... you are." He hoped his remark did not sound as artificial as he knew it was.

Bobbie smiled broadly. "How sweet! See? Now that's true love, honey cakes. And from a creature who travels so close to God."

"Thank, you Thomas," Deborah said. "I guess you can still propose to me if you want. I'll probably say 'yes.'"

"Yess! Do," James Dean said. "Bobbie can plan it. That's what he used to do. Plan weddings."

"Not anymore," Bobbie said a little dismally.

Thomas felt consumed by a shuddering sweat. "Not...yet," he breathed.

"We should celebrate in The Den," James Dean said. "The Den" also known lovingly by Glitz & Glitter Club insiders as "The Fruit Cellar," was a smaller room off to the side of The Cavern. During The Cavern's days as a speakeasy, the Den was the large, thickly guarded vault where the booze was stored away from the marauding cops.

Silva, Bobbie, James Dean and other regulars used the room to escape to other worlds. Bathed in a moist, cool darkness, save for a few candles, The Den was now a private room away from where people sat gathered in The Cavern to listen to music. It was where more potent drugs than pot could be imbibed in darkness and in private. Deborah, happy with her bourbon and occasional joint, chose never to go there, and she knew it was not right for Thomas.

"We'll just stay here," she told the rest of them.

"We know you will, Hera," Silva said. "How about you, Camille?"

"Thomas, you really shouldn't..."

"Let Camille decide for himself," Silva said.

Bobbie placed a hand lightly on Thomas's good shoulder. "You two aren't married, yet, sweetie. So she can't order you around like a real wife. Come with us just once. It will help your pain to be gone."

Thomas wanted to flee the trap set by the conversation of his marrying Deborah. "I suppose...drugs are...part of...all this," he excused.

James Dean giggled through his high.

Thomas looked over at Deborah, as though for permission. "I don't...like ...drugs."

Silva leaned back and took a deep inhale on the joint. "Like that kid sings in his folk songs: 'Don't criticize what you can't understand.'" He passed the marijuana to Thomas. "Here, Camille. Take another puff."

Thomas took a languorous puff. "I s'pose...just this...one time."

"Hell and damn you!" Deborah said. "I really do hate you *all* tonight!"

"Not nearly as much as we love you, dear Hera," Silva said. "We'll go easy on Camille, and have him safely back at your place and tucked in bed in a few hours."

She looked at Thomas. "Thomas, are you sure about this?"

He nodded. "Just this…once…for the…pain."

She shook her head in resignation, knowing it would be more than just once for Thomas. She'd seen her share of people get a little bit scrambled from their encounters with the Den, only to return for more.

Chapter 23

The Fruit Cellar

Silva, Bobbie, James Dean and four others who blended into the darkness of the Den sucked on sugar cubes laced with LSD—a drug originally used for medicinal purposes in the war. Soft, hallucinogenic moans filtered above the low audio piped into the room from the stage. Thomas hadn't been ready for the full intensity of the sugar cube normally infused with 100 micrograms of LSD, so was given a more absorbent chocolate chip cookie laced with about a third of a typical recreational dosage. Still, he began to quickly feel the effect.

He didn't know how long it had been since he had chewed demurely on the cookie. Maybe five minutes or five hours. Time meant nothing, and though he sensed he was in a room with others, he felt alone and at rest— feeling no pain for the first time in more than a month. His injuries no longer mattered. Nothing mattered but the void that had enclosed him.

He felt a rapturous warmth swell throughout his body as he sensed himself as a corporeal spirit hovering above his physical being. He began to love what he had become; totally at one with his god. His god—from the form of a chocolate chip cookie—had embraced him. The euphoria he felt through the weightless moment was infinite.

He heard music, or some sort of music, not at all like Big

Eunice's singing from The Cavern, but the gossamer voices of angels—His God's choir. And then a light swirled gently around him in liquid colors he could not describe because they were beyond the realm of his color sense. They glowed from within to warm and soothe him.

He felt an electric surge through his hair as he closed his eyes and envisioned it as the feeling of the brush Mother would draw through his long hair as a child. Back then, he again felt the moist heat from the peat fire smoldering in the hearth of his Ballycannough home. Mother coalesced into his vision as she stroked his hair and hummed the com- forting Celtic lullaby she would sing to him when he was scared. The vision faded into a glow of lavender light.

The light swirled into green, intense infinite hues of green. A field coalesced, wavering about in a gentle swirl of wind beneath a fluctuating rainbow fringe. A figure mingled among the grassy flow and came slowly forward as she gathered sheathes of red wheat—a young girl, about ten years old. The green field turned from red to blue to purple—to lavender. The girl was now holding sprigs of lavender, cradling and rocking them as though putting an infant to sleep. The girl was himself. She was Camille. Thomas's feelings became numbed, taken hostage and renewed into something precious.

Where have ye gone, Camille? He wondered. Gone to thy mother on Beltane Morn? Be ye thy mother? Aye, ye are a lovely sprite of a child. The clouds, they swirl above ye young soft-haired head in colors spun of heavenly gold agin a yonder firmament flowing from deep blue to pink. Faster again the clouds swirl into a form. It is? It is not! Ye cannot be—The form took on a new life. No. It cannot be. Mother, I'm frightened! Please. Go away—go back! The sky turned black. The green field turned to black. The young girl extended her sprigs of lavender as she faded away home.

Thomas gently closed his eyes to languish in the moment. And then he realized that the young girl in the field on Beltane morn had been Regina.

He slowly opened his eyes to realize a darkness aroused by a corona of flame light, whose coalescence slowly divided into dim pin- points of light from the candles throughout the room. He knew he had found a new way into his god. Through the experience, he had liberated his own soul—cleansing it from the burden of his guilt. He knew he would have to experience this euphoria again.

He heard the echoing semblance of a softened voice though the scent of cherrywood tobacco. "As soon as you drop that crutch of yours, Camille, sweetheart," said Bobbie, "we are gonna take you shopping and make you over. We know who you are, and more than you might think. You want what we are, and we're going help you along." He felt the soft pressure of Bobbie's warm kiss nestling into his hair.

"Please," Thomas whispered from a deep honesty he had denied himself for decades, "help me. I need to be released—released."

Part 3

April 1964 – July 1964

The World's Fair

Chapter 24

The tiny-pond water-skier

Regina stared out of the airliner's porthole at the surround- ing activity on the tarmac and became momentarily soaked in the creeping feeling that she might not return to the lush mid-western farmlands of her youth. The thought unnerved her of course, but the idea also set her free. Besides her job, all she had holding here was Hellie…and Timbo, though she knew that her little boy was in better, more secure hands with Hellie. All Regina might pro- vide for him would be the life of a gypsy, for she'd already tired of Oklahoma City and was ready to move on. Hellie would assure Timbo a good, stable life. Nonetheless, she knew she'd always miss him and wonder how it might have been, had she been more prepared to be a mother. The scene out her porthole began to slowly move backward as the airliner was pushed into position to taxi.

She soon relished the thundering power of 13,000 horses shuddering and lifting the four-engine Constellation from the runway. Then, 20 minutes later, and nearly 25,000 feet below, 1,500 miles of increasingly cluttered landscape muted by haze and clouds slid beneath. On its northeastward journey, the plane flew over the southland quilt-work of new-tilled earth alternating with patches of grass, soil and foliage.

The mesmerizing distraction of passing clouds later fogging over the suburban complexion of the Massachusetts coast was interrupted by Trevor's whisper as the Constellation banked sharply right to begin its westward descent. "What?" she said. "I can't hear you. My ears are popping."

He leaned closer. "I got us connected rooms."

"Connected rooms? That's nice, Trevor," she said through a spice of condescension. She lightly patted his hand.

Over the past months, Dave Kiefer from the New York World's Fair office in Manhattan had been talking to her about the progress of the exhibit's construction, as he was instructed by Trevor to do. During March, his calls became more frequent—and more personal. He mentioned that he was one year divorced, and, on that information, Regina secretly looked forward to seeing him again since their first meeting back in November. Trevor had become a burden to her freedom as she became increasingly annoyed with him like the acute, concentrated ache welling in her ears and blocking her sinuses as the airliner lowered toward Manhattan.

As the plane continued its slow, shuddering decent over western Long Island, New York City materialized from the haze beyond the murky headwaters of the Long Island Sound. The plane flew low and slow as its flaps extended and its engines roared in preparation to land. The landing gear thumped open and jostled the fuselage a little and the city passed languidly below. The airliner banked again, seemingly at building-top level, over the Brooklyn Bridge and East River. New York City coalesced more distinctly below as a tightly knit, gray con- fusion of spires and cubes appeared intricately networked by streets dotted with red and yellow cabs.

Regina warily stared out her porthole as the plane's enlarging shadow rippled closely over the waters of Flushing Bay like an impending doom. Every flap on the wing seemed to open wide as the plane approached the La Guardia runway for landing. But there was no runway, only water, a few feet below. She became momentarily deafened as the plane's powerful engines complained loudly against an unforeseen peril as they feathered to down for a soft landing. She trembled along with the fuselage, feeling she had become a helpless part of it as she tightened her grip on the arm of her seat until her knuckles turned white. She also grasped Trevor's hand, as she was certain the plane was going to crash. Finally, the airliner bumped as the wheels yelped on contacting the runway, and every flap on the Constellation's wings was further extended to slow it down, indecently exposing the cables that operated them. Regina squeezed Trevor's hand harder. He got the wrong impression from her message and squeezed back.

Dave Kiefer was at The Queens-Astoria Hotel to greet the entourage from Oklahoma. The hotel, set halfway between the airport and the World's Fair site, had just missed the mark of being tony opulent with its lobby feigning the popular ambience of its newer competitors. Its former decor seemed to have been stripped down, then simply covered up with fresh paint and foil-based wallpaper, leaving behind some of its original mid-1940s-style cornices and fixtures. It smelled scantly of oil. Signs proclaiming: "Caution! Wet Paint-¡*Precaución! Pin- tura Húmeda*!" hung around, indicating the finishing stages of its modernization into the spirit of the Fair. Trevor stood at the reception desk talking to the clerk as he confirmed the reservations for 13 rooms for the 24-member pavilion staff. Trevor slipped the manager a pre-arranged $100 service fee for his arranging for the connected rooms.

Dave winked furtively at Regina as he stood next to her toward the back of the throng of visitors from the Wild West. Many of them gaped about in repressed awe like rubes. At the first sight of Dave, Regina realized her wait had been worth it. He was finer than she had remembered. He had beefed up, acquired a tan, and appeared to her as a blond Adonis. "Have a nice flight, Regina?"

She tried to yawn away the leftover pressure bubble from the flight, and then grimaced a tight smile back at him. "Now that I'm back on the ground. Good to see you again, Dave."

He put his hand lightly on her shoulder. "Me, too—I mean—to see you—again, I mean," he said.

She reached across to her shoulder and confidently patted his hand. "Don't worry. You'll get over it," she said.

"I hope so. Sometime I'll show you around this decrepit city. Maybe go out to dinner?"

Regina lightly disguised her gratitude over his offer by leveling a sardonic glance at him. "Sure, Dave. I'd like that," she said through an easy smile. "You know where you can find me—just look for the water-skier in that mud puddle out in the Okie-Pavilion."

She noticed that he seemed relieved from an anxiety through his return smile. She figured that he had probably built up his resolve to ask her out for the last month.

"Dave, I need you over here to sign something," Trevor called.

"Gotta go feed the boss," he said.

"Tell me about it," she said as he walked to the lobby desk.

The plot for the Oklahoma State Pavilion was nearly completed for the fair's April 24th opening. With one week to go, the band shell and the Will Rogers Pavilion were finished. The larger lagoon in which Regina would ski had been recently edged with plantings and some rocks over which falling water would trip from gouged-out little sluices. The grassy areas and the perimeter of the small park had been fringed and dotted with mistletoe and redbud saplings. The cement on the walk- ways was still setting, and one of them led around the fenced inset of the relief map of the state.

As some members of the Tourist Bureau's entourage, including Regina, were led around the grassy parts, Regina glimpsed the fair's feature UniSphere ringed by gushing fountains in the Court of the Presidents directly across from them. A white pickup truck with the logo reading: Dantana Contractors, Ltd. on its door was parked near the lagoon.

Then she spied the exotic-looking, copper-skinned woman standing near the lagoon several feet away. She was intrigued that this woman seemed to be confidently in control of her staff of burley men. Her manner came across as Hellie-esque, reminding her how much she al- ready missed her aunt-turned-sister. Deborah caught her glimpse and flexed a little smile. Regina nodded in return.

"It'll be a real challenge to ski around in that little pond," Regina said to no one.

Betsy Maglin, one of the members in her group, said. "It looks so *tiny*, Regina."

"It'll seem a lot bigger once the water's in it," Deborah called over to them as she approached. "This thing takes up more than a half-acre. Looks are deceiving here in the construction stage."

"This is Regina, one of our water-skiers!" Betsy announced to Deborah as she pointed to her co-worker.

"We'll be putting the water in it day after tomorrow, after I pad it. You can take some practice runs then—Regina, is it?"

"Uh, yeah," Regina said.

"We'll take a final look at it then. I'll be here, just in case we need to add more around the edges."

"And you are...?" Regina asked.

Deborah touched the brim of her painter's cap. "Debbie Dantana, your official pond builder."

She tipped a smile in Deborah's direction. "In that case, I'm Regina Barragan, your official tiny pond water-skier." She noticed

Trevor motioning her to the Will Rogers Pavilion where she would also be working the front desk when she was not water skiing.

Except for a few electrical plates, the pavilion was ready for tourists. Oversized, deeply saturated photos depicting the state's natural beauty, some oil derricks in sunset and portraits of the down-home humorist who had made Oklahoma famous hung on the pine-studded walls. Above, redwood beams were adorned with Oklahoma memorabilia, including western saddles, steer horns, cowboy hats and oil-drilling bits, which Regina hoped would not fall on her head. The pavilion had the feel of a theme restaurant without the tables, though there were plush leather and cowhide couches arranged around steer horn-legged, smoked-glass-top coffee tables placed on the polished flagstone floor.

"Well, sweetcakes." She inwardly cringed over his chummy moniker for her. "Here's your base of operations."

"Nice."

"That's all? Just 'nice'?"

She smiled for him. "Really, Trevor. I like it, honestly." She looked up at the beams. "I'm just afraid one of those drill bits or horseshoes you have tacked up there are gonna fall on my head, or something."

"Ah, not to fear, sweets. They're only plastic, more likely to bounce off anything they hit. But they won't fall. They're pretty well spiked in." He motioned over to the counter. "Here's where you'll be sitting."

She observed a plushy, cowhide cushioned swivel stool on redwood legs. "I feel like I should saddle it," she said.

He leaned closer to her ear. "You've got me for that," he whispered.

Oh, for Christ's sake! What a dwink! she told herself as she managed a coquettish smile. "So, where are the cattle we'll be pretending to auction off?"

"They were dropped off last week up at a farm up in the country.

About thirty miles north of here."

"There's actually country around here?" she said.

"So, Trevor," Dave interrupted as he approached them, "your cows arrive up in Ossining in one piece?"

"Cattle, Dave," said Trevor. "And they arrived, each one perfectly healthy. All twenty head."

"Ossining. So, you put 'em up near Sing Sing Prison. At least they'll get three hots and a cot and sixty minutes of exercise a day in the yard. I thought you were gonna be bringing up fifteen cows, not twenty."

"Five of them are second stringers, in case some poop out on us," Regina said.

"Let's hope that doesn't happen, at least not here during one of your mock auctions."

"Yeah, Mr. Kiefer," Regina said to Dave as she leaned relaxed against the receptionist's counter. "It's not like they're, like, raging bulls or anything. They're all kind of old and toothless."

"They won't, Dave. They're all being well-cared for, and well-pastured."

The cattle had been selected for their age and docility. After the stint at the fair ended in October, they were to be shipped back, not to Oklahoma, but to Kansas City to be slaughtered for gelatin. Regina thought it sad, but at least they would have passed after their memorable performances at the World's Fair. This cattle's younger, meatier kin were most likely to be unwittingly rounded up and penned for their final journey down the ramp to their doom as rare to well-done steaks for the sake of human enjoyment. Poor damn cows, cattle, whatever, Regina thought.

Once Regina got to her room; a cavernous boudoir whose walls glittered up the place with even more garishly printed foil than in the lob- by, she unpacked her suitcases. She took a hot shower and then lay on the firm king-sized mattress. Moist and naked, she had covered herself loosely with a coarse-feeling bath towel. For a moment, she just stared into the silence, which seemed to be manufactured as one of the hotel amenities. Her relaxation was interrupted at times by the thundering rumble of landing planes, the far off, muffled honking of horns and the metallic clatter of construction equipment.

She already missed the soothing chatter of cicadas and the distant howling of coyotes and soft moaning from the cattle she heard from her little bedroom back at Hellie's house. She turned on the bedside radio, turned down the volume, picked up the phone and placed it next to her on the bed. She then dialed Hellie's number.

"Well, Reg, how're you finding the Big City?"

"Way up and to the right from Oklahoma," she answered. "I don't know. This place seems so dirty and, like, fake."

"Well, honey, you're gonna be there 'til October, so you'll just have to get dirty with the rest of 'em. Just don't go all fake on me once you come home, 'cause I can read you like some sorta Farmer's Almanac."

Regina heard Jamie's voice in the background. "Is that Re-*geee*-na?"

"Shut up, Jamie, you damn man-whore!" Hellie squawked back at him.

"Yee-hah! Ride 'im cowgirl!"

"How do you put up with him, Hellie?"

"I don't know. Maybe it's 'cause he's such a jerk; a loveable one, usually, but a jerk, nonetheless. Guess I'm jus' naturally attracted to the type."

"Me, too. The thought of spending the next five months with Trevor makes me wanna fuckin' puke at times."

"You dug your trench on that one, cowgirl. Now you're forced to take a few tumbles with the guy just to keep your job, I guess."

Regina clamped the receiver to her ear with a shoulder as she fidgeted with a ring on her right middle finger. "He got us two connected rooms."

"You're *kiddin'* me!"

"Yeah. He did. He acted like such a dickhead about it, like he owns me, or something."

"Not so, Reg. You own him."

"How so?"

"He's married, so you own his guilt. That'll be your ticket outta him."

"So, how's my new Caddy doing'?" Regina said to change the subject.

"Sittin' out in the driveway all by its lonesome."

"You can drive it you know, Hellie. You should, actually, to keep the oil flowing, along with all its other juices. Right?"

"Uh-huh."

"Just as long as you don't let that cowboy boyfriend of yours drive it. I'd kinda like it left in one piece."

There was a silence. "Uh-huh."

"Hellie?" Regina asked suspiciously. "You didn't let that maniac drive my car!"

"Just one time. Today after we let you off at the airport." "Shit! Hellie?"

"Uh, it was a special occasion."

"How can anything you do with that tumbleweed be called a special occasion?"

"Uh, we were driving back from the preacher."

"Oh, well, why were you doing th—? "

"Reg? Jamie and me. We got married."

Regina bolted up from where she lay. The towel slipped toward her lap, exposing the small globes of her breasts. "Shit, Hellie!"

"Timbo will have a proper father, now—we'll be a real family."

Regina realized that Jamie might make a better father to Hellie's adopted son than his natural father, John Bass. But still. "Timbo won't have a proper father, Hellie. He'll have Jamie Robertson." Then she thought about this, as she clamped the receiver harder to her ear and drew a tickling strand of wet hair back over her shoulder. This caused her towel to slide further downward to expose her stomach. Then, as if having reached an epiphany, she whispered to Hellie, "As in 'Flapjack' Robertson, the old coot owning the land he took from your father, along with all that oil?" she said.

"Exactly. And allll that cattle," Hellie said. "And Flapjack's got some sort of really bad dementia. He ain't long for the world." She whispered close to the phone. "Jamie's all he's got left in the way of family."

"Shit, Hellie! You sly beagle, you! Do you, like, you know, really love him?"

"I could learn to, I 'spose. But I sure *do* love the idea of that land."

"I just hope you know what you're getting into, Hellie. You and I don't have the best record when it comes to men."

"We'll just have to s—," Hellie began.

"Re-*geee*-na! I love you, sweetie!" she heard Jamie shout over the flushing of a toilet in the background.

"May as well put him on, Hellie, so I can pass on my congratulations to that goofy new husband of yours."

As she waited for Hellie to fetch Jamie, the music from the radio shifted from "My Guy," by Mary Wells, to "Anyone Who had a Heart," by Cilia Black. She heard a loud knock on the door connecting her room to Trevor's, then the low, concentrated voice behind it. "Hey, in there! I'm ready, sweetcakes. I hope you're not decent!"

Regina rolled her eyes and turned up the volume on the radio.

"Give me a minute, Trev. I'm on the phone!"

As Jamie answered the phone, he cried out: "Re-*geee*-na!" "Congratulations, Jamie. You go ahead and treat her right, now."

"Ya know ah weel, sweet thang!"

"Yeah. And if I find you've been driving my El Dorado again, I'm gonna have you castrated."

"Sounds like fun."

"You won't like it." Then she was seized by an oddly heartfelt afterthought. "And Jamie?"

"Youser, sweet thang?"

"You take care of my Ti—," she caught herself, "Hellie's Timbo, you hear me?"

"Ah weel, ah promise, li'l darling."

Trevor flung open the door looking like a flabby Sinbad with a stupid grin, as he stood there wearing only his poofy purple silk pajama bottoms tied at the waist. "I'm *here*, sweetcakes!"

Regina let out a sigh. "I guess I gotta go, now. Call y'all in a few days," she told Jamie and then hung up the phone

Chapter 25

The ghost in the closet

A faint rain started falling as Regina walked with Dave down the Avenue of the States. It was a comfortable and unobtrusively warm rain, which rendered up a soft, oily scent from the pavement. Like most everything about her new environment, even the weather seemed manufactured. Oklahoma rain smelled earthy fresh. This rain smelled oily, old and secondhand. She slung her arm loosely through Dave's as she sidled her head against his shoulder.

Her contentment when she was with him seemed as natural and honest as a Sooner rain. Trevor, now back in Oklahoma City for the week, was more like a twister to her; a desperate frenzy of activity until having sex relieved him to a point where he seemed anxious to leave. Slam, bam, thank you ma'am, she thought. Dave had become her solace in this strange place, a world away from her accustomed comfort zone in the Plains. She felt comforted that maybe she at last had found the hug she had been yearning for since she lost her mother.

"Quiet," he said.

"Hmm?"

"You seem quieter than usual."

"I've nothing to say, I guess." She tightened her arm around his. "Just enjoying the moment, now that my goofy boss is away."

"Your boss and roommate," he said.

"Oh, yeah. Anyway, today I'm with you, Dave. I'm trying to forget all about—that."

"He can be kind of intense."

"Okay, you can shut up about him now. This is my day off from everything that bothers me. Buy me lunch," she said.

"Yes ma'am!"

"Steak and champagne. Use your World's Fair influence."

He glanced up toward the elevated restaurant of the New York State Pavilion. "They have the best steak up there. Gallagher's, I think. And champagne. I know they keep a private stock."

"Okay," she said, as she looked up at one of the multicolored cantilevered streetlamps glowing ineffectively through the mist. "Let's eat and get soused before bedtime."

He looked at his watch. "It's only eleven in the morning."

"What? Suddenly you've got something against drunken mid-afternoon sex?"

"Absolutely not," he said.

The World's Fair grounds had taken on the appearance of a murky blueprint smeared with clots of desaturated color through the rain streaming down the restaurant windows. Regina had eaten only half her steak. She squinted at Dave through her highball glass.

"What are you doing?" he asked.

"Seeing what you look like through a sea of vodka and Seven-Up."

"You're getting all weird on me, Reggie. I'm cutting you off."

She put down her glass and conjured up a puckish smile. "I guess it's nap time, then."

"You haven't finished your lunch."

She glanced down at her plate. "Too much fat. I'm trying to maintain my girlish post-adolescent figure."

"Now you're worrying me, sweetie. You sure you're over eighteen?"

"So, you're carding me, now?" She sighed as she lifted her oversized purse from the floor to her lap and began to rummage. She placed a hairbrush and a packet of tissues on the table and then a stubby candle. "Ah," she said as she pulled out her wallet and flipped it open to her driver's license and pointed to the date. "See? March third, nineteen forty-four. I'm twenty. You're safe." "What's that?" he said to the candle. "Uhh, a candle?"

"In your purse? Are you expecting a blackout?" He lit a cigarette, then fluttered out his match.

"Well. You never know. Actually, I'm keeping it for later."

"Later," he said through a plume of smoke.

She leaned forward to confide. "For us. It's a sexual artifact. I like having sex by candlelight."

He smelled the taint of vodka in her breath. "It looks burned down a lot."

Her plush lips bloomed into a smile. "Like I said, Dave. I like making love and I've got a lot of it to give."

He leaned back in thought, then exhaled a slow stream of smoke and then called the waiter over for the check.

The wavering light from the three candles on the dresser filled the atmosphere as Regina and Dave's naked forms coalesced as glimmering silhouettes through the semidarkness and the tumble of bed sheets. The candlelight wavered through the muted darkness onto the print across her room. It was a stereotypical hotel room piece, a gross con- figuration of geometric and drooling muted earth and sky tones. She gazed into the painting and twitted a private smile. She liked the painting better in her mind's eye as it metamorphosed from a blue, gold and orange abstraction into a wavering golden cornfield in twilight. She reminisced over the Oklahoma plain fronting Hellie's house, and then her smile fell as she remembered the view of the cornfield through the picture window of her former home in Hanson. The cornfield where Connie had been found dead in November.

"Shit," she muttered at the memory.

"What, shit?" Dave muttered from his drowse. "You're awake?"

"Yeah, Reggie, I'm awake." He yawned, and the headboard creaked as he lumbered himself up against it. He lit a cigarette.

"Offer me one, please?" She asked while scissoring her index and second fingers together.

"You don't have your own?"

She curled down her index finger, leaving the second one rigidly extended. "Greedy bastard," she said. "They're in my purse. Way out there over in the bathroom."

He handed his to her, then lit another for himself. "What were you 'shit'-ing about?"

"Oh." She heaved a sigh, then picked a stray piece of tobacco from her lower lip and held it up toward the flickering candle as though to examine its insignificance. "I was just thinking of my — father," she said. That thought was never one she would admit to Trevor.

"You know? You've never told me too much about yourself. What was he like?"

"My father?"

"That sounds like a good start."

She scooted up against the headboard and huffed out a sardonic laugh. "Believe me, Dave. He's never a good start to a conversation."

"What was he—a murderer or something?"

"Yeah. Maybe."

"You're serious?"

She stared down toward her cigarette. "Let's just say my mother disappeared under, uh, mysterious circumstances. He might be the only one who knows because they were alone when he might have killed her."

"Well, *that's* a conversation starter."

"I'm a preacher's daughter, you know. I was brought up in Ahty, Ireland where he had his little church out in the country. I was too young to remember all that. I was only eight when we moved to Iowa. Anyway, I was an uncomfortably righteous kid. All prim and proper on the outside, yet boiling over with frustration inside."

He ran a finger through her hair. "Poor child of God."

"God had nothing to do with it," she said as she leaned her head against his shoulder and inhaled deeply in a dramatic gesture. "You've just gotta be brought up by a preacher like him to understand that God has nothing to do with things."

"And you think he killed your mother? What's that about?"

"He killed her spirit, for sure." She leaned over to snub out her cigarette and then nestled her head back against his shoulder. "I was only ten," she said to the picture on the wall. "My mother drowned while the three of us were on vacation in Jamaica. All the cops and everybody thought it was accidental. She and my father were sitting on the beach at sunset. You know—a romantic kind of setting, if my parents were so inclined, but they weren't. At least he wasn't. He was a cold fish to me and to her. Like it was a sin to show affection toward another person, even your wife and child. Maybe especially your wife and child. He was just so fuckin' weird." The hoarse crackle of her voice slithered from another private world. She choked up with the distant remembrance. "She went for a swim."

"Nothing wrong with that. She's on a beach in the Caribbean."

"Thing was, my mother didn't even swim. She was really scared of the water." She looked slowly up at him. "She told me once. One time when she was growing up in Oklahoma she watched while her mother drowned a litter of barn kittens. It's the kind of thing kids remember. Those poor little things mewing away as the water killed them. My mother used to tell me every time she saw a big body of water, like a lake or an ocean, all she could hear in the waves was that help- less meew—meew, like those kittens." She picked another stray strand of hair from the top of her breast and pulled the sheet up against a swell of chill from the air conditioner. "Anyway, it wasn't likely that she would decide to take a sunset swim a mile out into some fuckin' shark-infested waters."

"Probably not. Why did your father let her do it?"

"I don't know the reason. As to the how, he could have hypnotized her to do it."

"Oh, Regina!" said Dave as he realized that she still had a child's imagination and wondered if he was not doing the worst thing in this world by sleeping with a girl nearly young enough to be his daughter. He readjusted himself, and then subtly made to slip out of bed and into his clothes, then to make his apologies and leave. But instead he stopped and repositioned himself on the bed.

"No, Dave. It's true," she insisted. "He could hypnotize people."
"That's too, I don't know, Reggie—out there."

"He would do it during his church services, and it worked. He could convince those old fogies in the front rows to do anything. To believe anything."

"How the hell would he do that?"

She realized that she might have ventured a little too far out, but it was too late to reverse the track of their conversation. "He'd hang this little mirrored ball, like those ones they sometimes hang over dance floors, from a turning ceiling fan above his pulpit and he had this way of speaking his message to the reflection of purple light from the sparkly ball. After mom's death he spent years perfecting this—thing—he would do every Sunday." She slowly wagged a finger in front of her nose and followed its metronomic movement. "Stare into the moving light, so I can change you into thinking you're a toad," she cooed sardonically, "or at least to extort your life savings to put in my wallet for the good of the church." She then brought her hand to her lap. "Any- way. My aunt Hellie back in Oklahoma thinks he might have hypnotized my mother to go swimming and then watch her drown. I'm kind of starting to think she might have a point."

"And why would he do that?"

She smiled into the distance. "I don't know. Probably never will. I just remember he didn't seem to like my mother so much toward the end." Regina recalled how Thomas would secrete himself away from Jillian, even as she would try to reach out for him as she played the part of the concerned wife. Regina glanced at Dave. "And he changed his fuckin' behavior toward me afterwards—drew into his shell." A fluffy strand of ash dropped from Dave's cigarette to the bedsheet, leaving the tip of his cigarette to glow like a dim beacon in the candlelight. "You'd better put that thing out, Dave, before you set the place on fire."

He leaned across with a groan to tamp out his cigarette. She ran her fingers down his arm, then slid out of bed to remedy an annoyance across the room. "Where're you going?"

"To close the closet door."

He squinted toward the darkened patch revealed by the partly opened door. "I hardly noticed it."

"Well, I did." She remembered spying her father dressed as Jillian through his partially opened bedroom door. "Those kinds of things creep me out. Open doors for no reason."

"Afraid there's a ghost in the closet, Reggie?"

"No. Well, maybe," she said as she closed the door and padded back. "I'm just bugged by things like that." She slid back into the bed and cuddled next to him. "After my mom died, my father used to dress up like her."

"You're kidding."

"Really. I caught him a few times in the act when he didn't think I was watching. He used to sit at her dressing room table and put on her makeup, wig and everything. The guy was too creepy. I had to get out." She stopped short of telling him about her relationship with her alter ego John Bass, and the son she bore through him. She found herself wondering what it might have been like to cuddle little Timbo in her arms to relieve her of all of her slithering memories. She stared at Dave through the undulating darkness. "Let's fuck now. I need to fuck and be loved." She slipped her hand under the covers and into his boxer shorts to feel the rise of his response.

Chapter 26

Inga from Helsinki

Even though Thomas had spent years trying to perfect himself as Jillian, he was captivated by the sultry, emerald-green-eyed blonde reflected in the mirror at Pauline's Beauty Cotillion off Christopher Street, a makeover shop catering to the neighborhood's most discerning transvestites. Pauline, one of Bobbie's many relationships, had worked diligently on Thomas's conversion to Camille. "I must tell you, sweeties," Pauline told them. "Camille's required a lot of work, but she's turning into one of my finest creations."

"You look utterly bewitching, Camille!" James Dean proclaimed as Pauline delicately touched a peach-tinted gloss onto Thomas's full lips. The hue matched that applied to his nails, which had been tipped and were now drying as he twiddled his fingers out at his sides. "Doesn't she look absolutely enchanting, Bobbie?"

"Absolutely," Bobbie said.

"She'll do," Silva said indifferently as he examined his own bitten-down nails. He had had just about enough of the three days of attention lavished upon this creation of Camille.

"Goodness, darling. I'll date this creature myself, once you're done with her."

"Quiet, Bobbie," Pauline shushed. "You are such a *vamp*!"

"Such is as I am," Bobbie confided in Thomas's ear.

"I can't thank you all enough," Thomas said.

"Shhh! Darling, quiet!" said Pauline. "Try not to flex your lips while I'm coloring them."

The three-day process had been a painful ordeal, which left Thomas' skin tingling from three agonizing sessions of body waxing. Bi-hourly doses of Pethidine for his lingering body pains, along with some deep puffs of marijuana had helped to suppress the sting of the heated slabs of wax being rudely ripped from his body. The soreness was then soothed by thick applications of cool mud and aloe—one of Mother's recipes for bee stings. All of this resulted in his skin feeling softer and suppler than ever. "You may never have to shave again," James Dean told him, "or at least for the next week or so."

Bobbie patted Thomas on a shoulder. "We committed types have waxing done once a month. The first time is always the worst. Poor baby. You'll get used to it."

"I wouldn't know," Silva said. "I like sticking to my natural gender. You girlies have to work too fucking hard at it."

Pauline daubed at a spatter of gloss on Thomas's upper lip. "And you love us this way, Silva, don't you, dahling? Okay," he drew the smock away. "Done for now. Camille, dahling, you are now ready for your close-up."

Bobbie drew a waft of the blonde wig across Thomas's right eye, to lend a mysterious accent. "There, now you look like Veronica Lake!" "Camille should be on the cover of Vogue!" James Dean gasped. "I'll take that as a thank you, dearies," Pauline said. "What do you think, Camille, about the new you?"

Thomas brought a finely manicured finger to his soft, faintly blushed cheek. "I—I never thought this would be possible," he said as he felt the welling of a tear.

"No-no, dahling!" Pauline said to Thomas as he daubed it away with a tissue. "No tears now. You'll smudge! No crying allowed for at least two hours."

"Deborah can't know about this," Thomas said.

"Hera," Bobbie qualified to Pauline. "Camille's 'significant other'." "And she won't," said Silva as if he was struck with an idea. "The four of us are meeting her tonight at The Glitz and Glitter. All you have to do, Camille, is keep your mouth shut."

"Great idea, honey!" James Dean gasped. "She'll never recognize our Camille!"

"Oh, come on. Really," Thomas said. "You can't do this."

"Of *course* we can. She'll eventually find out anyway, so it won't be exactly a lie," said Bobbie. "It's Just like 'My Fair Lady.' You can be our Pygmalion!"

"This I have got to see, dahlings!" Pauline gushed. "Can I come, too?"

"The more the merrier," Silva said.

As Marie Trudeau sang a low, mellow French-English mix of the 1958 Brenda Lee hit, "I Just Want to be Wanted," the five of them sat around their usual booth in various degrees of womanly dress and accessories. The low light glowed through their drinks. Thomas was dressed in pair of loose gray flannel slacks and wrapped in the comfort of a white angora turtle-neck sweater, both from Pauline's closet. He wore a purple silk scarf tied around his neck, and some glittering hanging earrings as adornments. The lengthy blonde wig seductively hiding the right side of his face topped off his disguise. He brushed away a tickle on his right cheek.

"Doesn't she sound absolutely divine?" Teddie said leaning over Bobbie's shoulder as he made his rounds about the patrons of The Glitz and Glitter. "She's Marie Trudeau, a chanteuse I found up in Montreal in October. Love at first sight—or sound. Anyway, I brought her down and contracted her here to sing three nights a week."

Teddie sometimes had a memory issue. "We know, Teddie. You've told us already," James Dean said.

"A million times, "said Silva.

"And she's as gorgeous as she sounds," Teddie went on. "She was utterly made for our Bonne-Aires. Don't you agree?" He looked over at Thomas made up as Camille. "Speaking of gorgeous, who's our new little outlaw, here?"

Thomas started to announce himself.

"That's Inga, my *cousine* from Helsinki, over in Finland," James Dean interrupted.

"Why, J-D! I never knew you had Finnish connections. She's *ravishing*! Welcome, darling! *Bonjour et bienvenue!*"

Thomas nodded and flashed a tight smile. "Ya!"

"She doesn't speak much English," said Silva.

"Well, her drinks are on me, tonight," Teddy said as he patted Bobbie on his bared shoulder and then made his way toward the next table.

"Score one," James Dean said to Pauline.

Thomas shuddered nervously. "I feel really uncomfortable about this."

"Quiet, sweetheart," James Dean said. "Just speak in Finnish tonight, and you'll be fine."

"I don't know Finnish."

"Exactly," said Silva.

Deborah soon emerged from the smoky darkness behind Pauline. "Sorry I'm a little late. I had to spruce up my delivery for a conference in Anaheim next week." She pulled up a free chair from a nearby table and wedged in between Silva and Bobbie.

"Why, Hera, darling. I didn't know you were going out to

Disney-land," Bobbie said. "And why so? When we have so much of all that right here?"

"Complete with mice, cockroaches and fairies," Silva muttered, as he sipped the remains of his martini.

"Oh hear-hear to that, poopsie!" Bobbie said from behind his raised glass.

"Annual architectural designer's conference," Deborah said and then glanced at Pauline. "Hey-yah, Pauline. What brings you here, tonight?"

"Oh, just—something, dahling" he said coyly.

"Well, it's been a while. Good to see you. Bobbie, you got a ciggie?"

"You really should invest in a pack of your own sometime, Hera, darling, instead of always bumming from me."

"You kidding? If I ever bought a pack, I may take up smoking again on my own. And I don't want to do that since I gave it up for good last month, when Thomas took it up. It's bad for you." As she took one of Bobbie's Parliaments from the pack on the table, she noticed the tight simper on James Dean's face. "What's that look on your face, J-D? You look like you're holding back on a trip to the loo."

"How do you like the sound of Teddie's *chanteuse*?"

Deborah strained to listen to Marie's rendition of "I've Never Been in Love Before," as she flagged a passing waiter in the distance. "Marie? Yeah, I like her voice. It's really nice. I feel like I'm back in Marseilles." Finally, she spied Thomas as Camille. "Who's our new arrival?"

"This is Inga, my Finnish cousin," James Dean said. "And she doesn't speak a word."

Deborah smiled at Thomas as Camille. Then her stare turned skeptical. "Is she mute?"

"No," Silva said. "She's Finnish."

"Ya!" Thomas blurted enthusiastically.

"Um-hmm," Deborah said thoughtfully, as the waiter showed up.

"Oh, good. I need a Chivas. Double."

"Johnny Red with water," Bobbie said.

James Dean nodded neatly. "Pink squirrel, please, darling."

"Dubonet," Pauline said.

Silva simply pointed to his empty martini glass. "Ya—scosh—Ya." Thomas said through a frozen smile in a voice two octaves higher than usual. Deborah toughened another glance at him as she shook her head.

"No! No, Inga, sweetie," James Dean said through a nervous laugh. "You only drink vodka." He turned to Deborah. "Poor Finlandish dear. Has not a stitch of the English language in her. She thinks 'Scotch' means 'vodka.'" Then to the waiter, "You can bring my poor, confused cousin a vodka." He glared furtively at Thomas, then enunciated: "Her homeland's national drink."

"Non!" Thomas said. "I vant *scosh!*"

"Scotch or vodka? I'd like to get the order in before closing time," said the waiter.

"Just bring the broad a Scotch!" Silva groused.

"Danke you," said Thomas as the waiter left for the bar.

Bobbie turned to Deborah. "So, Hera. How's your World's Fair gig going?"

"Hera is building some sort of pond at the Oklahoma pavilion at the New York's World Fair," James Dean informed Thomas.

Deborah glowered at him. "I thought you said she doesn't understand English."

"I didn't say *that*, sweetie. I said, she doesn't *speak* it. Isn't that right, cousin Inga?"

"Ya!" Thomas said with a fortified nod.

Deborah bit on her lower lip. It was all she could do to keep from blurting into laughter—had the situation not been so pathetic. "It's going fine. I guess they do a lot of water sports in Oklahoma, so it's not all cows and oil fields, after all. The pond's gotta be big enough to tow Regina, the water skier, around in it."

Thomas's smile congealed at the mention of the name "Regina" in the context of Oklahoma. He felt a chill flush through his body.

Pauline sipped the remains of his Dubonet. "Water skiing takes up a lot of room, doesn't it, darling? Sounds like you should've built a lake. I didn't think they give a whole lot of space to those exhibits."

"About an acre and a half."

"Ya?"

Deborah licked her lips. "Uh, Inga, right? I've got to, uh, powder my nose, as they say here. Why don't you come with me to the little girl's room?" She cringed at her own uncharacteristic use of the term, little girl's room.

Thomas aimed a feckless look toward Bobbie. "I think she's fine here with us. But you go ahead, Hera." James Dean said.

"Ya! You go!"

Deborah stood up and grasped Thomas's healing arm, causing him to cringe. "Nonsense, boys! We need to talk girl talk." Thomas looked helplessly at the rest who stared back frozenly as Deborah drew him away into the darkness.

Once they were in the vestibule of the restrooms, Deborah tightened her grasp. "Jesus, Thomas! You want to tell me what the fuck is going on here?"

Thomas's shoulders drooped in the realization he'd been found out. "We didn't think you'd notice."

"What? That they laid this ridiculous disguise on you? Doll you up into some sort of dame out of a Raymond Chandler detective story? Besides you're the only one I know who orders a 'scosh' when you're nervous or soused. You forget, Thomas. I love you, every bit of you, and you can't fool me. This was a nasty little trick, and a mockery of what you and I are. I'm totally offended."

He puffed out his cheeks. "I'm sorry, Deborah."

"Where have you been? I've been calling the church for days. Even Francis didn't know where you were."

"I—I was spending some with James-Dean and Silva."

"Well, I can see that." Her grasp softened into a light stroke of his arm. "Anyway, you *oughta* be sorry! You think you really could have fooled me? Silva and J-D, and now even Bobbie have been threatening to make you over ever since that fucking Halloween party. And bringing Pauline, that trashy makeup artist, along was a dead give-away.

How could you let them do this to you?"

"I just wanted to try it," he admitted.

"Cross-dressing disguises only work in Shakespeare, and in some other places around England, I guess. It's legitimate for some of these guys here, but not for you. It's not your nature."

"Isn't it?" he said.

"No. It isn't." She smiled and then drew him into a hard kiss.

A transvestite emerged from the men's room. "You go, girls!" he bellowed in throaty guffaw.

Deborah responded by waving him away and holding Thomas more tightly. Then she drew away. "That's to remind you who you are, and what you are." She patted her hair back into shape. "Okay. Right, Thomas? Now, go home and change back into your man clothes. Then meet me back at my place so we can do what God intended a man and a woman to do. Once I get back from California we'll go to the World's Fair and I'll show you that lagoon I built in Oklahoma. We'll make a day of it. Just the two of us, like kids on a date. I think you'd love the Ford Motors place. They have mechanical dinosaurs. One of the pavilions has an Abraham Lincoln robot. He talks to you."

"When are you leaving for California?"

"I guess they've taken away your memory, too. I told you last week. I leave day after tomorrow, and I'll be back in two weeks, unless I decide to take an old college friend up on her offer to visit her in San Francisco. Which I may do. When I get back in early July we can put everything aside for a day and act like kids. It's a much more sensible idea than dressing up and acting like a woman."

Thomas managed a smile. "I'd like that," he said. It was less about going to the World's Fair than using Deborah's time away to dress and polish up his act of becoming the woman he yearned to be.

Chapter 27

The Scarecrow

Thomas suffered an irksome loneliness since Deborah left for Anaheim three days before. He craved another cigarette from Juan, but his key reason for venturing back into the under-belly of his adopted neighborhood was that his soul ached from emptiness. Though he still smelled of lavender from his role as Camille at The Glitz & Glitter earlier in the evening, he now wandered about in the post-midnight gloom of the Two Bridges as the person he was presumed to be—a man of God. He'd taken Bernardo's stiletto from his dresser drawer and slid it next to the amulet in the pouch of the bodice of his cassock for protection.

He trudged through the cool darkness cast by the overpasses toward where Juan, Milio and Spider spent their idle time. The humidity of late May seemed to shroud him in its airless grasp, reminding him of his sweltering welcome to New York City almost a year before. It really didn't seem so long since his arrival as a country bumpkin into the big city morass of Manhattan, but so much had happened. He became absorbed in the recollections.

He had built his church. He had enriched his soul through the liberation of a few nameless and forgotten men amid the shadows of his adopted neighborhood. He had grown a network of shadow-dwelling compatriots through Juan and Milio and had helped in the taking down of *Los Lobos Solitarios*. He had felt the special euphoric bliss of having liberated Angelina's soul into his. He had endured, with difficulty, the relentless assault of those White Cobras upon him. He had found and nurtured a growing cultural network of friends at The Glitz & Glitter, where he now felt at home among his new-found cross-dressing peers. Best of all, he had emerged from the chrysalis of a Jillian look-alike

into the stunning Camille. And, oh yes, Deborah. What to do about the slushy quagmire their relationship had become? It had been a long year after all.

"You here to save my soul, preacher man?" a whisper seethed from behind his right ear. "Well, we're gonna take *yours!*"

Thomas turned briskly to see a face, half in shadow. The man's scalp shined dimly through a short bristle of hair. He then felt a sharp point burrow a little into his left ear canal and glanced at a tattooed swastika on a hand wielding an industrial grade ice pick. He turned partway to answer a light pat on the front of his shoulder, and felt the pick enter a little deeper into his ear along with a dull surge of pain, which seemed to emanate from deep within his brain. "No, no, preacher man. It's not a too good idea to, um, turn too quickly. You don't want that long ice pick to go all the way in your ear to puncture your brain before I've had a chance to introduce myself to you." His unctuous tone flowed as lethargically, as a leakage of thick blood. "Turn the preacher to me, Rat," he directed his pick-wielding lieutenant.

As if the shaft of the ice pick were a handle, the one called "Rat" guided Thomas around to face a muscle-bound, harsh looking thug in his early 30s. His features were skeletal, with his cheeks and eyes sunken into shadow. His white-blond hair was in a bowl cut, like that of a monk, and inked onto each of his temples was a tattoo of a small red swastika. His assailant grinned widely, exposing a crop of perfect, white teeth, as he raised a chrome-plated, snubbed nosed

.38 pistol to the center of Thomas's forehead.

"I haven't had the pleasure of meeting you, preacher. I am the *Führer*. Maybe you've heard of me, no?"

"I—" Thomas groaned. He winced in pain as he felt a deeper surge and then a slight retreat, of the pick in his ear. His assaulter held the pick in place as, with his free hand, forced Thomas down into a kneel. "Talking hurts, doesn't it? Anyway. Now, what's this I hear about you and your team eliminating two of my troopers, hmm?" Thom- as felt the point of another pick wielded by a second trooper tickle the rim of his other ear. "Hmm, seems as though Prick, here, my little Himmler, is contemplating where to stick his, ice pick. Look, preacher man. I've got some good news for you, I guess—depending on how you take it. I'm probably not going to kill you. Isn't that nice of me? No.

What me and the troopers are going to do to you is incapacitate you. Permanently. See? Trooper Rat's been taking up the study of human biology. Right, Rat?"

"Uh," Rat muttered bluntly from behind, as he twisted the pick a little.

"AGGHH!" Thomas cringed

"I mean, you should see it, preacher man. Biology books all over our place, like some sort of, um, college dorm room. Imagine that. Rat going to college. If you knew Rat at all, you'd be very proud of him. But the problem is, with all those biology books, he hasn't had a subject to practice on."

While all their attention was focused on his nearly skewered head, Thomas instinctively inched his hand toward the knife in his cassock's bodice.

"Rat's been paying particular attention to studies of the human brain. Apparently, there's a place in the middle of the brain that you can reach through the ear. If Rat's eight-inch pick finds this place, and then…let's just say you'll never be able to feed yourself again, uh. Am I right so far, Rat?"

"Uh! Yes, *Führer*!"

Thomas lightly grasped the knife in his cassock, and slowly began to slip it out.

"And, well, not feeding yourself will be only the best part of your problem. It will take away all your abilities to move around. Any- where. And—if he puts his pick in again, where I know he probably can, then you will be blind, too. Now, Prick, here, he's Rat's best student and he specializes in the throat. So, what he knows how to do is *really* cool. Once, Rat's done with his little surgery, and you're mostly, well, helpless and not dead, Prick's gonna operate on your throat right down the old gullet.

"Now, preacher man, I'm telling you this because, A: There won't be any surprises, and, B: We can take away your eyes, your movement, voice, and, oh yes, your hearing, of course. Matter of fact, you've lost hearing in your left ear already thanks to Rat's pick now in it. Isn't that cool? Oh yeah. And, um, C: In that you won't be able to talk—or see, or move. The only thing you'll be able to do is to lie in bed, or maybe sit in a chair all day, paralyzed and hearing out of one ear. All you'll be able to do is remember how you got there and who did this to you. Now, there's always the chance that you might want to, um, not let my troopers operate on you. Maybe you'll want to try something stupid." He choked back a moist, macabre laugh. "Like you really can, right? Anyway, there's always this more merciful option." He cocked the .38 touching Thomas's forehead. "Okay. Boys, I guess you can start operating on the preacher, here."

"Holy SHIT!" Rat gasped as he clenched at his gushing neck and tumbled to the ground as he bled, leaving Juan standing above him with a blood-glittering straight razor in each hand.

"FUCK!" Prick burst out almost simultaneously as he reeled back- wards to the ground after being struck in the backs of his knees by a swing from Milio's baseball bat.

With the hilt of Rat's ice pick still protruding loosely from his left ear, yet firmly lodged into the cartilage of his ear canal, Thomas rapidly stuck the *Führer* in the stomach with the spike-stiletto, withdrew it, and then quickly stabbed him again.

Almost immediately, he heard the pop of a close-range gunshot, and the Führer's gun-hand flew up in the air as his chrome-plated pistol clattered to the ground. Thomas quickly picked it up as the Führer wheeled backward in momentary shock. He choked out expletives and harsh cries of pain in German and English as he gripped the gashes in his stomach with his bleeding right hand. As he tripped back and fell upon the asphalt, another one of his troopers rushed forward from the shadows. Juan then gradually crumbled into a heap next to his fallen porkpie hat as the Führer took him down with two shots near the heart from a second pistol he carried. Thomas rose to a stand and saw the Führer starting to writhe on the ground while holding the .22 pistol he'd used to take Juan down, in his un-damaged hand.

Powered by adrenaline, Thomas picked up the Führer's fallen .38, and then walked stoically toward Juan's killer. He fired the silver pistol five times. He watched with cruel indifference as the Führer jerked convulsively as each close-range shot entered his body: one to his stomach, two to his heart, one into the bridge of his nose, and the final round into his testicles.

"Bastard minuit! El Diablo Negro interfecistis. Juan occidisti!!" Milio roared angrily in a voice Thomas never knew existed within him. Milio's next action telescoped his rage as he brought down his metal baseball bat rapidly and hard on Rat, first on his legs, then four times in his abdomen. Milio's Yankee cap tumbled off his head, and

he stopped pummeling Rat long enough to stoop down to place it back on. He then drove the bat twice into his chest, and finally, as he convulsed into death, three times on his head, until it burst like a smashed pumpkin.

Spider stepped in front of Thomas and cocked his head as he looked him over. "Stand still, preacher man, don't you move, now," he breathed confidently. "I'll pull that out of your ear."

Thomas was unaware the pick was still sticking in his ear. "What?" Then, as the adrenalin started to recede, he winced as he felt a searing pain in the middle of his head.

"Stan' still, preacher!" Spider said as he tenderly reached for the hilt and began to slowly pull.

"God-DAMNIT!!" Thomas shouted, which only sent a relentless, fiery pain reeling throughout his brain and then down his spine.

"Shhh, preacher. It be almost out, now."

Thomas felt the slide of the ice pick from his ear. "Oh, *shit*! JEEE-zuss!" he gasped. The mention of that stranger, 'Jesus', meant nothing to him beyond an expletive release.

Spider held the pick with its bloodied spike in front of him. "See?

All out," he said close to Thomas's ear.

"What, Spider?" Thomas breathed harshly. His own voice thundered through his head. "I—I can't hear you."

"Milio and me, we'll bring you back to the church. Francis, he'll bring you to the hospital. We'll take care of all this mess, here!" Spider shouted as he stood away, so Thomas could hear him in his good ear. He took off his dingy ball cap, crumpled it up and handed it to Thomas to hold against his bleeding right ear. "Hol' this tight to keep the blood from flowing too much." Thomas humbly thanked him with a nod, as he noticed tears streaking down Spider's cheek, leaving lighter tracks against the grime on his face. "Shit, preacher. That fuck-head took Juan away from us!"

"Shit," was all Thomas could say, as he looked over at the *Führer's* body. His stomach, chest and face were a pulpy mass surging out a glistening welter of black-red blood into the shadow in which he died. He then looked over at Juan's body, cast in the wavering light from the headlights of cars passing ambiguously above. He lay in a single, enlarging pool of blood near where Milio crouched, crying irrepressibly over the body.

Thomas glanced down at the pistol in his hand with which he had killed the Führer. He knew what he had to do, now. He felt a warm trickle of thick blood and some other pulpy mass from his deadened left ear, and tightened Spider's ball cap against it. He then felt another searing head pain as, with his free hand, he rolled the gun he still held in the deep folds of his cassock to wipe the stock and barrel clean of his prints. He eased slowly over to Juan's body and crouched next to Milio. He reached to lift Juan's right hand by the wrist.

"NO!" Milio cried tearfully. "NO, preacher. No touch him!"

"S'okay, Milio," Thomas said, as he gingerly placed the pistol on the ground to lay his hand lightly on Milio's shoulder. "I would never hurt our brother, Juan. You know that." Thomas picked up the gun, placed it in Juan's limp hand and tightened its grip around the stock. "Blessings, dear heart. May you find your own god," he said in a voice choked by tears. He leaned closer and whispered, "You have won the fight, my brother!" He kissed Juan's cooling forehead. He felt the trick- le of a tear rolling down his cheek, as he stared solemnly at Juan's peaceful, countenance. Finally, as if the porkpie hat were a holy sacrament, he laid it respectfully upon Juan's face.

The Legend of *El Diablo Negro*

The Miracle—and Massacre—on South Street: Vigilante Revealed!!

By Frank Malone, Senior Editor, The New York Knickerbocker

New York City —May 28, 1964

Five slaughtered bodies were found by cops from the 5th precinct yesterday morning in the Two Bridges District of the Lower East Side. All close-range killings, the bodies were scattered around a small area near the Brooklyn Bridge, under The FDR Drive, near the Fulton Street Fish Market. Four of the five victims were gang members from The White Cobras, a feared band of low lifes who model themselves after the Nazis, and were the kingpins for the drug trade in the Lower East Side. Among the dead were Sam 'The Rat' Fredericks, Alan 'The Prick' Marion and Lars 'The Lion' Ericsson.

The 'Rat' was beaten into a disgusting pulp by a baseball bat or a heavy pipe and could only be identified by his prints. The 'Prick' was sliced twice and deep in the neck by a sharp knife or, more likely, a straight razor found at the scene (guess you could say the scum cut him- self shaving!). The 'Lion' caught a few shots from a .38—one to the head and another to the stomach. This weapon was not found on the scene.

The best score of all, though, was the taking down of the White Co- bra leader, known adequately as the Führer, a.k.a. Philip Sturber, wanted in New York City, Elizabeth, New Jersey and Bridgeport, Connecticut, on eleven charges ranging from drug dealing and car theft, to manslaughter and first-degree murder. For the last seven years, his crooked lawyers have managed to outsmart the system on technicalities, making this creep untouchable.

Until now.

The Führer—Sturber—was stabbed and shot multiple times with a .38 caliber handgun. He took one shot, along with garish knife wounds, to the abdomen, two shots to the heart, one to his hand and the killer shot to the head. A sixth shot was fired into his groin. The police lab has been examining the bullet casings and has reported two of them to have been from that second.45 caliber pistol.

Now this brings us to the fifth victim, shot twice in the heart by a third pistol, a .22 caliber. This victim was still holding the gun that finally took Sturber down.

Deep questioning of the 'non-existent' unwashed, who huddle on their cardboard boxes in the damp shadows of the overpasses, have revealed Sturber's killer as a street person known as Juan Trout,

a.k.a. 'El Diablo Negro' ('The Black Devil'). Little else is known about El Diablo Negro, except he was also 'present' at the Los Lobos Solitarios killings and disappearances last summer, and almost two months ago, when two other White Cobras were killed. Another thing about El Diablo Negro. This reporter was told that his trademark was a porkpie hat he always wore. Someone, perhaps one of his fellow homeless lieutenants, placed his signature hat over his face as a sign of respect.

Readers? I can now reveal to you our vigilante, responsible for bringing down the two major gangs in the Two Bridges District, one of the city's most notorious crime spots. I respectfully reveal to you Mister Juan Trout, about whom we know nothing except that he is our vigilante hero, "The Scarecrow."

On the following day, the legend of Juan having almost single-handedly relieved Lower Manhattan of two of its most violent gangs within a ten-month period appeared on page two of The New York Post. It also showed up on The New York Times front page, below the fold.

Chapter 28

Maddie Peck's

A muddle of noise swirled through Thomas's mind like a swarm of gnats. The cacophony seemed magnified by the oversized bandage covering his punctured left ear, but they soothed out like waves on a shore when he eased into his LSD-induced visions. He placed another communion wafer, lightly soaked with the drug, on his tongue. The resulting hallucination brought his god to him, and Thomas saw and heard him more clearly through his increasing number of dosages. The visions also brought a tender relief to the incessant, hot flow of his migraines.

Tonight, as he relaxed in his office chair, his god dissolved into view. As usual, his features were amorphous—the surging cloud of a face cast equally in shadows and dull glows—but his clothing appeared overly distinct. He was surrounded by a pulsating aura of colors swelling in and out of brilliance. In this visitation, along with Juan's tattered porkpie hat, his god wore a battered leather bomber squadron jacket with a sheepskin collar open over a red checkered chambray shirt adorned with mother-of-pearl buttons. His god also wore a pair work-worn blue jeans and cowboy boots.

Thomas reasoned that the cowboy getup might have been a holdover from his nagging remembrance of Deborah having mentioned Oklahoma and the name, "Regina," at The Glitz & Glitter Club nearly three weeks before. The bomber jacket was something of an inconsistency, but there were certain nuances in his god's appearance that Thomas found wisely convenient not to question. The sum of his god's visible parts represented something past, future and significant. He spied a red swastika glowing through the vapor where god's cheek may have been.

Contained by his thickly bandaged ear, the sound of Thomas's own muffled voice echoed smoothly within him. "I see you've gotten a tattoo."

The mist of god's hand touched the glowing red swastika through the dim miasma of his features. Normally, to those who never listened, god's voice came across as a cacophony of garbles sounding as brittle as breaking glass, but Thomas understood his god's measured and casual words. "Oh, you mean this. Some of those among you believe this symbol has some sort of evil connotation. Actually, three thousand years before the Nazis set the arms of the transepts of the cross to point counterclockwise, it was a Greek religious symbol with the transepts pointing clockwise, like I'm wearing here. It's also the ancient basis for the cross upon which you nailed the imposter, Jesus Christ." The cloud of god's head slowly rotated back and forth, as though he were shaking it in despair. "There's a misconception of human nature for you! Normally I get a kick out of sitting up here watching you all prattle through your failures. But I'm not enjoying this love affair you people seem to be having with the symbol of the cross. How much significance you have made from nothing!"

Thomas's hallucinations tended to bring out a casual feistiness. "I haven't!" he defended.

"You may think not, Brother Thomas, but you have one on your church door, and one behind your alter."

"Only to give our followers something familiar to relate to. Besides, the symbol was Deborah's design."

"Ah yes, your nonbelieving little friend. Pass the blame onto her, why don't you?"

"I prefer her as a nonbeliever. You sound jealous about her." God's glow turned red with annoyance. "She is not yours to 'prefer,' Brother Thomas," he said. "Anyway, I haven't visited you here tonight to perform philosophy. Philosophical thinking is only a tool for some bloviating fools to inflate their egos enough to smother those of others. It's worse than any religion!"

Thomas placed another acid-laced communion wafer into his mouth, and then settled back in his chair and into his vision. The space behind his god tossed smoothly in waves of aqua blending down to a deeper blue; the cooler colors he visualized when his god dissolved more peacefully into his vision. "I'm listening," Thomas said.

"You've reached a turning point, my friend," his god told him. The mist of his hand reached into his cowboy shirt and extracted a cigar. He put it to the haze of his face and lit it from thin air. The cigar smoke flowed light red as he puffed it deeply in, then blue as he languorously exhaled. He casually brought the cigar from the cloud of his mouth and held it up and off to the side. The movement of its glowing tip punctuated his comments. "Now that you've liberated those souls of evildoers for the good of the forgotten and decrepit ones living in shadows, you need to up your game to liberate yourself.

"So. For you, Brother Thomas, it's time for a slight personality change. As of now, you'll be liberating only women to fulfill the needs of your deeper soul. You'll like that. You remember the liberation you preformed on that waif, Angelina, this past winter? Remember how she lingered within you to warm your soul, even through your pain?"

"Oh, yes. I've never felt so enriched."

"That's because, brother-sister, you're truly the woman within yourself that I, through your mother, Molly, designated you to be. So only through your liberation of woman's souls can I accept you as complete." His god's tone now took casual turn. "Anyway, you've pretty much tapped out your own neighborhood, so I suggest you go elsewhere to carry this out."

"Where?"

"Hell, man, it's a big city. You figure it out. I hear the Upper West Side's a pretty good hunting ground for young women, but that's just my suggestion."

"But Heaven's Doorway is way across town, about, I don't know, three, four miles away from the Upper West Side. That's a little bit of a commute for a baptism, don't you think?"

His god took another puff on his cigar. "Ah, you know? I do love these Cubans!" he exalted. "You all don't know what you're missing through this Cuban embargo."

A dull pain surged deep within Thomas's head, as he began to feel the effects of the LSD lightly wear off. "What do I do? Hail a cab to bring these women down to the soggy bottom of the Lower East Side to liberate them in my baptism pool?"

"For my sake, Brother Thomas! Don't be such a damn whiner! Your office follows you. Don't you know that? You wear the costume of the church, so use it. You are the church for the needy to blindly trust you, no matter where you happen to be standing." As he took another puff, his image began to fade. "Look, I've gotta go. Just use the free will I gave you. Go to the Upper West Side and seek out the woman you were born to be. Good hunting! —And Brother Thomas?"

"What?"

"Lighten up a little! It's all part of our plan."

Maddie Peck's, a singles bar on 84th Street and Amsterdam Avenue, was doused in semidarkness and a thin dissonance of conversation rising through the clink and clank of glasses and dishes. The Beatles' "Hold Me Tight" wailed out loudly from a jukebox crouched far off in the haze and the thin, mellow edge of cigarette smoke. For three minutes Thomas had been staring at a woman in her mid-20s sitting stiffly alone at the end of the long stretch of bar amid the disparate cliques of people ignoring her. She seemed to be staring down into the bottom of a void as she absently clutched her glass.

Thomas sipped the remains of his Scotch and then reached beneath his black shirt collar and revolved the black band around his neck until the white tab marking him as a priest showed. He lowered himself from his barstool and picked up the small rucksack that he had placed at his sneakered feet. Among its contents were some chocolate chip cookies he had baked and then injected with a small dose of 70 micrograms of LSD.

As he approached the young woman, he noticed her features were pretty, though drawn and narrow, even though the hint of her plumpness. Her ivory skin enforced the severe darkness of her hair. Her weary eyes had a touch of Asian about them—like Deborah's—and her lips were set in a concentrated pout. She had not needed any make up, save for the red gloss on her nails that sparkled through the darkness. Though the late June evening was blending from hot to warm, she was dressed for late autumn in a heavy green sweater, blue jeans and light-green sandals.

"You look as though you could use a cigarette," he told her.

She eventually measured out her words. "I don't smoke."

He canted his head to angle his hearing right ear toward her. "What? You don't smoke? I'm sorry. I have trouble hearing."

She looked up at him with her glistening deep-brown eyes. "I don't smoke," she enunciated hoarsely, then saw the bandage covering his ear. "What happened there? To your ear?"

He smiled easily. "Damaged eardrum. Deaf as a post, there." He craned his left ear more toward her, as she narrowed her gaze.

"You're a priest," she said.

"I'm a priest," he answered. "Can I buy you a drink? You look as though you might need one."

She held up her full glass. "I don't drink."

"Don't smoke. Don't drink. And yet here you sit all alone in a smoky, crowded bar," he said as he subtly drew the medallion from his jeans pocket and placed it on the bar while cupping it in his hand. "This seems to be a happy place, yet you seem so, I don't know—morose."

She smiled wryly. "And you're here to serve up some salvation for me."

The bartender stood near them, pulling beers from the tap. "May- be. But first I need to serve myself a drink." He turned to the bartender and ordered a neat Johnny Walker Black.

"Should you be drinking?"

"Why not? Just because I wear a collar doesn't mean I'm not like anyone else in here."

"Oh right," she said. "All of us molded in His image and all that."

"I hope not. No one can tell us what God looks like. What if He's some sort of three-headed hydra with a bad case of psoriasis?"

She suppressed a chortle. "What if 'He' was a 'She'?"

Thomas would have liked that concept if he had not realized how much his god enjoyed Cuban cigars. The bartender placed his drink in front of him. "All I know is that His son changed the water into wine, not the other way around." He raised his glass to her. "So, bottoms up and God be with you."

"Cheers," she said dourly, then demurely sipped her drink. She placed her glass gently back down on the bar and contemplated it. "For a priest you're a bit of alright. I like you," she said.

"I'm a preist. You're supposed to like me, if you want to go to Heaven. Anyway, then I like you, too, uh…"

"Oh," she said looking over at him. Studying him. "I'm Zina."

"Interesting name."

"Yeah. Don't know where it came from. My parents are card-carrying White Anglo-Saxon Protestants from a faraway land known as New Canaan, Connecticut. All the girls I went to high school with had names like Sally, Jane, Priscilla, Marianne and the like. But, Zina? Where the hell did that come from? Persia? Anyway, I was always on the outside looking in. Still am, I guess." She took a deep sip from her drink.

Thomas reached into his rucksack, fumbled below his little silk cosmetics bag, a bottle of lavender *eau de cologne* and the fibrous fluff of his blonde wig and then pulled out a waxed envelope containing five LSD-laced cookies. "Would you like a chocolate chip cookie? I just baked them myself. Or don't you eat, either?"

"A man who bakes cookies?"

"And a preacher, at that." He grinned. "Go figure."

She smiled pertly. "Sure. Who doesn't like a chocolate chip cookie from time to time?" She took one from the packet, bit into it. "Um. Good," she said as she took another bite. "Thanks. You're a good cook, there pastor. Maybe you missed your calling."

Thomas smiled back at her as he carefully re-wrapped the package. "Now, Zina. You want to tell me what's bothering you tonight?" he asked. He slowly revealed the amulet and started to gently twist it, so it caught the scant light from above the bar. He angled it so its dim blue and gold glows wavered across Zina's face. She hardly seemed to notice as the light passed up and down over her eyes.

She sighed out a sad little laugh. "Why? You taking confessions?"

"No, Zina," he said calmly. "Just trying to help you unload your burden. Clearly you're upset about something."

"Of course I am. I'm upset about my life and my rat-fink ex-fiancé."

Thomas smiled privately. "I guess we all have one of those rat-fink significant others."

"Hah!" Zina laughed gently as she stared into her drink. Her voice was starting to slip into a slur. "So much for your vows of celibacy."

He smiled lightly. "I can dream, can't I? Anyway, that celibacy's only for Catholics and Shakers, which explains why there aren't any more Shakers left. And too many Catholics. That's why I'm a preacher and not a priest—we're allowed to act human."

Zina looked over at him and widened her eyes to take him in. "I really never understood why you ministers play the part of giving up so much to help others. I've always wondered what draws you types to your practice."

"I don't know. Maybe because vaudeville is dead?"

"Good answer," she said through a faraway smile. "Can I have another one of your cookies?"

He motioned to the opened package. "Of course. Now answer my question, Zina. What's bugging you about your rat-fink fiancé?"

She slipped another cookie into her mouth. "Same old story, 'cept this time it's mine." She began tearing up as she stared down at her drink. "He left me after six years for some eighteen-year-old child trollop. Didn't even tell me. I had to find out in the worst way."

"You found them together in bed?"

"No. Worse than that. I sensed it through his beginning to

ignore me, and all our plans. He just dropped out of my life, slowly. No re- turned calls. Stood me up on more and more dates. 'Leaving town' for weeks on end. That sort of thing," she sneered dourly. Her eyelids began to relax into a drowse from the effects of the drug and passing light from the amulet. "I had to find out las' week from one of my girlfriends who he told to tell me during his current disappearance. He wen' to Nassau to marry his now child-harlot-bride. They stayed on for a hon'moon. Rat-fink din't have the guts to tell me, his-himsel'." Her voice fell off. "For some reason, I'm sud'nly star'in' to feel notzo bad 'bout it all."

Thomas's tone became a gentle cadence. "Perhaps, Zina, there was a reason he did that. It could be that after six years he was becoming tired of you."

"You're pro'lly right." Her voice had become fluid as she softly repeated what Thomas had told her. "He be- came tire' of me."

"He wanted another woman. You're not getting any younger, Zina, and it's starting to show on you. Your fiancé is probably a vibrant young man, and deserved someone younger, more exciting."

Zina's hands slid down the sides of her glass and nearly tumbled it upon the bar as Thomas subtly reached to keep it from spilling. "He deserve' someone youn'er 'n me," she repeated.

"This was God's will for you."

"Goz' will," she gasped lightly as her eyes dulled and her features relaxed. She placed a hand gently on his knee, and looked sleepily over at him. "Can you help me?" she said.

He recognized the effects of her semi-trance as he smiled calmly at her. His voice flowed peacefully. "Let's go to your apartment, and I will." He pocketed the amulet, and then quickly splayed his fingers open before her eyes, jarring her into wakefulness.

"Let's go back to my place," she suggested.

"Good idea," Thomas said as he began to calculate how he would liberate her.

She anxiously, but clumsily dismounted her barstool, then took a swig of her drink. "You pay, preacher. I'll go out an' get us a cab."

Chapter 29

What is life?

Zina Harper's death may have looked like a suicide, but Marty Cohansen felt obligated to weigh other possibilities. She'd been keeping a journal, which his team found at the scene on her bedside table.

She had written that she was depressed over her job and, most recently, her boyfriend leaving her. So, there was that. There was a bottle of antidepressants tucked away in the bedside drawer, but of the 30 pre- scribed pills, 28 were still left. There seemed to be no sign of a struggle. Though it still smacked of a suicide, it was Cohansen's investigation to keep open.

He reluctantly decided to re-question Henry, the doorman. Henry had not been that helpful the first go-around, as he was still too shaken about having just found the body. But maybe the generosity of time would have restored his memory by now. Cohansen ignored the incessant chattering of typewriting as he gazed across at his partner, Jake Barnaby, who was absorbed in yesterday's New York Post cross- word puzzle. "Yo, Marty. This is drivin' me *nuts*! I might-could solve the whole puzzle if I can get this. What's an eight-letter word for a 'Saltwater clam'? First letter is 'c', fourth letter, 'm', and last letters 'e' and 'a'?"

"Hell if I know, Jake. I ain't big on clams." He gathered some paperwork together on his desk, then stood. "C'mon, let's go."

Barnaby peered up from the puzzle and over his rimless half-glasses. "Where we goin,' Marty? Way too early for a toot at The Back Page."

"I mighta got a pebble in my shoe over this Zina Harper thing," Cohansen said as he struggled into his seersucker jacket.

Most cops hated homicides, especially all the paperwork. "Marty. It was a suicide. Jus' like that," Barnaby said.

"Probably. C'mon, now, Jake. I wanna talk to the doorman one more time."

"Shit, Marty, okay." he grumbled as he laid down the crossword puzzle.

Henry's shift had just started so he had the benefit of sleep. It hadn't made him any less aloof as the two cops led him aside into the lobby. "You guys know just about everything I know."

"Maybe you'll remember more at the station house," Barnaby challenged.

"S'okay, Jake," Cohansen said. "Listen, Henry. Think back. Did Miss Harper come in with anyone?"

"I tolt you, already. Some guy. I was kinda, like, distracted at the time. By sompthin' goin' on acrost the street."

"What was that?" Barnaby pressed.

"Nuthin', it turned out. Towed car, or sumptin'."

"Or something?"

"Towed car, no big deal. Looked like some mambo-jambo pimp-mobile."

"What about the guy Miss Harper was with? Was he big? Small? Thin? Fat? What?" Barnaby asked as he wrote in his pocket notebook. "He was a little bit medium, I guess. But kinda well-built. Yeah, like medium," Henry decided. "He was wearing black; black shirt and some sorta black turtleneck sweater. And blue jeans, I think. Short brown hair. A little gray, I think."

"See, Henry? You *do* remember more than before," said Cohansen. "A turtleneck sweater?" Barnaby said. "On a hot night like that was?"

"Yeah, actually, it was, like, black and white. The sweater had like a white patch on the neck," Henry pointed to his throat, "on the front." "On the front of the collar," said Cohansen as Barnaby wrote in his notepad. "Like a priest?"

Henry became enlightened. "Yeah! Like a priest. He carried some sorta knapsack. Now, I remember!"

"That's good, Henry," Cohansen said. "Now. Do you remember if he said anything?"

Henry leaned back against the marble wall of the lobby with his arms folded as he tried to recollect. "Nuthin'. Just Miss Harper saying: 'Henry, I'm drunk.' He didn't say nuthin', just kinda seemed to, like, rush her to the elevator."

"Rushed her? Like pushed her, or something?" asked Barnaby.

Henry did not like Barnaby very much. "Not really," he answered caustically.

"So. She wasn't forced. Have you seen her drunk before?" Cohansen said.

"Actually, no. I don' think Miss Harper drinks, drank, whatever. But in my twenny years, here, I seen enough folks come in here after a toot. Even if Miss Harper was drunk, she wasn't, like, weaving around and stuff. She walked straight. Jus' slurred her words a little, now I think about it. As I say, she din't talk much."

Barnaby mulled this over. "Like she was in a trance?"

"Sorta, yeah."

Barnaby glanced at Cohansen. "Drugs? Maybe the other guy she was with sold it to her."

"A priest?" Cohansen said.

"Or maybe he was trying to help her down from an overdose." "Yeah, twenty-two floors down," said Cohansen he turned to the doorman. "Henry, this is important. Did you see the priest leave?" Henry scratched his nose in thought. "Ungh-ungh. Only person I saw leaving after Miss Harper came in was about a few hours later. Some long-haired blonde. Face kinda covered up. But I still could see it, I think. This one had a real bad makeup job. Smeary red lips. I 'member that 'cause it was after ten. Don't get too many comers or goers after that. 'Specially goers."

"So, it was around ten?" Barnaby asked.

"Jeeze, I dunno, I guess. Musta been around ten, ten thirty. The Yanks was playin' the Tigers on the radio in my office. Seventh inning." Then he added dejectedly, "Lost three to seven, them freakin' jerks."

"Anything else?" Barnaby asked. "Was this blonde carryin' any-thing? A purse?"

Henry had another epiphany. "Hey! She was holding a big mambo-jambo purse or sompthin' close to her chest, like tryin' to hide it, like this," he said as he huddled his arms together. "Ya know? It mighta coulda been a knapsack. Maybe the same one I saw the guy carryin' when Miss Harper came in. Jezzuzz! Ya don' think it coulda been—?"

Cohansen looked askance at Barnaby and sighed a little. "Guess we gotta keep this one open, Jake."

"Yeah," he said.

"Henry. Me and my partner's gonna take another look around the crime scene."

Henry flushed white. "Miss Harper's apartment's a crime scene, now?"

Cohansen nodded as he puffed out a sigh. "Probably, maybe, yeah, I think," he said.

Barnaby had gone back to their unmarked black cruiser to call in a team to join them at Zina's apartment. Three of them, including the coroner, arrived in 10 minutes. The coroner and his partner remained below to snap more pictures of where Zina had hit the pavement as another cop taped out the relative position of the fallen body.

The air in the apartment had turned moist over the last day-and-a-half since Zina's body was found, but there was one prevailing fragrance.

"Jake. What do you smell?" Cohansen asked his partner.

"I don't know, Marty. I been fighting this cold. I'm like the dumbest guy in New York for catchin' a cold in this heat."

"C'mon. Take a whiff."

Barnaby did. "Smells, I dunno, like flowers? A little?" he answered hopefully.

"Ya know, Jake? It does. What kind of flowers? To me it smells kinda familiar."

Jake took a deeper sniff. "Greta and me had this plant near our front door in Yonkers before we moved. Big honking bush, with purple plants, blossoms, whatever, all over it. Lilac. That's what it was. Lilac."

"Lilac," Cohansen repeated as he wrote in his notebook. "Funny, I don't see no damn plants around here. Not a one."

"Maybe it was her perfume."

"Yeah. Go check the bathroom. See if there's anything she has might smell like lilacs. I wanna take another look at the balcony."

"Okay, Marty," Barnaby said as he shuffled toward the bathroom.

The balcony was pristine; none of the tightly clustered porch furniture was out of place. There were no scuff marks or sign of a struggle. Cohansen looked over the edge at the coroner in miniature snapping pictures around the circumference of the tape surrounding the remaining bloodstain marking the body's impact 22 stories below.

Jumpers from high places are never a pretty sight once they hit their mark on the sidewalk. If Zina had not landed on her back, she would have been an unrecognizable pulp, another Jane Doe. As it was, her body had been half-splattered; pancaked out around her sides and squeezed out like toothpaste from a tube. The impact had broken her skull open, so the right side of her face was splayed out to half again its normal width. It took three industrial snow shovels to carefully lift her remains onto the ambulance gurney. Cohansen shook his head, then heard Barnaby and turned to face him where he stood in the open balcony door.

"No perfume at all, Marty. Nuthin' like that."

Cohansen still did not want to rule it a homicide. He wished Ray Nealy hadn't taken time off to go up his to his cabin in Maine. He might have had some insights. Oh, well, he reasoned. After about eight years of work and recreational drinking, Nealy needed the break to clear the cobwebs, and Cohansen was glad his best friend had finally found a cure in Francesca. Zina Harper's death could wait until it be- came so much discussion over booze, but love cannot wait.

Still, Cohansen decided to keep the case open as a homicide.

"Well? How'd it go, last night?" Thomas's god asked from his apparition from where he sat in the reeds across from his host in the Holy Water Soaking Tub. Tonight, his god wore a blue-striped bathing costume from the 1920s, and a Yankee ball cap. He had extracted another fat cigar from beneath his tank top and the red glow of its tip through the dull gold oscillation of his cloudy form punctuated his points as he spoke.

"Don't you know?" Thomas said as the effects from the acid-laced communion wafer he had taken 15 minutes before took hold

---

over him. "You're the one who's supposed to be all-seeing."

"Well, I did see that you had one too many of those cookies of yours. You smudged your lipstick all over your face. You should know better by now."

"I was in a hurry to get out of there."

"No, Brother Thomas, you were stoned out of your mind, and you know it. Anyway, I meant how did it go for you? Feeling any different?"

"I am. Really.

"That's good. But I sense you need another shot. And soon. To-morrow's Sunday, the Sabbath, and even I like to take the day off to listen to your little diatribes from the pulpit of this so-called church of yours. I suggest you make your next liberation sometime this coming week." He took long another puff. "Damn! That's a good cigar!" he said through a plume of blue smoke.

"But, don't you think it's a little too soon? I mean, Zina's body must have already been discovered. Maybe the police will be suspicious."

His god held the glowing cigar near to his indistinct face, and the miasma of his head tilted as though he were examining a rare find. "I think this one was soaked in one-hundred-and-eighty-proof rum. Un- der the influence of a smoke like this, no wonder Fidel was able to seize his island as completely as he did."

"You're not paying attention."

"I am, Brother Thomas. I always pay attention. I'm *God*, for Christ's sake!—Hah!—That was pretty funny! Not sure whether that one was an oxymoron or an enigma, or maybe one wrapped within another."

"You're drunk," Thomas said.

"Must be the cigar." He took another puff. "Brother Thomas, you worry too much. Zina's death will assuredly be considered a suicide, and the cops don't pay attention to suicides. Anyway, you're not fully complete yet. You're about halfway to where you need to be, and what you started tonight has to be acted upon right away. So. I'm going to do you a favor. I'm going to help you out a little on this next one by sending her to you. She'll be needy for advice from the cloth, as it were. The rest, though, will be up to you."

"Well that's very nice of you, but I'm still numb and shaking from Zina. I found it—sad." Thomas sighed as he sensed the warmth of Zina's soul within him. Where Angelina's soul had been anxious and unsettled, Zina's was soothing, yet tenuous.

"You're growing a conscience along with your new personality, all of a sudden? No brother, you should feel that way. You've taken the first real step in tapping into your abundant and hidden feminine side."

"I just can't get that sound of her body hitting the pavement out of my head."

"As, I said. Your feminine side. Driving your emotions. Your soul feels more fulfilled, right?"

"It does," Thomas admitted as he sank down lower into the tub water.

"Then I have faith in you, Brother Thomas. Listen. Try not to feel any remorse for those whose lives you liberate. What is a life anyway? Do you really know?"

"I'm sure you do."

"Yes. And well I should know. It's simple when you think about it. There is no sin. There's no virtue. At the end, it is only a life— nothing more than a mist of memories dissolved away in the filigree of time. A life is merely a collection of circumstances weighted down by some bad decisions. A life is nothing more than a test of free will. You win some, then you lose some. It's the ones going through the process of living who complicate the hell out of it all.

Me, almighty! No wonder everyone enters this world screaming in terror. The lives I choose for you to liberate to nurture your own soul are those that have already been lost, anyway. They are like still-borns being carried to term."

"How poetic," Thomas said.

"Well, of course. I am who I am, and I've driven the creation of poetry from Gilgamesh to Ginsberg." He drew a puff on his cigar. "Some of them bad."

"The poets?"

He languished in an exhale. "Well, some of them, but no, my son. I mean the memories within the lives you liberate. Memories hold their people within an emotional prison, so liberating their souls is the only thing that will free those unfortunates. You serve them—and me—well in your calling."

Thomas looked pensively at the water. "How about when I liberated all those lost souls around the Brooklyn Bridge? Did you have faith in me then?"

"Ah, ye of little faith. Of course I did! I helped you nourish a real void within you, to prepare you for these next steps in your completion. Like I said, it's all part of our plan."

"Why did you hide yourself from me, then? I've just started to actually see you after all these years. Where were you when I acted alone in the hope that I might, I don't know, get some sort of sign? Some sort of endorsement? I needed you then."

His god drew in another puff, then leisurely exhaled. "I was there right with you."

"Really? Where?"

The cloud of his god's head shook slowly in discouragement. *"Dei tui non inducitis in Yankees de hanc stupri 'ludum!* No—yer godwindo canno' bring th' Yanklados outta this fuggin' gamiata! May stan' a chance wit' meo Bagadda Intradato!"

"You *weren't!*" Thomas said. "Milio?"

"More like Milio was me." He took another puff. "I'm your god, Brother Thomas. Your conscience and protector. Besides, who else but God would go around spouting bad Latin? I'm also fluent in Aramaic, but that's another story. I can be anywhere I want—and anyone I want to be. Though it really made me feel itchy to live the way Milio did. Literally. At least I became a die-hard Yankee fan. Maybe I'll have them win The Series this year, if I can ever get Pepitone to wake up out there." He held the cigar up again to examine it. "*Damn!* Gotta love them Cubans. This is one helluva good cigar!"

Chapter 30

The invisible woman

The drizzle that softened the view a half-hour before had now reinforced into a splattering rain. Clothed in the trappings of his calling, Thomas sipped his watery coffee as he took in the scene from across the street drooling through the restaurant window. He eyed the rush of pedestrians from the warm, dry comfort of his booth of as they hastened their pace between 80th and 82st streets, past a row of clothing boutiques, a neighborhood pharmacy, two bars, an Asian food store, a laundromat and The Intermezzo Book Store above it. Some were shielding the tops of their heads against the sudden rain with umbrellas or the day's evening edition newspapers.

Even through the rain, the light escaping from the lowering sun beneath a belly of deep gray clouds over the Hudson River bathed the storefronts in the orange reflection of its retreating light. Thomas took another sip of his coffee, which brought him back to why he was waiting here.

He reasoned that Zina's body had to have been found by now, so he could not chance going back to where he had sought her out at Maddie Peck's a week before. Though her death may have been ruled a suicide, there might have been questions as to where she had been before she decided to kill herself. The bartender would most likely re- member his patron, who didn't drink, suddenly get drunk and leave with a preacher sporting a big bandage over his left ear.

That bandage was the mark of Cain. Thomas wasn't scheduled to go back to the doctor to have it removed and replaced with a smaller one until the following Thursday. And then, two weeks later, that smaller bandage would be finally replaced with a hearing aid. It would not do much good, as the hearing in the left ear was gone forever.

There was some good news, though. The migraines had abated almost completely, at least for now, though he indiscriminately still took his pethidine pills. He attributed the cure of his incessant migraines to Zina's soul within him. The moment he had felt her spirit flowing through his body, almost like a balm, the searing pains ceased. He believed what his god had told him—that her soul had nourished his yearning woman within. And although his core had been sated, he hadn't felt completely fulfilled.

So, on this rainy, twilit evening, Thomas's god had led him here to the Dutchland Coffee Shop on Amsterdam Avenue to await a sign for his next liberation. Thomas wondered what the old fellow might have planned as he acted as his puppeteer from behind the haze of his Cuban cigar.

Soon, a plea wrapped in a Boston accent came from the edge of his table. "Fathah? Cahn I tahk to you for a minute?" The husky voice be- longed to an oversized woman, whose glistening pink, porcine features were lightly traced with the wrinkles of advancing middle age. Her curly, mousey-brown, rain-soaked hair was matted loosely around her jowls. She was dressed conservatively neat with a modicum of care.

Thomas knew this woman was his god's doing, as promised. "Naturally, sister," he said, now playing the part of a priest as he motioned to the chair across from his. "May I get you a cup of coffee?" *And a brick of fruitcake?* he was tempted to add. *Come on. Be nice, now!* he scolded himself. *She seems to be in need.*

"Ahctually, a haht tea would be nice," she said in a breathy, rapid tone, sighing as she lowered herself into the little chair opposite his. She opened her purse. "Heah, let me pay—"

"Nonsense," said Thomas. "This one's on God. You can pay Him back later." He ordered another coffee for himself and a tea for his corpulent guest.

"Thank you, Fathah," she said as she settled back in the seat across from him with difficulty. The seat cushion sighed as she sat, or was it a fart? Her breaths issued out through tight, urgent wheezes.

"Now, how can I help you, sister?" A tear flowed down through the shimmer on her cheek as she thought about her answer. Thomas reached across the little table and put his hands on hers; warm on cool. "I can see you're very troubled," he consoled her, trying to come across as Catholic as he could remember. "You can tell me."

"Oh, Fathah," she sniffed, "I just don't know wheah to begin." "Have you sinned, sister? Maybe a confessional—"

"No. I don't think I've sinned. Well, I hahve as we all do, but—" The waitress placed her tea and Thomas's coffee before them. "Thank you," said the woman. Thomas noticed his supplicant's aqua-blue eyes were beautiful behind the swells of her plump face. She then looked back at him from the hardship she must have been feeling. "No, Fathah," she admitted privately through a croak. "My only sin is carrying on my life as long I hahve."

Thomas's lips formed into a tight simper. *You sly devil, you!* he beseeched his god, *how do you think I'm gonna be able to drag* this *one to her balcony?* He secured his grip on her hands. "No, sister, please don't think that. There's surely no sense in dying so young. Our lives are precious. God has seen to that."

"You think so, Fathah?" she asked hopefully as an easy smile spread across her face. "I knew you could help me." She drew her hands from his and sipped her tea.

Oversell! Thomas said to himself. "Well—usually," he said as he glanced up at the concentrated bright light above their table and then slid a hand into his pocket to draw out the amulet. "It depends."

"Depends?" Her tea mug chinked hollowly against the Formica of the tabletop as she placed it back down in front of her.

"Well, yeah. It does. There are some who are destined to be unhappy in their lives." He placed his hand over the amulet as he drew it from his pocket and onto the table. "What troubles you, sister?...Ah! I can sweeten your problem." He reached into his rucksack and brought out a little package of chocolate chip cookies. He realized that the LSD cookies he had tried out on Zina had been much too dense for the opiate needed for the subtle task of liberation. So, unlike his last batch, these had been generously infused with marijuana, from the recipe files of Alice B. Toklas. He unwrapped the package. "Here, sister. Try one of these spicy chocolate chip cookies. I made them myself. My parishioners tell me they're quite good. Please. Try one."

"Why, thank you, Fathah," she said as she took one and greedily placed it in her mouth. She then slumped her shoulders back down into her despair. "I hate who I ahm," she said through a mouthful of cookie, then took another. "Do you mind?" she said through a chew.

Thomas smiled benignly and then nodded as he slid the bag of cookies closer to her.

She continued. "I'm nearly fifty-two-years-old, and I've accomplished nothing. Trapped in this—body of mine. Nevah married, nevah had a chahnce to mothah a child, why, I've never even hahd—hahd—"

"What, sister?"

She blushed. Her beautiful, glistening eyes met his as she leaned toward him. "Sex—I'm still a virgin, Fathah," she whispered disdain- fully. "No man has evah been interested in looking my way. I feel so...invisible."

Believe me, you're not! Thomas's inner voice intervened. *Shut up! Concentrate, damn it!* He took a sip of coffee. "No, sister...sister—?"

"Gwen," she told him. "Gwen Perkins."

"No, Gwen, dear heart. That's simply not true. God has looked your way. God is interested in you."

She shook her head as he subtly angled the medallion to catch the light from above. "Fathah, I think I've given up on God. I sawr you sitting heah as I pahssed by and decided to tahlk to you as my lahst hope." He subtly rolled the medallion in his fingers until he noticed its refracted blue and gold rays cross her intense gaze at him. "God has not given up on you, Gwen," he said.

"I'm a mistake, Fathah," she said. "One of God's sick little jokes!" She took another little cookie and placed it whole into her mouth.

"Oh, no. Why do you say that, Gwen, dear? Why would you even think such a thing? God doesn't make mistakes with his children." He complimented himself on playing his role as a Catholic priest so convincingly. He noticed her eyes relax as she was succumbing to the marijuana in the cookie and the soft, passing gleams from the amulet. "Look at this hideously faht and ugly body God has...trahpped me in! Since I was a child I've...I've been this way. My...own pahrents hated me...fah it." Her whisper began to fall off to a slur. "I learned to hate...myself...fah...who I am...I was...bahn this way...Fathah... Try as I...might...I have nevah...been able to...shed this disgusting... ugly...body. I wahnt to...die!" her voice fell off in a soft, hoarse crackle. "Gwen. I can help you to find God—to make you new. Would you like that? I've, uh, just left from a house call for communion, and happen to have my sacramental kit with me. We can go to your apartment and I can administer Holy Communion to you. I guarantee that you will find your god."

"Yes, Fathah," she said. "I would…like thah…so mu…much!" She brushed away a stray curl from one of her ample cheeks.

He pocketed the amulet. "Wake, now, Gwen," he said as he abruptly splayed his fingers before her sleepy eyes.

She eased into wakefulness. "Cahn you offer me the Holy Sahcrahment back at my apahrtment, Fathah?"

"Of course, Gwen," he told her. "And God will be with you." He rolled his eyes. You'd better be serious about this! he warned his god.

Breathing heavily after the cumbersome ordeal of having liberated Gwen, Thomas went into her bedroom to search through the make up on her little dressing table. Her palette of lipsticks was doleful, but there amid the dull reds was passion pink, which had suited him yesterday while Pauline was giving him beauty lessons.

"Applying lipstick is an art that so many of us girls have never learned," he had told Thomas. "You've got to emphasize the structure of the lip without making a point of it. Small lips can be enlarged; large ones reduced. You have a lovely little indent leading from the base of you're a-*dor*-able nose and that ex-*quis*-ately pronounced crease on your upper lip. We can call attention to that," Pauline said as he had begun to apply the color to Thomas's lips. "You have such delicate lines, Camille. I hadn't noticed until now…large innocent green eyes and a slender neck, like Audrey Hepburn. Such soft, supple skin. I'm sorry, Camille. I can't help myself!" He leaned over and kissed Thomas fully on the lips, to which Thomas heartily responded. They exchanged a balmy twiddling of their tongues. Pauline closed her shop and they spent the rest of the afternoon discovering and fulfilling each other as they embraced warmly as one. Later, secure and lost within the ambiguous amnesty of the night, they bonded.

Thomas's precious memory of their day together lasted only a moment until he realized he was running short on time here in Gwen's apartment. He crossed the room to search through her dresser. Gwen kept her diaper-like undergarments in the top drawer, and he extracted one of her sizable bras, which he managed to wrap loosely around his chest. He stuffed the cups with some of the underwear and winter socks he had found in another drawer.

He rifled through the scant collection of grim-looking dresses hanging in her closet. Finally, he found something thing that appeared to be a leftover from some sort of wartime USO show: a droopy-collared green dress covered with big white gardenias. He took the dress, more like a muumuu, from its hanger, slipped it over his head and tied it snuggly at the waist.

The rainfall had begun to patter more intensely against the bedroom windows. He found a pink umbrella in a corner of Gwen's closet, and then placed it on her bed to remind him to take it with him when he left.

He then heard the water still running from the tub and surely onto the tiles, by now. He sloshed through the billowing light pink water on the floor and turned off the taps. He gazed down at her corpse. Gwen really was quite beautiful and at peace in her death. Her body had slipped down, and only her face emerged like a little pink island in the surrounding water made crimson by the deep vertical slices in her left wrist. Her short, brown curls floated loosely around her head like a halo of the angel he had just made of her. He kissed her lightly on her chilly lips. "Blessings, dear heart," he whispered. He brushed a curl from her cheek. He went back into the bedroom reached into the pocket of his pants laid out on the bed and brought out the vial of lavender concentrate. He went back into where Gwen lay, and anointed her forehead to consecrate her liberation. He prayed that she died grateful that she had found the inner being within that had been crying so desperately to get out of its blubbery prison.

Chapter 31

The lie in the center of life

Thomas continued to make himself up from the scant pickings of Gwen's cosmetic tray, and his own traveling supply. He carefully treated his green eyes with just the correct subtle balance of thin liner and light-aqua eye shadow. After plucking a few stray hairs from his eyebrows, he blended in a bit of mascara to his thinned-out brows with a delicate touch of his index finger. He had found a nylon hair net crumbled up on the corner of Gwen's dresser, which he capped tightly upon his scalp. He applied a faint hint of Gwen's rouge to his lanolin shimmered cheeks, and then picked up her umbrella from the bed. He glanced at Gwen's bedside clock, then rushed to the tiny living room to gather up his rucksack. He took out a sassy, au- burn-colored wig he had bought at Elizabeth Arden's, and positioned it as expertly as he had learned to do.

Finally, he turned to the couch side table and flicked on the little plastic radio and tuned it to 1420, WYOR, the same old-jazz standard station he had left playing from Zina's radio. He found Gwen's raincoat and threw it on, more to hide the hideous dress he wore and not just to protect him from the drizzle.

Before he closed the door behind him, he took out a spray bottle of lavender fragrance from his satchel and anointed Gwen's apartment as he had Zina's a week before. He then set off downtown to The Glitz & Glitter where Pauline had told him they would meet around midnight.

He arrived in the Cavern and found Silva and James Dean seated at an undersized table. Silva had dressed up from his usual working-man's garb into a blue pinstripe suit and wide-brimmed fedora.

Departing from her commanding brassy style, Big Eunice was singing a bluesy, heart-felt rendition of George Gershwin's "Someone to Watch over Me."

"Well, Camille. You look ravishing, as usual," James Dean said. "I hate the dress," Silva said.

"Well, it is a little overstated," James Dean said. "I was just trying to be cordial."

"Overstated and oversized," Thomas agreed.

"Really," Silva said, "All those gardenias. It looks like something Billie Holiday would have worn on a bad night. She had a thing for gardenias, right? Maybe you should put one in your hair."

"That hair looks gorgeous on you, though, sweetie," James Dean said. "Sort of, I don't know, expensive."

Thomas twittered a grin. "Two hundred at Elizabeth Arden's. The hair's just about the same color as my ex-wife's. Except ten times more stylish than the way she'd worn it."

James Dean was seized by a momentary state of shock. "Jesus, Camille!" he said. "I never knew you'd been *married*!"

The absorption of Gwen's hefty soul and LSD wafer he had slipped on his tongue on the cab ride over had made him unusually casual— and careless. "Long, sad and boring story, J-D. I also have a daughter. Somewhere. And a grandson, I think."

"Holy shit, sweetie! And you *survived*?"

Silva showed one of his rare smiles and patted Thomas's knee.

"Our darling Camille's full of surprises. But why not? How can anyone find who they truly are without experiencing the sullen, darker, hetero side of things?"

"Coming from you, Silva," said James Dean, "that's very insightful." James Dean's brooding was not lost on Thomas. "Are you two spatting again?"

"Oh, are we ever not?" James Dean said, and then spied the approaching waiter. "Oh good, here come our drinks. We ordered a Scotch for you, Camille, even though we didn't know when or if you'd be showing up, or what you were in the mood for tonight."

"Scotch'll do fine," Thomas said as he shuttled his body around in his seat, not knowing where to stuff the overflow of Gwen's dress.

"Camille's in the mood for Pauline. Or so we've heard," James Dean said and then noticed a look of awe shadow Thomas's face. "Word travels fast in this neighborhood, sweetie."

"Oh, shut up, J-D," Silva said. "Let the girl have a life."

"I'm happy for our Camille," said James Dean. "Aren't you at least happy for her?"

"No," Silva grumbled. "Happy people make me sick. They always seem so—retarded."

"Jeeezuz, Silva," James Dean said. "You are such a grumpy puss tonight."

"Dark Scotch. Neat," Thomas said to the waiter. Then to James Dean, "How the hell did you find that out about me and Pauline? We've only just started seeing each other."

James Dean's lips blossomed into a sly smirk. He arched an eyebrow. "Why, darling. You didn't know? You've partnered with the Village fog-horn."

"Who's the Village foghorn?" Pauline said as she planted a kiss on the crown of Thomas's head. "Love it, love IT!" he said about

Thomas's style as he sat down next to him. Pauline was wearing oversized dark glasses, the kind popularized by Jackie Kennedy and Holly Golightly. "Why, *you* are, sweetie," James Dean said. "You're the town crier."

"Just as well," said Pauline. "*Someone's* got to keep you Village idiots in the know." Pauline was traveling as a brunette tonight. He took a reflective second look at his partner and then twiddled the chin-length hair of his own wig in thought. He lowered the bulky glasses on his aquiline nose, which served to accent the rest of his Romanesque features. "Holy mackerel, Camille, my darling. Where in God's name did you ever find that dress?"

"A garbage can," Silva said.

"Or Maybe it was your ex-wife's?" James Dean said tacitly.

"Ex-wife?" Pauline gasped. "You have an ex-wife?"

"We all have a past, dear heart." Thomas said as he glanced at Pauline. "I'm sure you have one, too."

"That's not all," Silva said.

"There's more than that?" Then to Thomas, "Oh, of course," he surmised dourly, "Wife means you also must have a child."

"A daughter, somewhere," Thomas said. "And a grandson I've never seen."

"A grandson! But, sweetie, I thought I knew all about you, every little nook and cranny. Why, I've waxed every little part of you."

"You didn't!" James Dean said. "Even down...there?"

"*Especially* down there, J-D. And we loved every minute of it. Didn't we, dear? Anyway, Camille, you don't look nearly old enough to have a grandchild."

"Just goes to show you can wax someone all over and still not know them," Silva said.

"I married young. I don't really care about any of them, anymore.

My ex-wife, daughter or her bastard son." "Touchy-touchy," James Dean said.

Silva downed the remains of his martini and motioned to his glass and toward James Dean's, as the waiter nodded and placed Thomas's Scotch before him. "And whatever she's having. She probably needs one, right now," Silva said as he motioned to Pauline.

"Silva's been a bad boy today and he's making up for it by buying all our drinks tonight," said James Dean.

"A claret. No. A martini. Double," Pauline said. The waiter blended into the smoky gloom as he went to fill the orders.

"What did you do to rile up J-D this time, Silva?" Thomas asked as he was overcome by a yawning swell of weightlessness.

"Oh…nothing," Silva said.

"Oh, the usual," James Dean said.

Pauline, still stuck on the idea that his new partner had been married with a daughter and a grandchild, turned to Thomas. "Well, sweetie. That *is* a shocker. You are a person creeping with many identities, Camille. You're like a sweet little chameleon. Huh! Camille, the chameleon."

"I like that!" Thomas said. "Camille, the chameleon."

"Cam-a-*lee*-on," Silva said.

Chamelea! Thomas thought to himself, as he stroked his cheek and recalled the many identities he had assumed over the past two years to finally bring him here. "That's neat! I really like it."

"Oh, don't take us so seriously, Camille. Chameleons are ugly little things, darling, and you're far from ugly. You're absolutely *lover*-ly." Pauline said, and then lighted a comforting little kiss on Thomas's cheek. "Oh, behold, darlings," James Dean said. "Our comedian-poet is taking to the stage."

James Dean was referring to one who called himself Ishmael, as the poet positioned himself and his guitar on the chrome-plated stool on the dais. He drew a cigarette from the breast pocket of his vest and held it like a little baton as he signaled for silence.

"Oh, Christ!" Silva said. "When's that guy *ever* gonna realize how pretentiously bad his stuff really is?"

Thomas was grateful for the change of subject. "Shhh, dear hearts. I like his readings…most of the time."

"That's because you're from Kansas or one of those square states in the Midwest," said James Dean.

"Iowa," he said while condescendingly patting James Dean on the shoulder. "I don't think I ever caught our poet's name."

"That's because he rarely throws it out," Silva said. "I think it's 'Ishmael,' the world's first bastard, biblically speaking."

"Honestly, Silva, where did you come up with that? You never held the Bible in your hand in your life," James Dean quipped.

Thomas was momentarily stunned as he recalled liberating an Ishmael from his couch in the Cherry Street Hotel almost a year before. "Silva's right. Ishmael was God's first bastard," he said reflectively.

"One in a line of many," Silva glowered at James Dean. "One of them is sitting right here among us."

The poetry read in the Cavern was as conducive to the ambience of the place as its atmosphere was to the poetry. Tonight, as usual, the smoke of anything that was lit up stung the eyes, even those hidden behind dark glasses. The house lights dimmed to a single spotlight shining down on Ishmael. The gardenias on Thomas's dress became iridescent through the gloom. Ishmael, set far away into the darkness, spun some spontaneity from the six loose strings of his guitar as he recited from memory and a darkness from within. The dry, chapped, bass of his voice contrasted against his occasional, emphatic whispers:

"Death— D-E-T-H—

DEATH— is the center of

—LIFE.

For In D-E-T-H—

In death—we are born

— At least to die again!

For at the center of the lie of LIFE—

is IF."

"Oh, for Christ's sake!" Silva said after Ishmael's drawn out pseudo-intellectual torture treatment. "What a fucking lumber-jack."

"Oh, yes!" Thomas said in a dry whisper to Pauline after a moment or so of silence. "Yes! That was be-*eu*-tee-ful!" He raised his hands above his head and joined some others in the audience snapping their fingers like castanets in approval, while some others flicked their lighters aflame in the semidarkness.

"Are you nuts, Camille?" Silva said as he lit up a joint. "That was brazenly awful. That neophyte hasn't read his Sartre; doesn't know his Nietzsche from his Ginsberg."

"And you do, my little boo-boo?" James Dean said.

"No. Of course not, that's how I can know what Sartre is telling us. Existentialism is not knowing. It's *being*." Silva took a reflective puff. "You don't have to know life deeply to *be*. But death— That's too much work for the living. Too much thought goes into it."

"Bra-*vo*! That's what I love about you, Silva," James Dean said. "You're so smart. Too smart for what little knowledge you have."

"Why, thank you, dear. I'll take that as a compliment."

"*Ree*-lee!' James Dean said. "You must've been reading your World Book Encyclopedia, again. Criminy, darling, I've never known anyone to know so little and so much at the same time."

Silva took another inhale, and thrust the weed toward Thomas.

"Okay, Silva." James Dean said darkly. "You can knock off the act now. I forgive you."

Ishmael continued to extemporaneously strum the guitar from his own world.

Thomas took a greedy puff from the joint, and then sipped his Scotch to cool its sweet harshness as he allowed its effect to carry him back to the mythical Ballycannough of his youth, and back to Mother. He could not reminisce over death without thinking of Mother. "Death is the most natural thing on earth. Nobody I know can live without it," he said, "and the fear brought on by its mystery. Death has no part in life. Death doesn't discriminate. It can't. It just…happens in the end."

"Oh, *Gawd*! Not you, now, too, Camille!" James Dean said.

"Y'all forget, dear hearts. I'm a preacher. I deal with death as part of my job. Or at least to diminish its effect on those I've preached to who think it's unfair. Death can't rationalize its existence. So, people turn to someone like me because, to God-fearing souls, the great be- yond is the snake oil remedy sold by the Bible, along with God. And I'm a man of God," he said. He took another languorous puff. "I know first-hand."

"Jesus, girl!" Silva said. "And I thought *I* was the bullshit artist!"

"At least you're admitting it," James Dean said.

"Now, about that dress," Pauline said to diffuse the topic.

"It's hideous and you know it," Thomas said as he handed the reefer back to Silva.

"Well, it's not exactly Peck and Peck," Pauline said.

James Dean sipped his pink squirrel. "It's strictly E.J. Korvette's, and you should exchange it tomorrow. Better yet, burn it so no one else buys it and pollutes les haute couture."

Thomas adjusted the dress's sagging bodice. "I'm changing back into something more masculine at Pauline's place."

"My place?" Pauline raised his trim eyebrows in hopeful expectation, as he demurely raised his dark glasses to rest further on top of his head. His dark-blue eyes glistened seductively through the darkness.

Thomas placed his hand under the table and placed it on Pauline's inner thigh and stroked. "Why, yes, dear heart. I'm in the mood for a full body lanolin rub. Aren't you?"

"Well, then. Forget about hearing the rest of Big Eunice's set tonight," Pauline said. "Let's finish our drinks and go right now."

What Thomas had just said shocked him immediately. It was as though his entire character had changed in the last five minutes. He reasoned it must have come from Zina's and Gwen's souls meandering about within him—one wanton, the other desperate—both women.

Chapter 32

A catharsis

The trembling thrust of its 165-horsepower radial engine carried Night Bird above the shimmering, pristine blue surface of Rangeley Lake in western Maine. Nealy usually preferred to fly low and slow. *Night Bird*'s ambience had more the elegant feel of a fine motorcar than a typical airplane. Nealy glanced at the chrome-appointed instrument panel set into the dash of burled walnut. The burgundy carpeting felt thick under his feet.

Wavering rays from the lowering sun flickered through the crisp dense pine forest on the shores of the lake. Even though he viewed it from a distance, Nealy felt embraced by a near-perfect world. Through the opened side window, he breathed in the soft fragrance of spent oil along with the fresh smell of the lake water. The scent was tinctured by that of the spruce trees lining the shore. He gazed ahead, northeast, into the settling dusk toward the lush and craggy Whites, dominated by Mount Washington. And then he looked south, to his left and at the abundance of foliage and the rocky fringes of the northern New England woods.

For the first time in as long as he could remember, even before his marriage to Alice, he sensed true satisfaction and felt fully at ease. Francesca had brought him to this place in his mind as they had re- laxed into a comfortable relationship. It made him happy enough to giggle openly as a child at the imagined feel of the lapping wavelets 80 feet below *Night Bird*'s pontoons.

The plane jinked a little in a low gust of a headwind, causing Ham- let, only guardedly asleep on his blanket in the backseat, to shake himself fully awake. "Yee-Hah, boy!" Nealy exclaimed with infantile excitement, as he pulled back on the polished mahogany control stick.

He angled *Night Bird* up into a gentle 25-degree climb to 3,800 feet, where he cut the manifold switch to turn off the engine. The plane glided in weightless, luxuriant silence for a few minutes until it dipped lackadaisically forward, then more rapidly down toward the water. Nealy felt the G-force as a numbing rise in his stomach and a swelling in his ears.

Even under the influence of half a Dramamine, Hamlet acted uncomfortably impatient when his master did this and let out a frustrated groan along with a little dog-fart to show his annoyance as he scram- bled for footing within his blanket. Finally, Nealy flicked on the starter switch and the engine coughed into action as the plane trembled and then leveled off 100 feet above the water. He brought the plane into an easy 25-degree bank to the right, and then east toward home.

Nealy cut the engine and lowered the pontoon's water rudders. He then brought the plane into a gentle glide as he flared up against the wind at ten feet over the lake's surface. He relished the thrilling comfort of the pontoons chattering and shuddering the plane upon the wavelets. Hamlet circled within his blanket for his long body to find purchase enough to once again lie down. He rested his head on the ledge of the backseat window and stared out longingly in anticipation for an end to the manic joyride. He let flee another fart of displeasure as Nealy flicked on the magneto and the engine rumbled to life so he could steer *Night Bird* to its dock.

Nealy guided the plane toward its berth, which jutted out from

Koehler's Point, a small peninsula named for his maternal grandmother, who had owned the ten-acre family plot on the Rangeley lakeshore. Now it was Nealy's land, soon to be shared with Francesca, his future wife.

He had come to this final decision during his flight.

Carrying two iced teas, Francesca approached him on the pier as Nealy tied Night Bird down, securing the plane until tomorrow when he would take it up again. He opened the passenger door, flipped the seat forward and forklifted the grateful Hamlet out in his arms as his short legs flailed in readiness to run away from the madness of his in-flight experience. As he placed Hamlet on the dock, he scampered urgently toward Francesca.

She handed Nealy his tea as Hamlet took his side by her. She reached down to stroke his body. "What did you do to Hamlet up there, Raymond? His heart's beating a mile a minute."

Nealy sipped his tea, one of the remedies now used to swear off most of the booze. "He loves flying, Frannie. Always has."

She glanced down at Hamlet shuddering against her legs. "Looks like he's learned to hate it."

Nealy schemed to delicately tell Francesca of his decision about their future as they walked toward his worn-shingled, green-trimmed house at the end of the dock. "I love flying that plane."

She wrapped her free arm around his waist as she sipped her tea. "I know you do, sweetie."

"I really have a chance to think up there. Clear my mind. Put things in perspective."

"When you're not doing those aerobatics and scaring me and your dog half to death! Don't think I wasn't watching you up there."

"That plane can't do aerobatics," he said. "That was just a standard climb and descent to clear the plugs. I do it all the time."

"Scared the shit outta me, Raymond. Really. Don't try that crap when *I'm* sitting in the right seat," she said.

"Stalling a plane like that is one of the first things you learn when you begin to fly. You still want to learn?"

"Of course. I love flying. I just would kind of like doing it on my own terms."

"Ya, gotta stall before you learn to fly, Frannie. You want to start tomorrow? Your first lesson?"

"Raymond? *Really*? You *mean* it?"

"We leave the dock tomorrow at eight-thirty a.m. sharp. You're the pilot. You take the left seat. It'll be your plane for an hour or so while I guide you."

She hugged him tighter and stood on tiptoe to kiss his cheek. "Oh, Raymond. Thank you! Boy, do *I* love *you!*"

"Okay, then, there's something else I've been thinking about," he said as they walked into the shade of the front porch and into the cool house that smelled of Maine—musky, moist and piney.

The phone was ringing. Francesca slipped her arm from behind him and answered it.

"Marty!" she said excitedly. "Raymond's gonna teach me to fly!" "Oh, shit," Cohansen said. "The skies will no longer be safe for the

rest of us. I need to talk to the galoot of the house. Is he in?" She handed the phone to Nealy. "You're gonna teach Frannie to fly? I thought you valued that plane of yours. If she flies half as bad as she drives—" Nealy decided to break his news. "Marty? What're you doing this December?"

"With any luck, I'll be slumming it in Tahiti. How th' fuck do *I* know what I'll be doin' six months from now? Probably a lotta cop stuff and other paperwork. Christmas shopping for all my ex-wives. Why?"

"Well, I'm gonna need a best man."

"What th' fuck ya talking about, Ray?"

Nealy looked over at Francesca in her bare feet, sipping her tea. "You may want to make us a Scotch, honey. I'm asking you to marry me."

Francesca stared dumbstruck at him for several seconds while this registered. Then she screamed: "HOLY *SHIT!*"

"Jesus, Ray!" Cohansen said. "About fuckin' time! I kinda knew this was comin'— *hopin'* for it, even. It's been, what, since you've known her, twenty years?"

"HOLY SHIT, Raymond! YES, yes, yes. YES!" she dropped her glass of tea to the floor as she lunged into him. "Marty! Did you hear that?" she shouted into the receiver.

"I think they heard you alla way out in Weehawken, Frannie," Cohansen said.

"He heard you," Nealy translated. "Is December an okay date for us?" "Shit yes, Raymond!"

"My friend, I'd be honored to be your best man. Thank you, and congrats. Now we need to talk about what I called you about."

Nealy cupped his hand over the receiver and sent Francesca to make a couple of Scotches and then get ready for dinner at their favorite place over near Sugarloaf. "Okay, Marty. Speak."

"Ray," Cohansen said, "I got this particular pebble in my shoe."

"Maybe if you changed your socks every once in a while—"

"Yeah, well. There been a couple of suicides in the precinct."

Nealy's expression became serious as he read Cohansen's tone. "But you don't think they're suicides."

"I really don't know. They *do* kinda smell that way. I really wish you was here to prove me right—that suicides *was* what they were. Both victims were female; one a jumper, the other one a slasher."

"So, they just *might* be homicides?"

"Honestly I still wanna think they're suicides. The Two-Oh and the Upper West Side in general has been pretty clean the last year. Obviously I wanna keep it that way. But, shit, Ray, there're too many similarities in these two. My worst nightmare, any cop's worst nightmare, is some sorta spree's in the works."

"Try not to get ahead of yourself, buddy. It probably is just a couple of suicides."

"It's the jumper that mighta turned the key in the opposite direction, Ray. The doorman saw her come in with someone who mighta been a preacher. Didn't see him leave. In the case of the slasher, the downstairs neighbor found her in the tub, the water was still running and dripping though his ceiling. Cheaply built apartments."

"What are the similarities?"

"Both apartments smelled the same way. Like lilacs, for one. I need you here to put together the pieces for a coupla suicides."

"When were these, Marty?"

"The jumper? About a week ago. Late Friday night. The slasher, three days ago. Ray, I could use your help on this. Just like old times."

"You kept the apartments as crime scenes?"

"Yeah, for now. But I'm on the clock. Captain's giving me only one more week. Then I'll happily take down the tape, rule these as suicides, and be done with it."

Nealy found a pack of stale cigarettes in the hallway table drawer and lit one up. "The bodies on ice?"

"Both in the morgue. I'm waiting on tox reports." "You're running forensics on suicides?"

Cohansen puffed out a laugh. "We run forensics on everything nowadays, Ray. The department has some new scientific toys for analyzing bloodwork. Using the stuff like so many new playthings." Nealy heard him sip a coffee—probably laced from the bottle of Jack Daniels he kept in his bottom desk drawer. "Anyway, Ray, I don't hold much stock in all that science. I like what I can see with my own bleary eyes."

"It's where the world is goin', Marty."

"I hate to ask you this, buddy, you know, like rain on your Fourth of July and all these good things ya got goin' on around you with Frannie and all."

Nealy took the Scotch Francesca handed him. He put it down on the phone table and wrapped an arm around Francesca's waist. He felt her plush warmth. "You want me down there. Like, soon," he said.

Francesca heaved a sigh of disappointment.

"Could you? We'll pay you as a consultant," Cohansen said.

"Damn right you will, Marty. Time-and-a-half. I'm s'posed to be on vacation."

"We'll talk about the time-and-a-half thing. I just need you down here for a day or so. Then you can go back up there to The Yukon."

"Maine is not The Yukon."

"Same place."

Nealy puffed out a sigh and sipped his drink. "Okay, Marty. I'll see you in a few days. And congrats, again," Cohansen said and then hung up the phone. Nealy looked at Francesca. "Gotta go, I guess. Marty may have a case for us."

"You're lucky I know our business as well as I do, Raymond, and how strapped for cash we are," she said. "Otherwise, I'd be jealous of the time you're spending away. Is he paying us time-and-a-half?"

"I'll make sure."

"I'm gonna miss you, but God knows we could use the work. You flying or driving?"

"Oh. Driving." He kissed her on the forehead, then picked up his drink and rushed a sip. "Early morning, tomorrow. I gotta pack."

"Just pack lightly, sweetie," her voice echoed behind him as he ascended the narrow stairs. "I want you back soon. We've got plans to make!" She looked down into her drink. "You owe me," she said. She could tell his mind was now churning with Cohansen's case, and she already missed him.

Chapter 33

From 22 floors up

Twenty-two stories over the Upper West Side, the wall-sized windows in Zina's apartment revealed an un-obstructed, fog-shrouded panorama of lower Manhattan. Nealy slid open one of the balcony doors and let in the muffled street noises from be- low. He still had some leftover Maine within him from when he left a few days before, and he needed some air, fresh or otherwise. He sipped his cooling coffee as he stepped out onto the balcony. The noise and disorder from down on street level was transformed into a quieted, organized design of traffic inching through the network of streets, which at closer scrutiny would be peppered by the anxious, yet barely perceptible bleating of car horns.

Though New York was the same as it ever was, the place seemed no longer to be Nealy's. His New York had seceded into something else—something beyond during those formative years when he was a detective on the force with Marty. Like him, the city was dissolving into maturity while still wearing the hopeful disguise of youth. He lit a little cigar and reasoned from within in the recesses of his logic that his inner euphoric fool may have started to play a trick on him. He was certain he did not deserve the good fortune of his developing life after those sullen years of depression. If there was such a thing as an effortless love, he felt he had discovered it with Francesca.

"...was a rich kid," he heard Cohansen saying of Zina's lavish two-bedroom apartment through the open doors behind him. "This place had to set her back at least, what? Five-fifty? Six-fifty a month? She pro'lly had some help, maybe her parents or a rich uncle out there in Connecticut. She couldn't have sported this place on the salary she made at that print shop we found out she was working at." He walked over to the big 21-inch roll-around console television, whose dark- green tube convexly reflected Nealy entering the living room from the balcony. "I mean this TV alone's the size o' Rhode Island. It had to cost, what? A thousand bucks? Maybe more?"

Nealy turned his attention to Zina's desk as he glanced down at a neat grouping of framed photos behind an efficiently arranged pen set. He picked up a recent photo of her and an older woman, too old to be her mother—probably her grandmother. Zina appeared spunky, and wore the smile of someone who loved life; not the one of a young woman depressed enough to want to kill herself. The grandmother also beamed through her own happy smile, making the two of them appear comfortably unified. He knew this old woman would now be painfully grieving the loss of her granddaughter. It was another re- minder that the loss or disruption of anyone's life digs deeper into the fleetingly secure happiness of others.

Another photo showed a very pretty, beaming Zina and someone who was perhaps her boyfriend. He was a robust, seasoned country boy in a work-worn ball cap. Next to her slight frame, his was of medium build, yet brawny. Sharing her infectious smile, he appeared to be just an average, confident guy, happy to be in the presence of his sweetheart. Not even a truly depressed actor could appear as much at ease as did Zina in these pictures. All of it only suggested that perhaps there might have been foul play in her death, and that Cohansen's squad had become too comfortable in the conviction of their duties, if not their lack of willingness to fill out all the homicidal paperwork.

Nealy picked up the photo of Zina and her boyfriend and stared into it. "It looks as though Zina had a boyfriend. Did you question him, Marty?"

"Ray? I don't know. Like I say, my head wants to tell me this is a suicide. The rest is all maybe just something like a hunch I have. I kin- da didn't wanna open up any department can o' worms 'til I got your feel on this. So, no. No one beyond the doorman got questioned, here."

Nealy held back on his conviction that Zina's easy smile betrayed any thought of suicide as he replaced the picture.

Cohansen sniffed in the faint, leftover aroma of lavender. "Anyway, buddy. Whatdaya smell?"

Nealy sniffed. "I don't know. Violets?"

"Oh, I thought it was lilacs. It's the same smell in the Perkins woman's place."

"Perkins woman?"

"Gwen Perkins. She was the one who slashed her wrists over on Seventy-Sixth Street. We're goin' there next."

Nealy glanced around. "And you didn't find any matching lilac scent here in Zina's perfumes."

"Nothin', just stuff like Chanel No. 5, and something else from Elizabeth Arden. Tiffany's. Expensive stuff. Like I say, this one came from a little money. But that wasn't any sort of motive. We found fifteen hunnered in twenties and fifties stashed away in her top dresser drawer where anyone coulda found it."

Nealy stared at the couch for a few moments as he tried piecing the scene together. "I'm guessing she could have been lying on the couch, with nothing on under the robe you found her in. She might have taken off her bra and panties right where she was sitting, maybe like some sort of afterthought. Maybe getting ready to have sex with someone." "How do you know that? I mean she was nude with just the robe, but what makes you think she undressed then lay down there on the couch?" "Well, Marty. Those are her clothes piled in the middle of the floor, like she was in a hurry to get out of them. All the couch pillows are bunched up on the near end of the couch, and even now they're still a little crushed, like she might have been lying down." He leaned over to sniff the subtle indent her head had made in the pillows. He smelled the herbal, soapy residue of shampoo. "She was facing away from where she'd be lying if she was just watching the TV, which is aimed away, anyway. And then there's these," Nealy groaned as he crouched down to reach under the middle of the couch from where the tips of her bra strap and panties had been poking out. He pulled them from beneath the couch. "I'm guessing she was sitting in the middle of the couch, as though she might have been waiting for something to happen with someone else who might have been here, then took these off, dropped them to the floor; then kicked them under the couch. Then she might have poofed up all these couch pillows and moved them to the end so she could lie down. You say there wasn't any evidence of sex?"

"None. Preliminary coronary reports confirmed that. No fluids, nothing. Dry as a bone."

"Anyway, maybe this so-called priest who the doorman said he saw Zina with got off on watching women undress in front of him. You know, those priests and all that repressed celibacy. I once had a case where the wife was sure her husband was screwing around with some chippie. He'd leave the house at the same time every night," Nealy said as he glanced over the coffee table for clues. "Turns out he rented a room in a building right across the street from the chippie's apartment, so he could watch her through binocs while she got ready for bed. For some guys, the joy's only in the journey, I suppose. Maybe your guy was the same way." His voice trailed behind as he made his way toward the bedroom.

Cohansen heard him rumbling around. "Glad I brought you by here, Ray," he said, realizing his ex-partner was tending toward thinking murder. "You always did have some sorta sense for the emotional slant of things."

"Yo, Marty! Come on in here to the bathroom." Cohansen found Nealy poring over the vanity and the sink.

"Whadya find?"

"All around the rest of the place is pretty neat."

"I would say Zina Harper was a, whatdaya call it, fastidious person." "Yeah, well, this bathroom sink looks like a tornado went through it. I'd hate to think your guys made this mess." "No way. It is what it was when we found it."

Nealy lit up another little cigar, shook out the match, ran it under a dribble of water from the tap and then put it in his pocket. Cohansen followed him into the bedroom. "So, Marty, now there's this."

Nealy stood near the open door of one of her two clothes closets. "There's a gap here in this dress closet. Look. All the stuff in the closet over there is hanging just so and orderly, but in this other one, some clothes are pushed roughly aside, and the rest are still hanging neatly. There's one empty hanger in the closet, and another one thrown on the bed, and no dress for it. From what I see, this Zina doesn't strike me as one who would rifle through her dress closet as if she were in some sort of hurry. It might have been someone else." Then he added for Cohansen's benefit, "If it wasn't a suicide."

"So, our Zina was short and you're saying her maybe killer was her size. Well, at least-wise small enough to fit into her clothes."

"He wasn't exactly a halfback," Nealy said. "How 'bout this, Marty!" he uttered chummily. "Now we're starting to think like the cops we were back in the day!"

"Yeah, but I'm not convinced as you are on the homicide angle. That's the difference." Nealy was seized by an idea and offered a thoughtful smile. "What I'm suggesting is that the perp—"

"C'mon, Ray," Cohansen said. "I still gotta play devil's advocate, here."

"*Alleged* perp—wasn't driven by the luxury of choice, as Zina might have been. Those clothes were gone through a little too rough by someone who needed something to wear, to shield his identity completely. I'm thinking that your priest made himself up and dressed like a woman to get away." Nealy puffed on his cigar, then picked up a bottle of *eau d' cologne* from Zina's dresser and stared into it. "Anyway, if she had killed herself, this Zina seemed in a hurry to get out of her clothes in the living room, then she sure seemed to be in another hurry to get dressed in here. Like she wanted to get dressed twice, and fast. Then, strip down, change into her robe, and jump from her balcony." He put down the bottle and looked over at Cohansen. "The evidence doesn't stack up as a suicide, Marty. Hate to tell you this, buddy, but this all definitely points to another person here doing this. Everything's all over the place in that bathroom." He went back into the bathroom and concentrated at the uncapped lipstick container. "Isn't the point on the lipstick supposed to be chiseled? This is worn almost flat, broken off, kind of like an amateur or a kid applied it."

"Jeezus, Ray," Cohansen said. "What?"

"That guy, Henry the doorman, said he saw a really badly made- up woman with sloppy red lips leave the building after midnight. Said he'd never seen her before. Didn't see her come in."

"Maybe. In like a priest, do something bad, then out like a dame.

Who's to know?"

"There's still a lot of guesswork that needs to be cut through. Let's go out to where she fell."

The balcony revealed nothing new. There was no sign of a struggle, but if little Zina had jumped on her own, she would have most likely needed to climb up on a footstool or low table to step up onto the railing to do it. There was a small table next to the chaise lounge that might have served this task. The only way for the five-foot-tall girl to go over a three-and–a-half-foot tall glass-paneled railing would have been to have tumbled herself over—a doable, but awkward, way to fly off into the night.

Finally, as they were leaving, Nealy noticed two faint drag tracks about one foot apart in the carpet. They ran in and out of the footprints of activity from the cops that had shown up to assess the scene a week before. Nealy crouched down and looked up at Cohansen. "Look here, Marty. Looks like she was dragged to the balcony."

Cohansen squinted to notice the tracks. "Son of a bitch! Goddamn it to hell!"

"Marty," Nealy said as he rose, "why don't you go and bag that lipstick and test it for prints? If our guy was this sloppy in disguising himself as a woman, then he might have been sloppy enough to leave his prints all over that thing."

"Yeah," Cohansen said. "Now I remember, there was sompthin' else the doorman told me." He chucked his chin as though it itched. "He thought he saw the priest coming in carryin' a knapsack, and the broad with the bad makeup job leaving with maybe the same knap- sack, big purse, whatever."

"Really?"

"Yeah, I think this priest-into-dame-theory is startin' to settle a little."

Nealy spied a big Telefunken radio. "Alice and I used one of these radios," he said. "These things aren't cheap."

"See? Now that you n' Frannie are hookin' up, you don't have to go around reminiscing about past wives and their radios. But, I will say that thing put out one hell of a rich sound."

"How do you know?"

"Oh, it was on when the team got here. Some sorta big band music."

"Huh," Nealy said. "Doesn't seem like the sort of stuff a twenty-two-year-old girl would be into." Because it seemed this was becoming more of a crime scene, Nealy picked up a napkin and grasped the power button to turn the radio on, just as the call letters: "1420 WYOR," were announced by a mellow, mechanical-sounding voice. This was followed by Glenn Miller's "Moonlight Serenade."

The music and its genre bubbled up a desire in Cohansen to go to The Back Page once they were done. "Yeah, nice sound, Ray. Kinda like the stuff we'll hear on the juke at the 'Page,' when we're finished over at Gwen Perkins's apartment. I'll buy."

Nealy didn't hear him as he made a mental note of the frequency and then turned off the big radio.

Chapter 34

Detective games

The superintendent of Gwen Perkins's apartment building rifled through his key chain for the one to unlock her apartment for the two detectives. A door across the hallway abruptly creaked open and a piney swell of linseed oil mixed with turpentine insinuated itself upon the standing redolence of stale cooking smells and too much garlic. "A woman died in there," said a substance-affected slur from the open door. "Do something."

"Sorry, Paul," the super said as he found the key. "Shit like that happens sometimes."

"I won't pay rent in a building where someone died, Sal," Paul the artist said. "Bad karma. Bad joss. Poisons my creative process."

Paul hadn't paid his $95 rent for three months, but he usually paid about three months of his rent every fourth. Sal, the super, figured it would cost more to fumigate his apartment of the concentration of severe and asphyxiating oil paint and drug smells that had accumulated over the last seven years.

Cohansen turned toward the gristly, emaciated-looking painter, who, in his own splotched coating of random colors, looked like a painting from a disturbed mind. "Did you know the woman?"

Paul blinked at him. "Are you the FBI?"

Cohansen showed his badge. "Cops. And don't worry, this ain't about you. It's about the woman who died."

Paul considered this for a moment and then finally answered. "Hardly ever saw her, even though she was hard to miss when I did."

"Whatdya mean by that?" Cohansen pressed.

Paul spread out his arms. "Fat. Like one of Picasso's spherically-constructed cubist bathing beauties."

"You know if she had any sort of boyfriend? Girlfriend?" Nealy asked.

"I don't think she knew any-one, man. She really wasn't any sort of—let's just say she didn't care about her looks. Kinda scraggly looking and, like I said, utterly fat."

"Now, Paul, respect the deceased," said Sal. He half-opened her door and then turned to Cohansen. "She kep' pretty much to herself most of the times. I saw her goin' off to Mass most mornings and maybe off to do some grocery shopping."

"Grocery shopping. Probably lots of that, man," Paul said.

"Can we be done with him?" Sal asked.

"Yeah," said Cohansen. "Thanks, Paul. We'll let you know if we need you for any more about this."

"Glad to be of help, man," Paul said, and then slid back into his apartment, relieved to be free of any further inquisition from the police state.

"So," Nealy said. "Mass every morning?"

"Just about," Sal answered. "She definitely was a religious type. Pro'lly spent the day here praying the Rosary."

"You know which church?"

"I think it was Our Lady of Assumption, down the block on Broadway."

"Priest," Nealy reminded Cohansen.

"And you're sure you didn't see her coming in that night?" Cohansen said. "Maybe with a priest?"

"I wasn't even here, then. Took Mary and the kids out to dinner.

Mary's my wife. Didn't come back until I got a call from Emilio Rodriquez, the downstairs neighbor, about the leaking through his bath- room ceiling."

"When was that? The call?"

"Maybe eleven-thirty at night?"

Cohansen turned to Nealy. "We already talked to Rodriquez. Not much new there."

"Okay, gents," Sal said as he swung the door wider. "It's all yours. I gotta couple o' faucets to fix." He turned and walked back down the stairs. Gwen Perkins's cramped apartment smelled of old stuff. Like in a lot of turn-of-the-century brownstones, the rooms were small. The kitchen was partitioned off by a low counter like an after- thought to divide the living room. The stout, uninteresting furnishings were festooned with woolen throws and doilies. The overheated place needed a deep cleaning. It smelled musty—and aromatic with a slight trace of lavender. "There's that lilac smell again," Nealy said.

"Her bedroom's a mess, too. Clothes all over the floor," said Cohansen.

Nealy heard a faint hum behind him. He turned and noticed a little plastic radio on a couch side table. He brought his hand closer to it. "Jee-zus! This radio's hotter than a solar flare. It's been on all this time?"

"Shit. My guys must not have turned it all the way off. It was blaring out more of that 40s music when we got here."

"Lucky the place didn't catch fire." Nealy picked up a doily and turned the volume up. Glenn Miller's "In the Mood "was playing. He made a note of the station setting. 1420, WYOR. "Same radio station," he said, then turned it off.

"Must be The Glenn Miller Hour, or something." Cohansen said as he glanced at his watch. "It's almost noon. I'll buy us lunch after this." "You think there might be something our guy is using to tie this radio station into that lilac smell? I mean is there something about big band music and lilac?"

Cohansen shook his head. "Kind of a stretch, Ray," he said as he pulled a pack of Pall Malls from his breast pocket, tapped one out and lit it.

Nealy surveyed the couch and noticed the coffee table was set unnaturally away from the couch with the cushion on the floor between them. "I think she may have been sitting on this couch cushion on the floor. Maybe just before she decided to slice her wrists."

"Okay, Ray. What makes you think that?" Cohansen said, continuing to play against Nealy's findings. It was something they had since they were rookie detectives. If the evidence seemed to fit too well together, one of them would question the other's findings as he played the part of a doubter. The process helped to firm up their conclusions, while keeping their sleuthing objective. The same tactic never seemed to work as well with the dour Barnaby, as Nealy was better at playing into Cohansen's acting the part of the skeptic. It was what had made them so good at their job, which caused Cohansen to miss working with him even more.

"Okay, Marty. If you're gonna be that way about it." Nealy strained a little laugh. "First of all, our last victim may have been coerced to lie down on the couch, somehow. Zina was short. This one, Gwen, was large, and her couch seems too small to support her size. This coffee table—you may want to dust it for prints—looks as though it was pushed away to make room for putting this cushion here for her to sit on the floor. Following me, so far, Marty?"

Cohansen puffed his cigarette. "Yeah, okay."

"And this cushion is soft foam rubber." Nealy looked down at the cushion. "You can still see some sort of faint, latent indents. Two small ones, like from her knees."

Cohansen thought through an exaggerated exhale. "Like she mighta been kneeling? Like, praying?"

"There you go!"

"Another stretch, but okay. Assuming that's what happened." Nealy spied three pieces of broken wafer on the carpet. "*Hul*-lo. What's this?" He crouched down to pick them up.

"Looks like part of a cracker," Cohansen said. "Obviously she liked to eat. Probably millions around here, if you look."

Nealy turned a piece of the wafer as he examined it. "Too thin. I think this might be—a Communion wafer."

"There's that priest thing again. Surprised you even know what a Communion wafer looks like, Ray."

"I've had my shots of redemption over time. Not many until recently, but I'm pretty sure that's what this is." He placed the pieces of wafer on the table like the holy relics they almost were. "You should bag these and see if those crime analysis guys of yours come up with anything on them."

Cohansen had used up his only evidence bag for the lipstick from Zina's apartment. He mumbled some displeasure as he went to the kitchenette to find something that would do. Nealy went to the bed- room and into the bathroom as Cohansen came back to the coffee table with a fistful of waxed paper sandwich bags. He carefully picked up the wafer pieces and put it them in one of the little bags. He decided that he and Barnaby should question the priest at Our Lady of Assumption. Nealy stared at the freestanding tub in the middle of the bathroom. There was a dark, peach-colored stain diminishing down the insides from just below the rim left by the watered-down blood in which she had been lying for the few hours before the coroner took the body. It had been a resolute attempt. A thorough suicide through bleeding is quickened by the flow of warm water and the vertical cuts Cohansen described.

Nealy stared down at the stain on the floor left by the tub water displaced by Gwen's big body. "Did that guy the super said found her say that the water was running when he discovered her?"

Cohansen let out a hefty sigh of exasperation as he entered the bathroom to flush his cigarette down the toilet. "The neighbor said the water wasn't running."

"Who turned it off, then?" "She probably did?"

"I see," Nealy said, playing into Cohansen's fatigued agnosticism. "She's nearly dead, but has the strength to sit up and reach for the tap with four seven-inch gashes in her left arm to turn it off because she has the consideration not to bother the neighbors."

"She turned it off before she got into the tub?"

"That's not the way it's usually done, Marty. You know that. Besides, even if that was the case, she wouldn't have filled the tub to the brim like that. Especially someone her size, who displaces a lot of water."

"Okay, there was some water on the floor."

"Enough to seep down into the apartment below." said Nealy, continuing to enjoy Cohansen's doubting cop routine. "So, Marty. She turned it off after she was dead."

Cohansen rolled his eyes and then stared vacantly at the two frayed toothbrushes and the nearly expended tube of toothpaste on the left ledge of the sink.

"Well? Isn't that what you're suggesting?"

"Of course not." Cohansen conceded. "Okay, Ray. You win. Well, we still need to wait on the coroner's report and the blood work. But you're right. These both look like homicides."

Nealy sighed as he stared at the pink rim around the tub. "Worse. The lilac smell, the priest connection, the radio tuned to the same station. This may stink more of a serial situation, and our perp is leaving messages behind, like some sort of challenge."

The 20th Precinct had been about the cleanest one in the city for two years running. Violent crime had been down nearly 40 percent. "Fuck!" Cohansen whispered to himself as Nealy brushed past.

Nealy went to the bedroom and to the dressing table. Some bottles of nail polish, closed containers of lipstick, a can of hair spray, a box of face powder and a blue and white box of tissues with a puff of a paper tissue blooming from its top were on the left side of the table. The loosely capped jar of lanolin and uncapped lipstick, this time with a chiseled tip, were on the right. He remembered that the couch side lamp had been on the table next to the couch's left side. He looked behind him at Gwen's mussed up bed and realized she had slept on the left side of her queen-size bed, where she could easily reach the phone, her water glass, Bible and her eyeglasses, still there on the left side table, with her left hand.

"Marty. Which arm were the slices on?"

"The left." Cohansen called from where he had remained standing in the bathroom, dreading all the paperwork.

The fatal slices were in the wrong arm. "Gwen was left-handed," Nealy said.

"So are a lot of people," Cohansen said as he walked into the room. "My first ex-wife was a southpa—," then he caught himself. "The cuts were in her left arm," he said. "You sure she was left-handed, Ray?"

"Look here, Marty," he said to the dressing table. "All of her makeup, hair spray, face powder, tissues and these three lipsticks are on the left side of the dressing table, so she could have reached them from the side that was convenient for her. The couch reading lamp is on the left side table, and she slept on the left side of her bed so she could reach for the stuff on the table there, even half-asleep in the middle of the night when she could grope around for the things she needed."

"What about the uncapped lipstick and cold cream? I mean it looks like she coulda used that stuff with her right hand. It's on the right side of the table."

"Just like at Zina Harper's...Gwen wasn't the one to use it." Cohansen said, "So, some guy came in here and sliced Gwen Perkins's left arm, then turned off the water and made up his face and dressed up like a dame so he could leave. I still gotta wonder. Why'd he do the left arm and not the right?"

"Maybe because the perp didn't notice that Gwen was left-handed, or that he did know she was, and that the heart pumps more strongly to that side for left-handers. Anyway, he was probably right-handed. I think he stood behind her and sliced her arm. With the tub in the middle of the room like it is, it would have been the only convenient way to get any leverage."

"He talked Gwen into lying down in a tub of water, so he could slip a blade into her wrist?" Cohansen asked as he sat down on the edge of the bed. "Maybe she was, whadayacallit, ambidexterious."

"Ambidextrous," Nealy corrected as he leaned back against the dresser. He loosely folded his arms and gazed at the floor. "I don't know, Marty. But, if she was left-hand dominant, when it comes to some primary act like slitting her wrists, she would have used her dominant hand. I'm inclined to think this was all somehow arranged."

"Fuckin' serial killings," Cohansen pouted.

"Sorry, buddy. You asked me in on this," Nealy said. He offered up a smile of remembrance. "This is what made us such a great team." Cohansen lit another cigarette as he rose from where he sat on the bed. He stared reverently at his former partner and grimaced a hopeful smile at him. "You know, Ray, I kept your tin and piece in my desk drawer. Maybe like a memento. Anyway, somehow, I couldn't retire them things."

"No, Marty. I can't come back. You know that."

"Internal Affairs Department cleared you. Completely. You know that, and, yes, you can come back. I want you back."

Nealy lit another cigar, snuffed out the match between his fingers and slipped it into his breast pocket. He stared down at the floor as he sighed out a puff of smoke. "Problem is, Marty, I.A.D. may have cleared me, but I can't clear myself."

After over 20 years of their friendship, Cohansen was shouldered with the curse of knowing his best friend too well. "Door's always open. You know that. We did good."

"We did good," Nealy confirmed as he placed a reassuring arm around Cohansen's beefy shoulders. "Okay. Did I hear something about you buying me a lunch? Then I gotta go back north to my child bride. I promised her flying lessons."

"Yeah. Lemme know when she's flying around up there so I'll have the sense to stay indoors. You sure you wanna bring her kinda drivin' up into the skies?"

"Yeah. I do. And don't forget about you being my best man in De- cember. Frannie has a big family, and she wants a big wedding. So study up and buy a nice suit."

"Couldn't just do the Vegas thing, huhn?"

"You're talking about Frannie here. She's Italian, and all that implies. Besides, I did the quickie Vegas marriage once, remember? It may have lasted six years, but it didn't work." Nealy looked over at the dressing table. "And, Marty?"

"Yeah?"

"Don't forget to bag that open lipstick there on the dressing table. I'm pretty sure you'll find matching prints on the one you picked up at Zina Harper's place."

Chapter 35

The Holy Water Soaking Tub redux

Daylight streamed through the basement window behind Thomas as he slid luxuriantly into the Holy Water Soaking Tub. He felt the flowing warmth of the water caress into every previously waxed pore of his hairless, naked body. The sensation put him to sleep.

He didn't know how long he'd been resting until he was awakened by a whispering slosh and surge of the warm water next to him. He wearily opened his eyes to find Deborah, naked, cuddling up to him. "Hi," she said into his good ear. She planted a soft kiss on his cheek. "Rise and shine, Thomas. Miss me?"

"You're back."

"Thank you for noticing."

He wrapped his arm around her cool, dampened shoulders. "I couldn't help but. How was your flight?"

"It was on a 707 jet. Never flown on a jet-plane before. Coast to coast in just six hours. Left at two o'clock in the afternoon San Francis- co time and arrived at eleven o'clock at night New York time. It was— interesting. I'm still processing it."

He kissed the top of her head. "Well, that's the Jet Age for you."

"Sorry I tacked on a few extra weeks. I went to visit with Sarah, my old roommate from Pratt."

"Really, Deborah. It's okay. You apologized when you called two weeks ago to tell me." He lowered his hand in the water to stroke the side of one of her small, muscular breasts and imagined it to be his.

She nuzzled more deeply into the crook of his arm and shifted her body around. "It got boring after a while. A person can only discuss art for so long. I mean it's not like Pratt has a football team, or anything.

I came 'round to thinking only of this—" Her hand wandered down to the now hairless works between his legs. She no sooner drew her hand away and up out of the water in shock, as though she had just touched a mouse. "*Jee*-zus! What did you do to it?" she flared.

"I shaved it."

"That felt a lot softer than a shave, Thomas! More like a waxing, or something. Why did you do *that*?"

He thought about his answer as he lightly ran his fingers across her hardened nipple. "It's a gift—my surprise to you,"

"Jesus H! Well, happy fucking *birth*day! I suppose that body waxing is another beauty treatment I can thank those Cretans at The Glitz & Glitter for." She reluctantly lowered her hand to touch him again. "Well, you do feel soft down there." She worked her fingers around his limp sex. "Like a baby."

"I thought you'd like it."

"No. I don't." The water sloshed about as she rose and then straddled him, while massaging his parts more vigorously. "Come on, baby," she said into his right ear as she nibbled lightly on it. "Rise for me. I want you so much."

"I'm trying, Deborah. I can't. I don't know why."

She loosened her light, fondling touch on his scrotum, and moved her fingers to his penis started to masturbate him. "Oh, yes, Thomas. I know you can."

"No, I don't know—maybe my—uh—uhhh. I just can't feel it, to-day. God, I'm so sorry."

She kissed his temple and then eased herself away from him. "May- be later, then," she breathed as she lowered her hand down her body and to her groin to vigorously ease her acquired frustration. "Just— just—just a—justaMINute!" she breathed heartily and then eased further down into the water.

A damp little fall of her hair became glazed to her cheek as she positioned her body against the wall of the tub. She closed her eyes and swallowed as she began to rub her fingers against her sex. She started to work her jaw, then swallowed more purposefully from an ecstatic place far away from the tub, New York, the continent, the planet. She opened her mouth and heaved an irregular breath. Her breathing intensified as she moaned quietly though her wide-open mouth as she groped for breath. The sound of her breathing through the light sloshing of the water seemed to embrace the silence. Little by little, she arched her head back against the edge of the tub and gasped irregularly. Gradually she crooked her knee above the slithering surface of the water. Her breathing became more panicked, as if she was suffocating and groping for air. She finally extended the full length of a muscular leg and cried out pleadingly. She splayed her toes widely as she came to orgasm. Her breaths diminished to drawn out sighs as she slowly lowered her leg below the tub water.

All Thomas could do for the ensuing three minutes was to watch her work up to orgasm. He soon felt a shuddering stir forming in his own parts, but it smoothly abated. He felt no longer as motivated by Deborah into a blindness of heterosexual passion as before. The two souls he had absorbed while she was gone must had liberated him. As he'd become aroused to a conviction that emotionally he'd finally felt more like a woman than a man.

"Ho-kay!" she sighed breathlessly. "That's better, for now."

"I'm sorry, Deborah, I really am," he sighed in a whisper.

"S'okay, Thomas. Whew! Just give me a minute to catch my breath." After a short while, she let out another sigh. "Whooo— I feel better now. But you better promise me. Next time."

"I promise."

"Okay." She turned and looked intently at him, kissed him hard on the lips, then leaned back to look him over more casually. She stroked the bandage on his right ear as if she had just noticed it. "How's the ear feeling? Jesus, Thomas, I can't believe one of those cotton swabs could cause so much damage. You poked it right through your eardrum?"

"Next time I'll read the warning label."

"Next time you'll let me do it for you. Those things are not meant to poke into your ear like that. And the doctor says you've lost all hearing there?"

He nodded. "Anyway, I still have my right ear."

She softened her gaze and lovingly stroked his cheek. "When's that big honking bandage gonna disappear?"

"Well, actually, I'm going in on Thursday to get a smaller bandage. He'll be fitting me for a hearing aid."

"Poor baby," she mothered. "Why're you even getting a hearing aid if you lost your hearing, anyway?"

He wandered his hand gently down the smooth hillocks of her body as he wished he had one like it. "He thinks I may get some limited hearing back in my left ear eventually, so it might help."

"Let's hope so," she said as she stood up. The water flowed down her form in little rivers to the inverted tiny dark delta of her pubis where it collected and coursed as a single, silvery stream down her right thigh.

"You really are a beautiful specimen of a woman, Deborah."

"Hah!" she smirked as she reached for a towel and began to dry her- self. "You make me sound like some sort of high school science project." He smiled mischievously. "I wish you were. I love to do some poking and prodding. Just not today."

"You'll get over it—I hope," she said as she stepped from the tub and began to pat herself with the towel. "Oh, yeah. Thomas," she added as if remembering a lost thought. "We need to go to the World's Fair next Saturday. We really should see Michelangelo's Pieta at the Vatican Exhibit, then take that Ride into the Past, or whatever they call it at the Ford Pavilion. There's something else I need to see there. Plus, I've got a meeting scheduled at the Oklahoma Pavilion that day."

He recalled Deborah's reference to "Regina, the water-skier," when they were all sitting around the Glitz & Glitter Club before she left. "Oklahoma," he said indolently through the remembrance of Regina leaving Hanson to blend anonymously into flat plains of that dull place. Then He dismissed the thought. There had to be a thousand Reginas in Oklahoma. Even so, his expression drooped. "Sure. Why not?"

Chapter 36

Dad-damn!

Deborah realized that "The Magic Skyway" exhibit at the Ford Pavilion was just another commercial for the company's products. Sitting in a Ford car body, they were drawn along a track through history from animatronic dinosaurs to the dawn of man to the invention of the wheel and finally into a future showcasing a display of Ford's concept cars.

Thomas gawked in subdued panic at the robotic pterodactyls, brontosauruses and the scary Tyrannosaurus Rex who was cyclically attacking a lone stegosaurus that seemed to be losing. But this was a Disney creation after all, and each beast among the plastic prehistoric foliage seemed to be insinuating their treacheries though a kindly smile as though they were simply playing. Deborah was unfazed by the show off to the side, as she turned repeatedly to squint over her shoulder through the near darkness at the newly announced Ford Mustang convertible body being drawn behind them.

On the way out, she stopped to admire the Mustang featured just inside the pavilion's main entrance. It rotated slowly on its dais as though furtively revealing more of itself with each pass, like a stripper. The car body's chrome highlights and deep-red finish shimmied under the caress of the beams from the slowly moving spotlights above. At nearly $4,500 the fully loaded model was almost twice the price of the trending Volkswagen "bug," but the

Mustang was so much more car than the cute little "Beetle." Anyway, the Mustang was less a car than it was a statement announcing the id of an emerging generation.

Deborah continued to stare wantonly at the revolving car. "I'm so sick of driving around Manhattan in a pickup truck. It's so, I don't know—working class. Sarah showed me one of these Mustangs out in San Francisco. She's on a waiting list for one. I've gotta get this," she proclaimed. "It's so—me."

"I thought you were working class. Being in construction, and all."

She batted him playfully in the ribs as he delicately winced from the pain inflicted upon him from nearly six months before. "Please, Thomas! I'm not a construction worker. I'm a lifestyle designer. That's what Sarah and I decided that I was: A life-style designer."

He smiled wryly. "Looks like your college roommate hooked you right in your conceit." He touched the small bandage covering his ear. It was much less intrusive than the one it replaced, so he was able to cover most of it with a swatch of his filling-out hair.

"Well. I deserve a new car. I've worked hard for it. And I don't need your permission. Shit, and I really like this one, the same color, everything."

He followed her as she made her way around the revolving car, leaning forward at times as if to smell it. "Well, then, get one, dear heart. It's up to you. I'm beginning to wonder why anyone needs a car in this city, anyway, now that I'm starting to discover the subways to get around. They're not nearly as frightening here in real life as the thought of them was back in Iowa."

She hadn't heard him. "I'm getting one. This one."

"Where are you going to park it? Well, I suppose you could park it behind Heaven's Doorway, but in that neighborhood, this car might have a life expectancy of—what? Five minutes?"

She still hadn't heard him as she absorbed herself on the

magazine-sized brochure she'd picked off the rack. She pointed to a picture on the page. "A dark red convertible with a black top, just like this one. Four-thousand dollars. I can easily afford that. I mean, it's not like it's an eighty-thousand-dollar Ferrari."

"Have you been pricing those out, too?"

"No. Thomas, of course not. It's just that, here I am. I have money—lots of it—and I just hate spending it."

"Get the car, then, dear heart."

"I'm getting the car. A red Mustang convertible," she insisted.

He started to lead her away. "Okay, Deborah. Let's go see the General Electric exhibit."

"Right after we see The Pieta at the Vatican Pavilion." She looked at her watch. "But first we gotta stop off at Oklahoma. I need to check with the manager there about the waterfall and some plastic coping I put around the pond I built for the water-skier."

"Oh, yeah," said Thomas. "The water-skier. What was her name? Regina?"

"You remembered her name? I think I only mentioned her to you once."

Thomas stared back at the Ford Pavilion girded with high, vertical windows, and then around at the assortment of people strolling along the Avenue of the States. Clots of people gathered and roamed around in the blanching late morning sun and the numerous cantilevered, primary-colored street lights. "I guess there are certain things I remember," he said.

"You remember the name of someone I mentioned in passing, but you forgot my birthday."

"Really? When was that? Your birthday?"

"Ten days ago."

He was with Pauline, making love. "You were in California."

"That doesn't mean it didn't happen, Thomas."

"Well! Look who's here!" Deborah said as they approached the Oklahoma Pavilion. "We were just talking about you."

Regina had recently finished a bout of water-skiing and was preoccupied with drying herself. Though her vision was momentarily blurred from the water, she'd recognized Deborah's distinctively crusty voice. "Oh, hey, Debbie. You were talking about *me*? Why?" She tilted her head and cupped her right ear to dislodge some moisture through her left. Her damp and stringy auburn hair was plastered to her shoulders and face, disguising her for the moment. Her richly-tanned athletic body was clothed in a frilly, shocking-pink two-piece bathing suit. Three inches of the birthmark on her stomach showed faintly over the brim of her bathing-suit bottom.

Thomas had also been distracted, as he looked back at a woman in high fashion promenading past on the Avenue of Nations toward the gushing fountains ringing the UniSphere on the Promenade of the Presidents. He coveted the large, white floppy hat she wore above her immense dark glasses, such as those Pauline had worn when they met at the Glitz and Glitter Club right after Thomas had liberated Gwen a little over a week before. He vowed to take Pauline to Bergdorf's next week to find a pair for himself.

He then went numb as he heard a distantly familiar voice behind him: "Thanks for taking me, Trevor and Dave out for drinks before you left for the west coast. How was California?"

"No earthquakes, so I survived. How's this pond treating you?"

"Haven't fallen down yet," said Regina. "It's really good. I love these plastic edges. Glad you...changed...them," she said as though she had become mesmerized by familiar form of the man standing near Deborah.

Thomas cringed as he heard her voice fall off. No! It couldn't be! Couldn't! Impossible! He looked down at his feet and then furtively aimed his gaze toward the voice.

"Oh, Regina. This is my friend, Thomas Deavers."

"Thomas..." Regina said after a pensive pause, "...Deavers." The likeness of her father materialized before her as she brought her hand from her ear to her mouth. "Oh-shit!" she gasped. "DAD! Damn!!"

"Dad-damn?" Deborah said. "That's a new expletive. Must be something Oklahoman."

"Dad-damn!" Thomas spouted reflexively through a sharp breath as he slapped his arm. "Dad-damned bee!" He slapped his upper arm and then waved his arms frantically about his face as he quickly looked away. "Get out of here, dad-damned bee!"

Not knowing quite how to handle this, Regina reluctantly played along as she turned away from them and lightly swatted her thigh. "Dad-damned bees! I hate those things!" She glowered at Thomas. "There's this one in particular—"

"You two okay?" Deborah said. "Yes!" Thomas shouted.

"No!" said Regina.

"I think I told you about him when we all went out before I left. He certainly seems to remember you, Regina."

"No shit?" she said to the puddle at her feet.

"Well," said Thomas. "Not really."

Regina stood as she slowly looked around in quiet desperation. "No shit." Her quiet voice churned hoarsely as she scowled at her father. "No—fucking—shit," she muttered at him.

"I designed Thomas's church downtown. One of my best creations. I'll show you sometime," Deborah offered chummily.

"You don't have to, Deb," Regina said as she narrowed her stare at Thomas. "Thanks, though."

"Anyway, he's a preacher. So, watch your dad-damned language," Deborah said through a weak smile. She became suspicious about some inexplicable wound she might had uncovered.

"Preacher, eh?" Regina said.

"Do—you two already—*know* each other? I mean, that would just be *too* weird—"

"No!" Thomas emphatically said.

"Yes," Regina seethed as she backed away. "It would be—too weird." Trevor interrupted them from behind. "Oh, there you are, Deborah. Welcome back. I see Hollywood didn't grab you before I could have a chance to talk about the waterfall in our little river over there." "I, uh—" she said, not knowing what to make of the terse interplay between Thomas and Regina.

Trevor motioned her over. "Come on over with me. It's more of a gush than a trickle. I think we need some more stones, or something." "Yeah. Okay, Trevor," Deborah said uncertainly as she walked to- ward him. "Uh, I'll be back in a minute. You two get to know each other, or catch up...or something," she said to the two who seemed to be staring each other down like cats before a squabble. "Thomas? *Thomas!*"

He jolted his attention toward Deborah. "What!"

"We need to be at the Vatican by two. I have tickets for the showing of The Pieta, and you owe me a lunch, so be ready once I finish my dad-damn meeting with Trevor, here. Remember: Vatican. Two." She followed Trevor in the direction of the water spill she had built for the pavilion.

———

For a few moments Thomas and his daughter avoided each other through the swelling pressure of silence—even through the incessant, gaggling din of voices, gleeful and crying children, the tinny music from the speakers strung around the fair grounds and the landing and departing of airliners to and from LaGuardia. The environment was doused in the sweet aroma of cotton candy, popcorn and the passive, light carnival fragrances of Bavarian pastry and chocolate.

Regina finally spoke as she wrapped her towel modestly above the tight little swells of her breasts. "The Vatican. You get a promotion, or something? Anyway, I thought you were dead."

"As you see, I am not."

She padded closer to him. "Well, dad, you look like shit to me, so you ought to be," she challenged.

"Uh, how's your son?"

"Your grandson, you mean. I let Hellie take him."

"Hellie?"

"My mother's and your dead wife's sister. Probably you don't remember her. The little boy I gave birth to—he needed a mother. I am not a parent; never could be. I never learned from example."

He stood staring blankly Regina's light-green eyes.

"So," she said as she placed one hand on her hip, while holding the towel in place with the other. "You're a preacher. Still. Even though you're dead. Well, I suppose being a man of God does have its privileges. But I never put much stock in that resurrection crap, until now, I guess. Or maybe you're more like a Lazarus than a Christ—all ugly and shit."

"I had to leave Hanson," he said after a pensive silence.

"And leave behind a suicide note?"

Thomas bit his lower lip, as Regina suddenly appeared more familiar. She did not look to him like the pre-adult teenager who left Hanson a little over two years before, but instead as the sunburned, 10-year-old girl with a familiar birthmark squinting into the sun in the snapshot taken of her and Jillian on a Negril beach on the morning of his wife's death. She had even just covered up the same style pink bathing suit she had worn in that fading photo that he kept in his Bible.

"Well?"

"Well, what, Regina?"

"Everyone thinks you killed yourself," she said. "Does this make your suicide note null and void? Do I have to, like, return your house, and shit?"

"No. Of course not."

"I mean; I've already spent the money. Well, some of it."

"Whatever you've been left is yours. For all the world, Thomas Barr—" He choked on the mention of the name. "Reverend Thomas Barragan is dead."

"O-kay," she said as she sat down on a webbed chair, unwrapped her beach towel and patted her wet hair with it. "But Reverend Thom- as? What was that? Deavers? Reverend Thomas Deavers is alive. And that's supposed to change everything? Because, for better or for worse, here you are standing in front of me."

He had not noticed when he was serving as her father, but now, thinking as the woman he had become, he saw how youthfully beautiful she was. He fixed a burning gaze upon her, as though peering within. "I created you," he finally said.

This intimidated her. His tone had been a coarse, piercing, almost threatening one. She stopped drying her hair. "You—what? No! Mom had something to do with it. More than you, actually. *Much* more than you!" Still refusing to look at him, she fixed her stare away from him and on the glimmer of the pond's water. "I just really am sad I never got a chance to know her. Things would have turned out so— differently." A tear trickled down her cheek. She waved a hand loosely toward him. "Please, Reverend Thomas Deavers—Barragan, whoever you are now, just, go—please go. I never want to see you again."

He sighed deeply and turned and walked on shaking legs toward where Deborah was still talking with Trevor.

Chapter 37

Barrel riding

Time slipped leisurely into the afternoon as Regina tried to resist the temptation to break away from her performance to run back to her hotel room and call Hellie. The excuse of a headache would not have done it, as Trevor had heard that defense far too often during their after-dinner trysts. She finally realized this cushy water-skiing gig would take her mind off having seen her weird father. There was little art involved in the act of being towed around in a half-acre pond by a 9-foot, 25-horsepower sports boat going less than 15 miles an hour. But there was a technique that had to be followed. Though she may have bobbled few of her acts, she had not fallen as Barbara Hinkley, one of her co-skiers, did two weeks ago and broke her arm.

What stuck to the goo of the experience was Deborah. She seemed so self-confident and in control without having to give up her worldly class as a woman. Certainly she was more than worthy of the former Reverend Thomas Barragan from li'l ol' Hanson, Iowa. The thought of her deranged father with another woman, especially one of Deborah's stature, only led her to wish that she might have had the chance to know her mother longer.

Finally, at 6:45, she closed her hotel room door and sprinted to the phone to call Hellie. She crimped the receiver between her shoulder and ear as she began unbuttoning her shirt. The phone rang in her ear as she kicked a toe of one of her white sneakers against the heel of the other to slip it off. She then repeated the process on the other sneaker with the toes of her now bare foot. "Come on, Hellie! For shit's sake. Pick up the fucking phone!" she urged in a whisper. Finally, Hellie did. "Hellie!" Regina shouted breathlessly before Hellie could say anything.

"For iced cake, Regina!" said Hellie as Regina continued to occupy herself with wrangling off her shirt. "Where's the damn fire? You okay? I was out in the field training for a barrel competition. Jamie went'n signed me up for the damn Pottawatomie County Rodeo next month. Sheesh! I haven't rid barrels since I was seventeen, and now he's got me on this little sorrel called 'Shotzie'. Says he named her after a whore he knew when he was stationed over in Hamburg—"

"I don't shiv a git about all that right now, Hellie," Regina said as she flung her shirt on the bed. "Listen. I saw him. I fucking saw him!" "Saw who?"

"*Him*! The fuckin' Reverend fuckin' Thomas fuckin' Barragan. Your brother-in-law. My fuckin' *father*. I *saw* him!"

"Aw, hon. That's just your mind playin' tricks on you."

"No, it was him. I spoke to him, and he spoke back to me. It was fuckin' weird, I tell you. He's fuckin' weird."

Hellie met this with a hard, mounting silence. "You're sure?" "Fuckin'-A, I am. Shit!"

"So, the bastard was resurrected, after all," Hellie said in a dumb- struck whisper.

Regina chortled. "Yeah. I told him that. Well, that he was more Lazarus-like than Christ-kinda risen from the dead. More from the grave, really. Like all gross and leprosied and stuff."

"He had leprosy? Oh, hon, now I get it. You just had a realistic dream, nightmare, whatever."

"No, Hellie. Honestly. I did see him. He's dating one of our contractors. She builds ponds and swimming pools, I think. Anyway, this definitely wasn't a dream. It was a real-life fucking nightmare! Shit, Hellie. Why couldn't the bastard have just gone and died like he said he was?"

"Hoh-boy!" Hellie sighed.

Regina heard Jamie's voice in the background. "Is that Re-*geee*-na? I love you, Re-*geee*-na!"

Hellie must have cupped her hand over the receiver because her voice sounded muffled when she spoke at Jamie. "Shut up, there! We gotta *crisis* goin' on, here, cowboy!" Then her voice sounded clearer as she spoke back to Regina. "What a cowboy-jerk I married. Freekin' rodeo clown is what he is."

"What're y'all doing at your house, anyway? I thought you'd be living in his by now."

"It ain't really his. It's Flapjack's house. At least until Flapjack dies. Which oughtta be soon, 'cause he's startin' to turn. Well, in the light of what you just told me about the Incredible Reverend Barragan, I can't believe even *Flapjack's* passing'll be real."

"Oh, it's Deavers, now. He changed his name to Deavers."

"Oh, like that'll bring 'im back to life? Well, I guess it did, then. What about your inheritance? The El Dorado? You think we'll have to give it all back now he's alive?"

"No. He assured me that was all still mine. Some sort of gift. Besides. To everyone else, the guy who left me the house and the money is dead."

"What a mess! Maybe when he's done visiting that fair of yours, he'll crawl back inta whatever hole he came from. Then we can forget all about this."

Regina sat on the edge of the bed and lit a cigarette. "I'm pretty sure he lives here in New York." She shook out her match and plunked it in the bedside ashtray. "He's still a preacher. With a church. His girl- friend built it for him."

"He doesn't give up, does he? I guess dying does funny things to some people."

"I wouldn't call this fuckin' funny, Hellie." "Right. I'm not thinking too straight, now."

"Hellie. I need you to do me a favor. Can you call information in New York City and find out Reverend Thomas Deaver's number and where his church is at?"

"You got no phone books in New York City?"

"I need you to help me here, sis. I could ask his girlfriend," she cringed at the thought. "But I'm too chicken-shit. Besides he doesn't remember you."

"How do you know that? Hell n' damn! You told him about *me*? Oh well, what difference would it make that he doesn't remember me? It ain't like I'm gonna call him and reach out."

"That's what I want you to do."

"Hell, *no*, woman!"

"Hellie, listen to me. There's something creepy, about him."

"Like *I* don't know that?"

"No, really. I'm starting to think like you do. I can't help thinking there's something, like, unsettling about my mother's—Jillian's—disappearance. It's just a feeling I have, after something he said. Some- thing very spooky."

"What'd he say?"

Regina puffed on her cigarette as she tried to recall that part of their meeting. "Well, he had this way of looking at me, kind of through me, with this dead-looking stare." She paused.

"And then what?"

"Then he said something really fuckin' weird. He said: 'I created you.' He didn't mean it in a good way. Sounded almost like some sort of threat."

"Jesus H! You want me to come out there and hog-tie 'im? I mean, I hate New York City, but if you want me to—"

"I just want you to find out about him and this church of his. Just find the number, then call and find out the address. From there, we'll figure something out. For now, I'm like you. I just have this weird feeling he knows something about my mom's death he's not telling. Call it, I don't know, daughter's intuition."

"I suppose I could just tell him I'm Mrs. Jamie Robertson from Oklahoma City."

"Maybe keep Oklahoma out of it. Might make him suspicious. Tell him someplace like, Iowa. Hanson, Iowa."

"You don't think that would make him more suspicious?"

Regina snuffed out her cigarette. "It'll probably just drive him crazy enough to want to talk to you."

"No. I won't use Hanson, Iowa. I'll say I'm from Phoenix or something."

"Thanks, Hellie. In the end, this might help us both out with a little, I don't know, closure, about Jillian."

Hellie let out a loud sigh. "Okay, sure. I'll help out in any way I can. Now, Reg, hon. Just try to rest easy tonight."

She knew that after having talked with Hellie, she could rest a little easier.

It helped for Thomas to have turned his deaf ear toward the music surging from the stage of The Blue Note Café in Greenwich Village.

―――――――――――

Tonight had been amateur night, a chance for jazz hopefuls to take to the big-time stage. A cacophony of extemporaneous tenor sax notes in a loose interpretation of John Coltrane's style had been served up through the density of the din. Now he and Deborah could finally relax at her apartment in the cool, serene sanctity of her bed.

"Well, that was interesting," she said.

"I've heard some bad jazz in The Cavern, but never as bad as that," Thomas said. "It was shrill. Even my deaf ear hurts."

"Well, that, too, I suppose. But I was talking about today at the Oklahoma Pavilion." She inhaled a healthy dose of pot and then passed the glowing-tipped reefer to him. "I mean, did you and that girl, Regina, know each other?" she said. "You sure acted like it."

Thomas drew in a puff, held it, and then breathed. "No. She was just a girl. A total stranger." He handed the joint back to her.

"Kind of cute, I think. Don't you?" she asked. "Who?"

"Regina. Cute."

"If you like cute. I prefer my women a little more seasoned." She drew in a puff. "Like me?"

"Like you."

She exhaled. "So, Thomas, I'm 'seasoned,' now. Like some middle-aged harpy."

"You're not a middle-aged harpy." He touched her leg. "You're just right."

"I'm not even a little cute? Like Regina? Actually, she looks a little like you, in a way," She handed the reefer back into his loose grasp. He dropped it on the sheet. "Shit! Thomas? Watch it! You're gonna waste some perfectly good weed. You can't get this Californian stuff here."

He picked up the joint and frantically brushed off the sheet "Sorry. Let's just not talk about Regina, any more. Teenagers give me the willies."

"She isn't a teenager. Anyway, weren't you one once? A teenager?"

"I suppose. I just—put those years out of my mind." "Well, I used to be cute like that."

"You still are."

"I thought you said I was seasoned and dried up."

He inched his hand up her inner thigh to try to take his and her mind away from the subject of Regina. "You're not dried up," he breathed into her hair. "Far from it. Now let's pick up where we should have when you'd just gotten back." He kissed her on the temple near the corner of her eye.

"Oh, yeah, Thomas," she pleaded softly as she started to massage his soft, pliable scrotum. She nuzzled into him as he dropped the extinguished joint into the ashtray between them. "I've been holding myself up down there since before I left." She then huffed a soft smile. "Well, I wasn't a totally good girl out there, but I tried. For our sake."

"Okay, Deborah." He helped her to roll over on her back. "I'm ready now." He eased himself on top of her, then slowly in, then out, then in. He clenched his teeth as he cruelly thrust and parried the weight of his weapon into the moistening, responsive sheath between her legs. Her desperate moans shrilled into primal cries of pleasure mixed with pain. Their loss of breath roughened into frantic gasps. He would have done just about anything to take is mind away from having seen his daughter. Even this.

Part 4

July 1964 – October 1964

Chamelea

Chapter 38

Going into battle

Cohansen huddled like a paunchy beaver over his Jim Beam while he waited for Nealy to show up at The Back Page. He thought of the weight he had put on as he tried to adjust his body to relieve the binding of his shoulder holster through his shirt. He had not felt that chafe about a month before and the two killings on the Upper West Side. He ordered another bourbon as a backup for the one he had half-finished, and then lit up a Pall Mall.

He glanced at his watch again—10:35 already, and then 10:40. Nealy was almost 40 minutes overdue. It had become increasingly com- mon for Nealy to run on a different clock since he had made Francesca the center of his life. Cohansen had called his ex-partner three hours before and mentioned little except to say the coroner and blood work reports were in and to meet him here. The lab results had been held up for almost a month by a paperwork snafu, followed by a water pipe break that closed the research area for a week. So much for scientific forensics, but at least this abnormality allowed Cohansen to keep the cases open as homicides.

The detailed reports confirmed some commonalities in the two deaths that pointed at what he had begrudgingly come to know in his gut—that the two women's deaths were homicides committed by the same perpetrator. Though someone dressed as a priest was still part of the equation, Gwen Perkins' 82-year-old priest at The

Church of the Assumption had been immediately ruled out as being too feeble.

In addition to the physical evidence Cohansen and Nealy had come up with, the lab's blood analysis showed traces of marijuana and lysergic acid diethylamide—LSD—in both victim's systems. There had also been a trace of LSD in the communion wafer pieces Nealy had found in Gwen's apartment. Then there was the damning evidence of the prints on the two lipstick containers. They matched, yet were un- traceable. Cohansen led his team back to both scenes for a thorough dusting and found some of the same prints on both apartments' coffee tables, bathroom sink fixtures, a sherry glass and the tub's edges in Gwen's apartment.

He glanced up from his drink at the grime-smudged screen of little black and white television above the mirrored horizon of bottles be- hind the bar. It was a bad day for New York City sports. Through the misty murk of static flittering out in all directions on the screen. The hapless Mets had losing 3-4 against the San Francisco Giants at the top of the 9th inning.

Finally, Nealy's voice sounded over his hunched shoulders. "Who's winning?"

"Don't ask," Cohansen said into his drink. "You're late."

"I was on the phone with Frannie's sister about the wedding."

Cohansen glanced at him. "Sounds unmanly of you, Ray. I thought the dames were s'posed to take care of all that wedding crap."

Nealy sat in the adjoining stool. "Ah, so." He lit up one of his little cigars. "I'll have a ginger ale, Fred," he called to the bartender.

"Jesus wept!" Cohansen blathered. "*Ginger ale*, now? Not even a belt of Scotch? What's come over you?"

"Frannie's orders. No drinking after dinner."

"Jesus, Ray! She's already got her hooks in ya. I'm beginnin' to think you ain't gonna be no fun, anymore."

"She wants me fit and sober for when I meet her family in a few weeks. No more plundering and pillaging until after the wedding."

"Ya know, Ray? What 'chure goin' through's divided into two parts: The Wedding, where everything is bluebirds an' unicorns; an' then the rest of it—all those years of marriage, where it ain't so much. But I guess I don't need to tell you that."

"Guess not," Nealy said as Fred placed a ginger ale before him. He took a sip. "So, Marty. What did the reports say?" Cohansen heaved a bulky sigh. "Pretty much what we been thinkin' all along. Two homicides; same perp." He sipped the remains of his first drink.

"Shit. So it's a serial."

"I hate these fucking situations," Cohansen said after a follow-through of his gulp. "But, yeah. Looks like it might be. The prints on the two different lipsticks are a match. And get this. The tox report says there was LSD in both blood samples, and in them wafers you found. And some pot in both their systems."

"Jesus. There's an unexpected twist!"

"No shit, Ray. And we dusted both apartments. Found the same prints on the Perkins sink and tub fixtures, and on the sliding porch door handle of the Harper balcony. Couldn't find a print match on any records we had. We'll be sending the prints to the Feds tomorrow."

"At least you're covering the bases."

The ball game ended in the Met tragedy it was bound to become. Fred switched the channel to the late national news, which preempted the regular local news in preparation for an impromptu Presidential address. A small crowd, featuring The New York Knickerbocker's editorial crew of irregulars, had begun to gather behind them. Nealy brushed away the stale odor from Frank

Malone's cigar, which had invaded his space from behind.

"I need you on this, Ray, as a consultant. 'cause I don't think my regular guy, Jake Barnaby, has the chops for something like this."

"I'll help if I can, Marty. But I'm kind of busy right now. I can say that, because I'm not married to the force anymore." He swept away another waft of cigar smoke. "Jesus. What is that shit Malone is smoking over there?"

"Like you just said, Ray—shit. Anyway, you're about to be married in a worser kinda way that's bad for business. At least Frannie's been in the soup with you for this sort of work. So, since you asked, I'll pay you that time-and-a-half you wanted, and double for the day you al- ready gave me. You and me got more done in them few hours than my knuckleheads coulda figgured out in a week."

"Quiet in front!" Malone bellowed wetly around the stogie in his mouth. "Fred! Turn up the TV! We're pro'lly goin' ta war with them commie jungle gooks!"

Nealy leaned into Cohansen. "There goes Frank Malone, starting up his rumors, again."

"Jus' workin' his usual beat of rumor and innuendo." Nealy sipped his ginger ale. "You know? Maybe we should try to draw him out," he said.

"Who? Malone? That shouldn't be too hard."

Nealy then lit one of his cigars to counter the stench of Malone's. "I was meaning our perp. I may have a way. Let me think a little." Cohansen brightened. "You'll ride shotgun with me on this, then?"

"Thinkin' about it, Marty. For time and a half. All those wedding petit-fours can be expensive."

"Jeezzus! Now you gotta buy *underwear* for the broads?" Cohansen smiled sullenly into his drink. "Ya know, Ray. I really wish you'd come back into the game at the Two-Oh. You'd be getting a regular paycheck like the family man in suburbia you're about to become."

"Who'd never see his family," Nealy grumbled. "Marty, I already told you. It wouldn't fit right on me anymore."

Cohansen raised his voice. "Damn it, buddy! And I tolt you already. You was cleared. Com-pol-*leet*-ly. Cleared."

"Keep it down, you two freakin' gumshoes!" Malone groused. "We gotta watch all this what's happenin' here on the TV!"

Cohansen showed him his middle finger. "Rotate on this, newsie!" "Back at you, Marty!" Malone said respectfully.

"I'd feel totally un-right about coming back in, Marty," Nealy said.

"I shot that fifteen-year-old unarmed kid, and I was drunk."

"You only winged him. They fixed what you did to that kid before they sent him to jouvie for B and E, where he was taught to live a life of street crime, and has, for a long time, been back out. Anyway there's this: A. The kid was armed. He had a knife aimed at you."

"A pocket jack-knife."

"A *knife*," Cohansen said. "And, B. You weren't freakin' drunk. Your tox report showed you was under the limit."

"By a tenth of a point. I'd just split with Alice. I wasn't thinking straight."

"I.A.D. cleared you, Ray."

"Still, Marty. I think I'd be better for you here in the private sector. That way I can work outside the department."

Cohansen sipped his fresh drink, then tamped out his cigarette in the tin ashtray on the bar. "I suppose you got me there, buddy. Fuckin' paperwork. It's all become fuckin' paperwork. And fuzzy science. Anyway, Ray, you know the door's always open."

"To be considered. That aside, I might have an idea to draw our guy out, but it's gotta be on my terms. We can and should work together on this. You can collar the guy and pick up the bones if my idea works."

"I'm listening, Ray. What's your idea?"

"It's in my head, so I'm not fully clear on what it is yet."
"Damnit, Ray! Will ya stop leadin' me on like this?"

"Shaddup, will ya? Listen to the TV!" Malone said.

The crowd around the bar quieted as Walter Cronkite began his report. As it had come down from the White House, the tension in Southeast Asia had become more threatening with the news that two days before, three North Vietnamese swift boats had fired torpedoes at the *USS Maddox*, a surveillance destroyer they claimed was operating within the murkily defined territorial waters of the Tonkin Gulf. Two torpedoes missed their mark, and the third, which struck the *Maddox*, was a dud.

Today, the *Maddox*, and an accompanying destroyer, USS *Turner Joy*, had been ordered by the President to fire back upon any further aggressions from the North Vietnamese Russian-supplied gun boats, regardless of territorial water. And that happened. Late at night the U.S. destroyers fired back at a cluster of radar blips they had assumed to be advancing swift boats in the storm-chopped Tonkin Gulf. It was the opening salvo that transformed the South Asian conflict into what could become the Vietnam War.

"Now begins the shit," Cohansen said.

"Well, they fired first," Nealy said.

The whole topic of who drew first reminded Nealy again of why he chose to leave the force. The vision of the cornered kid's terrified expression coalescing from a corner in the gloom of midnight had plagued Nealy ever since. Fact was, Nealy was drunk and depressed over his divorce, and the 15-year-old kid, scared enough by the sight of his gun drew his jackknife. He probably had a family who cared about him enough to try to shelter him from a life on the mean streets—a losing battle in the South Bronx.

The remembrance prompted him to look over at Frank Malone, who had originally broken the story as another example of unjustified police reaction. He never named Nealy as the shooter, perhaps to call in a favor someday. *Malone, you fucking ambulance-chasing bastard!* Nealy thought. It angered him enough to consider ordering a Scotch. Frank Malone—Frank Malone—Frank—Malone! Nealy thought as his mood shifted from resentment to a thin epiphany. He looked over at Cohansen.

Nealy's look was not lost on his former partner. "What, Ray? What? I see them little wheels turning in your head. A very good sign."

Nealy paused in thought. "Frank Malone."

"Okay. Frank Malone. He's an asshole. So what?"

"He may be an asshole, Marty, but he could be our ticket to the killer."

"Th' fuck ya talkin' about, buddy?"

"What if *he* broke the story about these two homicides?"

"I don't like it. But it pro'lly wouldn't do much. A: No one reads that rag o' his, anyways. And, B: He ain't credible, and, oh yeah. C: He's an asshole."

"You already said that." "Beared repeatin'."

"Marty, hear me out. What's the main motivator for a person to go out and kill someone?"

"I'll give ya three," He ticked off the three points on his stubby fingers. "A: Jealousy. B: Rage. And C: Greed."

"How about when he kills more than one, and they're not related, like the Perkins and Harper killings? Let's assume for now they were strangers to our guy." Nealy looked at Cohansen's dumbfounded ex- pression as he waited for him to continue. "Okay,

Marty. Our guy is either a sloppy amateur or—" he paused.

"What's the punch line, Ray?"

"He leaves all the clues behind because he wants us to find him."

"Like, what? He's got serious head issues goin' on and he wants us to take 'im down? To take 'im away from his demons?"

"Maybe. Or maybe more likely he's needy and craves recognition. It's worth a shot."

Cohansen looked up at the Mr. Clean commercial on the television as he tried to piece together what Nealy had planned. "Okay, lemme see if I got this straight, Ray," he said. "You mention Asshole Malone along with a killer needin' to be recognized in the same thought, like you're stringin' them two things together. So my guess is you want us to break the story to Frank Malone and risk a panic about a serial killer bein' loose in my precinct."

"Well, don't you think the women in the Upper West Side need to know this, so they can protect themselves? Lock up their apartments and be vigilant? I mean, Marty, this is all gonna get out eventually. If the truth about these homicides comes from any other source than the Two-Oh, and my working on it with your blessing through Malone's paper, it'll look like you're not on top of it—we're not on top of it. Malone can be the mouthpiece, and it might irritate the killer enough to state his case."

"It's a long shot, Ray, and it ain't our job to control the news like that. You know we can't go around leakin' stories."

"Even if it can draw our guy out?"

"To what? Do more killings? Anyway, it'll just scare the hell out of everyone. They'll lock themselves up in their apartments. Look at that Kitty Genovese killin' out in Kew Gardens last March."

"That was different, Marty. No one wanted to get involved with helping her. That was a singular killing, and that guy, Moseley, is going up for life. That was a case of neighborhood apathy. Ours could be one of neighborhood concern."

"Yeah. But out in the world it made New York look like a crime center. So much so that none of our citizens cared. I don't want that kinda press spreading about my precinct, or any precinct in this town." "But, Marty, this is happening now, bad press or not. Listen. Maybe you don't want to break the story. But I can, because I'm a professional acting privately, so here's an example of where I can help you out from where I am. Nothing will stain you guys, at least for now. Let me talk to Malone."

"Lemme think on it," Cohansen said, then answered, "Okay. But I don't know nothin' about you telling Malone. Okay?"

Nealy took another sip of his drink.

"O-*kay*, Ray?"

Nealy aimed a gloating glance behind him at Malone. "Okay. Thanks, Marty."

"Okay, then, Ray," Cohansen said. "Now. This ain't a bribe or nothin' 'cause you owe me from the Knicks game last March, but because I'm letting you do this off the record, I just wanna remind you the Yanks are playing the BoSox next week."

"I'll see what I can do."

"Baseline seats?"

"Jeezus, Marty! You don't ask for much, do you?"

"Thanks, Ray. Anyway, I don't know nothin' except right now the President's on TV. He looks like shit, as usual. He always looks hungover, or something."

President Lyndon Johnson looked as if he hadn't slept in a month, pouched and drawn. The darkened bags beneath his eyes, accentuated under the harsh TV lighting as it shadowed and glinted his thick eyeglasses, emphasized his hound-dog sadness. He looked the opposite of that of his vigorous predecessor. "My fellow

Americans," he drawled tiredly, "as President and Commander-in-Chief, it is my duty to the American people to report that renewed hostile actions against United States ships on the high seas in the Gulf of Tonkin have today required me to order the military forces of the United States to take action in reply..."

Nealy took a pull on the remains of his ginger ale and slapped his glass down on the bar to signify he wanted a Scotch. "The hell with the eating part. Drink and be merry, for tomorrow we go to war."

Chapter 39

Fabricated truths

Slimmed down for his wedding and dressed smartly as if for vacation in a white sport shirt and khaki pants, Nealy drank a club soda and smoked his little cigar as he told "Stogie" Frank Malone what Cohansen had officially warned him not to leak out.

Nealy spoke with a guarded candor to the itchy reporter, who seemed to repress a perpetual urge to drool as he sat in Nealy's favorite old couch now placed, at Francesca's insistence, in the middle of the room across from his desk. He told Malone he was speaking unofficially as a private detective under good authority, and to keep the incident of their talk under wraps from Marty Cohansen and his precinct, no matter how drunk he might get at The Back Page. "Agreed?"

"Okay, agreed," Malone said.

Nealy told him about how the two unrelated female suicides in the Upper West Side within 12 blocks of one another had been linked as homicides. There were matching third-party prints found at both scenes, along with the unifying scent of lilacs, a fragrance which neither victim had in their perfume collections. He also told Malone about the traces of LSD found in their blood, and that there was nothing psychologically or socially pointing to their use of the drug. Nealy mentioned that one of the victims, the Harper woman, was seen arriving at her apartment on the night of her death with a man carrying a knapsack who was a priest, or at least dressed like one. A Communion wafer, laced with LSD, had been found on the floor of the Perkins woman's apartment, so there might be a connection there. Finally, Nealy told Malone to mention the fact that police were homing in on the presumed killer, who had been sloppy and left prints everywhere.

"Why are you telling me all this, Ray?" Malone asked over his notes, as a fat, two-inch ash tumbled harmlessly from his cigar to his lap. It added to the mess of older fallen and forgotten ashes on his pant legs. "I mean, if Marty Cohansen wants this on the Q-T? I thought you two were, like, tight. You know, working together."

"Let's just say that Marty and I had a difference of opinion, and I think the story should get out and—," he bit his lower lip to hold back the thought of how Malone was such an annoyance to him. "You should be the one to do it, Frank. Your story could be a bridge of in- formation to keep New Yorkers vigilant, especially in the Upper West Side." He took a swallow of his club soda. "One thing we don't want, though, is a panic. You'll treat this information with, uh, discretion. We really are close to finding this guy, and you can help us here, if you handle it right."

"You know I will, Ray," said Malone with detached confidence as he closed his notebook.

"I know you will, Frank," said Nealy, as his conscience grew wracked with doubt. "And one more thing. Whatever you do, don't mention my name. Yet."

"I get it."

Francesca came into the office glistening in perspiration and dressed in her running outfit after having taken her morning jog along the East River. "Phew!" she heaved through a breath, as she patted her running towel against her face. "Six miles today. In this heat." She looked up and noticed Malone. "Oh, hi, Frank. What brings you here?" "Nuthin', Frannie." He glanced over at her as he stood up from the couch and sent a shower of ash drifting down to the rug. "Followin' up on a dead end. I was jus' leavin'."

"He was just leaving," Nealy confirmed as he glared back at Malone leering at Francesca's legs, then at her breasts unencumbered by a bra. They jounced stoutly in time with her steps as she went to the new little office refrigerator for some water.

"I was just—leaving," he repeated as he walked to the opened door. "Oh yeah. And congrats, you two. I heard the news. You want I should supply Nickie as your photographer?"

Along with his reporting, "Double-Talking" Nick Pesipio moonlighted as a Knickerbocker crime photographer, and the thought of him covering her wedding had registered a welling freeze through Francesca's nerves. "Thanks anyway, Frank. But no."

"You sure? The guy's a regular Weegie."

That was the problem. "S'okay, Frank," Francesca reassured him. "We got my cousin, Danny Flannigan, taking pictures. He does weddings for a living."

"An Irish guy your cousin? I thought you was somehow I-talian."

"What can I say?" she said with a shrug and the tweak of a smile. "Mixed marriages."

"Okay, then. Congrats all the same," Malone said loudly as he left.

"What was he doing here, Raymond?"

"Taking part in a well-organized plan," Nealy said. "I hope."

***

Milio hunched over Thomas's desk in Heaven's Doorway to concentrate on the pictures in the sports section of The Daily News. Because of his various mental compromises, he did not read the words as much as peruse the pages for one of the few he could read: "Yankees." It was a difficult task for him and required most of his concentration until he was jolted away by the abrupt ring of the desk phone. His telephone manner was decidedly non-existent, and this sent him into a minor panic, and he was the only one in the church this morning.

The phone rang again. He stared at it as if it were a monster ready to pounce. It rang again. The phone metamorphosed before his eyes into a trembling, hairy little devil. It screamed at him again as it sprouted the quills of a porcupine, and then bristled as it leveled him in its sights. "Inna gonna be disapperito, little demonarino!" he muttered in a threat. Another scream from the monster. He stepped back, ready to defend himself. The devil's beady yellow eyes glinted over an intimidating Cheshire cat grin blooming on its face where there had once been a dial. The monster roared again, preparing to gobble him up. "*Licuit vobis nothus! Non comedetis es* me!" he said to the little black demon with its grating scream. He was not going to let it eat him. He swiped the new Yankees cap Thomas had brought him off his head and began to gnaw on the brim. The demon monster confronted Milio's defiance with another banshee's screech. "Ah! Shitata-cacca!" He said and reached frantically for the receiver to grasp the top of the head from the spiny little black demon. "AH-LOW?! AH-LOW?!" he shouted into its ear. "Ya canno eatrata me up! I eatrato you firstio!"

"Hello?" came a perplexed, hardened, female voice from the other end. "Who—is this?"

"*Meum nomen est Milio*," he proudly announced. "I seen da warrino and fight enta Europea in worl' warrino two, twenty year ago. I seen blood."

The voice on the other end didn't seem to care. It came equipped with a distinctly western drawl. "Is, uh, Reverend Thomas Deavers there, please?"

Milio didn't know who Reverend Thomas Deavers was; the

only reverend he knew was the preacher man. "Me no knowen Tomato Deavernsio. *Homo solus est praedicator.*"

As he said this, Francis lumbered through the front door busying himself over the manipulation of the three grocery bags he carried. He had never seen Milio on the phone before and shot him a perplexed glance. "What? Wha-dya say?" the agitated voice on the other end said. Milio said nothing as he thrust the demon's decapitated head toward Francis, happy to be rid of it. The curate placed the bags on the floor and took the receiver to hear the drawled voice saying: "Ah have no friggin' idea what 'chure sayin'! Speak American English!"

Francis sighed toward Milio. "Hello. This is the Heaven's Doorway church. How can I help you?"

"Well, praise the Lord and pass the ammunition! A voice ah kin understand."

"Sorry, miss. Our, uh, secretary is still learning to speak English. So, can I help you?"

"Yes, please. Is this Reverend Thomas Deavers?"

"No. I'm the curate here; Reverend Deavers is out on a call. Can I take a message?"

"Uh, sure. Ah guess. Mah name is Helen Robertson from Phoenix?" Hellie said in a tone muzzled in uneasiness. "Mah husban' an' me is comin' out to New York City from heah in Phoenix, in Arizona? We're looking for a church to do our Sunday worship in, an' we came across yer all's Heaven's Doorway."

"Yes?" Francis said during Hellie's pause.

"Well, we'd lahke to know where y'all're located."

Francis wondered why a couple of western state God-fearing Christians might take an interest in Heaven's Doorway down in this dystopia of the Lower East Side. "Are you sure you mean this church?"

"Absolutely. We think we'll be staying around where y'all are, and we just wanted ta be sure. Ah jus' need yer all's address, is all."

"Okay, Mrs. Richardson—"

"Robertson."

"Robertson. We're at twenty-one Front Street, just off Pearl Street in the Lower East Side. I guess you'll be driving. You'll be driving, right?"

"Whah, yea-as."

"So, you'll probably be driving south on the FDR. Best you take the Manhattan Bridge exit, then your first immediate left."

The instructions were something of a muddle for Hellie to under- stand. "Hold a minute while ah wraht all this down. The Heaven's Doorway Church, twenty-one Front Street, near Pearl. Manhattan Bridge exit of the F.R.D.—"

"FDR Expressway," he corrected. "And it's just called 'Heaven's Doorway', not "The Heaven's Doorway Church.'"

"Heaven's Doorway. Thanks, y'all been very hepful, Mr—"

"Oh, my name is Francis."

"Thanks, Francis." She paused again as she gathered her thoughts.

Her voice tightened. "There's one more little thang, if y'all don't mind."

"Okay."

She sighed uneasily. "Could y'all leave a message for Reverend Deavers that Jillian's sister, Hellie Laine, called?"

"Jillian's sister, Hellie Laine," Francis repeated as he found a pencil and wrote it down.

"Ye-as. Ah think ah might have met him once."

"Okay, I'll give him the message. Where can Reverend Deavers reach you if he wants to call you back?"

" 'preciate it, Francis. Good-bye." She quickly hung up.

Francis held out the receiver and glared at it as if it had offended him. Then he turned and saw Milio staring at him from where he had skulked away into a corner. He was wide-eyed and ashen in fear as Francis held the top of the head of the trembling little black demon in his hand. "What?" Francis said.

"Puddit don, now! Before it eaten you away!" Milio warned him.

"What the hell you talking about, Milio?" he snarled as he put the receiver back in the cradle and Milio relaxed. He motioned toward the grocery bags in the hallway. "Now come on and help me put up these groceries in the kitchen."

Murder Spree in the Upper West Side?

By Frank Malone
Senior Editor, The New York Knickerbocker

New York City —August 9, 1964
What originally appeared to be two suicides occurring nearly a week apart on June 24th and 29th are now being looked at as homicides. Zina Harper and Gwen Perkins, both residents of the Upper West Side, and living twelve blocks apart, had been thought to have taken their own lives when their bodies were first discovered. Miss Harper, 24, appeared to have jumped more than 20 floors from her balcony on West 66th, near the new Lincoln Center Project. Miss Perkins, 47, was found dead in her apartment bathtub on West 79th after having slashed her wrist.

Though the police originally classified both deaths as suicides, further evidence has linked them together as homicides. Toxicology reports showed both victims to have had small amounts of LSD in their systems. Both apartments, even days later, still smelled like lilacs, and neither victim had lilac fragrance in their perfume collections. Also, our alleged "Lilac Killer," described by my source as being careless and sloppy, may have been disguised as a priest. The doorman in Miss Harper's building noticed she had arrived with a priest the night of her death. In addition, what appears to be a communion wafer soaked in LSD was found on the floor of Miss Perkins's apartment. This also suggests some sort of religious connection in the killings. In neither occurrence was a suicide note left behind.

My reliable source, with strong connections to the NYPD, has chosen this reporter as the spokesman for these diabolical killings disguised as suicides. He advised me to advise you, my readers, not to panic, but to be vigilant, especially in the Upper West Side, and to report any suspicious doings which may involve a man of medium height and stocky build. He may be dressed as a priest and carrying a knapsack.

Considering last March's Kitty Genovese killing in Queens, we fellow New Yorkers all need to be aware and look after our fellow citizens.

My source has assured me the police are already closing in on a suspect. So, take care of yourselves, my fellow compradors, and if you see anything suspicious regarding these heinous doings, report what you see to the cops at the 20th Precinct, or to yours truly.

Thomas's god sat next to him on the two steps leading to the altar in the chapel of Heaven's Doorway. He was puffing on a joint. Though it was before noon, Thomas was anguished enough to have taken two LSD wafers, one after the other, so his god appeared to him in extreme clarity, except for the usual undulating red-to-rust-colored vapor of his face and hands.

"You really mixed me upside and down on this one," Thomas rebuked him.

"Me?" his god said as he brought a misty hand to the area of his heart. "I gave you free will when I created you, Brother Thomas. The consequences of your actions are entirely on you."

"This isn't about my actions this time. This is more of a— situation. A ghost from my past."

"Meaning?"

"A message I found on my desk that my deceased wife's sister called. She wanted to know where Heaven's Doorway was."

"So?"

"You know 'So.'" Thomas felt a euphoric surge from deep within. "Yes I do. You watched your wife drown to begin your journey toward a bonding and understanding between us—a covenant." He took another deep puff on the joint and a vapor of bright blue swirled green into the red-orange of his face. "A momentous epiphany in my book," He took another puff on his reefer and held it off to the side as if to admire it. "Ya gotta love this California stuff," he croaked, then exhaled a puff in the colors of a sunset.

"Well, I don't know what to do. All I have is her name from back then—Hellie Laine."

"Simple answer. She said nothing, so do nothing back." His god rose and misted over to stand behind the pulpit. "So, this is the view from your Sunday Throne. Not as impressive as mine, but my room rates are higher."

"No doubt," Thomas brooded.

"Anyway, Brother Thomas, we've got bigger Friday fish to fry. Did you see yesterday's New York Knickerbocker?"

Thomas slumped deeper into his LSD trip, as it was starting to become uncharacteristically bland. "I did. Just more of the same. It disgusted me, so I threw it away."

"Well," his god said, "You should find it and read it again. It appears as though a reporter named Mr. Editor Frank Malone has divulged your two uptown liberations as murders."

Thomas had nearly forgotten he'd read that article. It hadn't seemed to register with him, as he'd been under the influence when he read it. His LSD euphoria dissipated by degrees as he shot upright. He stood to face his fading god. "Shit!!" he said from a sudden fright.

"Now, calm down, Brother Thomas. We can deal with this as an opportunity."

"How?"

"Go on back up there and liberate another young woman's soul."

"Are you kidding?"

"I'm serious, because god doesn't kid. You, sir, are no killer. We both know that. You're acting more as a savior for those you service to enhance your soul to save yourself in my name."

"I'm not any sort of murderer."

"Of course you're not," his god said again through another inhale. Then he added in a strained voice, "You're a Liberator of Souls." He exhaled.

Thomas nervously reached into his pants pocket for another wafer and popped it into his mouth.

"It's your calling," his god said. "You need to be known for that."

Thomas closed his eyes as he allowed the acid to take effect as he slipped back into a mild euphoria and watched his god's image solidify before him. God's face and hands remained as swirling vapors. This time, though, as he opened his eyes he noticed his god had now metamorphosed from his original garb of a green gabardine shirt, blue jeans and the Yankee ball cap, into wearing a commandingly impressive gleaming white robe. His long white hair and beard flowed from the now crystallized, glowing red-orange mist of his features like pennants propelled by a wind Thomas did not feel. He fell to his knees, and then was overcome with a need to genuflect in supplication before his god and master. The carpet into which he spoke muffled his voice. "What shall I do?"

"What you're best at, Brother Thomas," his god's voice boomed and echoed authoritatively. "Liberation. And I'll provide you with another soul, like the last time. Just follow the breadth of my instinct within you."

Thomas felt a warmth drape around him like one of Mother's plushy hugs. It made him feel secure.

"This time, Brother Thomas, you'll leave a note behind. You will write what I command of you from within. I will guide your hand." God's tone now slipped into a casually conversational one. "And this time—"

Still supine, Thomas waited for his god to finish his thought. It would undoubtedly be a pearl of wisdom, as only a god can provide. "Yes, Father?"

"Don't be so damn sloppy around these liberations. For my sake, man, clean up after yourself!"

Thomas gradually raised his head from the carpet and saw that his god was gone, but had left his Yankee ball cap behind on the lectern of the pulpit.

Chapter 40

Trouble in the Pit

Patti Nolan had been working slavishly in the bullpen of McAllister & Freidman Ad Agency's art department for nearly 5 years. The creative work she did should have been an inspiration, but instead had become a grudging ordeal, especially under the iron control of Ron Ansler, the Pit Boss. The agency had been known for promoting artists of talent to assistant or even full art directorships, where, working with a team of copywriters, creative ideas sprung from their heads like that of Athena from Zeus's. It was pure alchemy in a day of a new dawning in commercial advertising where less was more, and less was hard to come by except through the most creative instincts. As good as the emerging talents were, some agencies recruited promising prodigies right out of New York City's high schools of art before college could dull their young minds. Patti had been one of these exceptional children of talent, and after over four years at M&F, she might have been allowed to exhibit more of her creativity if only Ron had not kept her so entrenched in the bullpen.

Last week, he had gone so far as to steal one of her unique ideas as his own. It was not the first time he had done this, but enough was enough. This morning she finally went to M&F's Creative Director and openly challenged Ron's motives. Now it became a question of her word against his. She knew she was beaten and would probably be fired, as the customary policy of M&F was to own the work, including the rejects, of those creatives they fired. If she was fired, Patti feared she would have nothing to show for all the years she was there. Hers was just another case of a losing battle of politics over ethics, as was so common a case in the ad agency world.

Around Amsterdam Avenue and 96th Street, there was an eclectic mix of news stores, Italian delis, and laundromats. There were also a few bars. Patti's neighborhood was a sleepy district populated largely by moderately poor and ambiguously-starving Columbia University students. Patti did not look as young as she was, and even through the leftover plumpness of her adolescence as she assumed the slender lines of young womanhood. She wore her short, sassy, blonde hair just below her ears like a cap molded loosely to her head. Her features be- trayed an innocence through a certain kind of sassy, sly coyness as her sincere smile set a twinkle to her dark, innocent, wide-set eyes. Life in New York City had made her street smart, and she had learned to rely almost too often upon her control over her naïve instincts.

Tonight, here in MacMillan's Bijou, the moist, beery smells and din and chatter of the university students' voices rose above the heavy chinking of beer mugs and talk of ongoing summer finals. Patti sat apart from the gush of student spirit, hating Ron and hoping for a man's comfort to relieve her despair. She was only halfway through her first rye and ginger when this hope may have been satisfied.

She heard a confident male voice rise from the misty darkness over her shoulder. "Anyone parked here?" She turned to face a stout, well- built, prematurely gray-haired man with thin, yet pronounced features. Not bad, she congratulated herself as she innocently wondered, even in the murky camouflage of this darkness, how their children might look. It was a kind of game she played with herself to qualify the quality of her choice in men. "I mean," he said, "if someone's sitting here, I can just—" he waved his hand back toward the distant college kids.

"No. It's fine. You can sit here," she told him.

He smiled wryly. "Thanks." He placed his rucksack on the floor and sat on the stool next to hers. "I haven't seen you here before. I mean, it's not that I come here every night, or anything. It's just—." He shrugged his shoulders.

"I don't come here a lot either. I'm usually working late at the agency. I, uh, I'm an advertising art director."

"Really!"

She shot a demure glance over her shoulder. "Yeah, really." She smiled blithely and then chuckled.

"Now that's exciting stuff! Do you do any famous advertisements? Like for cars, cigarettes—anything I might have seen? So, I can say 'I talked to the person who did this'?"

Her smile faded. "Well, no. But I might. Someday I might, really soon."

"I'm sure you will. I'm Jacob, by the way. Can I buy you a drink?"

She held up her glass and smiled. "Halfway."

"Fine, then I'll back you up with another. What are you drinking?"

"Seven and Seven," she said to the bartender as she inclined her head toward the man who had introduced himself as Jacob. "He's paying."

The bartender nodded and went to make her a drink.

"What's your name? I like to know who I'm buying drinks for."

She faltered for a moment. She'd been told never to give her name out to strangers, especially in the light of the faint rumors of the "Lilac Killer" fluttering around the Upper West Side. She considered this man and then rendered him harmless as she sipped her drink. "Patti. Patti Nolan."

"Patti Nolan sounds like a nice substantial name for a nice, substantial person." He leaned closer to her as the bartender placed her drink on the bar. "Pardon me for being so casual, Patti, but I couldn't help noticing you looked a little down when I came in. You want to talk about it? I mean, I've heard that if you can talk about what's bothering you to a trusted stranger, it's a good thing. And you can trust me."

He measured out his words as though he were trying to stick to a script. She detected a trace of an Irish brogue in his tone. "I'm not down," she said.

"I'm really good at reading these things. Come on, you can tell old Doctor Jake." He offered a thin smile.

"It's not important. Something at work. I'll get over it."

"You sure?"

"Well—yeah. I guess."

"Come on, Patti. You really can tell me."

She sighed, realizing he might be right. "It's just that—well, I work for this guy. So do a lot of other people who want to be art directors—"

"So, then you're not really an art director—"

"Oh, no. I am—almost. You see, Jack—"

"Jake," he said through a quick smile. "Actually, it's Jacob"

"Yeah. Jacob." She picked up her second drink as he settled in to listen. "Anyway, where I work is in the Art Department bullpen. Every agency has one. We call it the 'Pit.' It's like some sort of creative sweatshop, and this guy who runs it is a real tyrant and isn't letting anyone advance. Well almost anyone. Lauri, she's a fat tub with B.O. He sent her away to work as an assistant for an art director who does transmission oil ads. Then there was Felicia, but we all think she slept with him. She was advanced to high-end cosmetics. And of course the guys, he always advances the guys; they're sort of like all in the same club. But the rest of us, unless we sleep with him." She sipped her drink and noticed he didn't flinch when she mentioned about other girls sleeping with the pit boss. Maybe this person really did care enough to listen. She felt better already. "Uh, we girls don't get advanced no matter how creative we are, and I think I'm pretty creative."

"I'm sure you are," he said. "I can tell by looking at you."

"Really? You can tell that just by —?"

"Looking. Right. There's a thing about creative people, some sort of aura. Anyway, go on. This is interesting."

"Well, I—oh, yeah. Late last week, on Thursday, this guy, my boss, Ron, stole one of my ideas and put his name on it."

"Oh, no."

"Yes, Jake, he did." "'Jacob.'"

"Jacob. I've said enough. I'll get over this."

"Oh, no, Patti, you won't," he disagreed with mild emphasis as he sipped his drink. She noticed he sipped demurely, almost as a woman might. "What you want to do is stuff all your emotions about this and make it go away. But, honestly, Patti, that doesn't happen. No. The feeling just grows and festers. You may end up lashing out at him and there goes your job—your career."

"I know. It happens, and I'm stuck in it now. This time I complained to the head guy, the Creative Director of the department."

"You can't really stop it. It's Kismet. Fate."

Though she knew this to be true, hearing it from someone else triggered a flow of panic. "No way to stop it? Not at all?"

He quickly smiled. "The way I see it; you've got a legitimate depression on your hands. And it can only get worse. You may end up losing your job—and your credibility. Is there any other job you can do? Maybe accounting or something? Other skills, you know, because, Patti, you're in deep trouble here."

"I can't believe this!" she pouted, her eyes glistening. "I love what do! I don't want to learn anything else."

Thomas, traveling tonight as Jacob, took a hard look at her. He assessed whether she was becoming ready and conjured up an easy smile to win her confidence. "I may be able to help you."

"How?" she asked suspiciously as a fear over Jacob began to set in.

"You have to trust me."

She smiled uncertainly. "I don't think I—."

"I know how to hypnotize people. I could hypnotize the fear out of you, but maybe not the depression. I'll do it for you as a favor, Patti, because I care, and I'm concerned about your problem."

"I don't know. How do I know you won't make me act like a chicken, or something?"

"Now why would I want to do that, Patti? I think you're very pretty just the way you are. Anyway, I get that question a lot. No chickens or anything foolish. That's not my game." Thomas had taken a wafer of LSD just before he stepped into the bar, and his god had begun to materialize in his mind's eye. His god was dressed like the Monopoly Man as if he was out slumming in the Upper West Side in a top hat and tails. He had a monocle set in his gaseous blue face. "I just want to help people in need. And here I think I can really help you. I feel fate has introduced us here with a higher purpose in mind."

"Kismet," she said. He nodded. "Kismet."

She considered his proposition. "I don't know."

"You want to get promoted, don't you? To be the youngest art director at —? Where did you say you worked?"

"McAllister and Freidman."

"I've heard of that agency," he lied. "They're big! Now it would be a real feather in your cap to overcome this fear of yours and get promoted. What do you say, Patti? I've done this before—helped lots of people."

She slowly shook her head as she pondered a little further. "Okay.

I'll try it."

"Good!" he brightened. "Do you live around here?"

"Yes, but can't we go to—? I mean, don't you have an office or something where you do this?"

"Strictly house calls. This kind of thing has to be done where the subject is most comfortable."

"Oh, yeah. Right."

He leaned toward her. "Patti. Listen to me. You have to believe two things."

"What?"

"One: That I can help you. You have to have faith in me. And two: That, take it from Doctor Jake, you are one depressed person, whether you know it or not."

She smiled sadly down at her drink and then sipped it. "Oh, I know I'm depressed alright, and pissed off. I've never felt this badly about anything in my life."

"Good," he reassured her. "Then we're off to a good start."

Chapter 41

Order out of chaos

McAllister & Freidman paid Patti higher than scale; enough for her to afford a small, tidy first floor apartment in a brownstone on 86th Street. Creative people characteristically tend to over-express their style as an extension of their individuality; all bangles, florid colors and beads. But Patti's taste in what she wore and how she had decorated her apartment was subtly stylish, only slightly bordering on the eclectic. Like Zina, she was organized and fastidious.

Thomas glanced around and considered his options. She lived on the ground floor so jumping wouldn't work. Hanging would have been too tedious and messy. Razor in tub? No. The thought of Gwen's fate had ruined the moment for him every time he tried to unwind in the Holy Water Soaking Tub. He reasoned that Patti, in all her creativity, deserved something of a statement with a little more drama. Though her problem was minor, she was young enough where every little thing seemed like a tragedy.

Thomas excused himself to go to her bathroom to wash his face, and to take stock. Her makeup was all roses and peaches. A dusty-pink satin robe hung behind the door. He saw the edge of a galvanized foot-tub jutting out from behind a partition separating the shower. He flushed the toilet for effect and then brought the robe into the living room.

He spied the lamp by the living room couch. The bulb was flickering a little; not so much that it would normally be noticed, but a second dose of an acid Communion wafer had heightened his vision as it kept him above the droll senses of normality. While Patti was in her kitchen pouring some wine, he unscrewed the bulb just enough so that she would notice its sputtering light.

"You want some wine, Jacob?" she called from the kitchen. "It's pretty rot-gut stuff, but it does the job, alright."

"Why, thanks, Patti, sure." As Patti approached him carrying two glasses of red wine, she furrowed her brow and squinted suspiciously one-eyed at Thomas. "What are you doing with my robe, Jacob?"

"I thought that you might want to get comfortable for this. Does that bother you?"

She put his wine on the couch-side table and then sat back in the chair and held her glass by its flute in both hands as she smiled coquettishly over its brim. "You're not going to try anything, like, funny while, you know, you have me under, are you? I mean if you are, forget it. You can go," she said, while leaving the possibility open for discussion.

"I honestly hadn't thought of it," Thomas admitted. "I take this all very seriously, dear heart. And I'm here to help you, not to take advantage of you. You'll just have to trust me."

Patti was starting to wonder why he might not want to do what comes naturally to most men in a provocative situation such as this. In her few years of experience she had dated a number of boys, but had slept with only three. Though the thought of sleeping with the pit boss had repulsed her, she'd come to trust this man, Jacob, enough to allow him the possibility of her bed. It wasn't her overwhelming desire for him to embrace her, but one that she wouldn't turn away. "I trust you, Jacob. I really do."

"The robe is meant only to make you feel relaxed here in your own place. It'll help the process."

She placed her glass on the table and stood up and began to feel woozy from the drinks she'd had. She held out her hand for the robe. "Gimme," she said flexing her fingers.

He smiled tenderly and handed her the robe. "You know, Patti, this bulb's about to burn out," he said as he indicated the lamp.

"Looks okay to me." She squinted at it. "Yeah it's kind of flickering. Funny. I just put a new one in on Saturday."

"Well, there might be a short in the cord. I think I could fix it while you're in your bedroom changing. I'm really good at fixing things."

"Let's hope so," she said vaguely as she padded toward the bedroom. "Yeah, fix it then, if you think it needs fixing. Knock yourself out." He bit his lower lip in apprehension. "Do you have rubber gloves or anything? I don't like fooling with electric things without them."

"Just unplug it, then. If you need a screwdriver, it's under the sink." She began to close the bedroom door behind her. "Near the rubber dishwashing gloves."

When she came out of the bedroom wearing nothing but her robe tied tightly around her waist, Thomas was working on the lamp. He had it apart in front of where he was kneeling on the carpet stripping the ends of the unplugged cord. He was wearing the yellow rubber gloves he had found under the sink.

"You don't take any chances, Jacob, hunh? You unplugged it and still wear gloves?"

"You can't be too careful," he said from the absorption in his work. The vinyl cushion sighed deeply as she slunk languidly down into the couch.

"I like careful men," she enticed him, then crossed her legs. Her thighs were still a little chubby, but her calves were well-formed. Her pink toe- nail polish glittered in the light from the lamp on the far side of the couch. "You really don't have to do this, you know. Fix the lamp and all."

"God, it was driving me crazy." He smiled briefly, still absorbed in his task. "You're the one who's supposed to be hypnotized, not me. There!" he said as he held the wire up to the light. The exposed, 5-inch leads sparkled in the remaining low light filtering through the room. Then his eyes fell upon her. Her plump features were drawn out from the smooth, surrounding shadows. She smiled wistfully as he lowered the wire back to the floor. "You know, Patti. You're very pretty."

"You think so?" she asked timidly. "Here. Let me show you." She untied the robe and drew it down her stout milk-white body. Her wide-set breasts were firm, with pert, chubby pink nipples. Despite a thickness in her waist, she had a flat stomach with a deep navel. A soft, scant fleece of blonde pubic hair thinly covered her sex. She drew her legs up beneath her. "You can touch me if you'd like, Jacob. Really. I wouldn't mind," she invited in a voice shortened by anticipation.

Thomas stood in place, wishing his body were more like hers. He reluctantly shook away the thought. "That's not why I'm here," he re- minded her as he lowered his gaze to the wire lying on the floor.

"Oh, really? You weren't using all that hypnotism talk just to get me up here alone with you? And the robe?" Her eyes darkened with anger. "Come on, honey. Who are you trying to kid?"

"I really do want to help you out of your fear of losing your job," he said dryly, still not looking at her.

"Unh-hunh. Well maybe I'd like to have you—oh, just come on. At least *look* at me. I'm told I have a nice body, and it wants to be touched." He looked up at her with his eyes glistening with tears about to shed over the woman he so wanted to be. "What are you afraid of?" she asked as she leaned toward him. "You not a queer, or something?" She reached out her hand and took his. "Take off those stupid gloves. Come on–" With both hands she peeled the glove off his right hand and drew his hand down her body and across a breast. "That feels niiice," she whispered lazily as she closed her eyes. He moved his hand down her side in frustration, then found the lapel of the robe and pulled it back over her body.

"Maybe after I've hypnotized you," he offered, and then bit his lower lip.

"*Christ!*" she muttered angrily. "What a killjoy!" She flung her robe closed and tightened the sash around her waist. "Alright, damn it. What do you want me to do? Lie down on the couch?"

"First, I want you to trust me," he said weakly.

"I trust you, alright? Now that I know you're not going to take advantage of me. What more about you is there not to trust?" She turned and plopped herself prone on the couch.

Thomas cleared his throat and then pulled the medallion from his trouser pocket. It glittered out a purple reflection in the thin light as it radiated its flow across her face. "Okay, Patti, now concentrate on the jewel," he said softly as he swayed it before her wide-open eyes. "Soon you'll get sleepy," he crooned as the pendant's glitter reflected off her deep-brown irises. Her dark-lashed lids began to relax.

Then she quickly opened her eyes. "This is stupid," she muttered in a sleepy drawl.

"Close your eyes, now, Patti, and sleeeeep."

Her lids slowly fell, this time in earnest. He reached into his satchel for three 150 microgram wafers. He slipped one into his mouth as he continued twirling the pendant.

"Are you sleeping?"

No answer.

"Are you asleep?"

Her plush lips bloomed into a faraway smile.

"You are asleep, now." He brought an LSD wafer to her mouth. "And you must be hungry. Here, take a bite of this chocolate chip cookie I've brought you."

"Ohhh! I love chocolate!" she whispered, as Thomas gingerly placed the wafer between her lips. She let it dissolve in her mouth. "Ummm— sweet!"

"Yes, Patti," he told her. "Have another." He placed a second wafer in her mouth. "It's very sweet. Very rich." His god was guiding him well. He relaxed into a tender hallucination, as he closed his eyes and began to share her vision. "I can see you're on a chilly mountaintop—"

She shivered from deep within. "Cold," she muttered through a timbre of childish complaint.

Thomas's vision of her vision became more vivid. He sensed a glowing approval from his god. "Good, Patti. You are in my control and will do everything I tell you. Do you understand?"

"Ev—ev-ereee-thin' you tell me," she said in a drawn whisper. Thomas indolently slipped the medallion back into his pocket.

"You are very depressed about your career. About your whole life. You have nothing to offer in your life that is worth anything to anyone. What am I telling you?"

"My life—worthless."

EX-cellent, Brother Thomas! his god gloated. *Convince her of her weakness!*

"Yes. Good." Thomas said from his own trance. "If you lose your job it is because you deserve to; that your talent is valueless."

"Nooo!" she resisted from sleep as she tensed her lids.

"Yes, Patti. It is. Listen to me. What am I telling you?"

"Talent is value-lezz."

"Good. Believe that is true. Now believe I will take you to a place where your creativity has great worth. Where no one will dispute your talent. This is a place far away from your life here on earth. You will dream—now. Are you dreaming?"

"Yes."

"Yes. You are dreaming. You are dreaming of a place that is warm, where tropical breezes caress you and azure water caresses your pretty bare feet where you stand in the powdery white sand. A chameleon among the ferns growing near you blends in with the passing of sun- light through the shadows—" She stood naked in the slow-moving shadows of the palm trees just behind her. The air was laced with the fragrance of lavender and wisteria. The fresh, briny scent of the sea flowed with the reassuring regularity of soft breathing across the sand. A thick obelisk rose like a phallus from the water. It was bright white against the stark deep blue of the sky. Behind it, a flawless orange sphere slowly morphed until it floated freely in space and cast its soft, glimmering reflection upon the light blue water. Its shadow undulated on the ribbed white sand of the ocean bed shallowly below. She looked over her gleaming bare shoulder. The vivid simplicity of the colors and dimension of the geometrics of blues and whites in the sky along with the fringe of lush-green palms and ferns played out in a perfect orchestration of style.

She raised her hand and floated a glowing burnt orange pyramid into view. She turned again to face the water. She drew a circle around the sphere with her finger and it gradually turned bluer than the water. She reached out from her dream and then drew a straight path that turned the ocean a shade greener. She pointed to the sky and conjured up a golden cloud. She felt the power to design; to make order out of chaos, and chaos out of order.

Satisfied she was surely lost in the power of her imagination, and he half-conscious in his, Thomas rose slowly and then moved the coffee table away from the couch. He went into the bathroom then half-filled the galvanized tub with warm water and carried it to the living room, where she still lay deeply involved in her dream. He placed it before the couch where the coffee table once was. He put the rubber gloves back on and twined the bared ends of the wire together into a five-inch strand. "Now, Patti," he told her. "You are ready to step into this place you have so beautifully designed. Now rise from where you are lying and walk into the ocean." Slowly she obediently sat up on the couch and then stood. A breast inched its way through the loosening of her robe. "Now walk to the ocean."

She stepped from the shadows into the sunlight and felt the warmth of the sand beneath her feet. "Hot sand," she complained.

"The cool ocean is not far," he assured her. "It's right here." He steadied the metal basin and took her hand. "Now let me guide you up into the ocean." She stepped up into the basin as her robe loosened from her shoulders and settled down to where she had tied it around her waist.

"Nice." She smiled placidly. "SOOO niice."

He placed the bared wired end of the cord into her hand.

"Now take hold of the end of this rope as tight as you can, and don't let go until I tell you to. Point into the sky and show the world who's the boss. Now!"

"*Meee!*" she smiled brightly as she grasped the bared wires tightly in her right hand.

"Yes. You. Now, hold the rope tighter—as tight as you can. Don't let go of it. Let it pull you up. If you let go before I tell you, you'll lose all control over your creativity," he said as he picked up the cord's plug and brought it to an outlet. "And when the lightning strikes it will tickle you, cause you to laugh. It will send a soothing wave through your body, and you will feel more relaxed than you ever have. Now! Point to the sky and bring some lightning into the sunny day!" He plugged in the wire.

With the warm Caribbean water massaging her ankles, with her head proudly raised high as she pointed to the sky with her left hand, she drew lightning. The oceanic sensation made her feel totally at ease and at one with all nature until her knees gave way and she sunk into the soothing warmth of the sun-drenched sea, as she overturned the tub. She continued to clench the charged bare wires and smiled broadly from her newfound power over nature. After about a minute of shivering on her weakening knees, her smile fell as the reality overcame her imagination, and she crumbled against the couch. She dropped the hot, sizzling cord onto the rug as all the lights in the room continued to flicker.

Thomas quickly reached over to hug her moist, warmed, nearly naked body. He sensed the electrically charged entrance of her soul swell into his. His vision reddened. He was overcome by a grand mal, spasmodic orgasm, as he offered up a wondrous, wide, green-eyed gaze toward his majestic god. God's voice came across as tight; short of breath. *Well DONE, Brother Thomas! You have rewarded us well!*

Thomas gulped some air and tried to calm himself against the wave of emotion still coursing through him. He leaned closer to Patti's body and kissed her cool, darkening lips. He anointed her forehead with lavender oil from the tin vial he kept in his rucksack. "Blessings, dear heart," he breathed heavily in a reverent whisper. He became awed by power of her soul reawakening him fully from his vision as his god faded away.

Chapter 42

Dusting the keys

Annie King worked in the bullpen with Patti, and the two of them usually rode the downtown bus to work. The girls were close friends and shared the same dark suspicions about Ron, the pit boss. They ate lunch together, and often went out trolling for boys together. Except for last night.

This morning Annie didn't answer Patti's knocking on her door. She wondered if there was anything for which Patti had to be at work earlier than usual. Sometimes a deadline account would crop up with a problem, and either or both of them might be summoned at night like nurses on call to come in early the next morning. She knocked again, but there was no answer. They had exchanged one an- other's keys, so Annie fished Patti's out from her purse and stuck it in the lock, but the door was already open. A dark premonition coursed through her body as she eased the door open.

She saw Patti lying in rigid profile with her head propped up against the couch. Her disarrayed blonde hair, some of it sticking straight out, was darkened by a few shades; even blackened in places. The natural rosy-white color of her youthful skin had desaturated into a palette of grays. Her open robe unveiled the oddly light-blue, puckered aureoles of her breasts.

The mellow and harsh odors of burnt skin and electricity seized Annie with a need to throw up, which was soon overcome by one of sheer terror. She neared her dead friend for a closer look. Patti's right hand was swollen black-and-blue, and her fingertips were totally blackened, as were the soft edges of the pads of her soles. The metal basin was overturned near where she lay. A bared end of the electrical cord still surged weak pulses of power like a dying thing and had burned a smoldering hole even through the wet carpet. A light haze hung close to the ceiling of the little apartment. Its sulfuric smell was thickened with the stench of burnt hair and skin. This smell was oddly sweetened by thin traces of a fragrance she could not quite identify. Perhaps it was flowers? She was too stunned to classify it. The radio in the corner spewed out a faint soundtrack of big band music: "Tuxedo Junction."

"God! *Patti!*—SHIT! Oh no! *Shit!*" she gasped as she rushed to where the cord was plugged in and unplugged it. It was hot to her grasp. Only later would she feel the sting and see the welt of second-degree burns in the hollow of her hand, which for now she brought to her mouth as she gaped breathless at the sight of her best friend. Shock and morbid curiosity kept her bewildered gaze trans- fixed on Patti lying there with her mouth and eyes wide open; her tongue dark blue against the gray darkness of her lips.

Finally, she stepped over to the phone and dialed the operator to call the police. Adrenalin kept her calm as she kept her sight trained on Patti, hoping she may awaken back into life from her perverted sleep. In the throes of her sudden paralysis, Annie had not seen the note in the carriage of the typewriter on the little desk on the other side of the room.

Cohansen arrived on the scene within 20 minutes with Barnaby, a few other cops and a coroner. They found Annie huddled in a corner, knees to chin, refusing to believe that her best friend was gone. She had finally seen a note and tried to read it, but the words were just a blur through her tears. Cohansen hunkered down in front of her. He took off his hat and twiddled its brim loosely in his fingers. "This has probably been a long half-hour for you, Annie," he said softly.

Cohansen had learned not to offer any sort of consoling touch in matters like these, but to try to win her confidence. As the unexpected and violent death of a loved one can emotionally kill more than the victim, Annie's mind was most likely too busy making sense out of the most basic elements of life, like breathing. The sight of this horrible death through her innocent eyes might have crumbled all that was left of her reality.

"It's all over now, okay, Annie? Can I call you 'Annie?'" She did not respond. Cohansen kept talking, calling her "Annie" to try to bring her back. "Things might seem a little weird for you now, Annie, all topsy-turvy, and shi—stuff. But we'll try to make them better. We're here now to help, Annie. "

She did not answer him as she clenched tighter.

"Okay, Annie? Annie? Can you hear me?"

She nodded slowly while keeping her sight locked upon Patti as the coroner buzzed with quiet professionalism around her stiffened body, taking notes and pictures.

Cohansen listened to the silence, and the very faint strains of "Moonlight Serenade," from the radio. He had not heard the signature music when he had arrived. Now, he knew. That fuckin' bastard!

"Annie?" he continued softly to bring her out of her state of shock and back into herself. "Annie? I'm Lieutenant Cohansen. But my friends call me Marty. You can call me Marty. Can you do that, Annie? Can you call me Marty?"

"Marty?" she gasped timidly.

"Good." He looked up and summoned Sergeant Massio. "Now,

Annie, this is Sergeant Massio—Vern Massio."

The illumination from the flash on the coroner's camera swelled, then diminished; then lit up again as he took pictures of Patti's body. Though she flinched at the camera flashes, Annie remained transfixed in paralysis. To her, everything seemed to move in slow motion. The voices drooled around her like a 45 record being slowed to 33-1/3; a game she and Patti would play with her collection of hit singles. "She's my best friend," Annie said hoarsely as a tear inched down her cheek. "She left a note," she said meekly, oblivious to the tear.

"Yes, Annie, we know. We saw it."

From some place beyond where she huddled, she managed to con- jure up a distant smile, which then drooped to a frown. "I've got to get to work, now." She looked up at Cohansen and smiled sweetly. "Thank you for coming."

Cohansen returned her smile. "You should take today off, okay, Annie? Now, Vern is going to take you to that diner on the corner and buy you coffee and whatever you think you can eat, then I'll come down and join you. I just have a few easy questions for you."

"Marty?" She held open her right hand, displaying two long red welts. "I burned it. It hurts," she said as she awkwardly tried to rise. "I need my hands to be better so I can go to work."

"Okay, sweetheart. We'll get that looked after, I promise," Cohansen said as he stood and helped her up. "Now, Annie, Vern's gonna take you downstairs. Vern's a cop so no one'll hurt you. He'll protect you." He ventured a light touch and she settled into it by grabbing firmly onto his sleeve.

"I'll take her to that place over on eighty-second and Amsterdam, Marty?" Massio asked.

"Yeah," he confided to him. "Get her away from here. She's seen enough. Try to talk about anything but this, unless you feel she wants to talk it out. The thing is to get her talking at all, okay? I'll be down in about a half-hour, or whenever the ambulance gets here. Did anyone call those guys, yet?"

"Yeah. Way back when we were on the way over."

"Jeezuzz. They're late. I hope we didn't wake them." He then turned back to Annie. "Here, Annie, take Vern's arm. I'll be right down."

"Vern," she smiled up at him.

"Hi, Annie," Massio grinned as he guided her through the door. "Yo, Marty," Sergeant Frank Kennersly called out from where he was staring down at the typewriter. "You'd better take a look at his note." Cohansen put his hat on and pushed it back on his balding head.

"Yeah, yeah," he said as he watched Massio help Annie trundle toward the stairs.

"She didn't write it, Marty—someone called—" He squinted down at it. "Camella? — Camelie? —C-H-A-M-E-L-E-A. Strange name. You'd better read it."

Cohansen lumbered over to the typewriter and read the note, which was aromatic in that signature fragrance that seemed to follow the murders around:

To those who may have loved her or to whom it may concern:

Her name was Patti Nolan and she died gloriously, of her own choosing, with my help. Death came looking for her like the chameleon that it is; blending into life, hiding in life's bushes, sunning itself on its rocky terrain, where no one can see or expect it. It is openly in view, though. Always in view. And always watching. Just Like God.

Our dear Patti was one who looked searched for death through her own unhappiness with life. I am one charged by God as a liberator to do His will and to speed this beautifully horrible and natural process along. I

---

am the chameleon. You will not find me, so do not try. I will be the one to find you. Take comfort, dear hearts, that I am here to help you as I have helped Patti Nolan to find euphoria.

By the way, the fragrance you smell is that of lavender — not lilac! So please, dear hearts. Try to get your facts straight when you report my glorious accomplishments to Mr. Editor Frank Malone.

Blessings, Dear Hearts,

Chamelea

"Fuckin' shithead!" Cohansen seethed. "Dust those keys for prints, Jake," he ordered gruffly to Barnaby. Then he noticed a Communion wafer next to the typewriter. "Oh, fuckin' shit! Fuckin' son of a bitch!" he said to it as he carefully picked it up by its edges. He handed it toward Barnaby. "Bag this fuckin' thing, Jake."

Beyond the scene of Patti's death, all was immaculate, except for around the bathroom sink where she kept her cosmetics. Her clothes closet had not been disturbed. The arthritis in Cohansen's left knee began to flare up, as it often did when he was stressed. He limped back into the living room.

Tom Harris, the coroner, still believing it was a suicide, spoke out from where he was continuing to jot down his notes over the body. "You know, Marty. She meant business. The voltage's only one-ten, but by the looks of things, she must've held onto the wires, three, four minutes."

Harris had not seen the note. "You sure it was suicide, Tom?" Cohansen asked.

"Well, it sure as hell don't look like a homicide," he said. "I mean, no victim's going to stand still in a metal tub of water and let a murderer zap her for nearly five minutes." He took another picture, roughly advanced the film as if for emphasis.

"You sure it was electrocution, then? That this isn't some sort of cover-up?" said Cohansen. "Like she wasn't killed first, then zapped? We've got to think of everything, Tom."

"I don't see any evidence of anything but self-electrocution, Marty." "I'm not convinced. I wanna see complete autopsy reports on this one. I want this body going straight down to Bellevue, Tom, and I want you working with Tony on this." Anthony Vessiglio was the city's chief medical examiner. "Frank?" He called over to Kennersly.

"Yeah, Marty?" Kennersly called back from the typewriter.

"I want you to dust this whole fuckin' place. I wanna see powder everywhere before we leave!"

"Yeah, Marty. You got it."

Cohansen lit a Pall Mall then stared back into Patti's bedroom as he pondered a possible scenario. The pens and pencils were on the right side of her desk. She slept on the right side of her double bed for a convenient right-handed reach to the bedside table, so she was right-handed. Her right hand was burned, so that's where she had held the wire. Her clothes were still neatly hung in her closet, but there were two empty hangers. This time, though, the killer was in no hurry. He had time to write a note.

Cohansen puffed on his cigarette and then walked into the bathroom. Sure enough, one lipstick, a peach color, had been set aside from the rest and left uncapped. There were no bottles of lavender perfume, yet that same faint fragrance hung lightly in the atmosphere.

Harris appeared in the doorway behind him, holding the camera casually at his side. "Okay, Marty," he announced. "You ready?"

"Hunh? Oh, yeah," he puffed out his cheeks in a loud sigh, ran the tap water over his cigarette, dropped it in the toilet and then flushed it. "Let's do it." He followed him into the living room as

Harris checked the notes for his preliminary autopsy report.

"Okay," Harris said officiously as they stood over the body. "I put it as death by prolonged electrocution. There are no other types of wounds." He looked at Cohansen with conviction. "No ligatures or lividity on her throat, nothing to suggest otherwise." He referred again to his notes. "Her right hand is swollen black-and-blue. Judging by the multiple first-degree burns in her right palm and fingertips, she held the exposed wires tight in that hand for between four and five minutes, holding tightest with her fore-and middle-fingers. These finger- tips are burned black to the bone, extreme first degree. The heels and balls of both feet are blackened, and they also have slighter first-and second-degree burns where the flow of juice was conducted out to the metal of the tub she stood in.

"Also, there are some narrow second-degree blisters on her right forearm and left calf, ranging from four to seven inches in length—"

"Tom, close her eyes."

Harris looked up from where he had been absorbed by his notes, and blinked. "Huhn?"

"Close her eyes, okay? And her mouth?"

"Sure," he said and crouched down and brushed his hand down her face to lower her lids and close her mouth.

"Thanks," Cohansen said. "Anything else?"

"Nothing more than you see. Her body temperature's ninety-three point five. I put the time of death at shortly after midnight, maybe as late as one a.m., thereabouts. A little bit of rigor has set in. A little late, though 'cause the electrocution relaxed her muscles."

There was a rustle as the two ambulance E.M.T.s came in with a gurney and black bag. "Where the hell were you guys?" Cohansen barked annoyed, not so much at them as at himself.

"Barney thought you said eighty-fifth," one accused the other defensively. "Not eighty-eighth. We had to stop and call the precinct."

"Un-hunh. Okay, listen up, boys. Jake? Listen up here," Cohansen said as Barnaby stopped brushing for prints, which were coming up more like smudges, on the keys.

"What I firmly believe has happened here was another homicide, and it may be worse than it sounds." He looked at Barney, the ambulance driver. "I want you to drive this body over to Tony Vessiglio over at the M.E.'s office in Bellevue for a full autopsy. Take Tom with you. Jake? How're you doing over there?"

"Comin' up empty, Marty. Whatever prints were there have been rubbed off, or the guy wore gloves."

"What makes you think it's a man that typed that letter and not the victim under duress? I'm open to suggestions, here, from anyone. So, help me out."

Kennersly stared down at the note. "I don't know, first it's, like, worded like the perp wrote it. And the typing looks a little filled-in: the type is real black like the keys were stuck hard, and the ribbon looks really used up. There are a couple o' strike-trough's. Anyway, ain't women s'posed to be better typers than men?"

"Depends," Cohansen said. "You're askin' the wrong guy."

"I found a couple of patterns in the prints, though, Marty. Like the kind on rubber gloves."

Cohansen stirred in mild realization. Of course, the killer would have had to have worn rubber gloves if he was going to electrocute someone, and there would be clean prints inside the gloves. "Good work, Nick. Now let's find them gloves," he said as he walked to the kitchen to search the trash and beneath the sink. Here, too, they found nothing. They finally found the gloves on the floor of her clothing closet. On one of them, the middle finger had been snipped off.

After Cohansen had questioned Annie, who told him that the

only grudge Patti harbored was against Ron Ansler in the bull pen, he went back to the precinct to search his call list. Even if Nealy hadn't been on the list, he was on his mind to call.

He finally caught up with Nealy later that afternoon.

"Ray, I hate to interrupt your wedding prep, but we've got another one on our hands, a Patti Nolan." He awaited Nealy's response. "Ray? Are you there?"

He heard one of Nealy's distinctive, exasperated sighs.

"We're following every lead. Oh, yeah you mighta guessed. There was a lipstick uncapped off by itself and, this time, a note."

"She wrote a note?" Nealy said glumly.

"*She* didn't write it. It's from our killer. Calls himself 'Chamelea.' Apparently, you scored with your Frank Malone connection, but our perp was drawn out in the wrong way. Looks like he wants to play games. He even mentioned Malone in his note."

"Shit! God-damnit!"

"Listen, bud, I'm here at the station waiting for a pathology report on the body. Can you meet me at Back Page at three thirty? By then I'll need a stiff bourbon or more likely two. If you buy, I'll take you to the crime scene. See what more you can pull out of it."

"Okay," Nealy answered dejectedly. "Marty?"

"Hello, Ray."

"I'm upping this game a little. I'm gonna talk to Malone again."

"Okay. Just don't tell me you told me you were gonna talk to him."

Cohansen paused as he pondered this. "What the hell? You may as well. The news is out anyway. A reporter from Channel Five called and spoke to Mike Perry here at the station. So, these murders are gonna be on the local TV news tonight."

"Who's Mike Perry?"

"Oh. I never told you about him," Cohansen said as he rooted through his bottom desk drawer for the pint of Jim Beam he kept there to spice up his coffee. "Since the Kitty Genovese thing last March, some of the precincts have hired their own P.R. guys. Mike Perry's ours."

"So, the cops are sleeping with the media now?"

"Haven't we always? Look at the newsies and cops mingling at The Back Page. It's a dance we do. Now it's just goin' mainstream on TV. Things are changing about the way they're done anymore, Ray. You'll find out once I get you back working here."

Nealy dismissed Cohansen's ongoing invitation. "We're gonna get this guy, Marty." It sounded more like a dry threat. "We're gonna get him," he insisted.

Cohansen sipped his spiked black coffee. "Yes, we are, buddy," he agreed.

Soon after Cohansen hung up the phone, the call from the medical examiner's office came through. They were finished with their autopsy of Patti Nolan. He took a squad car down to Bellevue. A sallow, gray assistant led him to Dr. Anthony Vessiglio's office. Cohansen dutifully followed the boy into the dark, chilly depths he had always perceived as the "dungeon," where pathologies were performed true to the spirit of Dr. Frankenstein.

A dark interest brought Cohansen to look through the big window that exposed the examination room. Patti was lying on a table, and a sheet covered all but her head. There was a neat, bloodless incision around the upper circumference of her partially shaved head. Cohansen shivered briefly and turned away. His weak stomach was legendary around the department, and he hated this place. Dr. Vessiglio, paradoxically immaculately prim and tidy in his white starched frock, sat stiffly behind the desk in his bare office investigating the contents of a clear plastic bag in front of him.

Black-and-white photos of the body festooned the top of his desk.

"You going to be okay with this, Martin?" he asked officiously after the assistant had left and shut the door behind him.

"It's part of my job, Tony. Not exactly my favorite part, but we gotta do what we gotta do."

"Right, then let's get to it." He smiled with half his mouth. "The con- tents of her stomach revealed the evidence of at least two slices of pizza—pepperoni, I think—three hours before she died at around twelve thirty a.m. Her blood alcohol content was probably around point one six at the time of death. So, she was slightly drunk. There was also enough caffeine in her bloodstream to suggest one or two cups of coffee with her dinner or maybe before. She didn't smoke, if it matters."

"What about LSD? Did you find any of that?"

"I was getting to that. I'm guessing she had taken in about three-hundred micrograms, but I could be off on that."

"Figured," Cohansen sighed.

"There was no sign of sexual entry, no semen," Vessiglio went on. "She had orgasmed and urinated, most likely due to the electrocution. There were, as Tom Harris informed you, no grand puncture wounds, ligature discolorations, or any other marks to suggest anything other than electrocution. But we did find this—" He held up the clear bag, which contained what appeared to be a limp, deflated small, yellowish-brown party balloon.

"What is that?" Cohansen wondered.

"It's a severed finger from the rubber gloves you found. The kind commonly worn for washing dishes. It is, I'd speculate, the middle finger."

"I hope you didn't find that in her stomach along with the pizza."
"No. In her vagina," he stated as he put the bag back down on his desk. "It was dangling from it like a penis."

"A sex killing?" Cohansen mused.

Vessiglio shivered his shoulders. "Maybe. There is absolutely no evidence to suggest rape, though." He removed his glasses and busied himself over a speck on a lens. "If you'll allow me to editorialize. This act seems a little too complicated to have been a normal sex scenario. Too uniquely brutal." He put his glasses back on. "I would suggest that it was more of a ritual killing. Something religious, perhaps."

"Shit. *Witches*! That's *all* we fuckin' need!" Cohansen said through what might have been a laugh. "Listen, Tony. I need to see if our guys can pull any prints off the inside of that glove finger. I'll need it to send out with the rest of the gloves." He pulled a cigarette out from his breast pocket.

"Don't smoke here, Martin," Vessiglio warned gruffly as he handed him the bag with the severed glove-finger.

Chapter 43

Chamelea goes public

Nealy distractedly sipped his Scotch as he stood at his open office window and breathed in the faintly electric scent of the warm Manhattan evening. The bloom of light from his desk lamp softened the mood into something romantic as a backdrop to John Coltrane's soulful "Body and Soul" playing from the hi-fi. He looked out toward the East River. A thick blue swathe of twilight deepened into dusk beneath a billow of clouds, which seemed to radiate their shades of blue-gray.

Eight stories below, the rush-hour traffic leaked north along First Avenue. Two-toned red and yellow Checker and green and yellow Hudson taxicabs mixed in with other more streamlined cars varying in length and fin as they sluggishly prowled the street. He heard the muffled bleating of some of their horns, while others sounded hoarse, as if in the throes of death. The swelling of sirens overpowered the bed of traffic noises as they rose and retreated into the distance.

He recalled how much he liked where his office was here on the eastern edge of the city. It was quieter and less serrated than the western edge. In the middle, between the edges, grew an impersonal, ever-evolving undulation of lives. He wondered if a normal suburban existence wouldn't suit him and Francesca more meaningfully once they committed themselves to the game of marriage. After all, he reasoned, wasn't suburbia the place where married exurbanites were supposed to go to prattle through the rest of their lives? Or maybe he could retire from the woes of his work and they could move to Maine. His thoughts turned once again to the city belonging to people like Zina and Patti; kids trying to make something of themselves in a place that did not particularly care about them. And then there were those like Gwen, who may have felt invisibly and insignificantly crushed by an overbearing culture that passed them by as if they were wallflowers at a prom. Manhattan offered itself more to those impassively passion- ate ones in pursuit of their calling, like Marty Cohansen. And, for the moment, it belonged to this person, Chamelea, who likened himself to the death he administered. He had become a necessary evil in a place where, back in Nealy's father's time, murder hid in the shadows and was seemingly more discerning toward its choice of victims.

The investigation into the Chamelea killings had quenched a thirst within him and turned him toward a decision to rejoin the Two-Oh. At least the work, and the pay, would be more consistent. There would be a pension which could be picked up from his previous time on the force. But he would not tell Cohansen about any of this. Not yet.

The scene of Patti's murder had turned up nothing more tangible than Cohansen had discovered on the first go-around, but the note revealed factors that stirred up Nealy's intuition. Once he had been to Zina's and Gwen's apartments, he regarded homicide as a given, and now, with Patti's death, the mind of the person who had taken her had been offered up to him. The murderer thought of himself as death incarnate—a megalomania which, given enough time, might trip over its own ego. Serial murders, especially the more desperate ones, do not allow for the luxury of time. Chamelea had committed three killings in a month and a half. In Nealy's estimation, he was desperate.

Slender women wearing big floppy hats strolled along Fifth Avenue. Some of their faces were provocatively and mysteriously hidden behind the din of birdcage veils that flounced with each dainty step as they fluttered lightly in the warm, late summer breezes. Stylish women paraded primly past Saks', B. Altman's, Best & Company and Peck & Peck as the mannequins standing behind the stores' glass cast their cool, mesmerized gazes out at nothing, save perhaps their livelier muses passing them by. Some of the well-adorned ladies stared determinedly at the fashions behind the store windows as they watered their little poodles and shih-tzus at the sidewalk doggie bars.

The fragrances of morning dampness lingered, mingling with the added scent of oil from the street. Here, in a quiet Sunday indolence dappled in sunlight, everything seemed to slow down. Taxis slinked languorously by buses, whose diesel engine grinds seemed muffled in the rarified air.

Thomas sat on a bench near Tiffany's, partially hidden by the shad- ow of a hedgerow planted within a brick-walled well in front of him. He took in a breath of the lightly spiced hemlock scent of the hedge and then wrote in his red leather-covered journal:

August 23, 1964

I am Audrey Hepburn again today, living divinely within the shell of the man's body, which hides my true self. Playing the part of this man, I'm unhappily free to suppress the true and desperate desire of my spirit. The mannequins trapped under glass at Peck and Peck and Saks' are to me like idols masterfully sculpted by Donatello, gravid in the truth of my longing, while imprisoned by their necessity for secrecy, and I feel akin to them in their separate solitudes. I wonder if at night, when no one can see, they become alive in all their finery and waltz through the aisles of their stores shrouded by the comfort of darkness as am I when I prowl. I want so to be there, dear hearts, to be waltzing through the ubiquity existing beneath the torture of life, for it is life that has condemned me to death, yet without my feeling the sublime pleasure of dying.

You may, dear hearts, have passed judgment too quickly upon me. You may have made me out to be, shall I say, someone alternative to the appearance of my gender? Pray, no, my dears, I am not, contrary to your beliefs, queer. I sing of something far grander, as I am someone of no sex at all. I am Chamelea and I roam frustrated, misunderstood and undetected among you. I am not partial. I am only in search of the me that I am through those who forlornly pretend they are among the living. My soul—my god—tells me this so it must be the absolute truth.

Chamelea is pure!

Nealy stood off in a corner of an interrogation room in the Two-Oh, propping himself against one of its plain chipped brick walls, which had been painted over in a dull, intimidating green. A plane of sunlight flowed in grim striation through the bars of the dank room's only window, casting him in tines of shadow. Cohansen would have normally met him in the private office set aside for such get-togethers, but it was being painted and the stiff, overwhelming redolence of oil- based paint seemed to burn through his sinuses.

Cohansen sat in a gray, military surplus iron chair at the gray, military surplus iron interrogation table and grimly re-read Frank Malone's newest editorial on Chamelea, as Nealy had dictated to him. Cohansen aggressively chewed and snapped a wad of licorice gum he had begun to use as a cud to keep him from smoking too many cigarettes. He had already lost one filling to the gum, and his tongue repeatedly found the jagged edge of the hole in a rear incisor, causing him to occasionally bite it. "*Thit!*" he grimaced and pitched his head up from poring over The New York Knickerbocker. "Bid my fuhhing *tongue*, again!"

"Take an aspirin, Marty."

"Wha' I nee ith a stiff shot o' Kentu-hy's fineth." He took a cooling breath though his mouth to ease his pain. "Okay, Ray," he flicked his hand against the newsprint. "Did you really mean to hath that ath-hole Malone menthon your name in thith article?"

"Uh-huh. Absolutely," said Nealy. Cohansen's dumbfounded expression gave him cause to reason his actions. "I did. I'm trying to bait the bastard, Marty—give Chamelea a reason to come to me. You can see I made sure Malone dropped the 'detective' part in my name. I'm just Ray Nealy— 'a concerned citizen with some clout with the cops.'"

"What if he finths you and kills you off as a threat to hith M.O.?" Cohansen asked and then plunked his gum into a Niagara Falls souvenir ashtray on the table. "Lath thing I want to see is you laid out on one of Tony Vessiglio's slabs in Bellevue." He let out a hefty sigh and shook his head and then jolted. "*Thit*! Thith fuckin' *hurths*!"

"He tries that, Marty, I'll kill him right back. Go to your dentist, and get that tooth capped, will ya?"

To divert himself from the diminishing pain of the puncture in his tongue, Cohansen lit up a cigarette. "Easier thed than done, buddy. Anywathz, thith ballsey move of yours could just pith off that little thit-head just enough to go out again."

"I don't think he'd do that. I've got a feeling Chamelea's gonna try to reach out through the media. It's a way a lot of these perps work. Sometimes."

"Thumtimes, Ray. Only thumtimes. Thith ain't no run o' the mill tex-book case we're dealin' with here. Thath'z just my opinion." He bit his now-swollen tongue once again. He cringed deeply. "THIT!!! Fuhhin jeethus CHRITH!"

Nealy's account of Chamelea's murder of Patti Nolan in *The New*

York Knickerbocker had already gone the way of so much leftover burnt toast in Frank Malone's mind. This was particularly true now, since the story made last night's local TV news. Today, Malone huddled over his pre-war Smith-Corona typewriter and banged out some breaking story about an alleged kidnapping in Williamsburg, Brooklyn, which he conveyed as a God's-honest truth. The story served the purpose of filling up white space in the paper, even though it came in over the phone from a scorned and estranged female druggie who most likely chose Malone's brand of press power to get back at her ex-con boyfriend whom she had accused of stealing their five-year-old little girl. The only thing that mattered to Stogie Frank Malone was that it made for good press on an otherwise slow news day. Another flurry of ashes fluttered from his dying cigar to his lap as he continued to attack the typewriter keys.

Mighty Joe Kanowski leaned his head in from the echoing clatter of typewriters into Malone's door as he passed by. "Yo, Frank. Some- one here says he wansta see you. Don't unnerstan' a fuckin' word he's sayin' 'cept that he's got some sorta ad for the paper. I think tha's what he said, at least."

"Then send 'im down to advertising. I ain't got time for that kinda shit, Joe. We're closin' the issue in an hour, an' I'm busy on a hot one here."

"I canno' no 'member to do this," came a crusty rasp of a voice over Mighty Joe's shoulder. Malone looked up from his typing and spotted a hulky, wild-haired man with a three-day growth of beard over his wide, excessively pocked face. The gristle covered up a couple of lesions— the kind a person picked up from too much time on the street. "*Quis mihi hoc tribuat ut in nomine Malone praedicatoris operatur hic.*"

"What the fuck you *talking* about, fellah?" Malone sneered.

"Ye knowen Frankus Malone?" Milio asked.

Malone considered the translation of the question. "I'm Malone."

Milio walked around Mighty Joe and into Malone's office, extending a white business envelope. "Preacher man say I given to ye. *Ut procer in vestri amet.*" Milio took in Malone's perplexed stare. "For you papra to print. For preacher man. Says it be a-ve-tiche-mont."

"Advertisement," Mighty Joe translated.

Milio nodded and jiggled the envelope toward Malone. "From da preacher man."

Malone took the envelope and stared confoundedly at it. Typed on its front was: For Mister Editor Frank Malone, *The New York Knicker-Bocker*. When he looked up, he saw Milio, anxious to leave, brush by Mighty Joe. "*Hey!*" he shouted, but Milio did not answer as he made his way down the hallway. Mighty Joe simply shrugged his shoulders and then left to finish the story he was getting together for the edition's closing.

Malone didn't open the envelope right away. Instead, he looked down at East 24th Street from his third-floor window. He saw the odd fellow who was just in his office trundle out onto the sidewalk and turn left. He passed a few cars, then opened the passenger door of a waiting white-topped powder-blue Chevy Corvair, and got in. Still a little perplexed, Malone absently opened the envelope and lifted the letter. He held it in his hand as he watched the car pull cautiously out of its spot and head east toward Lexington Avenue where it turned to go downtown. He glanced down at the letter, which immediately caught his attention.

Hello, Mr. Editor Frank Malone.

I've been anxious to meet you even if only by letter. I am Chamelea. I've recently been the recipient of three souls, which you and now the greater media have brought to public attention. These three are only the most recent. There have been others, but you wouldn't care about them for they were destined to fall through the cracks of society, anyway. But these three recent ones, my darlings Zena, Gwen and Patti, have been the most nourishing of all. My god has enriched me through their spirits, which now happily reside in me.

Like some of those I've taken before, I, too, am very good at "falling through the cracks," —blending in, like the chameleon of my namesake. I can make myself very difficult to find, and though I can't be detected, I need a voice. So, I have chosen you for that task—and you're welcome. Just as sure as my soul needs nourishment, my voice—my reasoning— needs projection. This will be the first of what I perceive to be many such letters for you to publish; a prospect that I'm sure you will find inviting as my willing partner.

You may inquire as to my motives. What did these three angels I've issued into paradise have in common? Nothing—and Everything. They all wanted out of their lives, even without some of them knowing it. Gwen was the exception; she had become openly tired of the restraints that had shackled her to life. There are so many other women, young and older, in this city that could use my help. They unwittingly crave it almost as much as I crave my own fulfillment to myself and my God through them.

Will there be more? Oh my, Yes.

PS: The phone book is a wonderful thing. I was easily able to find the whereabouts of your informant, Private Detective Raymond Nealy, whose name you mentioned in yesterday's article.

PPS: My further missives to you will be addressed, as this one, to the 'New York KnickerBocker (underlined capital "B,") so you will know they came from me.

Blessings, dear heart, Chamelea.

Malone felt a little surge of accomplishment as he reread the letter. He rushed to his desk, grabbed up a black magic marker and redacted the postscript reference to Nealy, and the part about himself acting as Chamelea's "willing partner." The Williamsburg kidnapping story, still rolled up in the platen of his typewriter, would have to wait. Chugging like a steam engine trailing his cigar smoke behind him, he breathlessly hurried the letter to compositing. He would dictate his introduction to the typesetter.

Only after Chamelea's letter was safely tucked away into the evening edition would he call Nealy.

Chapter 44

Riding the range

"Flapjack" Robertson died peacefully in his sleep the day after Hellie had Made the call to Heaven's Doorway. She had reasoned it would be the dementia that might take him at the end of a long process, but instead it had been his heart. During the past few months, it seemed everything revolved around the prosecution of his Last Will and Testament, which ended up with Flapjack leaving all he owned to Jamie, along with the proviso that he carries on The Robertson Ranch's focus on oil over cattle. This was followed up by the tacit warning that his son learns more about oil and the business of running the ranch, rather than "gallivanting around like an idiot calf."

Jamie had taken most of his father's advice to heart, as he was now up in Tulsa with two of the ranch's lawyers closing a 60-acre lease with Sinclair Oil's European division that would guarantee him 30 percent of the mineral rights. Jamie had been feeling and acting more responsible now, partly due to Flapjack's admonition, but mostly due to last week's news that Hellie was three months pregnant.

As she held reins loosely in her right hand, Hellie relaxed back in Clarence's saddle and surveyed her newly-acquired 300 head of cattle. They grazed placidly in an 80-acre range of prime pasture with not one pumper in sight. Ranchers and oilers alike were required to have a sixth sense about the abrupt changes in the weather that was the signature of the Oklahoma plains. A barometer came in handy, but the real early indicator was the erratic behavior of the birds and livestock.

It seemed that nature had decided to rest easy over the Plains, and the cattle were as calm as the warm and gentle gusts that rustled the range grasses. On this balmy 73-degree early September morning, the prevailing scents were the sweetness of grass and muskiness of healthy earth mingling with that of the crude it held beneath.

She felt a tender warm surge deep in her abdomen—a gentle churning of the new life growing within her. She had started feeling these pleasant gaseous indicators a month-and-a-half after she was three weeks late with her period. The lateness was usual for a 37-year- old woman, when the internal workings normally started to settle into the early phases of menopause, but Hellie had never been regular in this way to begin with.

Aware of the delicacy with which she must now handle herself, she had started to go about her doings more cautiously in the realization that in a few months she might have to stop riding all together. She would dearly miss that. But now that she had field hands to work the cattle, she would need to concentrate her responsibilities on their management. She reluctantly reasoned that she'd spend more time be- hind a desk than in a saddle.

She felt a jostling motion followed by a tenuous cry from the large metal-framed papoose strapped to her back, as 18-month-old Timbo nestled into a different position. His growth had overflowed into a stubborn determination announcing the discovery of his little personality. He now was walking and sometimes falling and then getting up to walk some more. Hellie realized that in a month or so he would be too big for a papoose, yet still far from grown enough for a horse. His crying became more insistent. "You pay attention, now, boy," she said straight ahead as she adjusted her aged fedora with the eagle feather in its band. "While we got cattle to attend to."

She noticed one of the longhorn steers going through the motions of familiarizing himself with a cow. This time it wasn't Pedro or Juan. They had new responsibilities as the two longhorns stood majestically off in their separate corners of the range, overseeing the rest of the herd. Garbanzo circulated among the cattle, occasionally trying, though in vain, to bark some of the errant ones into back into the herd. Hellie gently urged Clarence into a trot. "Horney Texas immigrant!" she said crossly at the steer now folding himself over the cow. She languished meditatively in the moment as she rode, feeling the subtle breeze shifting from north to east in the crisp, pristinely endless sky. God, how she would miss her four hours a day on horseback. It was one of the few things she sensed that truly connected her to the environment.

Relaxed as she now felt, she resolved to call Regina tonight. There was a lot to talk to talk about. She had been guarded in their few discussions since her still-undisclosed call to Heaven's Doorway. She was not sure how to break the news to her surrogate younger sister. Wrapped up in the maws of Flapjack's Last Will and Testament, Hellie hadn't called Regina to tell her he'd died and that she was now running his ranch. Regina didn't even know about her pregnancy. No one did but Jamie. She knew he would be the boasting local town crier on that one. The cow and steer interaction had abated on its own, and the two beeves lumbered off, a little shaken, in opposite directions. Hellie took in her favorite mix of smells: earth, leather and horsehide, as she be- came one with the repetitive, soothing swell of Clarence's slow can- ter. The ebb and flow of his movement swayed her gently into the same submission that Timbo must have felt, as his cries had quieted. Through the peculiar abundance of silence, she closed her eyes and listened to the occasional lowing of the cattle; the rushing of breeze over grasses; the creak of her boots against the saddle; the high, nearly imperceptible drone of cicadas and an intermittent caw of conversation among the distant crows.

Regina was glad her workday was finally over as she trudged tiredly through the lobby of the Astoria-Queens Hotel. The air-conditioning was cranked up into an excessive chill as though the maintenance department had just discovered a new toy. It felt annoyingly refreshing. Fatigued from her perpetual rounds of water-skiing, she was equally fed up with serving as a mannequin behind the front desk of the Will Rogers Pavilion. She realized long before that she'd become nothing more than a convenience for Trevor and wondered if he would ever take her seriously enough to promote her beyond the object he had tried to make of her. He had been called back to Oklahoma City for a few days, and she yearned for another encounter with Dave Kiefer.

"Miss Barragan?" the desk clerk summoned as she walked by. "I have some phone messages for you." He held up three light-blue memo slips.

"Three?" she said, taking the memos. "I must be popular today." One was from Trevor, which she dismissed. The second was from Dave: "See you tonight, --D". The third, from Hellie, was marked "Important. Need to talk." She noticed Hellie's new number and would make that call first. Then she would call Dave.

The call to Trevor could wait until 6 a.m. in the morning when it would be an hour earlier in Oklahoma City. He hated being woken up before seven, so his wife would probably answer. Regina found a perverse amusement and an upper hand in these mistress-to-unsuspecting-wife conversations.

She sat on the edge of her bed with the receiver crimped

between her shoulder and ear as she lit a cigarette. "Hey, sis," she quipped perkily. "You called. What's up? See you changed your number. You been getting crank calls from all your old boyfriends?"

"Not really. This is Flapjack's office number. Or his old one. He finally went off n' died on us."

"Jeeze, Hellie. Sorry to hear. When did that all happen?"

"Almost a month ago. Jamie and me's been tied up in the will, and all. That's why I've been outta communication. Sorry, hon."

"S'okay. I've been pretty occupied, myself, skiing around in circles in that stupid little pond all day."

"Sounds monotonous. Is it makin' you dizzy? Goin' round and round like that?"

"No. But juggling my sleepover boss is."

"You still lettin' that guy poke you? I mean in the biblical sense of violatin' the Sixth Commandment, of course."

"Not for long, I hope. I'm beginning to feel like his personal Kewpie Doll."

"He'll get his, like they all do, sooner or later. So. I've moved into Flapjack's house. He left it all to Jamie, and I'm runnin' the place. Including three hundred head."

Regina gulped down the puff on her cigarette and daintily coughed. "Holy *shit*, Hellie!" she choked tightly. "That's great! I mean, he's gotta have, what, four-hundred acres?"

"Five hundred-fifty. Jamie's up in Tulsa closin' a really good sixty-acre deal on an oil lease. We get thirty percent in mineral rights. That's thirty percent of every strike. Should set us up pretty good."

"Yeah, I'd say...like millionaires."

"It would be Timbo's, too, once he reaches eighteen."

Regina was overcome with a numb and bittersweet silence. "Well, that'll be good for him," she said solemnly, as she choked back some tears.

"I thought you'd need to know that." Now Hellie was caught in a pause. "And also that Timbo's gonna have a live-in playmate. I'm, uh, about three months pregnant."

"Holy shit, sis! At *your* age?"

Hellie broke in with one of her characteristic little guffaws. "Yeah, hon. At *my* age. It can still happen, ya know."

Not to me. Not again, Regina thought. "So that puts him born in March?"

"Around then."

"I'll be there for it, then Hellie," she said and then realized she wasn't "there" for the birth of her own son for reasons that had begun to frost over.

"Hope so," Hellie said cheerily, as though to steel her to deliver her next parcel of news. "There's somethin' else I need to tell you, Reg."

"Wait. I just remembered." She tamped out her cigarette and wished for a cold beer. "Did you ever find out about my fath—that guy's church?"

"That's what I was gonna say. I did. Really strange." Her voice fell. "You wanna know, now?"

Hellie's tone made whatever she had found out to sound foreboding. "Good time's any, I guess," Regina said apprehensively as she settled back against the headboard to brace against what might be coming.

"Well, I did some research and found there was a Thomas Deavers in New York City. Actually, there are about ten of 'em. Only one had a 'Reverend' in front of his name."

Regina stared off to her right and into the frameless horizontal mirror above the blond-wood dresser. "Shit," she muttered.

"So." Hellie heaved a sigh. "I called the number." "Shit."

"Some lunatic answered the phone in a weird sort of language I could in no way construe as anythin' resemblin' English."

"Was it him?"

"Not unless he's taken to talking in tongues, which is quite possible. Anyway, someone else took the phone. Church secretary, or something. I mean, I sure hope the secretary wasn't that first guy who answered. You wanna write this all down?"

Trying to compose herself in her personal brand of contemplation, Regina furrowed her brow. She groped her hand around the night- stand for the Astoria-Queens Hotel pen and pad of paper. "Okay, Hellie. I'm ready."

"The secretary's name was, let's see…uh, Francis. He didn't give a last name. He had a lisp in his voice, like he coulda been a little light in the ol' Ropers."

"And you're sure that this Francis wasn't him? I mean, my ex-father's been known to, uh—disguise himself." She shook her head to dismiss the memory of having seen him dressed as her mother back in Hanson. "Don't think he'd have a need to do that with Mrs. Helen Robertson from Phoenix, who he wouldn't know from Eve. That's how I introduced myself, anyway. The name of his church is a place called, uh… 'Heaven's Doorway.'"

"Heaven's Doorway," Regina repeated sardonically as she wrote it down. "Figures. The shithead would name his church something goofy like that. 'Heaven's Doorway.' Who the fuck's he trying to kid?"

"It's in the Lower East Side, near the Manhattan Bridge exit off something called the FDR. Is this makin' any sense to you, Reg?"

Regina lolled her head back and pondered. "I think so. That's some sort of highway that goes along the river on the east side of the city." She heard a knock on her door. "Just a minute! I'll be right there!"

"You gotta go?"

"Not yet, Hellie." she said as she swung out of bed. "What's the street address of this Heaven's Doorway?"

"Uh, lessee…" Hellie said as Regina gathered that she was searching her notes. "Uh, oh, here. Twenty-One Water Street, off Catherine Street in that Lower East Side place. You gonna call him? Maybe you shouldn't."

"Probably I won't, but give me the number anyway."

Hellie recited the phone number as Regina wrote it down. She then went to her door carrying the phone. "Hon? There's somethin' else." "What more could there be?" She opened to door to the surprise of Dave bearing roses and champagne.

"Surprise!" he said. "Happy Birthday!"

"Oh, thank God!" Regina gasped at the sight of him. "My birthday's next week, but I'm not complaining." She pecked a kiss on his cheek as she ushered him in.

"I gotta tell you this, Reg," Hellie said. "It's been weighing me down. I ended up in tellin' that church secretary who I really was."

This stunned Regina. "You told him."

"I did."

"Shit! Hellie?"

"I told him to say that Jillian's sister, Hellie Laine called. I just couldn't let the bastard off without tryin' to make his life a little miserable, at least for a day or two."

It eased her tension to see Dave taking the ice bucket down from the closet shelf. "Okay, Hellie. Guess you had to do what you had to do. I gotta go. Dave's here."

"Who's Dave?"

"Tell you later. I gotta go. Thanks for everything, Hellie. And con- gratulations—Wait a minute." She held the phone away from her. "Dave? What do you know about the Lower East Side?"

"Where?" he asked, preoccupied.

"Water Street? Near the Manhattan Bridge?"

"It's closer to the Brooklyn Bridge. It smells like fish." He popped the cork off the champagne. "Pretty seedy neighborhood. Why?"

"Just wondering." Then she spoke back into the phone, "Dave says it smells like fish near where that place is."

"Figures," Hellie said dryly.

"Okay, sis." Then she added, pretending an afterthought, "Uh, how's Timbo?"

"Fine," Hellie said through a hint of surprise. "He's runnin' around all over the place, then falling down here and there, but I think he's gittin' the knack of it. Why?"

Regina became sullen in the remembrance of Timbo, and how soft he felt to the touch—how soft his touch felt to her. The sweet fragrance of mother's milk—her milk—and baby talc and the gossamer finery of his hair. "Just give him a little hug for—" she paused.

"For you?" Hellie asked hopefully.

"For you, Hellie," Regina whispered tightly. "For you."

Chapter 45

The ladies who lunch

Schrafft's restaurant on Fifth Avenue and 13th Street was an authentic memorial to a bygone metropolitan wartime culture that had since telescoped into the younger spirit of the Jet Age generation. Built in the height of the art deco age, this flagship of the many Schrafft's throughout Manhattan had remained uniquely unchanged with its high mirrors and cantilevered semicircular brass- railed balcony. Tall windows featuring a view of Midtown to the north up Fifth Avenue fronted the building's curved façade.

It was a small palace for ladies to delicately lunch, and its signature fountain treats were regarded as iconic. It was just the right sort of place for Bobbie, Pauline and Thomas to gather after a tiring morning shopping spree uptown at Bonwit-Teller. Bobbie had bought a small burgundy hat and wore it in a fashionable jaunt as he tried to discreetly angle a dainty wedge of his egg salad sandwich behind the fuchsia-colored birdcage netting covering his face.

"You know you can lift that up to eat, Bobbie," Pauline said. "Then there goes all the mystery."

Pauline lowered his fork down to his chicken-a-la-king in a puff pastry. "Suit yourself, sweetie, but you're about to drop some egg salad on your—" a dollop of egg salad tumbled into the lap of Bobbie's pink summer shift. "Whoops! Too late. There it went!"

"Damn!" Bobbie complained as he quickly swooped down a cocktail napkin to pick it up.

"There's an art to dealing with face netting," said Thomas. "Especially when you're eating."

Thomas could sense Bobbie's glower even through the veil, which he then lifted toward his hat to tuck it beneath the brim. Thomas could see why Pauline had once been so attracted to him. He was adorably clumsy and had done a fantastic job in making himself over with a pageboy auburn wig, light-peach lipstick and light-blue eye shadow complemented by a dark, thin liner of mascara. Bobbie's skin was so inherently supple he needed no other makeup.

Thomas played the sultry Veronica Lake blonde again today. He had drawn a long swath of hair to cover his right eye. His eyes were also hidden by a pair of large, very dark sunglasses like those he had spotted at the World's Fair six weeks before. Beyond that, he chose not to remember that day when even the magnificent Pieta seemed to have lost its marble sheen. He glanced past Bobbie at the mural depicting turn-of-the-century ladies in layered ankle-length dresses poised among men in top hats and tails in an impressionistic setting below a fringe of painted vines. The respectful clinking of forks against plates and the quiet din of conversation echoed as properly as the sweet aroma of pastry throughout the restaurant. Thomas took a distracted bite of his ham salad on lettuce. "A chocolate frappe for your thoughts, Camille," Pauline said.

"Just thinking," he said. He didn't know about what, though, be- cause, at least for now, his mind was blessedly empty. He realized how much he needed this day of mental rest. He looked over at Pauline. "How's your chicken?"

"Tasty—and yet bland. Could use a little more paprika." Pauline winked over at Thomas as he swiped a strand of his long black-haired wig behind an ear. "Those glasses really suit you, sweetie. All you need is one of those three-foot-long cigarette holders."

"How does anyone draw any smoke through one of those tunnels?" Bobbie asked.

"You don't," said Thomas. "They're just so you can show everyone how stylish you can be."

"Huh. Might have worked well for Holly Golightly. Didn't quite work out that way for Franklin Roosevelt," Bobbie said.

Thomas sipped his whiskey sour. "Depends on if you ask Eleanor, or her secretary who ended up sleeping with him—or her—whatever." "Lucy Mercer," Pauline recalled. "Maybe Lucy had a thing for long—things."

Thomas nearly choked back his drink, as the three of them chortled like school children.

Bobbie had finally given up on his sandwich. He lit his pipe. "I don't know about Eleanor." He shook out his match and deposited it in the table ashtray. "I've got a feeling she was more a he-she like us, though not nearly as trendy."

"Eleanor's stylist must've been a real hack," Pauline quipped. "I could have worked wonders on her, if she was so inclined. Oh, Bobbie, dear. I wish you wouldn't smoke that thing in public. It gives us all a bad name."

He blew a puff of smoke toward Pauline, then made an exaggerated face, which quickly returned to normal as he was struck by his own news to them. "Oh!" he gushed, "Did I tell you, Pauline? Somebody called me to get back in the business."

"Bobbie was a wedding planner in a former life," Pauline reminded Thomas. "That's great, boobie-kins! You gonna do it?"

"I don't know. Since Edward left—"

"Your ex-partner, the one you dropped for me, you little vamp," Pauline said.

Bobbie took another draw on his briarwood pipe. "Edward got married and went out to settle in suburban Lancaster, Pennsylvania, of all places. We thought he might have been smitten by the Amish. I think he was afraid he had crossed too far over the line in our direction—a real horror for the hard-core hetero he only thought he was. Shocked him right into religion."

"He'll be back," Pauline said. "They all come back eventually."

"How long were you doing it?" Thomas asked to keep the conversation going. He subtly slipped a pot-laced cookie into his mouth.

"The wedding planning business? About seven years. Right, Pauline?"

"Something like that."

"I was really good at it," Bobbie reminisced. "Edward and I had incredibly creative minds for coming up with themes."

"You really should get back into it, booby-kins. It's about the happiest I've ever seen you. How did you find out about this one?"

"A friend of a friend of a friend of a friend of mine's cousin. Bride's name is Francesca something-or-other Italian—I have it written down somewhere—she's getting married in December." Bobbie lifted the veil that had crept back down across his face and he held aside his pipe and sipped his Scotch and soda. "All sorts of theme possibilities; Christmas; the big Italian thing—she said about four hundred people were coming. And here's something really interesting—her hubby-to-be is a policeman or something up in Midtown. I was thinking I could do a nineteen forties cinema-noire theme for them."

"Sounds perfect," Thomas said distractedly as he let the weightless effect of the marihuana filter in.

"I'd take the job if I had someone helping me out. These big wed- dings take at least two people."

"Yeah, the bride and groom," Pauline said.

"Hardy-har, Pauline. Anyway, I won't be able to do it. Not alone at least."

"Maybe Camille could help you."

Thomas had not heard much of the conversation while the pot mingled with the scant after-effect of the LSD tab he had taken four hours before. He felt engulfed by a sea of the white cloths draping each of the small tables. The waves of white swirled within a small confusion of the black-and-white waitress' uniforms. Women's hats of all kinds ebbed and flowed within a snowy sea among the bobbing pink flowers in the waves. He reached out to touch one and felt the petals of the pink carnation in the white bud vase on his table. He looked out the tall, curved windows toward the street below where the roofs of cabs glittered in the bright sun as they made their way up toward the Flatiron Building and the angled intersection of Broadway. He turned his head in a slow stroboscopic motion toward the mural on the wall behind him and watched as its people became sluggishly alive—walking but not moving—as if on a treadmill. He took in the light, sweet redolence of sweet buns and chocolate.

Pauline brought him back into the conversation. "Camille, darling!" Thomas slowly arose into wakefulness. "Hunh?"

"I was saying maybe you could help Bobbie with setting up the wedding."

"That's crazy, Pauline! Camille's far too busy with her preaching and all to help me out. Wedding planning takes a lot of time, concentration and attention to detail."

"Whose wedding is it?" Thomas asked sleepily as the gentle hallucination faded smoothly from his mind. He really did not care whose wedding it was; he only wanted to continue to float away while Bobbie and Pauline carried on their conversation.

"A distant friend's distant cousin named Francesca," Bobbie

answered. "It'll be an Italian, Christmas kind of wedding. She's marrying a lawman, so maybe there's a police sort of thing in the theme."

"I think our dear Camille would be perfect for helping you, Bobbie," Pauline answered for Thomas. "She's really developed a style, and who knows? Maybe you two could restart the wedding planning business you loved so much."

"What about your church, Camille?" Bobbie asked, as if working with Thomas had become a forgone conclusion.

"I don't know," Thomas said.

"Camille's church attendance has fallen off. Hasn't it, dearie?" Pauline said. "Besides you have Francis to carry on when it's not Sunday."

"Pauline?" Bobbie griped. "Will you puh-*leez* let Camille decide for herself?"

Maybe the fog of drugs had spoken for him, or maybe it was his god, but Thomas smiled at Bobbie and said, "I 'suppose I could try it just this one time. But you'll probably fire me in a week."

"Really?" Bobbie gushed excitedly. "You'll do this with me, Camille?" "Sure. Why not?" He reached toward another flower in the vase as the hallucination wore away like a departing friend.

Bobbie leaned across the table and kissed him on the cheek, not caring about the fluted half-full glass of water he overturned in the process. "Thank you, thank you, sweetie!"

"What do I have to do?" he asked as Bobbie resumed his seat.

"I'll set it up right away. Just show up with me at the bride's apartment up on York Street next week."

Thomas brushed away the attacking plume of Bobbie's pipe smoke. "We're not doing this in dress, are we?"

"No, darling. We go as God made us—as boys." "Pity," Pauline interjected.

"Okay, Bobbie." He twiddled a bow on his big glasses. "But I don't want to go as 'Reverend Thomas Deavers.' I'd feel awkward about mixing religion and commerce, so to speak."

"So to speak," Pauline agreed. "So, what do we call Camille's male doppelgänger?"

Thomas had come down into the moment as he pondered over taking a final bite of his ham salad. "Ishmael. I can be Ishmael."

Bobbie's expression soured. "Ishmael? Like that dreadful poet at The Cavern?"

"Ishmael," Thomas accentuated with a nod.

"Sound's exotic," Pauline commented. "Does our dear Ishmael have a last name?"

"No. Just—Ishmael. A single name makes me sound more creative, anyway, don't you think? More exotic?"

Bobbie fidgeted with his napkin. "Fine. Ishmael, it is."

Pauline laid down his fork and summoned a waitress who wore a crisp, black uniform with a starched white filigree bib draped over her shoulders. "Anyone up for sharing a banana split to celebrate Bobbie's renewed passion?" he cheerily asked.

Chapter 46

Out in Casablanca

Thomas slouched uneasily in the couch next to Bobbie in Francesca's first floor apartment on York Street. Bobbie, resorting to using his given name, Robert Kavrovitch, had been absorbed in taking assiduous notes in the hope of selling the bride-to-be on his *film-noir* theme.

He had never seen Bobbie as a male before, and glanced occasionally in his direction to be taken in by his beauty as a man-child with clear soft skin and a dark golden, fleecy mane of hair. He sported a light saddle of freckles across the bridge of his nose, which he had unwisely chosen to cover up when in drag.

Francesca exuded a childlike charm to complement her plush, well-toned, innocent features. Her lusty black hair was hastily done up and disarrayed into indifference, as she had nearly overslept this meeting with her wedding planner. Though she was barefoot, she was dressed for a walk in the woods in an oversized, thickly yarned orange sweater, and misty-blue jeans on the way into tatters.

"So, Francesca," Bobbie asked deliberately. "How would you feel about…? Well, I was thinking of a theme wedding."

She sipped the remains her coffee. Her frayed, awakening voice echoed huskily into her coffee mug. Thomas noticed how smooth and flawless her hands were. "A theme, Robert?" She delicately cleared her throat. "That might be interesting. What sort of theme?"

"Well," Bobbie began, trying to mask his excitement. "Your hubby-to-be is a policeman."

"Private detective," she corrected. She raised her empty mug as if toasting them. "You sure I can't interest either of you in a cup of coffee?" "Oh, no. Thanks," said Bobbie. "I make it a rule not to drink anything after ten-thirty in the morning or before five in the evening."

Francesca chuckled. "Sounds a little boring. Just hook me up to a caffeine I.V. and I'm good for the day. 'Scuse me." She rose gracefully from her chair and padded toward the percolator to refill her cup.

Thomas felt an inexplicable effervescence sizzle up his spine. "If you have any, I could use a Coke," he said.

"Ah," she said from the open door of the fridge, as she searched for milk for her coffee. "Sure thing, Isaac."

"Ishmael," he corrected.

"Ishmael," she said into the little chill of the refrigerator. "No Coke. I have Tab," she offered.

"Perfect," Thomas said. "I'll have that."

The soda bottle chinked against its neighbors as she brought it out into the open. She flicked off the cap with a bottle opener and poured its sizzling contents into a water glass. "There's no ice. It's still making from last night, this morning, whatever. The soda's cold, though. Hope you don't mind. Your name's interesting, Ishmael. Is it Jewish?"

Thomas pondered this. "I don't know, but probably. Depends on who you ask. It is biblical, though."

"Oh," Francesca said distractedly. She carried her coffee and the glass of soda to the pinewood coffee table. She placed Thomas's drink in front of him.

"Our Ishmael is a very religious person," Bobbie said.

"Catholic?" Francesca asked in a tone thinly laced by hope.

Thomas tweaked a smile in remembrance of his seminary a long time back in Ireland. "I've, uh, taken a few courses in it." He sipped his soda. "I'm kind of a hybrid, now."

"Uh-huhn," Francesca smiled benignly. She settled into her recliner chair and tucked her legs beneath her. She turned to Bobbie. "So. What's your theme idea?"

"Well," he said heartily as though preparing to announce an event. "I'm thinking that because your hubby's a policeman—"

"Private detective," she reminded him through a sip of coffee. "—I had in mind a Raymond Chandler, film-noir sort of theme." "Film-noir," she mused. "I'd never really thought about doing any sort of theme wedding."

"I was thinking maybe the bride could dress in something slinky."

"Slinky," she said.

"Well, respectably slinky. Something cautiously elegant, with one bared shoulder. Maybe in red satin, or silk." Bobbie saw he had captured her attention and continued. "Your hair is lush and longish, Francesca. We could make you up so it hangs provocatively across your face. Like Lauren Bacall. I have just the person to make you up." He looked over at Thomas. "Pauline."

"I figured that."

"Lauren Bacall," Francesca stated. "Should I say 'I do' in that croaky voice of hers?"

Bobbie sensed her sarcasm and blithely laughed.

She noticed his defeated expression. "No. Robert," she said. "Go on. It sounds interesting. Really. You're thinking of dressing Raymond up as Bogie?"

Thomas flushed at her mentioning the name: Raymond.

Bobbie referred to his notes. "Fedora hat, black trench coat, gray pleated tux, patent leather Italian-looking pointed shoes. You in red satin stiletto heels."

She chuckled over her coffee mug. "I'd have to learn to walk all over again. I can hardly even handle pumps as it is. Aren't brides sup- posed to be dressed in white?"

"We can change the red to white, or off-white," Bobbie suggested. She leaned back in thought. "I think I kind of like it," she said. "I don't know about Raymond, though. He's not big on any sort of costume things."

"Isn't that what a wedding is?" Thomas volunteered. "A costume party?" Bobbie leered at him, then held his finger subtly to his lips in a "shhhh."

"You're right about that, Ishmael," Francesca said through a mischievous chortle. "One big costume party. Okay. I like it. Let's see how Raymond takes to it when he gets here."

Bobbie brightened. "He's coming by? How *wonderful*! When?"

Thomas tried to shiver away the sudden apprehension flowing throughout his body.

Francesca looked over her shoulder at the contemporary sun ray face of the kitchen clock. "About five minutes ago. He's famous for being late."

"Why, dear," Bobbie said. "Being fashionably late is all the rage nowadays."

"Late? Maybe. Fashionably? Never," she said. "My Raymond will never change."

Thomas glanced around nervously for an escape route just in case his worst fear came to light. He lifted his glass to hide his trembling lips. Bobbie looked down at his notes. "I don't think I—no, I don't have it down. How forgetful of me. What is your Raymond's last name? I know I should have taken it down, but—sorry."

"S'okay, Robert. It's Nealy. Raymond Nealy."

Thomas nearly choked mid-sip on his Tab. "You okay, hon?" Francesca said.

"No." He cleared his throat. "I'm fine." He cleared his throat again and fanned his hand in front of his face. "Just went down the wrong way," he said, realizing how true this was. "I'll be fine." He needed a Pethidine to salve the surge of another migraine. He cringed away a heated pain as he rose from his seat with a little cough. "I just need the rest room."

"Oh, sure, hon," she said. "Wait. The powder room in the front hallway is waiting for a plumber, so you'll have to use the one in the master bedroom, through that half-open door there. Pardon the mess."

"S'okay, Francesca," Thomas choked breathlessly as he made his way toward the bedroom door.

"So," Bobbie continued as Thomas left the room, "you want to get married in Oyster Bay, Long Island. It'll be pretty cold there in December, those breezes off The Sound being what they are. Have you chosen a venue, yet? Yacht club? Banquet hall? Anything like that...?"

Thomas felt trapped as he closed their conversation off with the bedroom door. His gut reaction was to climb out a window to escape and then realized the senselessness of it all. He gazed around the room: the king-sized bed, rumpled on both sides—his and hers—the clothing closets, hers with the wide-open slatted doors; dirty laundry scattered around a wicker basket and the vanity in the far corner, with its disorder of mostly dark-hued cosmetics. Through the open bathroom door, he saw a pair of panty hose hanging on the curtain rod of the shower. He headed there and closed the door to secure himself that much further away from the coming doom.

Held hostage by nausea and throbs of migraines, he fumbled

around in his pants pocket for his container of Pethidines. He scooped the three that were left into his mouth and swallowed. He then heard a muffled little commotion from the living room, accented with the low timbre of a man's voice. Mister Detective Raymond Nealy had arrived. Thomas swallowed another cup of water to steel himself while he allowed the Pethidines to calm his pain. He took two deep breaths and then left the bathroom for Francesca's living room.

Thomas had concocted an image of Nealy as a corpulent, cigar-smoking gumshoe, wearing a beat-up, narrow-brimmed, homburg hat on the back of his head like in the movies. But this was not the case. Nealy was taller and leaner, though full in body and, with his thinning gray- streaked immaculate hair, more patrician-looking than Thomas had imagined. He was dressed by Brooks Brothers in a gray seersucker jacket over a light-blue sport shirt, crisply pressed khaki pants and polished oxford leather loafers as if he were on his way to The Club for a round of cocktails before tennis. Thomas could hardly imagine him dressed as a *film-noir* wedding detective.

They were relaxed around the coffee table—Bobbie on the couch and she with her legs still tucked beneath her as she had settled back in her recliner. Nealy stood up from the couch as Thomas entered the room. "Ah, honey," Francesca said. "Say hi to Ishmael, Robert's business partner."

"Hello there," Nealy said amicably as he took Thomas's sweating palm firmly into his plump, welcoming, dry one. He had a professional handshake.

For a long moment, Thomas imagined Nealy's gaze searing into him as if he knew everything. "Uh, yeah, hullo, uh, Raymond," he said aridly as he looked down.

"Glad you could help us out," Nealy said as he released his grip. Thomas's soda had been placed on the side table next to a thickly cushioned side chair into which he lowered himself. "Ishmael. Now that's an interesting name. Is it, what? Greek?"

"No," Francesca answered. "It's biblical."

"Ah," Nealy said.

"But he's not Catholic. Ishmael's, what did you call it? Hybrid?"

"Being Catholic isn't like some sort of pre-requisite for planning our wedding, Frannie." He winked amiably at Thomas. "Look at me. I'm a card-carrying agnostic."

"Not like our children are gonna be," Francesca dryly insisted. "Actually," Bobbie interjected, overcome with joy and forgetfulness over Francesca's accepting his film-noir wedding theme. "Our Camille—er, Ishmael—is a very religious person. He even went to a Catholic priest's college in Ireland to study." Thomas wished he would shut up.

Nealy was intrigued by the accidental mention of 'Camille' in relation to Ishmael's name, along with the Catholic connection. He narrowed his gaze at Thomas. "That so? Catholic college. You mean like a seminary?"

"Me? Oh, heavens no!" Thomas chortled nervously from behind the soda glass he clutched protectively in both hands. "Nothing like that. I just sort of dabbled in it for a while."

"Dabbled," Nealy said.

Thomas put down the glass and smiled broadly. "So. Raymond. What do you think of Robert's theme for your wedding?"

"They've come up with a great idea for a theme wedding for us, Raymond" Francesca said.

Nealy looked cordially toward Bobbie. "A theme wedding?" His tone was cautious.

Francesca patted Nealy's knee. "Let him tell you, honey. Just listen. You might like it."

"Okay, Robert. Fess up. What is it?"

"Well, Raymond," Bobbie said in a voice sizzling in anticipation. "You're a policeman, right? A private detective?"

"Yeah, I am," Nealy said apprehensively. "Emphasis on 'private.'" "Well. I was thinking of a detective theme. Sort of like a film-noir detective story, like 'The Big Sleep,' something like that." He gazed at him for a reaction.

Nealy sipped his water, then answered: "Okay. So now I'm totally confused."

Francesca continued Bobbie's thought. "He thinks it would be kind of neat if I dressed in a, I don't know, slinky satin evening gown and do my hair like Lauren Bacall. I'm really beginning to cuddle up to this idea."

"And who am I supposed to be?"

"Humphrey Bogart," Bobbie answered.

Nealy forced back a laugh as he took this in. "Humphrey Bogart!" He lit up a cigar and then shook out his match as he thought the idea through. "Oh, I get it. Who's my best man? James Cagney? And the preacher? Sidney Greenstreet?"

"That was 'The Maltese Falcon,'" Bobbie said dejectedly.

"What?" Nealy said.

"Sidney Greenstreet was in 'The Maltese Falcon.' And 'Casablanca.'"

Nealy looked warily over at Thomas. "What do you think of this idea, Ishmael? You on board with it?"

"I think it's fine, I guess. Robert's been working it day and night for the last week." He motioned toward Francesca. "I, uh, think Francesca likes the idea."

"I'm really starting to love it," she said.

Nealy's remembrance as to why he left the force over five years before set the cop theme sourly with him. "I don't know. We don't need any sort of masquerade party. Why don't we just keep it as a traditional wedding?"

Bobbie heaved a ponderous sigh.

"What if I want to do our wedding Robert's way, Raymond?" Francesca said icily enough to cause Nealy to surge his shoulders in response.

"You like this theme idea that much, Frannie?"

"I do. Yes."

"Okay, Robert. We'll compromise." Nealy said. "You did come up with something I suppose I could live with, which really isn't that far off your idea."

"I did?"

"Yeah. If Frannie insists on a theme sort of wedding, even though I might prefer the standard bride and groom tradition at The American Legion, with paper cups and all the beer you can drink—"

"Raymond!" Francesca protested.

"Don't worry, sweetheart. That's just me, a soppy traditionalist. If we've got to do it a theme wedding, maybe we can make it a little less cop-centered. Let's try a 'Casablanca' theme."

"Really?" Bobbie brightened. "Yes, let's! Francesca can be Ingrid Bergman as Ilsa Lund. And Raymond, you could be Bogey as Rick Blaine!"

"Guess I'd rather be Rick Blaine than Philip Marlowe," Nealy said through a spirited laugh and then swiftly stood as though he had somewhere else to be. "Well, it was good meeting you both, but my bride and I have a lunch date."

"We do?"

"'Casablanca!'" Bobbie gushed excitedly as he stood while visions of potted palms and men in fezzes tripped happily through his mind. "This is gonna be *wonderfully* terrific!"

Thomas followed everyone's cue and stood. Caught up in

Bobbie's exuberance, along with his own about finally leaving, he said, "This is wonderful. Blessings, dear hearts!"

Nealy looked suddenly overcome with a freeze on hearing Thomas's parting comment. He held his smile as he gazed at Thomas and took his hand to shake it. "It was really good to meet you, Ishmael," he finally annunciated with calm deliberation. Thomas went numb in the realization that Nealy smelled the familiar hint of lavender in his cologne—the same he'd sprinkled the notes he left for him to find after the murders.

Nealy stared with calculation into Thomas's eyes. "Thank you for helping out, Ishmeal."

"The pleasure was mine, Raymond," Thomas said, hoping that all was right, now that this wedding ordeal had ended. Bobbie could take it from here, and he could submerge from the situation.

He withdrew his sweating hand and smiled shyly as he reached toward his glass. "You want me to drop my soda glass off in the kitchen on the way out?" Nealy looked down at the glass. Possible evidence? "Oh, no, Ishmael. Don't bother." He stared back at Thomas with a scant hint of intensity. "I'll take care of all that."

Thomas gazed at him as he tried preserving his own smile, even through the uneasy thought that, for some reason, he feared that Mister Detective Raymond Nealy had just made him as Chamelea.

Chapter 47

Morning in Dublin

Thomas huddled over his journal as he wrote. His longhand script was neat and stout; precise and deliberate:

Thursday, September 10, 1964

I hardly know where to turn in this gnarled thicket of my despair. My good fortune has suddenly twisted and knotted up my passions. Since my liberation of Patti Nolan two weeks ago, and since Mister Editor Frank Malone's editorial in his New York KnickerBocker, through which Mister Detective Raymond Nealy had tried to lure my dear Chamelea into the light, I've posted three letters for Editor Malone to publish and entice Detective Nealy to respond in kind through the press. Alas, I've heard nothing. Earlier today, though, by dumb chance (and my own careless stupidity!), I met Mister Detective Raymond Nealy, who, to all the world, has made it his project to expose my dear Chamelea. Worse, and I have no idea how, but I saw in his eyes that he knew he had found his mark. My darlings! It is far too soon for this—our dear Chamelea is not prepared to be unmasked! We must now suddenly leave New York, but where are we to go? I feel consumed, smothered by confusion. I am choked by the very embrace of my God.

Then, through the intervening wisdom of his god, Thomas brightened as he constructed a solution:

Wait a minute, my dear hearts! I still have my residence in Ireland! In Ballycannough. I can finally go home! It will be simply a matter of sending the rental tenants packing with a little sum of money to sweeten my indis- cretion toward them. Surely it wouldn't take much. Is there extradition in Ireland? I think not. Alas, this revelation has driven me to ramble. I need to take another communion wafer.

He delicately slipped an LSD-laced wafer onto his tongue and savored it as though it was a sacrament.

Ah, yes, my darlings! The world will not close in on us after all, as my God now cloaks me in assurance. I must call Seamus, my barrister, when it is morning in Dublin.

Work to do! I must go now.
Blessings, dear hearts!"

"*Toomas!*" Seamus shouted from over his phone in Dublin into Thomas's good ear. He'd forgotten how boisterous his barrister could be. He contemplated moving the receiver over to his deaf ear, now plugged uncomfortably by his new, ineffective hearing aid. "How *be* ye, lad?"

"Fine, Seamus. It's good to be talking to you, again. I should have called more often. Sorry."

"'Tis noothing, I ashoor you. What can I do for you?"

"It's about my house in Ballycannough. I was thinking about moving back to Ireland."

"Well, you may've called at the right time, Toomas. Ol' Mister O'Hiene has soofered a stroke."

"Really." Thomas held the receiver between his ear and

shoulder as he found a pencil. He twiddled it among his fingers to calm his anxiety. "Who's old Mister O'Hiene?"

"Why, Toomas. He's the one who be payin' rent on yer hoos for the last twenty years or so."

It shook Thomas a little that he had forgotten the name of his tenant. "Of course, Mr. O'Hiene. I nearly forgot. How's he doing?"

"I joos told you, lad. Not well. He had a bad stroke an' his missus is not up to keepin' up the place on her own. She wants to move to an ol' folk's apartment in Dooblin, wherein she can have help with tendin' to 'er hoosband."

Thomas could hardly believe the turn of his luck. He leaned back luxuriantly in his office chair and slipped a marijuana cookie into his mouth with one hand while continuing to work the pencil with the other. "Well, Seamus, I am sorry to hear that the O'Hienes want to move from my little *pied-à-terre*. And just as sorry to hear about his stroke."

"'Tis true, Toomas. They no longer have two ha'-pennies to roob together to affoord your hoos or the little apartment, 'specially in Dooblin, costs bien' what they are nowadays."

Thomas's pot-induced exuberance seethed into a generosity.

"Well, Seamus. Here's what we'll do, then. We'll waive any deposit cost they've made, and you can set it up so we can pay their moving costs and rent in Dublin for the next year while they get settled."

"Why, Toomas! Tha' is very generous of us."

He smiled sullenly and gazed down at his typewriter and the latest half-finished letter to Frank Malone rolled into the platen. "Well, Seamus. There is a slight price for our generosity." He laid the pencil next to the typewriter, and then leaned over his desk.

"As there shood be, I s'pose."

"I'll be needing to move back to Ballycannough pretty soon."

There was a reflective silence from the other end, until Seamus lowered his voice into confidence. "How soon?"

"Probably about two weeks."

"A fortnight. Are you in soom sorta trooble, now Toomas?" he stated suspiciously.

"Oh, no more than usual, Seamus. I just need a time away from all this preaching to get back to my roots. I need to return home to Ireland."

"Well that is good, Toomas, it will be good to finally meet you after all these years. Now, what do you need from me?"

Thomas tapped his fingers on the phone's receiver after his call to Seamus and then brought his hands back to rest on the typewriter key- board. He read what he had written so far in this, his fourth, letter to Frank Malone since he had liberated Patti's soul.

Hello, again, Mister Editor Frank Malone;

Today Chamelea is frustrated and somewhat annoyed. This is my fourth attempt at reaching out through you to those who have been trying to find me. Today I will again make my case. Dear hearts, I am not as cold-hearted as you might imagine. Indeed, my soul is filled with light — God's light — that I have offered to those I have liberated. Lost and desperate souls, all, I've chosen them wisely. I share a sublime intimacy with those I enfold in their last moments of darkness, for I'm imbued with permission from my God to offer them the light of redemption. I absorb the dark burden of their suffering to enrich my soul so that I might liberate others.

All darkness passes into light as sure as dawn is born from the night. I bring the darkness of those I have liberated into a glorious light where darkness can find no place to hide, as there is light beneath the surface of all darkness from where God's light shines through. Each broken

---

beginning is yet another beginning—a true renewal of hope—for which my liberated children have hungered. I have delivered them from death through death, so they may finally live a full life.

I am an innocent catalyst of God. Chamelea is pure!

Thomas liked what he had written, but it was incomplete. He started typing again, moving his fingers more lightly, more relaxed, over the keys. He had become energized by the idea of leaving for Ireland to renew his own life and to replace the one that he knew was now closing in on him to smother him in its gloom of uncertainty.

To Mister Detective Raymond Nealy, I conclude:

I know this game of silence you are playing. The absence of your response to my previous three attempts to reach out to you has not been lost upon me. Silence is just another form of darkness, and there is a light lurking behind your silence, seen only by me. The darkness hiding that light will consume you before you will ever find me. I work through the dark and into the light so that I may fade back into the ubiquity of the darkness once again, for I am, as I have said, like the chameleon. Do not delude yourself, Mister Detective Raymond Nealy, that you are close to finding me, for you are destined to the darkness, where only I can find you.

Blessings, dear heart, Chamelea

Gloating over the accomplishment of his letter, he slid it into the business envelope he had previously typed as he had the others:

To Editor Mr. Frank Malone,
Senior Editor, 3rd floor, New York KnickerBocker…

He heard Milio rustling around in his room above; a sign that he was waking as he usually did, at 11 a.m. As soon as he saw him making his way to his daytime residence of the spacious dumbwaiter near the kitchen sink, he would flag him down and drive him to the Knickerbocker offices, where Milio would deliver the letter to Frank Malone, as always.

Thomas leaned back in his chair and rubbed his tired eyes as he heard the muffled sound of a car horn anxiously bleating outside his window. He realized he would not miss all the anxiety of city traffic once he was settled out in the lush ruggedness of his roots in Ballycannough. The horn now sounded an insistently long blast, followed by two short ones. He rose with a broken sigh, and then went to the front door of the church and opened it.

Deborah was sitting in a gleaming dark-green Ford Mustang. Though a crisp chill meandered through the air, she had lowered the tan convertible top. She wore a light-green silk headscarf to partially cover her windblown hair. "See, Thomas?" she said happily from be- hind the wheel. "I got one!"

He did not know how to respond as he drew a hand to his chin.

"This is that car you wanted?"

"Yep!" She tapped the gas pedal and the engine sounded out a guttural swell. "Come on. Let's go celebrate!"

"Go where?"

"The country. I know of a place up on the Connecticut coast far away from this mess where you can buy me dinner."

Twittering a dubious smile, he approached the car and took in the sweet showroom smells of Naugahyde and new rubber. "Much as I'd like to, Deborah. I can't. I'm preparing an ad for a church supper for the Tuesday Knickerbocker. It has to be in by noon today. Maybe later?"

"With you, sweetie, 'later' means maybe sometime—but never. Come on, now's the time! Get whatever you're gonna give to the paper and we can drop it off on the way."

He glanced over his shoulder at the church doorway. "I, uh, don't like dealing with newspapers. Never did," he said absently. "I usually take Milio over to bring up the ads. He knows who to give them to."

"Thomas! Just get the damned ad and I'll run in with it. Jesus. How hard could it be?" She gunned the engine twice, which registered two warm twinges of power through his body like an assent from his god. "Let's make this one of our special days. It's time we got caught up on some things, anyway"

He looked at her, then at the church, then up at the blue sky decorated with high clouds as he considered her offer. He realized a trip out to the country might not only be nice, but required, to calm him down. It would be a gift from his god. "Oh, okay," he finally said. "When we get to the Knickerbocker, just run in, drop the ad off, and then come right on out, so we can get on with it."

The humid halls of the Knickerbocker were redolent in the moist smells of ham and cheese and pepperoni pizza. Deborah carried the envelope up the creaking wood stairs that led to the editorial offices behind a pair of filmy glass doors on the third floor. The doors creaked as she swung them open and then went to a glass-fronted counter, behind which sat an aged, hatchet-faced crone with loosely piled dry brown-gray hair. She wore rhinestone horn-rimmed glasses, which magnified her eyes to the size of saucers. She rested her cigarette in a chipped glass ashtray near her typewriter. She composed herself with a cough. "Yeah?"

Deborah peeked at the envelope. "I've got an ad here for Mr. Frank Malone?"

The crone went back to whatever she was typing. "Advertising's down the hall. Room three-eighteen."

"I was told to give this to Frank Malone," Deborah frostily insisted.

The woman said nothing as she stopped her typing and held out her hand for the letter. She spotted the inscription on the envelope with the underlined capital "B" in KnickerBocker that Malone had told her to watch for. She suddenly became attentive. "Oh. Okay, hold on, ma'am. I'll get him out here."

"It's okay. I was told just to drop it off. I'm in kind of a hurry."

"This'll only take a second, hon." She looked over her shoulder and down the hall behind her, where Malone's door was open. "Yo! FRANK! Front desk!"

No response.

"MALONE!! Front desk!"

Deborah heaved an aggravated sigh, as she rolled her eyes in exasperation. Finally, she heard the throaty grind of a toilet flushing, followed by a husky, rugged male voice from the dankness down the hall. "For criminy sake, Myrna! I was in the crapper!"

Myrna glanced back at Deborah and offered up what she might have thought was a smile. "Sorry, miss. Gotta excuse our boy, Frank. We been workin' on him for years, but it hasn't taken."

"What? What?" Malone grumbled as he materialized into the thin light.

"Got one of them messages for you," Myrna said, as she handed him the envelope.

He quickly stared at it. "Well, shit!" he whispered and then stared up at Deborah, as she wondered why so much attention was being paid to a three-inch ad for a church supper. Malone puffed on his cigar as he squinted at her, sizing her up. "You speak normal American English?"

"Of *course* I do," she said coldly. "This is an ad for your Tuesday paper, okay?"

"Okay, fine," Malone said as he lowered his voice. "I'll run it right down to advertising. Uh, who's it from, so's I can tell 'em?"

"Heaven's Doorway. It's a church. You've run ads for them before." Malone grimaced a little smile of accomplishment, as he wrote "Heaven's Doorway" on the envelope "Sorry, ma'am. Just protocol. Ad department needs to know who to bill. Oh, yeah. Our ad department always has questions. Who do they contact there, 'case they have a question?

We never got to run this info from that guy you usually send, 'cause he don't speak no English. I t'ink he must be Lithuanian or sumpthin'."

Deborah knew Malone meant Milio. "I understand. The contact at Heaven's Doorway is Reverend Thomas Deavers."

Malone was so pleased with himself that his cigar began trembling in his fattened lips. Ashes fell to the envelope and he brushed them away. "Oh, okay. Great. Oh yeah, one more t'ing. I'm gonna need a mailing address, you know. For the billing."

"Sure. Down on Water Street. Twenty-One Water." She gave him the phone number.

Malone wrote it all down and leveled a jovial glance at her, and then wondered if she was having some sort of thing with this guy, Deavers. He further wondered, if that were the case, what such a good-looking dame saw in someone like this Chamelea person. "Okay. Thanks, ma'am. Thanks so much!"

"You're welcome, I'm sure," she said icily and then left.

Malone rushed back to his office to call Nealy, leaving behind the stench of his cigar smoke, which Myrna routinely brushed away as she continued her typing.

The ride up the Connecticut coast went quietly. Caught up in the elation of her brand-new Mustang, Deborah never mentioned her banter with Frank Malone. Urban clusters had diminished into the mellow swells of the shoreline countryside. They took in the chilly stir of the coastal breeze as it rushed around them and through the current of passing traffic on I-95. The smell of the breeze had loosened with the passing landscape from one tightened by electricity and waste into the softening harmony of a developing autumn blending with brine. Thomas took it all in as he relaxed into a state of a relief. The wavering sunlight from above sent him into a doze.

They arrived in Essex, a quaint New England sea town, doused in maritime history, in eastern Connecticut. They walked down cobbled sidewalks past whitewashed clapboard, black-shuttered storefronts and venerable old homes. The roots of thick-trunked, roughened-barked oak and maple trees swelled up from the ground and buckled the sidewalk in places. The tree leaves, blending from summer green to faint early autumn yellows and oranges, dappled gentle interplays of afternoon sunlight and shadows along the street. The air smelled of earth, tinted here and there with salty gusts from the mouth of the Long Island sound. Thomas wondered if Ireland would be anything like this.

Deborah led him through the old doors of The Essex Hotel, a low- beamed-ceilinged building creaking in history. The darkened restaurant was aromatic with the moist comfortable fragrances of whisky, beer and seared beef. A primly dressed hostess showed them to a table near a large open hearth housing a crackling, well-tended, though un- necessary, fire. Deborah excused herself for a trip to the restroom, and Thomas ordered Scotches for them both.

She was a little late in returning. "Well, darling."

"Well, Deborah," he said.

"I got us a room for the night."

"Without asking me?"

"You just would have said 'no.' besides, we need to get out of that crappy old city more often. Don't you feel like it's closing in on you, sometimes?"

"Sometimes," he admitted, thinking of Ballycannough and the slim remembrance of his chilly childhood bungalow with its fairy-tale thatched roof, and peat-burning cooking fires. His eyes glazed over. "Sometimes," he repeated distractedly.

"And anyway, darling." She placed her hand upon his; stared intently into his eyes. "We have something to celebrate."

"Your new car," Thomas said, still lost in the thought of returning home, at last.

"Well, that, sure." She tightened her touch on his hand into a grasp. "Well, sweetheart. Thomas, my love. I'm pregnant. With our baby."

Thomas's day went suddenly dark as he froze in the shadow of what she'd told him. His breath shortened into gasps as he heard his god guffawing mightily from within. He felt Deborah's warm hand slide from his moistening, trembling one.

"Thomas! Are you okay? You're turning white as a sheet."

"I'm fine, Deborah," he said dryly. He heaved one final exhale of composure, then put his hand upon hers. He looked into her expectant gaze now welling with a rare onslaught of her tears.

"Are you sure I'm—?" he said nervously. "I mean, you told me you had a, I don't know, an encounter with someone a few months back while you were in California."

She blushed, then blanched. "Well, more than one, actually," she said.

Thomas breathed a silent sigh of relief. "Well, then. There you go." "It's you, Thomas."

"How do you know?"

She heaved a sigh and stared into her drink. "Because my encounters weren't with a man. Sarah, my roommate at Pratt, and I had a thing back then. It caused quite a stir." She smiled ruefully in remembrance, as her voice fell off into privacy. "We just decided to, uh, catch up on a few memories. Actually, I found it all pretty mundane." She looked up hopefully at him. Her eyes glistened. "Aren't you the least bit happy about this, Thomas? We're going to have a child. You and me."

He was sullenly relieved that Deborah had had a lesbian affair. It legitimized him and Pauline. "Yes, Deborah. I'm happy for you. I'm happy for us," he fibbed. In fact, he felt that he was drowning in a wave of self-loathing.

Chapter 48

Hello, Munchkin

The delicate strains of Eric Satie's "Gymnopedie Number 1" fluttered throughout Thomas's bedroom. The piano-piece playing from the little hi-fi was so innocent, so light, so pure. It had been Jillian's favorite and an apt accompaniment for the moment, as Thomas distractedly finished applying a light crimson coating to his nails. He waved and twiddled his fingers to his sides to dry the polish. Restored and framed in a light filigree of silver-blue, the timeworn portrait of Jillian now permanently sat near the dressing table mirror. Casually checking it for reference, he lightened the coating of rouge on his left cheek. He then glanced up once again at the mirror and his very-near likeness of her.

His hair was flattened and misted by the tight hairnet he wore in preparation for the wig he had purchased yesterday at Bergdorf's. It was nearly the exact fullness of Jillian's chestnut hair as it was when she died. He fitted the wig to his head and he remembered wistfully how she would sometimes wear her hair in a loosely gathered braid hanging less like a skein but like a feather down to her breast.

He smoothed the open collar of the pink-silk blouse, his favorite—her favorite. He left the two top buttons open to show the soft skin of his freckle-glazed chest. He accessorized this discreet disclosure with a lavender-colored silk neckerchief—one of Jillian's signatures—and fastened it with the gold and pearl clasp she nearly always had worn. Another glance in the mirror reflected that he was finished—he was 98-percent Jillian as he remembered her. He slipped on the large sunglasses he had bought at Bonwit-Teller. Was that just two weeks ago? It seemed more like two years. Nevertheless, the over-stated glasses were the only accoutrement he wore that Jillian might not have.

He tightened his larynx a little. "Blessings, dear heart," he said through an openly friendly smile, with just the right hint of shyness, but not quite. He tensed his neck muscles just enough to alter his voice once again. "Blessings, dear heart," he strained. "Peter Piper picked a peck of pickled peppers." That sounded a little better. It wasn't an exact match for how he remembered Jillian's voice, but at least it could be interpreted as that of a woman. "Blessings, dear heart." He felt an uncomfortable tightness in his throat but knew he wouldn't need to use the voice for that long. He would exercise his jaw on the way to his destination.

He nodded approvingly at his reflection, stood and then furtively slipped downstairs so Milio wouldn't see him. At any rate, Milio would have most likely taken to his usual roost as he huddled in the oversized dumbwaiter. Thomas reasoned that his new digs in the kitchen may have reminded him of his former home under the FDR Drive. Sometimes, he'd heard the softened sounds of a baseball game over the portable radio Milio hugged to his ear as he hid himself away. Sneaking past from where he heard the muffled re-broadcast of a Yankees game, Thomas went down to the common room and then out the back door to the grime spangled Corvair parked behind the church.

Fortunately for Regina, the weather had turned too chilly for waterskiing, so her job now took her indoors full-time to work the

Pavilion's front desk during the closing days of this year's fair. The crowds had dwindled along with her enthusiasm for New York City. She longed to get back to her routine in Oklahoma and see Hellie again for the first time in nearly five months. She felt a repressed, gnawing yearn to see Timbo. She missed her El Dorado. She hadn't even driven a car since she'd come to New York. Now that Hellie was married to Jamie and had moved into Flapjack's house, Hellie had offered hers temporarily to Regina, and she relished the independence that would come with having her own place—and her own personal life.

She was brought from her homesick daydreaming into the now by the vaguely familiar fragrance of lavender. She looked up from the desk to spot the back of an auburn-haired woman in a pink-silk blouse, a gray flannel calf-length skirt and trendy blue pumps. A mauve-colored silk kerchief loosely surrounded her neck. The woman was glancing nervously around at what few patrons there were, as though scheming something. "Welcome to Oklahoma! May I help you?" Regina asked in bland cordiality.

"I was wondering where The Ford Motors Pavilion was,"the woman answered huskily, her back still turned.

Her voice sounded withdrawn to Regina, but her appearance seemed to materialize into someone distantly familiar. "Oh. Sure. Just go right, down The Avenue of the United States, past Hollywood and under the Parkway. You can't miss it." Duly realizing her job was to lure patrons to Oklahoma rather than to send them away, she added in practiced professionalism: "Before you go, though, ma'am, why not take some time to relax here in Oklahoma?" The woman turned slowly to face Regina, to reveal herself. "There's so much—here—to—see." the woman removed her over-sized sunglasses.

"Oh, munchkin. I've been here before."

"Oh, *shiiit!*" Regina bristled, as she cupped her hands over her nose. Her chair scooted back as she abruptly rose. "You *bastard!*" she gasped. "You fuckin' *bastard!*"

"Hello, Regina. I've finally come back to you—"

"Get the fuck away from me!" she seethed.

Thomas flimsily reached out his hand as he advanced toward his daughter. "I've missed you so much. And I know you've missed me, too, munchkin," he continued, using Jillian's pet name for her daughter. Thomas appeared to have been in a trance and had not heard Regina's trembling protestations.

"I said, GET OUT!" she shouted. Some other patrons turned their attention from the glass-encased displays of rope lariats and Cherokee tribal trinkets and toward the commotion at the reception desk. Some advanced to help as Regina bellowed, "Get the FUCK out of my *SIGHT!*"

"But I'm your *mother*."

"You are *not* my fucking MOTHER!" she stared helplessly wild-eyed into the small crowd. "She's NOT my mother! This, this person is not even a fuckin' *woman!*"

Trevor rushed out from his little office. "Regina! Is everything alright?" He sensed the growing rush of anxious voices among the visitors as he went over to her. "Everyone please calm down. Is this woman bothering you, Regina?"

Thomas offered a benign, almost reassuring yet distant, smile. "But I created you, Munchkin" he said in a dry way, wound up lightly in the threads of ghoulishness.

"AGHH!" Regina said at him. "Fuck you! Fuck you ALL!" She grasped her purse and burst into tears as she vaulted confusedly out the front door into the bright autumn sunlight.

"Regina!" she heard Trevor call feebly from behind.

As all the attention had been turned to the front of the pavilion, Thomas put his sunglasses back on and slipped unnoticed through the side and then into the thinning clusters of fairgoers meandering along The Avenue of the United States.

Regina tried to collect herself as she made her way breathlessly to the Fair entrance cab stand to hail a ride back to her hotel. She waited anxiously in line, bobbing from one foot to the other. She felt the hardening hands of fear close her around her throat. She lit a cigarette, took two quick, nervous and desperate puffs and then dropped it to the pavement to crush it out with the toe of her cowgirl boot. Finally, a cab pulled up and she told the driver to take her to the Astoria-Queens Hotel. She scooted into the backseat and then collapsed into tears.

"You okay, there, miss?" the cabbie asked.

"No! Please, just—just shut up and drive!" she croaked.

Once at the hotel, she rushed through the fabricated chill of the air-conditioning, not up to her room—no time for that—but to the bank of phone booths in a darkened corner of the lobby. She slouched breathlessly onto the hard metal seat of one of them. Then she slammed closed its cantilevered glass door to seal herself away from the rest of the world. Finally, a little more composed, she slipped a dime in the slot to call Hellie collect. Her shaking finger misdialed, and she yanked down the receiver cradle to return her dime, and then dialed again. She let it ring for two—three—almost five minutes, and even over the grating buzz after buzz after buzz, all she could hear was the heft of her own breathing. Finally, exasperated, she hung up. She was then seized with an idea to call Deborah Dantana. She rummaged through the vastness of her satchel of a purse until she found Deborah's crinkled up card. She dialed. "Dan-tana Contracting," a male voice sounded happily through the receiver.

"Deborah! I need to speak to Deborah Dantana. Please! Hurry!"

The guy at the other end sensed the urgency in her voice that tele- graphed something must have gone wrong on a site. "Hold on."

"This is Debbie," she answered after a few rings. "Debbie!" Regina huffed. "Thank God! We need to talk."

"Who is this?"

"Oh, sorry. Regina Barragan? From the Oklahoma Pavilion?"

"Oh. Yeah. Everything okay, Regina? Is the pond okay?"

"It's fine." She heaved a breath. "Okay," she said more to compose herself, as she heard her voice echo into the stifling confines of the humid booth. "Okay. I'm fine. Listen, Debbie. We got to talk. It's about Thomas, Barr—Thomas Deavers, your boyfriend."

Deborah's tone was doused in suspicion. "What? You talked to him? Damn it! I knew there was something between you two. Well, *Regeena*," she threatened quietly, "did he happen to tell you I was going to have his baby? I'm pregnant. So back *off*, girlie!"

"What? No! Debbie, no…you can't do that. Shit!"

"Too bad, sweetie. Thomas and I are together, so steer clear, okay?"

"What the hell are you talking about?" Regina asked perplexed, and then put Deborah's presumptions together. "You think he and I—we?"

"It's over between you two, get it?"

"Debbie! Will you just fuckin' listen to me? I'm not, like, going out with him. I never have. Is that what you thought? Shit!"

"Well, I thought some-thing." Deborah said.

"We need to get together and talk. Can we do that? It's important." "Talk about what?"

Regina silenced into thought as she closed her eyes and wet her lips. "Well," she finally said, "for starters, I'm not his girlfriend. Not ever." She sighed again. "I'm his daughter, Debbie, his daughter."

"His daughter?"

"Yes. And there's more you need to know about my—father. He, uh, dresses like a woman."

Deborah sighed. "I know that," she admitted dourly.

"And you still *date* him? Debbie! Believe me. The guy's a fuckin' lunatic. Today he came up to me dressed like my mother, his, uh, dead wife." She heard Deborah catch her breath. "You didn't even know he was married before? He didn't even tell you that?"

Now it was Deborah's turn to be quiet. "No, I mean yes, I guess. If you're his daughter there has to be a mother-slash-wife somewhere in the equation," she said faintly. "Okay, Regina. You're right. We need to talk."

"Damn straight. When and where?"

"I'll be out of town in Charlotte, North Carolina, tomorrow through Thursday. How about Friday?"

Regina heard an insistent knocking rattle the booth doors and glanced up to see Dave Kiefer motioning her to hurry up. His voice was muffled. "I need to talk to you, Regina." He smiled. "So hurry up and finish!"

She showed her relief on seeing him through a thinly relaxed smile. She held up a finger, signaling him to hold on. Then she said back to Deborah, "Okay, Friday. Where?"

"The perfect place. Thomas's church. Twenty-One Water Street, downtown near the Brooklyn Bridge."

"I know where it is, Debbie. But that's crazy—I can't meet you there. The thought of that place gives me the creeps." Dave knocked again on the booth doors. She held her fingers to her lips to shush him. "Can't we just meet for drinks, or something?" She felt a welling of nervous- ness as her breath stiffened in her throat.

"He won't be there. He's never there late Friday afternoons. He's usually off somewhere, God knows where. I'm thinking we might find something there to, I don't know—I just think we both have a vested interest in him—good and or bad. Closure, maybe. Anyway, we've both gotta try to find out more about him."

Regina bowed her head and noticed how much her chest was heaving. "Okay," she said. "My father's church. Twenty-One Water Street. Around five? I don't get off work 'til three-thirty or so."

"Make it four?"

"O-kay, then—four." Then after a reflective silence: "I'm so fuckin' scared, Debbie."

Deborah's tone became smoothed by sympathy. "Regina? Listen, hon, it's gonna be okay. We'll get to the bottom of all this, I promise. We won't stop 'til we do. Okay?"

"Yeah, okay," she resigned tightly through a light ambush of tears. "Thanks for believing me."

"It'll be okay, hon," Deborah reassured her as she, too, had choked up. "Now dry those tears."

Regina hung up the phone and sat in the humid booth as she stared meditatively down at her lap to compose herself.

She was jolted into awareness by the hollow clatter of Dave's opening the door. Her lips quivered in the suggestion of more tears, as she rose to her feet and fell into his arms. "Let's go up to my room. Now," she commanded blithely into his shirt. "I just fucking need— some- thing," she sniffed.

"Sure, Reggie," he said understandingly as he stroked her sweat-dampened hair.

During their lovemaking, she was intent on wrapping herself around him, to feel the warmth of a caring soul. She stopped him every time he tried to tell her they needed to talk. She feared that maybe he wanted to tell her that his wife was back in the picture, or that he'd found someone else, someone more his age, perhaps, and would be getting married. She had

had enough bad news for one day.

Soon she listened to the stifled sounds from the bathroom where Dave was gathering himself together for a dinner at the Waldorf with the powerhouses of The New York World's Fair Commission, and where Robert Moses would be sitting at the head of the table. She sat up in bed, bare breasted above the nest of sheets that had gathered in her lap. She leaned her head back, and then absently lit a cigarette.

Her solitude was interrupted by the crashing open of the connecting door and the almost comical sight of Trevor simmering as he tried to com- pose himself while being intrigued by her nudity. His anger was softened by his western drawl. "What the HELL was that all about, Regina? You can't just up and leave like that!" He closed the door and loosened his tie.

She drew into herself in anticipation of his sordid plan to try to have sex with her. "And hello to you, Trevor," she said icily. "Forgotten how to knock?"

"I'm so fucking *pissed* at you right now. How am I going to explain what you went and did to the Commission?"

She snubbed out her cigarette as he sat on the edge of her bed. "Something very bad happened there, Trev. My worst kind of nightmare. That woman you saw —"

He reached out and put his fingers on her bare shoulder, which felt clammy to his dry touch. She smelled like the damp muskiness of sex. "Dammit, Regina. If she was giving you trouble, you could have just come and got me."

"It—it wasn't like that," she whispered as she turned away. "May- be you should just—go," she pouted quietly down at her lap. "We'll talk later."

"Why the hell are you whisper—?" Then they heard the sound of Dave's stream, followed by the phlegmy flush of the toilet. "What the *fuck*?" he said, as Dave opened the bathroom door while he casually buttoned up his shirt.

He looked up and spotted Trevor rising numbly from the bed. "Oh," he said calmly. "Hi, Trevor."

"What in the hell are you doing here, Dave?"

Regina offered a wry little smile as she wanted to respond with something like, *See, Dave? I* told *you he was stupid*! But instead she re- marked, "What do you think he's doing here?"

Trevor cast his dumbfounded look from Dave to Regina. Finally, he said to her: "You're fired. Pack up and go." He dejectedly trailed his silence back into his room and then closed the door, this time quietly.

Dave flashed a knowing smile at her.

"What the hell are you so happy about? I've just been fired and sent home to Oklahoma City on the worst day of my life. You'll probably never see me again."

"No, sweetie," he said as he draped his tie around his shirt collar. "You're *hired*. That is, if you want."

She drew her knees to her chest and leaned forward and wrapped her arms around them. "I don't—."

"That's what I came here to tell you. I got you a job working at the New York City Planning Commissioner's office in Midtown. " She shook her head in confusion. "What do you mean?"

"I mean you'd be earning about eighteen thousand a year working as an associate to Commissioner Moses, himself." He flicked a smile and kissed the top of her head. "Starts two weeks from Monday, just before the Fair closes for the winter."

"Well, shit! Of *course* I want it, Dave!" she gasped. She bounded forward and hugged him as the reality of his offer penetrated her confusion. "Hot damn and thanks!" she whispered enthusiastically into his ear. "Really though, I need a place to stay in New York at least until, I don't know, Sunday. There's something I—there's an old friend I promised to see. And I absolutely don't want to stay here…" she looked around what had become like a prison for her over the past five months, "in this room."

"You're right about that, Reggie. I wouldn't want you sleeping in a connecting room to Trevor's," he said pensively. "Well. Just so hap- pens I've got a nice little place of my own in Brooklyn Heights I think you might like. You can move in right now. I say we make a go of it. How about you?"

She kissed him heartily. "God, yes, Dave! Fucking-A yes!"

Chapter 49

Gumshoes and newsies

After bagging Ishmael's soda glass as evidence, Nealy rushed it over to Cohansen to test it for prints. Realizing this might take several days, he decided to fly Francesca to the lake house for a five-day weekend. On Sunday evening, they both sat in the large Adirondack chair on the apron of dewy grass leading down to the shore where the canvas-covered *Night Bird* bobbed lackadaisically on the water. Francesca's gaze was transfixed on Hamlet as he rooted intently for scents among the underbrush lining the lakeshore. "This is nice, Raymond," she whispered. She then rested her head on his shoulder as she shivered and clasped the neck of her sweater in defense of a billowing chill.

"Well, we've got a lot of work to do before December. We need this, now."

"Um," she smiled as she nestled closer to him.

"Uh, how do you like those—wedding theme ideas?" he asked.

"I think the 'Casablanca' idea's a really good one. Robert certainly seems competent enough to pull it off."

"And what about that other guy, his partner?"

"Ishmael? Seems nice enough, a little green and uncertain, but he follows Robert's cues."

"So, you're going with them."

"No, Raymond. *We're* going with them." She slipped a chilly hand into his open windbreaker to warm it. She twiddled her fingers play- fully against his chest.

"Okay, Frannie. Why?"

"Why? Because I say so. And, as you said, Raymond, the time's approaching." She sighed. "Anyway, I got a call yesterday from Robert.

He's already lined up a place for us near the old MacArthur airbase. An abandoned hanger. You should like that. Says he might be able to find a plane like the one they used in the end of the movie for a prop."

"Well, I would like that," he brightened. He wondered where Robert might round up a 1937 Lockheed 12 Electra, and then wondered if it might be up for sale after the wedding. Then he reminded himself that this conversation had a mission. "Honey? Why don't you let me handle the two wedding planners?"

She drew her hand away, sat up and glowered at him. "Christ, Raymond. I know you too well. You can hardly handle planning a tea party, much less our wedding."

"I just thought with the aviation theme, and all—"

"'Casablanca.' Your idea, remember?"

"All the more reason I should deal with the planners, Frannie. Besides, you have a lot of other things to do. Right?"

"I'll think about it," she pouted and then thought for a moment as she settled back against him. "Raymond? Is there something wrong?" "What makes you think that, honey?"

"I just know you. I can tell when you're upset about something. You wiggle your ears a little when you're nervous." She sputtered a cute little laugh as she touched his ear. "I can feel it. You're doing it now."

"Let's just say I'm a little concerned about—something about those two. I'm sure it's probably nothing. Just I want to be the one dealing with them."

"Raymond?" she worried.

"Let me handle it for now, Frannie. Okay?"

She thought a little. "You sure there's nothing you want to tell me?" He draped an arm over her shoulder. "Except that I love you? No. Not yet," he said. "Maybe later." He kissed the top of her head. Her hair smelled of fresh water and sweetly of hemp.

Once back in New York, Nealy did not go to his office, but spent the day in the Two-Oh's break room, waiting for results from the lab on the prints on Ishmael's soda glass. He scoured through the police reports about the three killings, searching for possible connections. He noted certain things: Ishmael's nervousness; Robert's slip of the tongue in referring to his partner as 'Camille,' and the reference to Ishmael's religiosity; the lavender scent of Ishmael's cologne—all of it set uneasily in one way. The solidifying thread was in Ishmael's unguarded signature: *Blessings, dear hearts*. This revelation rose above the rest of Nealy's intuitions and pulled him deeper into studying the reports.

Finally, at about 6:30, Cohansen came into the break room to wash out his coffee cup—a futile attempt, as it might never come clean. "I heard something, Ray. Lab results on that glass you brought in."

Nealy leaned back from the papers scattered on the table and rubbed his eyes. "Anything new?"

"Not really. Lots o' smudges is all. Getting anything from a glass is always a crapshoot. Moisture plays hell with prints; washes 'em right off. The guys found a partial they might be able to use, though. They'll need a little more time with it." Cohansen hung his coffee-crusted cup up among the other cleaner ones. "No one's ever gonna steal *this* fuckin' cup," he said to it. "Rumor goin' around my cup's got typhus, or something."

"I suppose a partial's better than nothing," Nealy said.

"Sure, buddy. Come on, now. I'm thirsty. Put all that paper up, an' we can go to The Page an' buy each other a few drinks."

A dim pall moistened The Back Page through the filmy smell of beer and whisky hovering among the perpetual odor of spent tobacco. Malone fecklessly dealt himself another poker hand, as he pretended not to listen to double-talking Nick going on about something involving his nephew's cousin's wife and the hot Indian curry pot roast she tried to cook the night before.

"So, what does that make her, Nick?" Mighty Joe wanted to know.

Will of the Hat cracked open a shelled peanut. "What does that make *who*?"

"Nick's nephew's cousin's wife?" Mighty Joe said as he took a pea- nut from the bowl on the table.

Nick thought it over. "I don't know, don't know. Some sorta cousin twice removed, or sompt'in'—maybe three times. I don't know. Someone who's, like, way in the distance. I was talkin' about her Indian pot roast, anyway."

"Okay," Mighty Joe said. "So?"

"Went down like a friggin' three alarm fire in my t'roat. One bite an' I hada drink four Schlitz's to put it out. Four of 'em."

"Okay," Will said. "So it was hot."

"Yeah, well wid all them beers. An' then some more. I got a little shit-faced. Really shit-faced."

"I believe this, Nick, what you are sayin'," Mighty Joe said.

"Yeah. I got shit-faced an' I went an' punched out my nephew's cousin. Punched him out. On account a' his wife's lousy cookin'," Nick bristled in a voice that dissolved into a phlegmy cough. "Really lousy cookin'. Spicy food has a negative kinda effect on me. Makes me wanna go out an' kill someone, I think."

"I like a little tabasco from time to time," Mighty Joe said as he un-shelled another peanut.

"So wha' happened after that?" asked Will. "The guy fights back and crushes you into pulp?"

"Nah," Nick said as he tried to rub away the hangover that had nagged him all day. "That woulda been too impolite a' him in his own house an' all. Like in fronta his wife, my nephew's cousin. Ya know, Willie? You haven't seen my nephew since he was, like, what? Four years old?"

"Jesus, Will," said Mighty Joe. "He's, what, eighteen now? You haven't seen Nick's nephew since fourteen years ago?"

Will shelled another peanut. "So? Same kid."

Malone drew a ten of hearts. "*Shit!*" he muttered at the poker hand he had ruined.

"'Cept for when you jus' said: 'Shit,' Frank, I hardly 'membered you was here," Will said. "Where'd you just been wanderin' off to in your head?"

"Nothin'," Malone grumbled.

"I beg to differ that it's som't'hin," Will said.

Mighty Joe sipped on his Wild Turkey. "Ah, he jus' got another love letter from his pen pal last Thursday."

"That Chamelea person?" Nick asked.

"Last Thursday? An' you din't run it down for the evening edition?" Will said. "*Jee*-zuz, Frank! Where's all that journalistic integrity you usta—?"

"Leave it be, Will. I'll run it tomorrow. Believe me. It's burnin' a hole in my head, I jus' need to check some—facts."

"Since when did *that* eveah stop ya?" Will asked. "You once tolt me: 'It's all only about the story, stupit! The facks are, like, incidental.' You tolt me that like them was words to live by."

The jukebox started playing Frank Sinatra singing "Witchcraft," as Malone dealt himself a three of clubs. "Shit!" he said again and threw down his hand.

Malone's luck hadn't been with him over the past few days since Deborah dropped off Chamelea's letter to him, and he was compelled to talk to Nealy about it. He owed him at least that before pressing it to the Knickerbocker's crime section. The letter now sat like ballast in the inner breast pocket of his seedy tweed jacket. He had to have tried to ring Nealy up 12 times, but he hadn't answered his phone, so Malone guessed he left for the weekend with his child bride. Today Malone had tried to call his office all morning, and still no answer. His effort now was to talk with him or Cohansen if either one of them showed up at The Back Page tonight. If not, he decided he would run the letter tomorrow without their blessing.

Double-talking Nick had just shifted his perpetual conversation to something about how his wife used paper cups of beer to ward away the mites from the rosebushes lining the front sidewalk of their row house in Yonkers.

"Waste of perfectly good brew, 'f ya ax me," Will commented. "Yeah," Nick agreed. "I think them damn rosebushes bin drinkin' it. They're scrawnier than my sister's Uncle Ralph. Scrawnier, even. An all dried out like. Dried out."

"'Scuse me, Nick," Mighty Joe finally realized. "'F the guy's your sister's uncle that makes him your uncle, too."

"Jumpin' Jehosiphat," Will said. "Here he goes again."

Malone shot up from his table as soon as he spotted Nealy and Cohansen walking in past the bar.

"Jesus, Frank," Mighty Joe started. "Wha'jya get stung by a freakin' *bee*?"

"'Pro'lly sumpt'in Nick said finally drove ol' Frank crazy," Will said dourly.

"Agh! That ship sailed, already," Malone said as he rushed to where Nealy and Cohansen had found their table. He pulled up a chair for himself.

"Why, hello, to you, too, Frank," Cohansen said. "Whyn't pull up chair an' join us?"

"Yeah, Marty." Then to Nealy: "Th' fuck you *been*, Ray? I been trying ta call you."

"Out of town for the last week, and with Marty at the precinct all day today." He noticed Malone wearing his anxiety like something he had to hold back before rushing to the men's room. "Why, Frank? Whataya got for me?"

"You guys owe me a fuckin' case of Four Roses for this."

"Good luck tryin' to collect on *that* one, buddy," Cohansen said.

Malone reached into his pocket and held up Chamelea's letter like a holy relic. "I think I found our boy." Cohansen leaned forward. "No shit. Speak."

Nealy lit up one of his cigarillos and flicked the match into the table's ashtray. "He sent you another letter," he guessed.

"Yeah," Malone breathed as he laid his cigar in the ashtray. "But this one's written to you. I wan-ned to hold off on running it 'til I talked to you." Nealy reached for the envelope, as Malone drew it back. "Jus' a sec, Ray. I think that what's inside the envelope ain't's import- ant as what's on the envelope."

Cohansen's expression soured. "If you're meaning his prints, Frank, holdin' the envelope like you are is destroyin' evidence. Besides we already got his prints, anyways."

Malone waved him off. "Jus' lemme tell ya, okay? Usually, this Lithuanian guy brings the letters to me. Speaks a little English, but it sounds like it's goin' through a meat grinder. Just leaves the letters and goes away. Anyway, this time some dame brings it by, an' she speaks perfec English. Tells me she's got a ad for the paper from some sorta church."

"Don't you just send those kinds of things to advertising, Frank?" Nealy asked.

Malone shook his head. "'Cause it was addressed to me personal. And this Chamelea has a code, sorta, so I know these are from him. Look." He extended the letter toward Nealy. "See how the 'B' in 'KnickerBocker' is capped up and underlined? That's how I know it's from him."

"Tricky," Nealy said as he squinted at the Malone's scrawl on the envelope. He brushed some cigar smoke away. "What's all this writing?"

"That's your guy," Malone said proudly.

Nealy handed the envelope to Cohansen, who held it up to the dull light as though trying to read what was inside.

Malone went on: "Look at what I wrote on the envelope, would ya, Marty? I'm pretty sure this Chamelea is a guy named Reverend Thomas Deavers, preaches at a place down near the Brooklyn Bridge on Water Street. I wrote the rest of the stuff down, includin' the phone number, in case you wanna call him."

"How the fuck did'ju *get* all this, Frank?" Cohansen asked as he handed the envelope back to Nealy.

"Far's I know. The babe who dropped this off thought it was an ad. Had to get the vitals for the ad department to bill, right?" "Good work, buddy!" Cohansen congratulated him. Nealy lifted the flap of the envelope. "Okay if I—?"

Malone picked up his cigar from the ashtray. "May's well. It's written for you anyways," he said as he puffed to re-ignite his stogie. "Well, Frank." Cohansen told him. "I gotta tell ya, this is like the first honest in-depth reporting I ever seen from you."

"Fuck you very much, Marty," he remarked congenially around his glowing stogie. "Asshole."

"Can't afford a case, but I'll buy you a drink, at least," Cohansen said summoning the waiter. He ordered a round.

Nealy seemed oblivious to their conversation as he concentrated on the letter. Finally, he folded it up. "Frank. I'm gonna ask you to do something you don't want to do. I don't want you to publish this."

"Shit! Ray?" he sputtered around his cigar.

"Frank? You do, and he'll kill again. He's all but saying it in this letter."

"Lemme see," Cohansen said. Nealy slid the letter toward him and he began to read it.

"It's news, Ray. I gotta do what I gotta do," Malone brooded. "This is, like, my job."

"Not if I confiscate this thing as evidence," Cohansen muttered as he read.

"Shit! Marty? Fuck almighty! I knew I shoulda ran it when I had the chance."

"Then we'd have another homicide on our hands," Cohansen said as he looked over at Nealy penning what Malone had written on the envelope onto a cocktail napkin. "What're you doin' Ray?"

"Just writing this down," Nealy said. "Jeezus, Frank. Thank God for typewriters. Your penmanship stinks."

"You better not be plannin' anythin' stupit, Ray, like a stakeout," said Cohansen.

That was exactly what he had planned. "Oh? I don't know." He handed the envelope back to Cohansen.

"Just call me before you do. You ain't stakin' out no one without me."

"Hey! Can I come, too?" Malone asked. "Promise, I'll just sit in the back with my yap shut."

"No!" Cohansen said emphatically. "Christ on a *crutch*!" he groused to Nealy. "That's *all* we need. Frank Malone on a stakeout with us."

"YO, MARTY!" Fred the bartender shouted from over from his station off in the murky gloom. He held the receiver in one hand, while he waved him over. "You gotta call! Sezzitz important!"

"*Fuck*! I missed another alimony payment," Cohansen grumbled as he groaned to raise his bulk from the chair. He looked down at Nealy and Malone. "You two: Sit. Stay," he commanded and then ambled toward the bar, grabbing his glass of bourbon from the tray the waiter was carrying toward their table.

Malone languished into the comfort of his whiskey as Nealy reread the letter.

Cohansen came back to the table five minutes later carrying his half-empty glass. He eased back into his seat.

"Ex-wife?" Malone asked.

"No, saints be praised," he said and then turned to Nealy. "We got results from that partial on the glass."

"And—?"

"It's a match to the lipsticks and prints at the scenes."

"Thanks for the story, lads!" Malone said excitedly. "What glass?" "Just shut up and drink your drink, newsie," Cohansen growled at him. Then he shot him a smile. "That's real good work you did, Frank.

Chapter 50

Friday begins

Friday, September 18, 1964—9:15 a.m.

I know they're out there. I've seen them parked in their police car—lurking like trolls underneath the B. Bridge overpass. There they lie in wait—three of them in their humped-back cruiser painted in the color of darkness, watching over me like snakes from the shadows. And like the snake of my God recoiling within me, no longer giving me guidance, preparing only to strike. I am not ready for whatever is to follow me into the gloom. I am by myself.

Dear hearts, for the first time in my life I am helplessly scared.

Your darling Chamelea has written four letters for Mr. Frank Malone to publish. Only one of them showed up in yesterday's KnickerBocker, and it wasn't even my latest one. All the salient parts were taken out. All that was left was my Chamelea's empty plea, crying like an insignificant child trying to be understood. They edited out all I wrote about my loving service to my misguided girls and how I have redeemed them into a happier life. Darlings, I say again. I have provided an invaluable service to them! What I perform is not murder. It is redemption!

I guess that our quasi-prestigious Mr. Editor Frank Malone has turned my letters over to Mister Detective Raymond Nealy, perhaps as the "evidence" that has resulted in the cruiser parked under the B. Bridge. Watching me; watching for me. I know Mister Detective

Raymond Nealy is there among the trolls, thinking he has found me. He has even gone so far as to direct Bobbie, as his future bride's wedding planner, to deal through him alone. If Mister Detective Raymond Nealy thinks he may have found our darling Chamelea, then I must act now. And then leave. Forever. So now I must do what I must.

Thomas's diary entry left him fussing over his nervousness. It took two trembling gestures to lay down his pen. He vigorously closed his journal and jostled it into the dressing table drawer. Gathering himself, he looked into the mirror, mussed up his hair, and then, with trembling fingers swiped some irregular smudges of mascara to dirty his sweat-dampened cheeks, chin and forehead. He swallowed a few Valiums and then bit down hard on a cancer sore on his lower lip to draw out a bead of blood.

He felt as if the lightness of a dream state had telescoped from the dressing table stool to support the weight of every insecurity that had come back to haunt him. Overcome by a weightless swell of dizziness and the sear of another migraine rush, he meandered over to his clothes closet. The hangers clattered overly loud on their pole as he moved them apart to select a heavy, tattered greatcoat Juan had once worn. He shivered within a warm, dull prickle of fever as he slipped the weighty coat over his shoulders. He heard only the irregular heaving of his breath as he stood stoically in place. Craving sleep, he drew his eyes closed. A few minutes of rest was all he needed.

But he did not even have a few minutes. The sound of his breathing, rattling as though it came though some dilapidated apparatus, was accented by the regular *thunk* of the pendulum in the stairway wall clock measuring out the rhythm of time. Thomas just wanted time to cease. It served no purpose but to flick away at his deteriorating mental state like the lash of an overseer's whip.

He felt a mushy sensation as he turned to retrieve a throw pillow from the bed. He cringed over the dull ache in his upper arms as he reached back to tuck the pillow between his shoulders and the coat. With a trembling hand, he slipped on a pair of lens-less black-rimmed glasses with a missing bow. Now looking like a myopic second cousin to Quasimodo, he glanced once more into the mirror. It took two tries to position a rumpled knit cap upon his head. This did nothing to salve the onslaught of another headache. "Blessings, dear heart," he muttered to his reflection, then left the room.

Making his way down to the kitchen, he heard Milio shifting his position within the dumbwaiter. Its opened door revealed him folded like a fetus as he hid himself from the known world. Seriated in shad- ow and light, he listened to some Klezmer music on his radio.

Thomas lumbered past to where six canapés in a cardboard tray sat next to the thick plastic, light pink Schrafft's bag they had come in. He opened a cupboard door above him and fumbled for a lacquered oak box he kept in the sheltering darkness of the top shelf. He took it down, then ran his fingers across the thinly embossed wood grain. He opened the box to reveal a small syringe and two rubber-corked vials of LSD tucked into plush, purple-velvet padding as delicately as any Communal host.

Thomas was startled by Milio's drowsy voice. "Why'd you dress like dat, preacher man?" he asked as he leaned out from the dumbwaiter.

"It's okay, Milio," Thomas said through his tightening breaths. "I'm just going—going to a costume party. You go ahead back to sleep, now."

Milio didn't have the capacity to wonder why the preacher man would be going to a costume party in the early morning on a Friday. Having no concept of time, he was not sure, or cared, what day it was. "I nuont be sleeping. I, *non dormiunt*. Jus hearing de musicia."

He yawned and then folded himself back into the wide dumbwaiter and into the realm of his inconspicuousness.

After plunging close to 1,800 micrograms of LSD into the syringe he held in his shaking, light grasp, Thomas injected a little into each of the canapés, doubling the dosage into the two center ones. Leaving the syringe nearly half-full with 1,400 micrograms, he replaced the vials alone on the top shelf and put the syringe in its velvet-lined box into the plastic Schrafft's bag. Taking a bottle of sleeping pills from a cluster of medications and vitamins on the lower shelf, he crushed and then pressed three of the small pills into each of the two center canapés to mellow out the dose of LSD without sacrificing its effect. Finally, he covered up the pastries in tin foil and put the tray into the bag. Fishing around in the damp, linty void of his chino pants pocket, he found his amulet and wedged it against the pastry tray in the plastic bag.

He fumbled for a clean dish towel from a pile of them near the sink, which, through another hot swell of a migraine, seemed 50 feet farther away than it was. Taking one, he folded it and laid it on top of the foil-covered canapés. Over this, he placed four different colored silk swatches he had cut from the inner hems of some evening gowns he had bought at Sak's Fifth Avenue in June. He tightened the drawstrings of the plastic bag and placed it in a large, crumpled grocery sack to disguise it.

Steeling himself to what he must next do, he left undetected from the backdoor in the parish hall sacristy and limped hugging the bag to his chest as a mother would her baby. He meandered past the Brooklyn Bridge and the watchers in their cars to catch the Uptown express subway to Grand Central Station.

The overheated environment of the dingy subway car smelled of vomit laced with the saccharinity of bubble gum. The subway's rumbling and shaking sent convulsive, humid stabs into Thomas's head to a point where he felt as though his body might burst into flame. His heart palpated with the tightening heaves of his irregular breathing as he fixed a vapid gaze on the little wall fan above the car's connecting door. Its blades, disconnected from any useful purpose, spun lackadaisically one way, then the other.

As the subway raged through the local stations, the clattering of its wheels against the track reverberated unbearably through the car's open windows and into the depth of his brain to the point where he felt faint. The sudden, harsh flickering of the passing platform lights registered the blast of their latent flares into his sight. He closed his eyes in defense of the illusionary assaults and leaned his head back to breathe open-mouthed toward the ceiling of this rude, moving cell. Finally, the train pulled into Grand Central and its sliding doors creaked open. Thomas rushed out into the bustle on the platform like a prisoner released.

He fumbled his way up the stairs and into the lower level of Grand Central Station, then headed into the men's room. The soiled bathroom with its sticky floors was like a tomb from antiquity in wait of being un- earthed. The rusty scent was acerbic with the odor of urine and blood, pungently sweetened by the asparagus-like under fragrance of shit. The walls were paved with cracked and missing terra-cotta tiles, which might have once been green, but now were filigreed with unintelligible graffiti and the grime of what seemed to be 1,000 years of abuse.

Men of all cultures, from suburban commuters to denizens from the underworld, stood busying themselves at the cracked, grayed sinks and urinals. Two of them, standing dispassionately at the urinals, watched one another in silent obsession while they masturbated as if they were caught up in a competition.

Thomas hustled into a free stall to relieve the fullness of his bladder, and then the weight of his overcoat, along with his filthy baggy chinos, under which he wore a neatly pleated pair of jeans. As he stuffed it and the pillow he'd used to hump his back into the big grocery sack, he realized that though his breathing was still labored, his headaches seemed to have misted away. Clutching the two bags, he rushed greedily from the filth of the men's room and out into the relatively fresh air of the station. Feeling lightened and rejuvenated, he breathed in the welcome stale air of the cavernous station as though standing alone and free on the prow of a ship at sea.

He still felt the weight of his legs as he hobbled partway up the low, vaulted ramp connecting the two levels of the station. Scanning the checkerboard arrangement of lockers against the ramp's left wall, he found an empty one where he stashed the old sack, swelled to capacity with the pillow and the mass of Juan's overcoat.

Now it seemed that the seizures of headaches and nervousness that plagued him since Heaven's Doorway had lifted. Dressed as Ishmael and carrying the Schrafft's bag, he jaunted as a normal human being up the ramp. He had time for a cup of coffee and to relax at the counter of the Chock-Full O' Nuts off the station's main level, where he could control the last remnants of his belabored breathing.

He relished the thought of the home awaiting him in Ballycannough as his hands eased out of their tremble. He recalled where he had placed the Aer Lingus ticket in his desk for his flight out to Dublin next Thursday — in less than a week. Until then, he would lose himself away from the trolls parked under the Brooklyn Bridge by staying with Pauline in the anonymous depths of The Village, making love to him. He twitched a smile and finished his chilling coffee. He laid down a dollar for the thirty-five-cent coffee on the sticky counter and then gathered up the Schrafft's bag and walked back down the ramp to the subways.

He joined the throng of mismatched humanity clustering toward the uptown subway platform to catch the Lexington Avenue local. From the 79th street station, he walked to Francesca's York Street apartment. He found a bistro across the street and went into the place to order a wine and to sort out his plan. The place was decorated with ferns and other foliage and seemed more of a loamy-scented greenhouse than a bar.

Thomas soon spied Francesca walking by carrying a few bags of groceries. He watched as she fumbled with her keys while balancing her grocery bags before she finally disappeared into her building's lobby. He sipped his wine and decided to wait a little longer.

Chapter 51

Silk

Once Francesca had put up her groceries and then made some coffee, she crossed the room, slipped off her shoes and then settled into the plush comfort of her recliner chair. She sipped her afternoon coffee as she flicked on the TV with the remote and began watching the 15-minute Friday cliffhanger episode of "The Guiding Light."

Nealy had directed her to spend less time at the office while she planned for the wedding, and she welcomed the respite away from nothing to do there. Last week, she had sent out the invitations to the printer and remembered them telling her that the proofs might be de- livered today. Other than that, there was not much to do as she nestled into a lazy routine more suited to a woman eight months pregnant than that of a bride.

She heard a knock on her door just in time for show's climactic end. "Ah, for Pete's sake!" she muttered and then made her way over to answer the door with her eyes trained on the show. Opening it, she expected to find the printer delivering the invitation proofs, but instead found Ishmael standing with masked impatience as he fidgeted with the drawstring of a plastic Schrafft's bag. "Ishmael!" she said, mulling over why he might have come. "Oh. Raymond's not here. He's in his office."

Thomas knew this not to be true, as he was lurking among the cops in the cruiser lying in wait across from Heaven's Doorway. His tone was tenuous as it filtered through the growing gnaw of a returning headache. He took in a breath. "I tried calling him there and he didn't answer," he said. "I was passing by, anyway, and I wanted to show you some dress swatches."

"Sure. Okay," she opened the door wider. "Come on in. Raymond wouldn't know satin from burlap, anyway."

"Actually," he said as he hustled himself into her living room. "They're silk."

"Oh, wow! Even better." She gazed at the sheen of perspiration on his ashen face. "You okay, Ishmael?" she asked as she closed the door behind him. "You look a little done in. Can I get you some water? Maybe a Tab?"

"Oh, thanks, Francesca. Yes. Water's fine. Suddenly I feel like I'm burning up. Nothing contagious, I assure you. Just allergies." He eased himself down onto the couch and placed the bag at his feet to keep it in easy reach.

"Heck, yeah, Ishmael," she sympathized in a tone hollowed out by the distance to the kitchen. "I've got 'em, too. This year's the absolute worst." She extracted an ice tray, clattered its contents onto the counter, picked up a handful of cubes and plinked them into two glasses.

He pulled the four silk samples from the bag, laid them on the coffee table and admired them. He shamed himself for having nearly ruined four of his best dresses—he hadn't even had a chance to wear them. "I think you'll like what Robert and I have chosen, here."

"Oh, I'm sure I will," she called over the running water as she filled the two glasses and then padded over to the couch. "I can't wait to see them."

He continued to stare down at the swatches as though mourning the loss of his evening gowns, until she caused a diversion by sitting next to him.

She handed him a glass of water and put hers down on the table. "Really, Ishmael. Take a sip. You're shaking. You want an aspirin, or something?"

"Sorry," he said as the headaches resurged. "No. No thanks, I'll be fine."

"Well, I heard somewhere that New York City water is the best in the country, and it'll cure all that ails you," she chuckled. "'Hudson River Champagne' they call it, though I find it hard to believe. I can't imagine it really comes out of that dirty ol' river." She spotted the swatches. "Oh, these *are* nice!" she raved.

"Aren't they?"

"Which do you like?"

Thomas stole another look at them. They seemed to be breathing back at him. He caught his breath. "All of them, really. I guess what matters is what you like, Francesca."

"Oh, please, Ishmael. Frannie. All my friends call me 'Frannie,'" she giggled. "Except Raymond, who calls me a whole lot of other things."

"Well, I'm glad to be counted among your friends."

She answered him with a pert smile, and then she concentrated on the swatches. "I think I like this light purple one," she decided.

"Lavender. It's lavender. Isn't it nice, though? It's my favorite, too." "'Okay, then. We'll go with that one."

He diverted his gaze toward the annoyance of a Carter's Little Liver Pills television commercial.

"Pretty awful stuff on TV, isn't there? Especially the commercials." She reached over to the easy chair, fished around its cushion and found the remote control and turned off the television as an Oscar Mayer Wiener commercial whined out *"Oh I wish I was an Oscar Mayer Weiner..."*

Thomas was amused by the remote control. "That's an interesting thing."

"This?" She held up the cigarette-pack-sized remote as though modeling it. "You've never seen one of these?"

"I don't watch much television."

"Yeah. It's called a TV remote controller. You can turn off the television from anywhere in the room. They've been around for a few years. A lot of people have them, now."

"Hmm," Thomas mused. "That much less exercise we need to do." "Guess you're right about that, hon," she chuckled. "They say there are some coming out where you can change the channel from where you're sitting, though I can't imagine how something like that may work." She put the remote down on the coffee table and then re- leased another little giggle. "Maybe if you click a button, a hand on the end of a very long arm comes out and flicks the channel knob around. Technology's full of these little surprises, I suppose."

Thomas had come to really like Francesca. She seemed so pure and balanced—so happy. He lamented over what a shame her loss would be. He glanced at the bag, and then reached down to peel back the folded dishtowel to reveal the tray of pastries. "Now that you mention surprises, Frannie, I have some chocolate canapés here. They're from Schrafft's."

"Really," she stated. "I have a big thing for chocolate."

He simpered a little through another cringe. "Well, I guess we all have one of those!" He pulled out the tray with his trembling hands, as though he were handling a bomb. She reached out to help support the goods as they both put the tray on the coffee table. "Thanks. Robert suggested we use Schrafft's to cater the reception, or at least some of it. There was an air of decadence floating around in Rick's American Café in Casablanca, so we thought we might play into that. And there's nothing more decadent than chocolate, right? Especially when it's Schrafft's."

"Well I like that idea! And I'm sure Raymond will, too."

Thomas tried another faint grin. "I hope he will. Or he might until he sees the bill."

"Not to worry, Ishmael," she joked. "Raymond may not fully realize this yet, but he's about to inherit some wealthy Italian in-laws who live for big family weddings. I mean, he's a good P.I. and all, but he some- times has trouble realizing some of the littler things closer to home."

"We all need wealthy in-laws," Thomas said. He hated the idea of taking Francesca away, as he reached with a wobbly hand for one of the center canapés. He caught his breath to quench a tear. "Here, Frannie," he said as he handed her the pastry. "Try this. It's *divine!*"

"Well, you don't have to ask *me* twice," she said as she took it.

Thomas took one of the end ones for himself. He winced anxiously as Francesca bit off a corner. He asked himself, *Why* this? *Why Francesca?* But he realized it was now beyond his control, as he put the whole canapé into his mouth. "What do you think?"

"Um!" she mumbled, waving a hand in front of her mouth as though she'd bitten into a hot pepper. "Dee-*li*-cious!" She ate the rest of the pastry. "God, Ishmael! We have got to have these!" she mumbled. "This is about the best thing I've ever eaten. And you're talking to a girl who's eaten a *lot* of chocolate in her life!"

"I hoped you'd like it," he brooded.

They talked some more about the style of her dress—Ingrid Bergman as Ilsa Lund, dressed in elegant simplicity like in the movie—what about a hat? Should Francesca wear a hat like Ilsa did in the famous "*'Here's looking at you, Kid'*" finale? —Should Raymond wear a white evening jacket or tails? Maybe a tuxedo? What about a Fedora or a homburg? —What was the difference between the two, anyway? Thomas listened as her voice started racing and watched as her fatigue set in. He cringed as she took up the second canapé from the middle of the tray and darted it into her mouth like a piece of popcorn. She soon yawned. "I'm so *tired* all of a sudden!" she slurred. She looked across the room at a world that was starting to swirl into itself. The refrigerator started to glow gold as it formed into a rough sphere against the now garish red foil kitchen wallpaper, which itself began to twirl into amorphous patterns of crimson. "My god!" she gasped as she rubbed her temples. "These allergies!"

Thomas took up a canapé for himself, while watching her slip away and huddle toward him for support. "You seem tired, Frannie. You want me to move so you can lie down?"

Her breathing had quickened as whatever she was looking at in the room, once so familiar, had rolled into abstract vaporous forms of vivid greens and blues. "Would you min', Iss-mal?" she garbled. "I dunno—wha'—," He stood and took up the Schrafft's bag as her body collapsed in small stages on its side upon the couch. She looked up at him with a hint of fright through her dampening dark-brown eyes. Thomas appeared diminutive to her, like a circus dwarf clutching a glowing, shocking-pink bag. She giggled aloofly at the sight of him, and then closed her eyes to see a swell of vivid orange and red hues flying and swooping around her with the grace of gulls. A tiny rose in the center of her vision telescoped forward to swallow her up in the advance of its mammoth bright-crimson petals.

Her head lolled between the cushion and backrest as Thomas noticed the wild wandering of her eyes beneath their quivering lids. This time he would not need the amulet for her. She was deeply entranced, controlled by the effects of LSD and R.E.M. sleep. He half-closed his eyes and concentrated the amulet he twirled before him as he eased into his own hallucination. It began melding into hers.

The gentle, kaleidoscopic swirls of dramatic colors that had seemed to comfort her sent barbs of pain into his brain. His breathing quickened and tightened to the point of nearly choking him as he tried to find his voice. He let the medallion fall onto the carpet. "Yes," he groaned as he fought against another stab of headache. "You are total-totally—" he gasped out a desperate breath. He felt like he was drowning. "—totally rela—relaxed." He swallowed a breath and tried again. "You are very—rellllllllassed—" he whispered, annoyed by the dim realization that he was no longer in control of himself. The roiling of colors in their shared vision had started to dull and languish into a putrid mass as though waiting for a further command.

"Reee-laassed," he heard Francesca sigh deeply.

Thomas felt a flush of fever course throughout his body, now clam- my and dampened in sweat. The hard, sting of another headache flared from where the White Cobras had slid the ice pick into his ear. The stab of pain, which networked its way through the mushy depths of his mind, was paralyzing his ability to think. A confusion of the misty, desaturated colors assaulted his vision. "Reee-lazzz your mind," he slurred.

Francesca whimpered, helpless against the onslaught of the swell of foggy colors. Still lying on her side, she folded her body into a fetal position. "I'm scared!" she shuddered as she envisioned an approaching gray cloud. Its core glowed in the rusty hue of old blood engulfing a beating heart, ebbing and flowing its glimmer to her own heartbeat. The cloud metamorphosed into a white stallion—an enraged stallion with bulging red eyes, which seemed to swell larger in their sockets. She flailed out an arm to push it away. Her whimpers became more like desperate pleas from a dark place in the folds of despair. "I'm, *sooo* sc-scared! Go 'way! *Pleeeeze* go 'way! Don' hurt me, pleeeeeeze!" she pleaded in a ragged whisper.

Thomas saw the darkening core of the cloud bloom open until it bled. From this womb rose a misty figure, clothed and shadowed in brown monastic robes. The infinite depth of his hooded cowl produced a rotting green glow as another churning cloud. His god. The entire figure morphed into a formless blend, then lifted its murky arms to draw back its hood, along with the colorless fumes that had hidden his face. Thomas drew back as he recognized a pustuled face resembling that of The White Cobra, the Führer. Thomas felt consumed by fire as the figure raised an ice pick from his frock and held it aloft in preparation to stab him deep into the heart.

Francesca's vision had taken on the form of a face afire within a black robe as she shot up and huddled away from it into the corner of the couch, knees to chin. From the flames churning within the hood emerged the head of the horse, now with the wrinkled snout of a crocodile. The sharp-toothed jaws yawned open and closed, as the head on its long neck, covered in layers of scales, leaned out as if to engulf her. "No! NO! Please!! Go a-WAY!" she cried. She writhed wildly to swat the vision away, then flailed her arms forcefully to fend the fetid creature away. The swells of her pupils were now stirring wildly around beneath her quivering lids, as she stood and kicked out at anything around her. She lost her footing and collapsed back to the couch. Now screaming through her tears, she pounded her fists on the couch pillows and toward Thomas, who was consumed in his own horror.

His god's eyes glowed yellow as he saw the extended ice pick arc down toward his heart, and then change direction to pierce the middle of his forehead. He screamed in pain over the banshee yowls of his god as a blazing agony seemed to slice his body down the middle. His god had kneaded their separate darknesses into one amorphous black cloud. Francesca's frantic screams stabbed into his fevered brain as he scrambled backward, shouting "Mercy! MERcy!"

NOW! his vision scowled in return. Redeem yourself, Brother

Thomas! For I am not your enemy. I am merely — The Other!

Breathing uncontrollably, Thomas dimly saw Francesca huddled back in the couch. Her eyes were open wide in panic. Her ink-black pupils had dilated to nearly the size of her irises. She lolled her head violently in defense of her own attacking creature. *She is dying in misery!* his god told him. *Redeem her soul for your own! Do it! Now!* Thomas groped out to find a pillow on the couch. He yanked her prone, seized the pillow in both hands and held it down upon her face, as she convulsed ferociously to fight back.

The banshee's screaming shortened into echoing bursts — howls from some nearer depth. He held the pillow down with more force until Francesca's frustrated energies weakened into submission. Thomas was overcome with a sharpness of pain now centered in his right calf. The banshee howls continued, followed by more heated bolts of pain in his leg.

His fevered breathing went on after he thought Francesca had slipped away. He lifted the pillow. Finding what little dying breath she could, she tried feebly to push him away. He caught his breath as though to dive underwater and clutched his hands around her neck, jabbing and pressing his thumbs hard into her throat until he was sure she was gone.

Lifting his hands away, he saw a tear roll down her cheek. He closed his own tearing eyes to drown out the harsh little screams continuing to echo around him. He felt his fever and breathing ease. He saw his god, cloaked in his monastic vestments, now with the hood drawn over his fathomless face. His god stated: *I created you. You are my son; in whom I am well-pleased.* He then dissolved back into gloom, returning Thomas to the afternoon daylight of Francesca's apartment. He stared into her wide-opened eyes. Her pupils had constricted down to normal, revealing her gaze as so very innocent, as though questioning: Why? He arched over with difficulty and kissed her cool damp forehead with his trembling lips. "Blessings, dear heart," he croaked in a winded whisper. He reached into the Schrafft's bag and brought out his vial of lavender. He dripped a few drops onto his thumb and drew it across her forehead to consecrate his actions. "I am so sorry." The harsh little screams in the background retreated into the braying bark of a dog. Off to the side, seeking his own protection, he saw Hamlet, whom he had encountered in passing when he and Robert had first visited Francesca the week before. Hamlet saw Thomas directing his attention toward him and cowered further away as his hoarsened barks became frightened as ethereal howls of mourning.

Thomas was not quite finished, and the dog's wailing, which seemed to be caught up in a loop, would not do. He thought about snuffing out the dog as well, but then realized that the absorption of a dog's soul would pollute those he had worked so hard to consume. Suddenly he realized in a little surge of panic that he felt nothing happen within him as Francesca died. Her soul had somehow passed around and away from him. He knew by this that his god had abandoned him.

The barking diminished to helpless whimpers as Thomas stood and advanced in the direction of Francesca's bathroom to relieve himself. Hamlet's howling bark found a new life in the panic that Thomas would now hurt him. Wondering what might quiet him, he took up one of the two remaining the canapés in the tray. "Here, boy," he urged in a spent whisper as he leaned over to offer him the pastry. Hamlet stood his ground but quieted as he inched forward and raised his snout in curiosity to sniff the chocolate. "You must try this," he coaxed him through a benign smile as Hamlet approached. "It's simply *divine!*" Hamlet sniffed again, this time with more purpose, and then nipped the LSD-laced canapé from

Thomas's trembling fingers before retreating back toward his protective corner.

As Hamlet concentrated on contentedly chewing the canapé, Thomas threw him the remaining one. Anxious to leave, he limped on his numbed, dog-bitten legs to the radio on the kitchen counter, flicked it on, and turned the dial to 1420 WYRK. The song was a duet, "Make Someone Happy." Hamlet, already starting to feel the effects of the LSD, was sniffling aimlessly around in his corner, ruffing out some low barks at something seen only by him.

Thomas went back to the couch, picked up the Schrafft's bag and then pulled out the lavender-scented envelope addressed to Mr. Detective Raymond Nealy, and placed it on the coffee table.

Chapter 52

The cost of love

Jake Barnaby huddled over his cup of black coffee in the front seat of the cruiser next to where Cohansen sat behind the wheel concentrating on the entrance to Heaven's Doorway.

"'S colder than a witches' tit out there," said Barnaby, "I mean, for September."

Cohansen puffed out some smoke from his cigarette. "Get used to it, Jake," he grumbled with disinterest. "It ain't going to get much warmer."

"Still," he said as he sipped his coffee, "last week it was, I dunno, fuckin' eighty degrees." He then became distracted by something else. "Man, oh man!" he brightened, as he raised his stakeout binocs to his nose for a closer look. "I gotta get me one of *those!*" He was referring to the dark-green Mustang with a tan convertible top that had slowed in front of the church.

"You going through a midlife crisis, Jake?" Nealy said from the backseat. "Looks like a little too much car for you. I've always figured you out as a Volkswagen type of guy. Maybe one of those little Italian Fiats." The mention of "Italian" brought an image of Francesca to his mind. And the way she smiled.

"Just shows to go ya, Ray."

"Hold, on, fellahs," Cohansen said, "It's parking right in front of the church." They all directed their attention to the possibility that the Reverend Thomas Deavers would emerge from the car.

Barnaby squinted through the binoculars. "Just one person," he said. "A dame. She's just sitting there, maybe waiting for someone."

Then a cab pulled forward from where it had been waiting up the block to park directly behind the Mustang. A girl with shoulder-length auburn hair and wearing a light alpaca sweater and tweed skirt emerged from the cab. She walked forward with a little uncertainty to greet the slightly older, taller woman with short, dark-brown hair who was now getting out of the Mustang. They talked briefly in a greeting. Then the two of them went into the church. One of the women, the older one, acted like she had been there before, while the younger glanced nervously over her shoulder as though not wanting to be found out.

"Looks like our Reverend is a chick magnet," Barnaby mused.

"Okay, Jake. Let's all keep our eyes peeled and wait. Looks like something is startin' to happen."

And then it did.

The police radio crackled to life: "*All units, One-Nine Precinct. Please respond. Code one-eighty-seven, Four Forty York Avenue, Apartment 4-A.*"

Nealy froze as he instinctively crushed his paper coffee cup, bursting its hot contents all over his right hand and shirt cuff.

"*Repeat: Code one eighty-seven; four-forty York—available units respond.*"

"*Shit!*" Cohansen gasped as he looked incredulously over his shoulder at Nealy. "That's **Frannie!**"

"Frannie?" Barnaby said.

"Ray's intended," Cohansen explained. "Ray? What the *fuck*?"

Nealy felt as though his jaw was locked into position. He took in a few gasps of air. "We gotta go!" he said. "I pushed the fuckin' bastard too far! We gotta go to Frannie's. NOW!"

Barnaby was still not able to grasp the situation. "What about our stake?"

"Shut the fuck up, Jake," Cohansen snapped as he started up the engine and the cruiser jolted into motion to race north, with its siren blaring, toward Francesca's apartment.

Silhouetted in the shadows of the Brooklyn Bridge overpass near to where the cruiser had been parked, a figure crouched in a filthy trench coat as he watched the police car hasten away. He puffed on his fat cigar, producing a glow to illuminate his chubby, grizzled jowls as he wrote on his notepad. Even if the cops were no longer on the scene, "Stogie" Frank Malone would be.

Milio was distracted by a dripping from the kitchen faucet. The close walls of the dumbwaiter had only served to amplify the trickle as the afternoon wore on. Drip-drip-dripdrip — Drip-drip-dripDRIP! "Shitata-*cacca! Madens aqua, tardus ut cruciatus!*" he muttered as he extricated himself from the dumbwaiter to the thump of Teutonic marching music from his radio. He hobbled across the room to rummage through the tool drawer for the right gizmo for the job. He found what he needed. Oversized screwdriver in hand, he muttered in disjointed Latin as he trundled over to the offending spigot. He inspected the faucet and its knobs for the screw that would tighten away the drip.

Finding nothing, he tapped on the faucet with the tip of the hefty screwdriver. The dripping continued, and he realized he might not be using enough force. He turned the screwdriver around and tapped its wooden handle on the bottom of the spigot's nozzle. "Shitata-Cac-ca!" he said and then batted the drip in the hope of hitting it out into left field. He stopped and caught his breath as he heard the door open and usher in the voices of two women. Still holding the screwdriver, he retreated quickly back into the dumbwaiter.

Deborah directed Regina into Heaven's Doorway and pointed her toward Thomas's office. "I guess we should start here. I gotta tell you, Regina. Now I'm starting to feel really weird about this."

Regina had done her best to prepare herself since their phone conversation. She drew her lips into a wry smile. "Nothing compared to how weird my father would make you feel if you were married to him."

"Well, I never said anything about marriage."

She nodded approvingly. "Good, Deb. Then don't." She hustled around to the back of the desk and tried the drawers. "Hmm. Not locked. That makes things a little easier."

"You sure this is necessary, Regina?"

She opened the top drawer and began to rifle through it. "I'm his daughter, or at least was. I lived alone with him for almost ten very fucked-up years." She found nothing but some Heaven's Doorway envelopes, stationery, a pencil, ballpoint pens and a fountain pen. "I know he's a man of many dark secrets."

"I think I'm starting to realize that," Deborah said morosely.

"I'm doing you a favor, Deb. Oh, hullo, there!"

"What?" Deborah said as she craned forward.

Regina held up a set of keys hanging with a pair of miniature dice. "My car keys. I can't believe he kept my lucky little dice." "His car keys? To that crappy little Corvair he drives?"

"*My* keys. And bite your tongue, sweetie." She tweaked a friendly grin. "That's *my* little crappy Corvair you're talking about." She pocketed the keys. "So, it's mine, now. Again."

Deborah nervously giggled. "Good luck with that, Regina. It needs a new—everything."

She stared down into the open drawer where she'd found the keys. "As long as the radio still wor—Oh. This is interesting."

"What? What now?"

Regina extracted an envelope with a plane ticket sticking out. "I don't exactly—know," she said as she drew out the ticket. "A ticket to Dublin, Ireland. One way. For next Thursday." She looked up at Deborah. "Did you know anything about this, Deb?"

"No," she whispered. "Not a thing. Why would he—?

"There's also some sort of letter." She pulled it out and opened it. "Looks official. From some law office in," she squinted at the address, "Dublin. You know of anyone named—Seamus O'Shea?"

"Sounds—Irish," Deborah said.

Regina simpered. "Yeah. Like someone you might find popping out of a box of Lucky Charms." She began reading:

Top O' the morning Thomas!

She glanced up at Deborah. "Oh, come *on*! 'Top O' the *morning*?' How phony is *that*?" She looked down and continued reading:

Here is your ticket for a 10:40 AM flight from Idlewild in New York to Dublin on Thursday, 1 October. It will be good to have you back home again after all these years. The O'Hienes are overjoyed with our arrangement to move them from your childhood home in Ballycannough to their brand new flat in Dublin.

Regina looked up again. "You didn't know about any of this, Deb?" Deborah looked at the floor and shook her head in gloomy resignation. Regina heaved a sigh and read on:

As soon as you arrive, contact me at my office in Dublin, and we'll restore your identity back to Thomas Barragan (no "Reverend"!), per your instructions to me. Passports, etc. are being prepared and will be waiting for you, as well as your actual birth certificate, which is still being held in my personal safe.

Regina glanced at Deborah and flexed her eyebrows. "The plot thickens."

We'll also begin to transfer your American funds back to consolidate with your existing holdings in the Bank of Ireland. We've made some wise investments over time, Thomas, particularly in the German, Belgian and French reconstructions since the war. With the addition of your American holdings, I trust it will value your assets to around eight million (in American dollars, of course!).

Regina faltered into a tremble as she glanced back at Deborah. "*Hooo*-ly fuckin' *shit!*" she gasped. "You *still* think he's not keeping anything from you, Deb?"

Stunned, Deborah merely shook her head. Regina continued reading:

It will be such a pleasure for me to finally meet you. Some of those charitable contributions you made to the Athy Cathedral in the Barragan name have made quite a positive name for you around here, Thomas. You will be welcomed back with wide-open arms! May the Luck of the Irish continue to be with you until we finally meet, lad.

Your everlasting friend and Barrister, Seamus O'Shea.

As she folded the letter, she noticed a postscript on the back. As she read it, she kept her stare on the words as though trying to freeze them as her tan deepened in a flush of disbelief.

"What is it, Regina?" Deborah croaked. "You look— "

Regina read on:

PS: We also need to rewrite your will, Thomas, as I was unclear on this point. Do you still want to leave your daughter, Regina, in as your sole beneficiary? I will not change this until we have a chance to talk about it. Until then, I'll remain your fiduciary conservator."

With trembling hands, Regina folded up the letter and slipped it back into the envelope with the airline ticket. "No...fucking...*WAY!*" she gasped as she folded the envelope and stuffed it into her skirt pocket. "My crappy little car suddenly doesn't seem like such a big deal for me, anymore. Shit, he's not going *anywhere!* I'm hanging onto these things."

Below where she had found the envelope, she spied Thomas's time-worn bible. "I don't think he ever read this thing." She mumbled as she opened it to where Thomas had marked Genesis 22.1, and then started reading about God willing Abraham to kill his son, Isaac, as a burnt offering. "I always hated this story," she said as the photo serving as a bookmark fluttered to the desk. It was her Hanson High senior portrait; probably a fitting marker for that passage. She picked it up and stared into it, noticing how gloomy she looked. She remembered that the photo had been taken the day after the brutal argument she and John Bass had when she'd told him she was pregnant. She had had to turn her head away from the camera to shield the resulting welt on her swollen cheek. That was about two weeks before she was willingly kidnapped away from Hanson by John's creditors after they cut off his ear in repayment and sent him howling into the night and out of Regina's life for good.

Another photo, a snapshot, slid out from where it had been loosely lodged into the flyleaf. She squinted at it and picked it up. It was a picture of her as a 10-year-old, standing gleefully next to

Jillian when they were in Jamaica. It had been taken the day Jillian died. Regina felt her eyes stiffen with tears as she realized once again how much she loved her mother, in this snapshot and in her heart. She was overcome with the warmth of finally finding a home; of finding the love she could not before define; a love that she had denied herself. Through this picture she finally sensed Jillian's permission to love, and to be loved.

"What's that?" Deborah asked.

"My past. Here. You want to see a picture of your boyfriend's wife?" She held it up to Deborah. "God, I loved my mother, and he took her away," she choked through some tears. "And he didn't even *care!*"

Deborah laid a consoling hand on Regina's trembling shoulder, then carefully drew her toward her in a tenuous embrace as Regina cried into her shoulder. "That fucking *bastard!*" Deborah snarled.

Francesca's features had involuntarily relaxed since Thomas had left, and her body lolled slightly on its side on the couch as though she were merely resting. Her full lips were parted slightly open as though caught in mid-speech through an easy smile. Her beautiful, innocent eyes were open in that expression of wonderment that made her even more beautiful. She seemed to be staring with childhood fascination into something wonderful beyond the future. Like whatever it was, it was okay and not to be feared.

She had one arm drawn above her head with its hand held in a loose clutch. Its rosy-pink palm resting within the soft russet-brown thicket of her hair splayed around her head. Her other arm was draped over the front edge of the couch, as it would sometimes fall over the edge of the bed when she slept on her back. Nealy often wondered how she could manage to sleep that way.

The skin of her legs shone smooth in the low light in the room.

One of her plush legs was stretched straight out on the couch while the other, like her arm, was draped over the front of the couch. Her bare foot touched the carpet. She loved walking around her apartment barefoot. The barefoot contessa, Nealy would sometimes call her. *Come to me, my barefoot contessa.*

He fixated on the little mole on her cheek, and the slightly larger one on her neck, below where the killing hands had reddened it. He then stared at the crescent birthmark on the heel of the foot touching the floor.

Yes, she might have just been sleeping, but the graying pallor of her skin revealed the truth. Nealy felt distanced. Numbed. Paralyzed. All he could do was stare—like a voyeur.

He then took in the whole picture of her lying there on the couch where they had spent so many happy hours drinking their drinks and eating popcorn over some dumb TV show. Here was the couch where they made out like teenagers to take their minds off the dumb TV show that had driven them to it—the couch where they had made love. Now she was there alone. Gone.

He might have heard voices around him. He wasn't sure.

"Some delivery guy found her." A cop was saying. "He called the super, who called us. Looks like she put up a hell of a fight."

"—Ligature marks around her neck," the coroner was saying from somewhere further off in the distance. "Body temperature around ninety-five. Time of death two, maybe three hours ago."

Cohansen kept his gaze on Nealy who stood over the couch as though he had turned to stone. He faced the coroner. "Let's go into the kitchen and talk about this, Ted. Ray shouldn't be hearing all these details, right now."

"What does he? Know her or something?"

"They were gonna be married in December," Cohansen told him.

"Oh, shit!" said Ted. "That's rough. That's *soo* fuckin' rough."

"Shit is right," Cohansen said. "Come on, now, Ted. Come with me." He led him to the kitchen.

Nealy broke his silence about a minute later, as he remained transfixed on Francesca's colorless body, save for the pink grip marks that, to him, seemed to have been burned into her neck. "Turn that fucking music off!" he shouted.

Cohansen glanced over his shoulder at the radio, still tuned to WYRK, now playing "As Time Goes By" from the movie, *Casablanca*. Cohansen bit his lower lip as he shut off the radio.

Hamlet, still entranced, started into a frenzy of barks and whimpers, as though he had just discovered there were strangers in the apartment. He circled around in opposite directions around smears of dog vomit and mounds of his poop, snapping at invisible butterflies and houseflies as though he must have sensed they were attacking him with their stings. "What's a matter with that dog?" one of the attending cops wondered. "S'like he's stoned or sumpthin.'

Nealy stirred at the sound of Hamlet's confused barking and went over to him. He stooped down. "Come here, boy, come on," Nealy implored Hamlet as he held out his hands. "It's gonna be okay." He knew nothing would ever be okay after this, that he would never share the happiness he had with Francesca—never.

Recognizing the comfort of Nealy's familiar scent, Hamlet ceased barking and, panting heavily, sauntered over to him, as though embarrassed, with his tail drooped between his legs. Between his rapid panting and whimpering pleas, he aimed his hot, dry-nosed snout toward Nealy's hand to lick it. He missed his mark as though he had been blinded. Nealy took Hamlet's trembling head in his hands and noticed that his pupils were dilated. Off to his right he spied a half-eaten canapé on the rug near a puddle of vomit. "Fuck shit!" he fumed, now suspecting his dog had been drugged. "That fucking-shit son of a bitch!" Hamlet was the only relief left for him. Nealy nestled his head close to his own and stroked him lightly behind the ears to comfort him. "S'okay, boy, S'okay," he soothed in a whisper as though he was talking to Francesca as well. He felt the trickle of a tear down his cheek as Hamlet continued to whimper. Nealy kissed the top of his quivering head. "Calmly, now. Calmly, boy."

"Ray? Hey, Ray?" Barnaby said quietly from over his shoulder. He produced a letter scented in lavender. "He left a note for you, Ray."

Nealy offered a vacant, purposeless smile as he stood and took the note. His hands trembled as he read it:

To Mister Detective Raymond Nealy,

For what it is worth, I'm terribly sorry it had to come to this. Francesca was such a dear heart, and I can tell she loved you very much. But in my defense, you have tried to take something just as valuable from me. It is something that lives deep in my heart, as Francesca must in yours. So, as you see, Death begets death, and it is never a victimless crime.

I knew you were closing in on me. I knew this because you had silenced me. We had agreed, Mr. Editor Frank Malone and I, that the KnickerBocker would be the voice of my useful purpose to those that suffer. By keeping these letters justifying my good intentions to yourself—for evidence—you have silenced the voice to which I am entitled. So, you see, dear heart. I had to recriminate against your injustices to me, for, as I have taken away your beautiful Francesca, you have taken away my beautiful voice of reason for liberating the souls of those who suffer.

Blessings, dear heart, Chamelea

PS— Do not be disillusioned that you will ever find me, for this is a

---

big city to disappear into before I am very shortly and forever gone.

Nealy's expression hardened into a hateful scowl as he crumpled up the note and flung it to the carpet so hard that it startled Barnaby. He stood and faced Cohansen's partner. "Make sure my dog gets to a vet and soon!" he ordered the room, and then stormed away.

As he trudged his way through the vestibule and toward the front door, he heard Cohansen calling desperately from the far distance. "Ray! Ray! Where the fuck you goin'?" Nealy did not answer as he flung open the front door. Cohansen knew exactly what his friend had on his mind. "God *damn* it, Nealy! Don't do anything stupid!" Nealy cut him off as he slammed the front door.

He plodded heavy-footed down the hall toward the entrance of the building. Cohansen followed him. "Wait up, wouldja Ray?" he shouted. His voice was nothing more than an echo in Nealy's ears. "God fuckin' damn. SHIT!" Cohansen wheezed as he caught up with him and grabbed him by the sleeve and turned him to face him. "Ray! You know who I am?"

No answer.

"Ray! God-damnit. Who *am* I?"

Nealy remained silent as the light glimmered in his eyes. His lower lip began to tremble.

"Ray! Am I your friend?"

"Friend?"

"It's me, Ray. Marty. It's me, and I'm with you, buddy. I've got your back."

"Marty?"

"Yeah. Me. Marty. I love you, you dumb son of a bitch!" Then Cohansen hauled off and slapped him hard. Twice. "Now, come to, you fuckin' son of a bitch!"

Nealy's expression flared awake. "Marty."

Cohansen relaxed his grip on him. "Yeah. Me, your best friend, Marty."

"I got to do this, Marty," he said as he turned.

Cohansen re-clasped his grip on Nealy's arm. Nealy wheeled around with a fire raging through his gaze. Cohansen recoiled away from any punches his best friend might throw at him. "What is your intention, buddy?" Nealy's lower lip began to quiver again. "Come on. What is it? To kill Chamelea? You think that's the solution? Fuck no! And you know it!"

Nealy's eyes welled with tears. "How did it come to this, Marty?"

"Shit, buddy," he said, as he released his grip a little. "How many times do we end up asking ourselves that same fucking question? It's all a Goddamn cliché by now."

Nealy then collapsed into tears. Cohansen held him as close as he would an inconsolable child. For a while they just stood together, as Nealy heaved and tried to sob away his anger. "It's gonna be okay, Ray," Cohansen reassured him as he also choked up. "Okay? It's gonna be okay, buddy. Not today, not tomorrow, not this year, even. But things get a little better, day by day."

"Sounds like something Francesca might say," he said.

Cohansen smiled knowingly. "Where d'ya think I heard it?" He eased Nealy away. "You okay? For now, Ray?"

Nealy brushed away some dampness from his cheek. "Yeah. No. But yeah, Marty. Thanks."

Cohansen pursed his lips in determination and patted him brusquely on the shoulder. "Good. Then let's you and me go haul this shithead in!" He twiddled a benign smile. "I'll drive. You never was any good at running them red lights."

Chapter 53

Blessings, dear heart

Thomas felt smothered by the press of rush-hour as he waited, fevered and sweating, among the throng on Grand Central's downtown subway platform. His headaches had returned as heated bolts of pain. His face contorted as he cringed against their assault, making him appear deranged, as some standing next to him kept at an uneasy distance. His humpbacked body, huddled beneath the mass and weight of Juan's greatcoat, completed the picture of him as a coiled-up lunatic.

A garbled announcement through the public-address system echoed that the downtown express had been delayed. As the local rumbled in, peevish throngs of urban commuters shepherded Thomas toward and into the waiting train. The nearly solid block of people within the car closed in on him, as, with a sweat-drenched hand, he grasped onto a support pole like it was the only thread connecting him to the living.

The minutes slid away like the slow undulation of lava. The 33rd and 23rd Street stops shed away some of the primly appointed Murray Hill and Gramercy Park passengers but took on the far more ragged downtown commuters to crush their weight around him as the car became stuffier and heated by bodies, many of whom Thomas envisioned as dead—not liberated, but dead. Sweat poured from beneath his wool watch cap and seeped out through his groin.

A feeling of white-hot spikes driven into the mush of his brain sent a rash of fevers pulsating unctuously through his pores. He pissed himself. It trickled down into a pool around his feet. At 14th street, the balloon of people around him deflated. He breathed a little easier in uneven gasps, as the fever and pains in his head diminished.

Thomas relished the thought of one last bath in the Holy Water Soaking Tub. After that, he would change into some fresh clothes, gather up his air ticket and vanish into the Lower Village for the next few days to live and lay with Pauline. Thomas knew he had to tell Pauline he was leaving for Ireland—maybe convince his lover to quit the beauty shop to join him in a life of misty, fresh-aired bliss among the open, moist aromas of earth and greenery—and the sweet fragrance of lavender.

As he finally exited out of the Brooklyn Bridge/City Hall Station onto the street, he burst into a bout of heavy breathing. It was as if, despite the surrounding dissonance of car horns, he had prematurely found the fresh air of Ballycanough. Hugging the big grocery sack containing the Schrafft's bag to his chest like a mother shielding her infant, he took another breath in the sheer joy of having found freedom in the waning sunlight.

The police cruiser was no longer parked in place under the bridge, but Thomas still chose to take no chances. He stole past the parked Corvair and through the back door leading to the sacristy vestibule to enter Heaven's Doorway for the last time. Once in, he closed his eyes for a moment as he relaxed against the closed door. He then stared at the ceiling as he breathed deeply and then exhaled into the safe, familiar solitude of his church.

Now relaxed, yet still wracked with mild headaches, he shed the encumbrance of the greatcoat and his sweat-drenched shirt. He remembered the syringe in the Schrafft's bag, and he meant to pack it back away on the kitchen shelf. He had decided to leave all the LSD paraphernalia behind. The last thing he would need to happen would be an arrest at Idlewild Airport for transporting contraband overseas. He wasn't worried about the drugs for he was certain that Seamus, through all his shady connections, would find him some more.

He made his way shirtless through the sacristy and set the bag down next to the pool. After taking the dish towel from the bag and placing it near the edge of the tub, he stripped off his urine-soaked pants and shorts and slid naked and luxuriantly into the warm water near the reeds. He bunched up the dish towel and then sighed as he relaxed his head against the pillow he had made from it. As he was trying to empty his mind, he heard a rustling from behind the closed accordion panel separating the tub from the common room.

"Hello?" he called. "Milio?"

There was no answer right away. Then he heard Deborah's dour voice as she slid the panel open. "It's me, Thomas."

"Ah!" he brightened, as he cringed away another headache. "Deborah, sweetheart. I'm in the pool. Come on in and join me."

The curtain clattered as she opened it and stepped in with caution as she glared at him. "You're back. You're usually not here on Friday afternoons."

He grimaced a smile. "I just thought I needed a bath—"

"You lied to me, Thomas!" she flared. "You've been lying all along!"

He tried soothing her anger as he leaned forward. The dish towel serving as a pillow slid into the water. "Deborah? What's wrong?"

"You never told me you had a daughter."

"A what?" he gasped.

"A daughter. Regina, your *daughter*! Shit! I knew something was going on between you two that day you saw her at the fair."

"Daught—?" he said incredulously as he realized there was no use in pretending. "I was going to tell you. I'm sorry. I guess I waited too long."

"When were you going to tell me, Thomas?" she asked as she walked slowly around the edge of the tub toward him. "After our child was born? *Hunh*? *When?*" Her lips quivered with rage as her complexion darkened. "And obviously you had a wife. You never told me about her, either."

"She died years ago," he said as he inched his hand behind toward the bag to pull it closer. "I didn't think it was important."

"Not *important*?" she said as she closed in on him. "Not im-*por*-tant? I trusted you, Thomas. I fucking trusted you! I've put up with so much from you—even to the extent of your going over to Pauline's to play dress up. What other woman would tolerate that sort of shit! Who else but me? Because I, stupid me, believed I could learn to understand you. And stupid me, again! I still loved you all along, in spite of all of it!" "I'm so sorry, Deborah, so sorry." But there was no sorrow in his apology, only the timbre of despair. He pulled the bag a little closer.

"So, so sorry."

"And then," she huffed as she crossed her arms over her chest.

"There's that one-way trip to Ireland next week." Thomas froze in place as he gaped at her. "Uh-huhn," she said with a curt nod. "And all that money waiting for you over there. When were you going to tell me about *that*? Huhn? Were you going to send me a postcard, Mister Thomas Barragan? No. Probably no—"

She yelped as he clutched her ankle and yanked her into the pool, then hurriedly spun her around in the water to hold her from behind in a one-armed hammerlock. Pain resurged in hot waves though his brain. "THOMAS!" she wheezed. "What the fuck are you do—?" Her comment ended in a gulp as he forced her underwater. With his free hand he groped behind into the bag for the syringe. She gasped harshly as he raised her above water. "SHI-SHIT! Fuck *you*, Thom-Thomas! HELP!!!" she screamed. He doused her again as he positioned the syringe in his right hand and poised it. He raised her up once again, jammed the needle into her neck and plunged nearly 1,200 micrograms of LSD—over 400 times the amount of a high recreational dosage—into her bloodstream. He drew it out and threw the syringe clattering across the tiles. "*Jesus!*" she cried in a hoarse plea. "Hel-HELP! HELP MEEEE!!!" He dunked her again and held her under as she kicked and fought him with all her waning strength. He reached for the wet dish towel floating behind him, raised her up and held it tightly molded over her nose and mouth.

The force of her resistance surged and retreated in diminishing power until he finally felt her slip away. He transfixed his attention upon her as he held her under one last time for maybe a minute, until he released her body to float face down upon the surface. He watched her corpse swirl lackadaisically in the current created by the underwater jets. Her short brown hair fluttered like a wavering fringe around her head.

He cringed away another bolt of headache, as he waited for his god to appear. No one showed up. He leveled a quizzical gaze at Deborah's floating body, itself having provided a home to her developing child, now, mercifully, also gone. Finally, through the heated surge of another headache he said: "Blessings, dear hear— "

Then all went pink. He was being smothered in pink, as he felt a thin, severe tightening bind of a chain around his neck. He heard a harsh breath that was not his own—a purposeful grunting. The chain tightened intensely as it bit in around his throat and started to cut off his air. Another angry swell of the chain's tension started to close off his trachea.

Now, too exhausted to fight back, he closed his eyes as the pink slipped into darkness and time gradually ceased to mean anything. From behind his closed lids, a gentle light emerged through the darkness. In his mind's eye, he shielded himself away from the glow's growth as it advanced. Suddenly the pain in his head abated, and his fever became oddly cooled in the warmth of the glow.

From it emerged a dim figure, who might have been a tall, middle-aged man, certainly no older. He appeared to be Middle Eastern—hollow cheeks, a slender aquiline nose and comfortably reassuring, widely-set, lush blue eyes below a thin growth of brows. His head was crowned by a ringlet of dark auburn curls, some of them graying. His jaw was similarly outlined in a fleecy growth of beard. His skin was lightly bronzed, and his visage featured a plush, benign smile, which might have been taken as one of understanding. Thomas materialized as a visitor to his own hallucination dressed like the other, in a loose, light-lavender robe trimmed in silver. Though Thomas's cowl was pulled up over his head, his visitor's was not. *Who are you?* Thomas asked, perhaps knowing the answer—while fearing it.

The other's smile broadened. *I am the one you have been seeking.*

My god?

No brother. I am not your god.

Whose are you, then?

I am the God of all peoples—the son of all.

For the first time in his life, Thomas recognized the one his god had forced him to ignore. He felt a trickle of warm tears tracking down his cheeks. *You are—the Christ?* he gasped innocently.

I am that I am, he answered softly.

Are you—are you love?

I am that I am, he repeated. His smile broadened as he opened his arms as though to embrace him. *For, even in death, you will find love*. Thomas walked toward him, yet never attained the embrace he so needed as the apparition receded back into the darkness.

The vision of the man who may have been Christ faded back into a glow and then into the distance of shadowed obscurity. The dark- ness glowed pink once again and he felt the biting pain of the chain tightening around his neck. He heard a woman screaming through a mixture of gasps and groans, as the chain tightened, then loosened, then tightened again harder with each of her inflections.

"You're *not* my father! You have *never* been my father! You killed my mother! You did *not* create me!! You're *not* my father! You're a fucking BEAST!"

A final searing tension around his throat broke the chain and freed it. With what strength he could muster, Thomas grabbed the humid, smothering, pink plastic enclosure free, as he gasped for air. The broken chain of the amulet, which had become tangled in the drawstring of the plastic Schrafft's bag, sunk into the pool.

He turned to face his daughter, shivering and staring blankly back at him, holding a now limp piece of the plastic bag. She retreated slowly back from where she had been stooping on the edge of the pool. She backed further away, eyes widened in fear as he rose from the water.

"I love you," he threatened in a dried-out tone as he began to get out of the pool as he reached toward her. "I—*love*—you, Regina." He tried to smile.

Suddenly, he was pulled back from behind as he suffered a deep stab of pain into his neck, then another as he lost his footing and fell back. He felt a warm, slow trickle of blood oozing toward his collar- bone. Another hard pang entered blow his ribcage, and finally a fourth into his stomach as he collapsed down into the water.

Regina stared confoundedly at a drenched, hulking man standing in the pool. He was wearing an assemblage of filthy rags and held a bloody screwdriver in his rock-solid grasp. Milio stared wild-eyed at Thomas's body floating face up in the surging billows of crimson. He then glanced over at Deborah's body and then up at Regina. He smiled benignly at her. "Da preacher man went a killen da pretty woman. *Mu- lierem pulchram, et occidit illum.* She did have love for him."

"Yes, sir," Regina said in a frightened whisper. "I think she did love him. Very much." *Maybe too much,* she added softly to herself, as she stared at Deborah's floating corpse.

Milio broadened his smile as he, just as frightened as she, stood his ground in the pool. "*Tu preacher man's filia?* You be preacher man's daughter?"

"I am," Regina said, her voice trailing a tremulous echo. "I'm his daughter."

"Den you go—*Tu, ad relinquam*—go to outside, an' hide. Not you come backen. Not worry. I not knowen you."

"Who *are* you?" Regina asked, as she checked her skirt pocket to make sure the envelope containing the ticket to Dublin, her car keys, the letter from Seamus and the snapshot of her and Jillian were all still there.

Suddenly another voice burst in. "What the *fuck* is going on h—? Hooo-lee *shit!*" Frank Malone gasped as he saw the two bodies floating in the pool and then Milio standing in the water near them. "Holy fuckin' *shit!*" He'd seen enough bodies in his time—enough to know that though they may be the story, they couldn't *tell* the story. He instinctively poised his pen over his pad and glanced at Regina. "Okay," he said in a stacatto rush. "Who are you? What are you doing here? And what did you see? It's okay. I ain't a cop. I'm a reporter."

"She be preacher man's—*filia.*" Milio said blankly. "She go away."

"Daughter," Regina answered tenuously. "His, uh, daughter."

"Shit almighty! Chamelea had a friggin' *daughter*?" He quickly jotted some notes on his pad. "Okay, then. What's your name?" He did not hear an answer, and when he looked back up, she was gone. "Oh, fuck shit!" he grumbled in defeat. Then he looked over at Milio and saw the bloody screwdriver.

"I killen de preacher man," he admitted.

Malone knew he was in for a long conversation with the person he could not understand. "Okay, Mr. Lithuanian," he sighed. "What's *your* name?"

Milio proudly stood at attention and saluted Malone with the screwdriver. "*Meum nomen est Milio!* I seen da warrinto and fight enta Europea in worl' warrino two, twenty-year ago. I seen blood. *Ete meum nomen stays to be Milio!*"

"Oh, great!" Malone muttered as he wrote on his pad.

Regina rushed out through the sacristy's back door and into the rear parking apron. There she saw her old Corvair, battered and dusty, but still in one piece. She fished around in her pocket for the car keys next to the envelope and then spotted the now misted and battered Hanson High Panthers sticker on the bumper.

She shook away her nervousness as she huddled into the long-ago familiarity of her car. She stuck the keys in the ignition and tried twice to start it. On the third try, its little rear engine turned over. She found she had to re-familiarize herself with how to drive it, but there was no time for any further formalities linking her to the past, not now. She looked up and saw a fog settling over the cityscape. It was low enough to mist over the two shrouded buttresses of the Brooklyn Bridge.

She backed the car up, headed out into the driveway and then right onto Water Street. As she waited for the light to change so she could turn onto Catherine Street half a block south, she heard a siren and a saw a confusion of swirling police lights in the rearview mirror. At first, she feared the cops were after her. She realized she did not even have her license; that it was back in the Brooklyn Heights apartment she had just started to share with Dave.

She breathed a sigh of relief as the police car screeched to a spinning halt in front of her fath—that church. She saw two men, who weren't dressed as cops, hustle into the place. She reckoned they must have been detectives, or something like that.

As she turned on Catherine Street to make her way to the Brooklyn Bridge's entrance and then home to Dave's place on Henry Street, she understood she could not accept his offer of the job. There were other places she had to be. The envelope containing Seamus's letter, the tickets to Dublin and the precious snapshot were the overwhelming prospects urging her to finally move on with her life.

It was the only choice she had.

Chapter 54

The fragrance of lavender

May 1, 1967 Ballycannough, Ireland — Beltane Morning

Regina settled back into the wicker chair on the recently re-constructed front porch of her whitewashed, thatched-roof, home in Ballycannough as she inhaled the moist, loamy chill of May in central Ireland. She gazed at the knobby green knolls bordering the hollow that nestled her newly modernized home. The promise of a sunny day slid up from beneath the low, brightening gray clouds against a silvery sky. Feeling the dash of a chill through the misty air dampening her rosy cheeks, she tightened her grip on the warm mug of coffee she clasped in both hands. She twitched her nose against the invasion of tobacco smoke from Hellie's rancid cheroot.

"I can't believe you're still smoking those foul things," she said. "Jamie doesn't let me smoke my hand rolleds anywhere in the house, or on the ranch property, or fifty miles there without," she said as she inhaled. "Though I don't know how that rodeo clown would know how far away I smoke 'em, anyway. Says it's a fire hazard for all the oil flowing beneath us. But my beeves love the smell of 'em. I can tell."

"Sure," Regina said. "It reminds them of their fucking stalls. Anyway, how's Jamie taking to the El Dorado? How long did I have a chance to drive that thing? Maybe four months?"

Hellie glanced down at her cheroot. "Well, o' *course* he loves it, as he's made it more his own. Two months back he went an' had it fitted with long steer horns over the grille and had the interior upholstered with black an' white steer hide. Gave the horn a 'Moooo!' sound. Makes me feel like we're drivin' Elsie the Cow aroun' town."

Regina chuckled. "Men will be boys, I guess."

Hellie stared out at her three-year daughter, Elvira, and four-and-a half-year old Timbo circling around each other in their happy innocence in the golden apron of field fronting the house—two little towheads picking at the hay. Timbo tickled Elvira's cheek with a shoot of it. "*Timbo*! You 'top dat *now*!" Elvira giggled in response. She flung one she had picked back at him and he ducked away in a gush of laughter.

"He's grown quick," Hellie said. "Elvira, too. She reminds me of me."

"Um," Regina said distantly from thought as she directed her gaze upon the children. "Almost *too* much, huhn?"

"You think ya might ever come back home, hon?"

"I'm starting to believe *this* is my home. My roots."

"Not yours, Reg," she scolded. "His, maybe—not yours."

"He's gone," said Regina as she sipped her coffee.

"Really? Ya *think*? Even in your memories?" Hellie asked. Regina could not answer truthfully, as Hellie watched the kids slip beneath the height of the hay. "Y'all stay where ah can spot y'all!" she shouted.

"We will, Hellie!" Timbo called back thinly from wherever he had hidden.

"Well, don't chu go pickin' up any ticks, now!" She turned to Regina. "Timbo developed a really bad habit o' pickin' up ticks. Made an art of it."

"There may be ticks, but at least there're no fuckin' snakes here, thanks to that Saint Patrick," Regina said. "Hell, they name everything after him around here, for what he did. Guess the Irish had a bad feeling about snakes."

"Garbanzo went an' corralled a diamondback in Clarence's stall last fall. Damn thing long as the Rio Grande," Hellie said.

"Jee-zus! What happened?'

"Snake struck at the ol' fellah in the nose, was what. And he died from it."

"Shit, Hellie! I'm sorry."

"Yeah," Hellie mustered up through her bravado. "Garbanzo always was dumb as a porcupine's foot. Leastwise he went quick." She mashed out the cheroot on the sole of her boot.

Regina settled back in her chair again and remembered how much Hellie had loved Garbanzo. "Still, Hellie. I'm sorry."

Maybe to distill the memory, Hellie asked, "Did you finally go ahead an' take care of that thing?"

"What thing?"

"That church thing. All the money that fuckin' asshole stole."

"Why, Hellie!" Regina said in amused amazement. "I've never known you to use such words. It's so not you."

"What? 'Fuckin' asshole'? I reserve such a designation for a few select people; the Reverend Thomas Barragan bein' one of 'em."

"Okay, then. Me, too." The rising sun had started to overcome the gloom by breaking up the clouds. "The Church of the Holy Waters in Hanson, Iowa," she reminisced, realizing how she had matured since those innocent and shadowy times less than five years before. "What an unfortunate place. All that money the fuckin' asshole stole from them, who barely had two nickels to rub together, no thanks to him."

"Y'all paid it back."

"Of *course* I did. I had Seamus finally send Deacon Barnstable a million dollars about four months back. And a half-mil a year for the next two. It's the least I could do. Those church people were innocent, and always tried to do the right thing for others."

"You did good for them, hon," Hellie said as she straightened and stretched.

"You all packed for your flight back tomorrow?"

"Yeah. Elvira hates to leave not just here, but anywhere. Claims flyin' goes an' makes her deaf an' blind. Too many monsters in the sky. Kids!" Hellie stroked some hair off her roughened cheek as she looked out toward the knolls, now a contrast of light and shadow in the slant of the sun's rays. She leaned against the railing. "Ya know, hon? This would be a real nice place, but it's missing something."

"What's that?"

"I dunno. Flatness, maybe. A view into forever." She smiled wanly. "Derricks. Cattle. Horses. All of it."

"Tornados, violent thunderstorms, droughts," Regina added.

"Agh!" Hellie said. "*Them* li'l 'ol things! They just add a little drama, is all. That's what it is. There ain't no excitement in a place like this. Just the same ol' dreary weather day upon day." She lit another cheroot and shook out her match. "It's all so, I don't know — un-American."

"Because it's Ireland, here. I think it's beautiful in its very own way," Regina said. "Anyway. We have ponies."

"*Ponies*!" Hellie laughed with a friendly disdain that only a sister might understand. "Who rides ponies, anyway? They rank right up there with circus clowns."

Regina thought for another moment as she sipped her coffee. "Do you think he killed Jillian, Hellie?" she asked distantly. "Do you think he really killed her?"

Hellie mulled the question over. "Knowing what you know now, Reg," she finally said, "what do *you* think?"

Regina squinted out into the field. "Honestly? Probably. But I don't think I'll ever know for sure."

"Me, either, then," Hellie mused, and then stirred as she heard Timbo and Elvira gushing in excitement as they approached the porch. "Mommee! *Mommee!*" Timbo shouted. He simpered as he held something behind his back. A surprise.

Hellie stooped to his level. "What, honey? Ya got somethin' fer me, there, son?"

"*Yeth!*" Elvira shouted bluntly.

"Mommee. I have a surprise for you!" Timbo said as he waddled past Hellie and went to Regina to huddle up against her leg.

Regina placed her coffee mug down on the deck and leaned over him and then stroked his fleecy blond hair. "What, sweetie? What do you have for mommy?" she asked.

"Here! I *love* you, mommee!" Timbo told her as he offered his gift. She leaned over to take his offering. She kissed his crown. "Oh, baby! It's *beautiful*! *So* beautiful! And I love you, too, sweetie. With all that I am. I love you *sooo* much!"

She held him to her as he wrapped his little arms as best he could around her neck. She felt a tear roll down her cheek as she absorbed an embrace she had longed for all of her life. She sniffed back more tears and then stared at the gift from her son—a sprig of wild lavender.

FINIS

& Etc...

"The Reverend" Playlist

Songs are lisited in the order and the venue in which they appear in the story.

"South Street" —

Artist/Inspiration: The Orlons

Venue in Story: Chapter 2— Regina in Hellie's pickup truck

"Da-Do-Ron-Ron"—

Artist/Inspiration: The Crystals

Venue in Story: Chapter 4— Maxie's DeSoto

"Foolish Little Girl" —

Artist/Inspiration: The Shirelles Venue in Story: Chapter 4—Maxie's DeSoto

"Allegro—Third Brandenburg Concerto" —

Artist/Inspiration: J.S. Bach

Venue in Story: Chapter 5— Tenement construction site

"If You Wanna be Happy (for the rest of your life)" —

Artist/Inspiration: Jimmy Soul

Venue in Story: Chapter 6— Tenement construction site

"In a Sentimental Mood" —

Artist/Inspiration: Dexter Gordon

Venue in Story: Chapter 10— Ray Nealy's office

"You Don't Own Me" —

Artist/Inspiration: Leslie Gore

Venue in Story: Chapter 11— Tenement construction site

"El Watusi." —

Artist/Inspiration: Ray Barretto

Venue in Story: Chapter 12— *Los Lobos Solitaros'* Buick 88

"I Wish I were in Love Again" —

Artist/Inspiration: Frank Sinatra Venue in Story: Chapter 13— The Back Page Bar

"Old Devil Moon" —

Artist/Inspiration: Tony Bennett

Venue in Story: Chapter 13— The Back Page Bar

"Sukiyaki" —

Artist/Inspiration: Kyu Sakamoto

Venue in Story: Chapter 14—Deborah in the holy water soaking tub in Heaven's Doorway

"Help a Good Girl Go Bad" —

Artist/Inspiration: Ruth Brown

Venue in Story: Chapter 15— Glitz & Glitter Club— Big Eunice and The Bonne-Aires Band

"Manteca!" —

Artist/Inspiration: Dizzy Gillespie

Venue in Story: Chapter 15— Glitz & Glitter Club— The Bonne-Aires Band

"Wives and Lovers" —

Artist/Inspiration: Jack Jones

Venue in Story: Chapter 15— Glitz & Glitter Club—

Dancing Eddie and The Bonne-Aires Band

"It Never Entered My Mind"—

Artist/Inspiration: Miles Davis

Venue in Story: Chapter 15— Glitz & Glitter Club— The Bonne-Aires Band

"You've Got Those Wanna Go Back Again Blues"

Artist/Inspiration: Ruth Etting (1926) / Leon Redbone (2010)

Venue in Story: Chapter 17— Glitz & Glitter Club—

Dancing Eddie and The Bonne-Aires Band

"Auld Lang Syne" —

Artist/Inspiration: Dixieland style

Venue in Story: Chapter 17— Glitz & Glitter Club —

The Bonne-Aires Band

"And the Angels Sing" —

Artist/Inspiration: Janet Siedel

Venue in Story: Chapter 17— Glitz & Glitter Club—

Marie Trudeau and The Bonne-Aires Band

"I've Never Been in Love Before" —

Artist/Inspiration: June Christy

Venue in Story: Chapter 17— Glitz & Glitter Club—

Marie Trudeau and The Bonne-Aires Band

"I Hear Music" —

Artist/Inspiration: Blossom Dearie

Venue in Story: Chapter 17— Glitz & Glitter Club—

Marie Trudeau and The Bonne-Aires Band

"It's all in the Game" —

Artist/Inspiration: Tommy Edwards (1958)

Venue in Story: Chapter 17— Glitz & Glitter Club—

Dancing Eddie and The Bonne-Aires Band

"Allegretto — Seventh Symphony"—

Artist/Inspiration: Ludwig Von Beethoven

Venue in Story: Chapter 21— Heaven's Doorway, Thomas's office

"She Loves You" —

Artist/Inspiration: The Beatles

Venue in Story: Chapter 22— Deborah's apartment

"Hound Dog"—

Artist/Inspiration: Big Mamma Thornton

Venue in Story: Chapter 22— Glitz & Glitter Club Cavern —

Big Eunice and The Bonne-Aires Quintet

"My Guy" —

Artist/Inspiration: Mary Wells

Venue in Story: Chapter 24— Regina's hotel room

"Anyone Who Had a Heart" —

Artist/Inspiration: Cilia Black

Venue in Story: Chapter 24— Regina's hotel room

"I just Want to be Wanted" —

Artist/Inspiration: Brenda Lee (1958)

Venue in Story: Chapter 26— Glitz & Glitter Club—

Marie Trudeau and The Bonne-Aires Band

"I Hear Music" —

Artist/Inspiration: Blossom Dearie

Venue in Story: Chapter 26— Glitz & Glitter Club—

Marie Trudeau and The Bonne-Aires Band

"Hold Me Tight" —

Artist/Inspiration: The Beatles

Venue in Story: Chapter 28— Maddie Peck's Bar

"Someone to Watch Over Me" —

Artist/Inspiration: Ella Fitzgerald

Venue in Story: Chapter 31— Glitz & Glitter Club Cavern—

Big Eunice and The Bonne-Aires Quintet

"Moonlight Serenade" —

Artist/Inspiration: Glenn Miller orchestra

Venue in Story: Chapter 33— Zina Harper's apartment

"In the Mood" —

Artist/Inspiration: Glenn Miller orchestra

Venue in Story: Chapter 34 — Gwen Perkins' apartment

"Tuxedo Junction" —

Artist/Inspiration: Glenn Miller Orchestra

Venue in Story: Chapter 42 — Pattie Nolan's Apartment

"Body and Soul" —

Artist/Inspiration: John Coltrane

Venue in Story: Chapter 43 — Ray Nealy's office

"Gymnpedie Number 1" —

Artist/Inspiration: Eric Satie

Venue in Story: Chapter 48 — Thomas's bedroom in Heaven's Doorway

"Witchcraft" —

Artist/Inspiration: Frank Sinatra

Venue in Story: Chapter 49 — The Back Page

"Make Someone Happy" —

Artist/Inspiration: Bobbie Daren

Venue in Story: Chapter 51 — Francesca's Apartment

"As Time Goes By" —

Artist/Inspiration: Dooley Wilson from "Casablanca" (1942)

Venue in Story: Chapter 52 — Francesca's Apartment

NOTE:

Marie Trudeau's singing style is based upon that of Janet Seidel, e.g.: "And the Angels Sing."

About the Author

David (D.H.) Robbins has been actively writing fiction for nearly 30 years. His first novel is a family saga centered around the 1960s, "The Tutone DeSoto" (2014), introduces eight teenagers growing up in Iowa during the veiled turbulence underlying The Kennedy Years (1960-63).

This second novel, "The Reverend" (2019) is set in New York City in 1963-64. The Greenwich Village Scene, Lower East Side and the New York World's Fair are featured settings.

The third in the saga, "The Weight of Indifference," is set place during the counterculture years (1965-68).

He's co-authored two media design books, "Motion by Design" (Lawrence King, 2007), and "Visual Effects Artistry" (Elsevier Press, 2009). He has also created and produces a 5-part lecture series, "The 1960's—Revisiting a Crucial Decade." Robbins has taught learning module design and is now teaching a fiction-writing course/workshop.

Robbins was born in Darien, Connecticut, and currently lives in Simsbury, Connecticut where he continues to type away on his short stories and novels.